12/19

D0616784

MURASAKI

MURASAKI

A Novel in Six Parts by

POUL ANDERSON
GREG BEAR
GREGORY BENFORD
DAVID BRIN
NANCY KRESS
FREDERIK POHL

Edited by

ROBERT SILVERBERG

BANTAM BOOKS

NEW YORK · TORONTO · LONDON · SYDNEY · AUCKLAND

MURASAKI

A Bantam Book / May 1992

Murasaki copyright © 1992 by The Science Fiction Writers of America.
Introduction copyright © 1992 by Agberg Ltd.
"The Treasures of Chujo" copyright © 1992 by Frederik Pohl.
"Genji" copyright © 1992 by David Brin.
"Language" copyright © 1992 by Poul Anderson.
"World Vast, World Various" copyright © 1992 by Gregory Benford.
"A Plague of Conscience" copyright © 1992 by Greg Bear.
"Birthing Pool" copyright © 1992 by Nancy Kress.
"Design for Two Worlds" copyright © 1992 by Poul Anderson.
"Murasaki's Worlds" copyright © 1992 by Frederik Pohl.

Book design by Harakawa Sisco Inc.
Illustrations by Jonathan Scott

Library of Congress Cataloging-in-Publication Data

Murasaki / edited by Robert Silverberg and Martin H. Greenberg

   p. cm.

   ISBN 0-553-08229-9

   1. Science fiction, American   I. Silverberg, Robert.   II. Greenberg, Martin Harry.

PS648.S3M87   1992

813'.54—dc20   91-39283

                           CIP

Published simultaneously in the United States and Canada

Bantam Books are published by Bantam Books, a division of Bantam Doubleday Dell
Publishing Group, Inc. Its trademark, consisting of the words "Bantam Books" and the
portrayal of a rooster, is Registered in U.S. Patent and Trademark Office and in other
countries. Marca Registrada. Bantam Books, 666 Fifth Avenue, New York, New York
10103.

PRINTED IN THE UNITED STATES OF AMERICA

RRH 0 9 8 7 6 5 4 3 2 1

CONTENTS

INTRODUCTION

ROBERT SILVERBERG

VII

THE TREASURES OF CHUJO

FREDERIK POHL

I

GENJI

DAVID BRIN

38

LANGUAGE

POUL ANDERSON

70

WORLD VAST, WORLD VARIOUS

GREGORY BENFORD

IOO

A PLAGUE OF CONSCIENCE

GREG BEAR

I4O

BIRTHING POOL

NANCY KRESS

I86

CONTENTS

APPENDIX A:

DESIGN FOR TWO WORLDS

POUL ANDERSON

231

APPENDIX B:

MURASAKI'S WORLDS

FREDERIK POHL

259

INTRODUCTION

This book is an anthology of new stories set within a single conceptual framework, produced jointly by a group of science-fiction writers—a kind of collective enterprise that is known in the world of science-fiction publishing as a "shared-world" anthology. Many such shared-world volumes have been released in recent years. What is special about this one is that all the writers involved in creating it were winners of science fiction's highest award of professional excellence, the Nebula. Never before has a group of Nebula winners been brought together to apply their very diverse talents to exploring the same set of ideas and characters.

Science-fiction writers are notoriously individualistic in their private lives, political positions, and professional demeanor. It's a field richly populated by lone wolves, libertarians, nonconformists of every stripe. They tend to think their own thoughts and go their own way. Most of them resist editorial tinkering with their work and are usually unhappy in the fundamentally collaborative atmosphere of a place like Hollywood, where writers are (rightly) considered to be nothing more than members of a large team, and not very important members of the team at that.

How very strange, then, that this collection of cantankerous individualists would have embraced with such enthusiasm the collectivist concept of the shared-world anthology. To work with other people's ideas—to volunteer for positions in what are essentially round-robin novels written by many hands—to take pains to make certain that their contributions to these books don't violate the previously determined conceptual boundaries of the project—it seems the antithesis of individualism in every way. And yet throughout the history of the science-fiction field such shared-world projects have attracted some of the most talented writers of each period.

One of the most famous of these joint enterprises was hatched in the earliest days of science fiction as a specialized form in the United States. This was the seventeen-part serial novel *Cosmos*, which was published in 1933 and 1934.

The contributors to *Cosmos* were the top-ranking professional science-fiction writers of the era. The roster included some authors whose names today are nothing more than trivia-contest items—Abner J. Gelula, Bob Olsen, Francis Flagg, J. Harvey Haggard. But also we find, among those who turned out the monthly *Cosmos* chapters, such titans of science fiction and fantasy as John W. Campbell, Jr., E. E. Smith, Ph.D., A. Merritt, and Edmond Hamilton, who wrote the spectacular final chapter, "Armageddon in Space."

Cosmos was a romp, a spoof, an exercise in sheer science-fictional playfulness, tremendous fun for writers and readers alike. But the next shared-world project that comes to mind was a very serious endeavor indeed.

This was a volume called *The Petrified Planet*, published in 1952, for which the scientist John D. Clark worked out the chemical and biological specifications of a planet where the basic element of life was silicone, rather than carbon as it is on Earth, and three outstanding writers of the time were invited to contribute novellas based on Dr. Clark's technical data. The results were outstanding: a trio of stories that bore no relationship to one another in plot, character, or theme, and yet grew organically out of the same set of scientific postulates.

Other shared-world books followed, over the years. The most remarkable such project of this sort, I think, was Harlan Ellison's epochal *Medea*, which was published in 1985 after a ten-year gestation period. It was Ellison's brilliant idea to create a science-fictional planet by a three-stage process: first, some of the field's top idea-men would produce essays setting forth the astrophysics, geology, biology, oceanography, and even the politics and theology of the hypothetical world. Then four other writers would be handed the booklets containing all this information and would go on stage (during a series of major science-fiction seminars held before a general-public audience at the University of California, Los Angeles), in an attempt to improvise plot structures for stories set on this world; and, finally, a group of writers including all of the earlier creators would be asked to do the actual stories.

Ellison used a formidable cast of major figures to bring *Medea* into existence. The underlying specifications were drawn up by no less a team than Hal Clement, Larry Niven, Frederik Pohl, and Poul Anderson. The quartet of intrepid writers who improvised story ideas before a huge audience at UCLA included Frank Herbert, Theodore Sturgeon, Thomas M. Disch, and Robert Silverberg. The stories for the book were written by Messrs. Niven, Anderson, Pohl, Clement, Sturgeon, Herbert, Silverberg, and Disch, plus Jack Williamson,

Kate Wilhelm, and editor Ellison himself. Many of the stories, first published separately, became Hugo and Nebula nominees, and at least one won an award. The book was an extraordinary achievement, fascinating and unique. Even where the writers strayed from the specifications, contradicted one another, created variations on the theme that grew from their own distinctive literary personalities rather than from the preset concepts, that in itself was significantly interesting. If *Medea* were the only example of such collaborative science fiction ever to have been conceived, it would by itself have justified the notion of the worth of collective activity of that kind.

Many other shared-world projects have followed it—a few of them ingeniously and coherently devised, others less impressive. In the main, a great deal of notable work has been done in these joint enterprises over the years. Which brings us back to the paradox I put forth on the first page of this introduction. Why are science-fiction writers, so deeply individualistic in so many ways, willing and even eager to take part in these projects, in which they have to subordinate their own creative impulses to some editor's a priori notion of what they should be writing, or, even worse, some *committee's* ideas?

The answer, I think, lies in their love of a good challenge. Of course, any good science-fiction writer would rather work from his own ideas than anyone else's, and, most of the time, that's what they do. But there's an element of sport—of risk, even—in being handed a prospectus and asked to fit one's own literary personality into preconceived modes and structures. And, too, there's the aspect of expressing one's creativity *within* the preconceived structures, by reinterpreting them, by transforming, by extending, by stretching the boundaries of what's been given. That's what I meant when I said, in speaking of *Medea*, that one of the book's many fascinations lay in seeing where and how some of the writers had deviated from the plan. Any hack can produce a lifeless imitative work-to-order; the test of a real writer is to breathe individuality and vigor into a story *even though the original creative impulse for it came from someone else.*

Which brings us to the book you now are reading.

Fifteen years have gone by since the unforgettable night when Tom Disch, Frank Herbert, Ted Sturgeon, Harlan Ellison, and I spent hours in front of that huge UCLA audience working out variations on the *Medea* concepts that Fred Pohl, Larry Niven, Poul Anderson, and Hal Clement had invented for us. Sturgeon and Herbert are dead now; *Medea* itself is out of print, a collector's item, for a tangle of reasons as inexplicable as they are regrettable, though I understand that a reissue is finally in the works. One afternoon in 1988, while we were attending the Nebula Award ceremonies of the Science Fiction Writers of America in Los Angeles, Martin H. Greenberg and I came up with the notion of trying to produce a new book that might come close to matching the scope and depth of Ellison's mammoth anthology: this time as an official project of the SFWA.

For *Medea*, Harlan had invited a de facto elite of science fiction: a group of writers whose accomplishments over many years had made them plausible candidates for such a book. For the new volume, we chose to limit the roster of potential contributors to an elite also, but not simply a de facto one. Since this was to be an official publication of the Science Fiction Writers of America, the ranking professional organization of the field, the only writers who would be invited to take part would be those who had won the Nebula Award that the SFWA presents each year to the writers of the previous year's four best stories and novels, as chosen by vote of the membership.

That gave us a considerable potential roster. Since the inauguration of the Nebulas in 1966, something like fifty writers have received the gleaming Lucite trophies. Invitations went out to all fifty. Some replied categorically that they never took part in shared-world projects; a few told us that they regarded themselves as fantasy/horror writers and found writing this kind of science fiction uncongenial; some said they were too busy with projects of their own at the time; others offered reactions ranging from the conditional to the enthusiastic. And, one way and another, we winnowed the list down to the group who produced the present volume.

To construct the underlying specifications we chose two veterans of *Medea*'s formative days, Poul Anderson and Frederik Pohl. Poul worked up a brilliant design for the double-world Murasaki System and sent his rough draft to Fred, who came back with suggestions of his own; then Fred produced an essay on the probable cultural traits of the Murasaki planets' denizens, and much else. (The original Anderson and Pohl specification essays are reproduced as an appendix to this volume, by way of showing the richness and depth of the material that underlies the stories. If you want to experience this book the way the authors of the stories did, I suggest that you turn to the appendix *first*, read the essays by Anderson and Pohl, then go to the fiction. You'd be wise to read the stories in the order they appear in the book, from that point on, unless you *really* enjoy challenges.)

Once the Anderson-Pohl conceptualizations had reached their final form, I wrote a "primary scenario," five or six pages long, setting out some fundamental narrative structures that would provide the book as much unity as a novel written by six different writers is likely to have. There's no need to reprint that scenario in full here: the six writers have put flesh on its bones with admirable skill. But perhaps a few brief extracts will give some notion of how one goes about the planning of a book of this sort:

"The basic notion is to build the book around two patterns of opposition: rational-minded humans vs. spiritualists, and the alien natives of Genji vs. their counterparts on Chujo...."

"The first level of conflict is between the two batches of Earth-critters—the science-y types on Genji, and the New Age sorts on or around Chujo. Each group detests the other and is miserably afraid that the other will spoil its party...."

"Of course, some kind of synthesis has to come out of all this eventually: a compromise between the Earth factions and a blending of the two alien cultures. What it will be, I have to leave to the writers of the final stories. My only stipulation is that it ought to be reasonably positive—that is, I don't want the book to be one huge demonstration of the thesis that the wisest way to approach intelligent alien species is not to approach them at all...."

And then the fat package of preliminary material went off to the writers. Fred Pohl wrote the first story; Poul Anderson did the second. They were the two guys, after all, who understood Chujo and Genji better than anyone in the universe, and we wanted them to establish through vivid narratives what these planets were really like. Then the growing bundle of manuscript was forwarded to Greg Benford, who did the third story, and David Brin, who did the fourth (although it's the second in the published book, because it was necessary for David to fill in a gap in chronology that had begun to develop). Greg Bear provided the fifth story, and Nancy Kress heroically drew the whole project together with the sixth and climactic one.

And there you are: the first shared-world anthology conceived and written entirely by Nebula Award winners. As you'll see when you read the appended essays, even these six top-flight writers didn't begin to exhaust the background material from which they worked; we could all go on writing Chujo/Genji stories for many years to come. Perhaps some of us will. Perhaps there will be other books of this sort. But such projects are a matter for the future. Here we offer you your first glimpse of the Murasaki System. Our deepest hope now is that Chujo and Genji will become as real to you as you read it as they did to us during the intricate process of assembling the book.

—Robert Silverberg
Oakland, California, September 1990

MURASAKI

THE TREASURES OF CHUJO

BY FREDERIK POHL

1

One of the advantages of Aaron Kammer's situation—there weren't many of them—was that he didn't have to worry about unpleasant surprises. There weren't likely to be many more of those for him, either. Ever. Kammer's situation was what the old physicist, Richard Feynman, called a stable system. Feynman said stability was what you got when all the fast things had happened, and all the slow things hadn't happened yet.

In that sense, all of the Spacer ship that was exploring the Murasaki planets was in a stable state, at least up to the moment when the first message came in from the approaching Japanese expedition. Earlier, there had been plenty of fast things happening. There had been the building of the ship and the recruiting of the crew—all of them, from Spacer habitats all over the solar system and even from Mars, like Kammer himself. There had been the launch, the long acceleration, the accident with the drive at turnaround (very fast things happening then, and very serious for Aaron Kammer—not to mention for the three crewmembers who weren't even as lucky as Kammer, but just died). Then there had been the arrival at the star, Murasaki, and the dispatch of exploration parties to the planet Genji . . . and, yes, there also had been a great many *personally* fast things among the crew, such as their repeated episodes of divorces and remarriages, and re-divorces and re-remarriages, as the accumulated boredoms and hostilities of the eleven years of interstellar flight took their toll.

There had also been some other things that had been, really, fast enough for anybody, by any objective measurement—the ship had attained velocities fairly close to the speed of light on the long trip from Earth's system to

Murasaki's, and certainly that has to be called *fast*—although they hadn't seemed fast at all while they were happening. (Four thousand time-dilated days! Long enough to seem an eternity to the nineteen surviving people who had been crammed into each other's personal space for all that time.)

At any rate, the ship had finally arrived safely. More or less safely, anyway, not counting the fact that Aaron Kammer was still slowly dying and the three other casualties had already accomplished the process. So all those fast things had happened. Now ship and crew were in the stable state of waiting for the slow things to happen.

There were a lot of those slow things that hadn't happened yet, even if you didn't get into the *very* slow ones, like the dimming of the sun or the heat-death of the universe. One of those moderately slow things would be completing the exploration of the Chujo-Genji system. Another—for those who lived to do it—would be going back to Earth . . . and, in Aaron Kammer's case, there was always that ongoing slow thing that was highly important to him. Namely the very slow, but not slow enough, process of finishing the business of becoming dead.

Then the ship's radio announced an incoming call on the hailing frequency, and it was the Japanese.

Aaron Kammer was tethered in the control room when it came, nominally occupied in monitoring the incoming picture transmissions from Genji's starside. He hadn't expected any calls on the hailing frequency, there twenty-some light-years from Earth. He certainly hadn't expected them from *strangers.* When the blast of Japanese language came over the speaker he jumped and jabbed himself with the needle in his hand. The only other person in the room was the captain, half drowsing over his autobridge board like a huge four-limbed pumpkin. Captain Darryl Washington had a different reaction. He lunged for the radio, slapping his game board across the room, and brayed, "Cut it out, Nicole! Use your lander frequency, if that's you."

There wasn't any answer. The captain glared accusingly at Kammer. Kammer, sucking his finger, shrugged. It would have been quite like Nicole to try to startle them, if she was in fact in space on her way back to the ship. But keeping track of Nicole wasn't his job—wasn't even, any longer, his right.

In theory, Kammer was on duty. He was supervising the ship's instruments as they scanned one more track of Genji's surface, adding false-color optics and magnetometer readings to the maps they had been building up ever since they arrived. It was the kind of job you gave to somebody who wasn't healthy enough to go down to the surface of Genji, since the instruments didn't actually need any supervision at all. What Kammer was mostly doing was sewing a bonnet for Bandit, his ex-wife Nicole's old seal point cat.

"Hey, Nicole!" the captain called, now really irritated. "I'm talking to you!" And, turning to give Kammer another accusing look, as though it were his fault: "She's supposed to stay in radio contact on the ascent!"

Kammer didn't respond. He bent back to his sewing, because he hoped to finish it before Nicole arrived. The fact that Aaron Kammer was making clothes for his ex-wife's cat didn't mean that he was loopy—well, certainly it didn't mean that among the crew of the starship, most of whom had found hobbies a good deal weirder over the long years of the trip. Kammer was doing it because he didn't have much else to do, since Boulat Kotsvili, the ship's main medic, refused to pass him as fit for a Genji mission . . . and also because he was fond of the cat . . . and also, to be sure, because he kept hoping wistfully that his ex-wife, Nicole, would once again divorce her once and present husband, the captain, and marry him again, if only for a little while before he died. Kammer was biologically thirty-two years old (though the birth certificate back on Mars said he had been born more than forty years ago), and unlikely ever to reach thirty-five. (That was because of the dying thing: he and the other casualties should have been more careful while they were changing the antimatter thruster block at the midcourse turnaround.) As he sewed the pretty little bonnet to put on his ex-wife's cat, he was tethered so that he wouldn't float away in the microgravity of Low Genji Orbit. He was completely absorbed in making the stitches neat and small, and Captain Blow-Your-Horn's yelling annoyed him. (Loud noises sometimes sent Kammer into convulsions these days.)

There were only three of the crew left in the big interstellar ship—Boulat Kotsvili asleep in his room—though a fourth was supposed to be en route up from Genji. That was the missing Nicole, who was bringing a sick fifth person back in the landing craft. Everybody else was hard at work on the surface of Genji, doing what they had come all this way to do. Aaron Kammer thought of them often, and with a lot of envy. Even though the sick Murqhad Fasbar was coughing his lungs out, the result of having tried to talk unprotected to the Ihrdizu at sea level, and the people still in the base camp on the high plain were bitter about the biting winds and the miserable cold—even though existence on Genji was perilous and nasty—that was where he should have been.

With, of course, Nicole.

Then the hailing radio spoke again.

It was a woman's voice this time, but definitely it was not Nicole. "Hello, Spacer ship," it said. "I'm Manae Nakahishi, and we just wanted to let you know you'll have company in about twenty-two days."

The captain swung himself around in his harness, panting at the effort of moving all that fat around, to stare at Aaron Kammer again. This time his look wasn't angry. It was depressed. "Oh, hell," he said. "The Japs have caught up with us."

Kammer took his finger out of his mouth and looked at it. It had stopped bleeding. "That's too bad," he called to the man he had nicknamed Captain Blow-Your-Horn.

"I didn't expect them for *years* yet," the captain grumbled. Kammer didn't answer that, because it was obvious. The spacers knew when the Japanese had launched their Murasaki ship, and they knew very well, none better, how long it took to make Murasaki orbit, having done it themselves. It was an unpleasant shock to find their competitors arriving early. The captain scowled and ordered Kammer, "Go wake Boulat up."

"He's awake already," Kammer pointed out, because the state-of-the-ship telltale on the wall was already flashing to show that Boulat Kotsvili's door was opening. "Darryl? Maybe you should call Nicole to let her know what's happening, if she's already on her way."

"I *am* trying to call her! Don't get all in a flap, Kammer," the captain ordered, waving his sausagey arms. "Do something useful, why don't you? Go change the cat box!"

If Kammer did as he was ordered, it wasn't because he respected the captain's authority. Captain Blow-Your-Horn didn't have any of that. It wasn't in the hope of the captain's appreciation, either, because there was no hope that the captain would ever like Aaron Kammer. Especially since the captain knew exactly how much Kammer wanted the return of their intermittently exchanged wife. Now that the captain was captain, after their real captain died in the same shower of radiation that was still killing Kammer, Darryl ("Blow-Your-Horn") Washington regarded Kammer's coveting of Nicole as something near mutiny.

Given a choice, Kammer would have preferred that the captain like him. It wasn't that he had any high opinion of old Blow-Your-Horn, it was only that Kammer wanted to be missed when he died. The only people around in a position to do that for him, now, were the people in the Spacer ship, because certainly no one they had left behind in Earth's solar system cared any more. They were all forgotten there as individuals by now. And Kammer couldn't be mourned by his own original wife, Priss, the one he had come aboard with in the co-Ceres orbit long ago. That wife had been killed in the same accident that was still killing him—although, to be sure, she'd divorced him before that, anyway.

Kammer would be dead for a long time, he knew—that was one of the *really* slow things—and he liked to think that when he went all the survivors of the crew would mourn him, and speak fondly of him, and wish he were still alive. Even the captain.

Time was when Aaron Kammer had been one of the most important members of the ship's crew, the head drive engineer, on whom the safety of every one of them rested. People respected him then, and the women looked on him with interest. Especially Darryl Washington's pretty brown-haired wife.

Since the accident with the thrust block, that time was over. Now that the ship was merely rolling around Genji in its one-hundred-minute orbit, the important people were the downside exploration crews. Time would come when the ship would turn around and head back to Earth with all the readings and films they had taken and hadn't had bandwidth to transmit completely back to Earth, and its freezers full of precious biological samples. But even then, Kammer wouldn't be important again. It was Kammer's backup who would have to be the engineer in charge on that long flight, because Kammer himself would not be alive.

He shivered. In spite of all his practice at it, he didn't like thinking about how he would be dead. But what was interstellar flight, in the first place, but a form of cut-rate suicide? You didn't really end your life; you just threw away about a quarter of it on your interminable trip. It wasn't an accident that four of the original crew had had histories of attempted suicide. When the screening board first began interviewing volunteers they had set pretty high standards for mental stability, but they had had to cut them back. Really stable people didn't volunteer to go to Murasaki.

But some people didn't have much choice. Like Kammer. When you were born on Mars you had the worst of all worlds. Poorer than Earth or space, not much in the way of natural resources; when the chance came to move to a space habitat you jumped at it, and when the chance came along to try your luck at an interstellar mission you took that, too.

Even though you knew what the cost would be.

So Kammer thought; and was glad to be interrupted when the cat, Bandit, sprang out of hiding and landed on his shoulder, rubbing up against his ear.

Nicole's Siamese had come aboard with all the others when the ship was launched. That was a long time ago. In those days Bandit had been a kitten, and the captain (who wasn't yet the captain) had been an energetic (and even thin) young space volunteer, doting on his young bride and tolerating her peccadilloes—that was, of course, before she became Aaron's bride, and then took another turn at being the captain's after Aaron got sick. Bandit was an old cat now. But when you thought of it that was one of her fringe benefits for going star-wandering, because if she had stayed in the habitats she would have been long since dead; it was only the relativistic time dilation of their trip out that kept her still going.

Changing Bandit's box wasn't particularly distasteful work. Kammer didn't have to comb the turds out to dispose of them, because there wasn't any place to dispose them to, anyway. All he did was take the metal tray out of its screened enclosure (screened because otherwise, in their microgravity environment, the cat would have scratched sand and excrement all over the ship) and put it in the high-temperature oven to turn everything back to a sanitary state. The vapors, of course, were sucked into the recycling tank, along with all the other stinks and scraps the crew of the ship produced each day. It didn't take long.

When it was done Kammer picked up the tray with gloved hands and set it back in its cage. The cat was crouched beside him now, waiting for the chance to soil the pristine sand. "Not yet, Bandit," Kammer warned. "Let it cool off." That wasn't necessary. Bandit knew very well that hot sand would scorch her paws, because she'd had a lifetime to learn.

Just to make sure, Kammer picked her up and stroked her while he waited. He was glad to see that his finger showed no sign of beginning to bleed again. That was good. Blood was one of the things he couldn't spare, not as long as his blood cells kept dying and the rejection rate kept getting worse each time he was transfused.

Dying wasn't just a slow thing. It was a hard thing, and he wasn't very good at it.

Of course, everyone knew there would be a Japanese ship along one of these days. It wasn't only inevitable, it was, really, quite *fair*. It had been the Japanese who had first probed the Murasaki System and found that it had two habitable (well, more or less habitable) planets. For more than a year after the spacers had sneaked their own hastily built ship into launch orbit, the crew had been subjected to furious recriminations coming over the radio every day from the Japanese.

Fairness didn't count, though. No one *owned* the star Murasaki and its planets. Even the Japanese didn't question that, though they'd named the system and fully expected to be the first to explore it in person. They only thought it was a dirty trick for the spacers to fit an interstellar drive onto one of their ships and send it off, while the Earth-bound Japanese themselves were still completing designs for the one they intended to build for the job.

All the same, Kammer was a little sorry that the Japanese ship was so close.

He thought about going back to the control room to talk it over with Darryl and Boulat Kotsvili—he could hear their voices down the hall. But he felt a quick jolt as he held the cat, and knew what that meant. The lander had docked.

He wanted to see Nicole, too, of course. He always did. But he hadn't finished making Bandit's little bonnet so that Nicole could, so charmingly, play baby-dress-up with the cat in place of the real baby she wasn't likely ever to have. Anyway, when he did finish the hat, he wanted to give it to Nicole in private.

So Kammer did what he did more and more of the time these days. He pulled himself quietly to his own room, closed the door and his eyes, and went peacefully to sleep. . . .

Awakening only in surprise when a sudden disconcerting rocking pressure against the straps that held him told him that the ship's drive was on. They were moving the big ship out of Low Genji Orbit! Another fast thing was happening, and a wholly unexpected one.

2

When an outside intrusion (as, for instance, the early arrival of their Japanese competitors) perturbs a stable system (like Captain Blow-Your-Horn's ship), the system doesn't stay stable. Then all sorts of fast things begin to happen all at once. The captain was experiencing several of them.

The captain's name wasn't really Blow-Your-Horn, of course, but only Darryl Washington. The unwelcome nickname was just one of the reasons the captain disliked Aaron Kammer. He didn't really need reasons. Darryl Washington had once been a reasonably amiable human being, but after living intimately among the other adventurers for the last interminable time-dilated decade, he didn't like any of them very much. Murqhad Fasbar, before he went down to the surface of Genji and got sick, had got into a roaring match with the captain once. (That was one of the reasons why he had left for Genji the next day.) In the course of it, Fasbar had told the whole ship, at the top of his voice, that Darryl Washington was not only disgracefully fat but a fundamentally insecure person. That was why he was so hostile all the time, Fasbar shouted, and the insecurity was the result of his unexpectedly having inherited the captaincy when the *real* captain died, so that Washington simply didn't allow himself to like or trust anyone at all.

Of course, that was nonsense. At least, Washington himself was almost certain it was. Washington knew perfectly well why he didn't like his crew. They didn't deserve to be liked, because they were a pack of undisciplined dipshits. They didn't respect his position. Anyway, he told himself, just to set the record straight in his mind, he did like *some* people—he was sure of that—particularly his wife, now that she had come back from her stupid escapade of marrying that particularly undisciplined dipshit, Aaron Kammer, for a while. Washington demonstrated that fact to himself as soon as the lander docked, by throwing his arms around her and whispering into her ear. But, being who he was, before he kissed her, he accused, "You should've been in radio contact coming up here!"

She pulled back and looked at him. "How could I? I was busy trying to keep Murqhad alive." She looked like hell, he thought. Her face was pinched and lean. "I thought if we got him to the high plain he'd be all right, but—" She shook her head.

It was time for a loving husband to be forgiving, Washington realized, so he kissed her ear tenderly. "Yes, fine," she said, distractedly releasing herself, "but won't you help me get Murqhad to bed? The fool thought he could go out without a suit, and he's wrecked his stupid lungs."

"Poor guy," Washington said with satisfaction. "Come on, Boulat, give Nicole a hand." He watched critically as the two of them helped the wheezing, coughing Murqhad Fasbar to his own room—another nasty little nuisance to put up with, Washington told himself. They'd be listening to those hacking coughing fits all over the ship. Nicole did look a little thinner, he thought critically, watching her. She had kept herself slim all through the flight—while he, like so many Spacers, had just let the kilograms pile on—but she still had a warmly curved, still-attractive figure. He was pleased about that, since he expected very soon to have the pleasure of experiencing it.

When they were gone, Washington strapped himself back in at the control board. He wasn't planning to do anything special there; it was just the right place for a captain to be. Washington reviewed his conduct for the last few moments and was satisfied. It was, he thought, just about what his hero would have done.

Darryl Washington's hero wasn't a real, live human being. He wasn't even a dead one. The person Washington most admired was a fictitious character from the works of an almost forgotten twentieth-century novelist, and the character's name (which, regrettably, was the source of Washington's undesired nickname) was Horatio Hornblower.

As a boy in the cis-Mercurian solar-power habitat where Washington had grown up, he had fed his childish fantasies with such heroic books. Kipling, Homer, Percival Christopher Wren—all the great old stories about people who traveled far to do great things, and always knew just what to do. Young Darryl had read every one of the Hornblower disks before he was twelve. That was why he had wanted so badly to be some kind of captain when he grew up.

And then, without warning, he was—when, halfway to Murasaki, the accident with the antimatter drive had killed the real captain.

Nothing is ever as good as its anticipation, is it?

Oh, there were good things about it. There was the thrilling, not to say shocking, discovery that even the old captain had not been absolutely honest with the crew, because there were "sealed orders" (Washington liked to think of them as that) that the captain had never even hinted at. But they were a real problem. Washington was not at all sure he wanted to carry them out. And the captaincy itself wasn't nearly as good as he had thought it would be. What was a captain now, in these soft times? Nothing! The kind of things a captain had to do were mostly just plain *boring*—absurd, petty things like checking the leaders of the planet parties to make sure everybody was keeping up his steroids and calcium intake; riding herd on Boulat Kotsvili to ensure that all the women were using their fertility blockers; nagging the supply chiefs in every downside party so no one would forget to keep their reserve supplies up—and not run out of medicines, say, or food supplements. Horatio Hornblower had it easy. And worst of all, from Captain Washington's point of view, people *argued* with him!

It had been a lot different with Horatio Hornblower. When the first Hornblower gave an order, everybody jumped to do it. They had to. He could hang them from the yardarm if they didn't. The only thing Hornblower had to worry about was making sure he gave the *right* order, and that was easy enough to do (in Darryl Washington's opinion) if only everybody else around would just shut up and obey.

For Washington himself, it was different. What he was forced to do was to give only the orders that people would be willing to obey . . . and what was the fun of that?

To be sure, there were a lot of ways in which Captain Darryl Washington's situation was a good deal more interesting than that of the mythical Captain Horatio Hornblower. Crew, for instance. A sailing-ship captain like Hornblower was lucky if a quarter of his crew could read or write, while the people under Washington's "command" included specialists in linguistics, petrology, archaeology (with a minor in theology), plant chemistry, sociology, zoology, and a dozen other -ologies and -isticses. (They hadn't all been expert in all those things at launch time—but it isn't hard to earn double doctorates in eleven years of monotony.) Washington didn't think of that. Wouldn't have considered it much of a break if he had, because all it meant was that they had a lot more ammunition to use in challenging his decisions.

Washington glowered around the control room, as though quelling a rebellious crew. Of course, they weren't there. Boulat and Nicole were caring for the sick man, Kammer was doing whatever he did when he wasn't in view—Captain Blow-Your-Horn didn't much care; it was just good to have him out of sight. Still the captain, in his own control room, felt the inaudible sound of them snickering at him.

There was a better place to be, where no one ever questioned his authority. Captain Washington set all the controls on automatic, unstrapped himself, and, wheezing with the effort of pulling his monstrously fat body through the corridors, went there.

The chamber that Darryl Washington had commandeered for his private office wasn't large, but it was a great luxury. When he locked the door he was a real captain. Supreme in his own domain, it was the kind of luxury no one on the spacer ship had been able to possess for all the subjective eleven years of their flight.

Once it had been storage space. Storage space was what most of the interior cubage of the ship was: room to hold the huge quantity of things that were necessary for exploring the new planets, like the two scouting planes, four of the six wire-wheeled surface buggies, the food machines, the camping equipment, two or three lander loads of trade goods to win friends among the natives. Those things were all gone now, painfully ferried down to the surface of Genji. Their storage space was empty. The ship now had surplus *room.* Anyone of the crew remaining on the ship who wanted it could appropriate a compartment of his own, and put a door on it, and lock it.

Naturally, everyone had immediately done so. Everyone had dreamed for years of the joy of possessing a personal place to scratch or pick one's nose or break wind in private. Washington, as captain, had asserted his right to first pick, of course. The only real difference was that Darryl Washington still used the locks . . . for that was the kind of person Captain Blow-Your-Horn was.

The first thing the captain had done with his "office" was to fit it with a duplicate of the ship's communications terminals. Everything that passed in or out of the ship appeared on those private monitors. He kept his own log on them, encoded so that no one else could read it. He could even use the system to monitor almost every compartment in the ship itself. He did so, often, especially when his wife was aboard and out of his immediate presence.

Captain Blow-Your-Horn had not mentioned this to any of his crew. He was aware that some of them would object to his prying into their privacy. Of course, he didn't agree. In his mind, it was simply the kind of advantage that it was proper for a ship's captain to have—how else could you make sure everybody was obeying orders?

Comfortably strapped in, Darryl Washington first turned his monitor to outgoing transmissions, just to make sure that Boulat Kotsvili had been doing his other job as ship's data-transmitter. He had been, of course. He might now be trying to patch up the sick Murqhad Fasbar, but the transmitter was still on automatic, busily pumping data back to the spacer habitats around Sol. Just at that moment it was shots of the carpet whales that were being transmitted— probably taken by Fasbar himself, before he had ruined his lungs. Washington didn't watch for long. No one did any more; it was too boring. To make the long trip back to Sol, the data bits that made up any message had to be transmitted slowly and repetitively, with redundancies and parity checks. It took more than an hour to transmit a minute's worth of recording, and then what showed up on those twenty-year-distant screens would be only a single frame, drawing itself dot by dot and line by line—and doing it three times, because each frame was transmitted thrice, as seen through the red, cyan, and green filters. That was the only way that the pictures could be reconstituted in full color back on the TV screens of Earth, Mars, and the Spacer habitats in orbit.

There was no reason to watch it. Washington knew of something more important to do, and was about to do it when the intercom sounded. It was his wife. "Murqhad's really sick," she reported. "Boulat says most of his alveoli are crushed and he may have to try transplants. I *told* him he shouldn't go out in that soupy air without a suit, but he wanted to try to talk to the carpet whales direct."

"So it's all his own fault," Washington said briefly, dismissing Murqhad Fasbar and studying his wife. She looked both tired and muscular. They all took steroids, of course, before venturing onto Genji; but the effort of dealing with Genji's high gravity had put muscles on her muscles. He said importantly, "I've got other things on my mind right now."

"The Japanese?"

Washington nodded peevishly. "They didn't finish their ship for three years after we launched. How did they get here so fast?"

Nicole's face on the screen looked patient—it was a way she often looked at her husband. "Boulat says they probably just went faster. They come from Earth, you know. They start out with a one-gee environment, so they could just put on more thrust—maybe work up to a gee and a half, so they'd be ready for Genji. Why didn't we think of that?"

"It would've killed us!" he snapped, nettled at the criticism. He believed it was true. The spacers weren't used to high gravity, even with steroids.

"It might've killed you," she said, pointedly gazing at his flesh. His first (and only) landing on Genji nearly had, with all that blubber to lug around. "We did increase the thrust gradually; otherwise we couldn't have landed in the first place. We just could've done more. Why didn't you think of that, Darry?"

"I didn't set the flight plan! Captain Markorian did that!"

"But—" she began, and then, gazing at him, stopped. She changed the subject. "Question is, what do we do now? I've been talking to Boulat, and he thinks we ought to do Chujo."

"Chujo!" he barked, nettled—how dare his crew think about future plans behind his back?

"It makes sense, Darry. We've already sent back a load of stuff on Genji, but we never touched Chujo at all."

He glared at her. "Because Chujo's a waste of time! Genji has *sapients.* They're what people are interested in, not plants and maybe some creepy-crawlies like on Chujo."

"But we ought to at least look—"

"We *have* looked," Washington informed his wife. "All those scans." He was on firm ground there, he was sure. They had their own robot satellite, still orbiting Chujo and sending back data, though none of it was very interesting. Scenery? Chujo had plenty of scenery, if that was what you were interested in: mountains, brackish seas, dried riverbeds, the "ring of fire" all around its globe where moonside and starside met; well, what about it?

To be sure, there was definitely some evidence of life. The "fuzzy" logic of the ship's computers had teased a few portraits out of the quick snapshots of the scans. The ones they called "trolls": tall, two-legged, toothed—and clawed, too, because one of the frames had shown a troll ripping the guts out of one of the long-legged things, like skinny kangaroos, they'd named the "high-jumpers." Well, how would you like to meet up with a troll in some dark Chujoan alley?

"There used to be something better there," she reminded him.

Washington glared at her silently for a moment. It was true enough. The scans had produced pictures to suggest it, and for that matter even the original automated Japanese probe had found signs that there had once been perhaps something almost like a civilization on the paired planet. At least, there might have been things that could once have been buildings.

"We couldn't do everything at once," he barked, feeling the challenge to his authority. Everybody had agreed that Genji was the priority target! Genji was where the real action was, with its himatids and carpet whales and all kinds of smart, or semismart, fauna.

She sighed. "We'll talk it over later, hon," she conceded. "First I'm going to take a shower."

And at last Washington had the chance to do what he had been setting out to do.

He had *sealed orders.*

Before he opened Markorian's old file there was something else he wanted to look at. They weren't really sealed, because they had come over the radio from cis-Mercury, and they weren't really orders. But he took them seriously. He slipped his own record capsule into the machine and set the program to his private decode mode. Naturally, no one's private messages were private if they were transmitted in the clear.

He played once again the last message he had received from his father.

It was interesting that, on the screen, the old man didn't look any older, but it wasn't surprising. The message had taken almost as long to get to Murasaki as the ship had. Though the captain had received it only a few days earlier, it was a voice across the decades, twenty years out of date. When Roy Washington stepped up to the TV cameras and sent it, the ship was still less than halfway through the acceleration phase of its journey. Johnny Markorian was still alive then—and still captain. Aaron Kammer was still hale and healthy. . . .

And Nicole was just getting ready to divorce him and marry Kammer.

The captain bit his lip and glared at the screen, where his father was beaming in pride. "I'm glad things are going so well for you, Darryl. If your mother had lived she'd certainly be thrilled to see you making something out of yourself at last. Nicole's parents were on the screen last night, and the three of us drank a toast to you two lovebirds." Then he frowned. "There's something funny, though. They heard the same rumors we did about coming back early instead of staying for the full ten years. I think it has something to do with the Japs—they're launching any day now, I hear. Well, this is expensive, so I'll just say that we all think of you, and miss you . . . and give that pretty bride of yours a kiss from your father."

Frowning, Washington switched to Markorian's private log and scrolled to the entry he wanted:

"My private instructions are that if the Japanese get their ship going ahead of schedule we are to turn around and come back as soon as they get to Murasaki. This is an economic necessity, because the first samples returned will be the most valuable—"

He let it run, but he wasn't listening any more. He was thinking about the damn Japanese. What should he do?

He knew what the real Captain Hornblower would have done when an enemy ship hove in sight. He would have tacked right up to the other ship, opened the gun ports and dismasted it, and then probably led a party to board the enemy vessel, cutlass in hand. Of course, you didn't do that kind of thing with spaceships. Even if you had gun ports to open, or guns of any kind. Even if you had the sort of loyal, brave crew that would follow you through the gates of hell, instead of this bunch of cripples and complainers . . .

"Oh, hell," he said out loud. He wondered what his father would think if he could see him at that moment. Probably that his son was doing the sloppy, inept kind of job both his parents had always expected from him.

It was simply unfair. They'd spent eleven years, one month, and twenty-two days in transit, trying to find something to do. Now they'd spent more than a year trying to do a tenth of one percent of the things they *ought* to do—all short on sleep, cutting corners every which way. . . .

And now this!

Still frowning, Washington reached to turn off the machine—and clumsily missed the switch. His fingers hit centimeters below the keyboard.

That was the first he realized that there was a slow buildup of thrust. The ship was easing out of Low Genji Orbit. It was moving somewhere else.

By the time Washington reached the control room both Kammer and Boulat Kotsvili were there before him, hanging on the captain's net. He knew before he got there who would be usurping his place, and of course he was right. "God damn it, Nicole!" he exploded. "What the hell do you think you're doing?"

"Shut up, Darry," she said patiently. "I started to set up the course for Chujo for you because that was the obvious next step for us to take. Then I saw that we were in a good launch window, and I thought we'd better not miss it."

"That isn't your job! That's up to the *captain*!" he shouted, but they were only looking at him patiently, Kammer sleepy-eyed, Kotsvili with a thermosonde dangling around his neck—Nicole, of course, with that offhand tolerance that drove him crazy. "Well, it isn't," he finished.

Nicole didn't even respond. She only said, "Everybody knows we've got to land on Chujo."

"Chujo's *worthless*," her husband said obstinately.

"Chujo's a whole planet," she reminded him. "There are buildings there."

"There are *rocks* there. They don't look like buildings to me. Worthless!"

She was losing her patience. "And how do we know it's worthless until we send somebody down to look at it? Back home they expect us to get there before anyone else, don't they? That's what being first means, so we've got to go there. The only thing we have to decide is who does the landing."

"Me, for one," Aaron Kammer said at once.

Everybody looked at him in surprise. Then they looked back at each other as though he hadn't spoken. "I can't go," Kotsvili said reluctantly. "I've got to take care of Murqhad."

The captain said harshly, "Let me see the course." Silently Nicole displayed it for him on the screen, with all the burns and vector changes. Washington glowered at it. "It's all right," he grumbled, "but, really, I don't think—"

Kotsvili spoke right over him. "It's a two-day trip to get to low Chujo," he pointed out. "Then we'll send the lander down, couple of hours each way; say six or eight hours on the surface to look around—"

"More than that," Nicole objected. "I want to spend at least one whole Chujo daylight there. Maybe more."

Her husband looked affronted. The Chujo day, like the Genjian, lasted forty-seven hours with a forty-seven-hour night following.

"That's practically a week we'll be away from Low Genji Orbit!" he complained.

Kotsvili added, "What if the people on Genji need something? And you've got the lander tied up?"

What the people on Genji might want was not what had been on the captain's mind; it was what his wife had said.

"So you think you ought to go," he said meditatively, searching for a reason to forbid it.

"I am going, yes," she told him.

"But not alone," Aaron Kammer said firmly.

They all looked at him again. "Oh, Airy," Nicole said without patience, "what if you get sick down there?"

He didn't argue the question. He just said, "I'm going. I have a right to that much."

"A *right*," the captain sneered. What did a ship's crew need with rights? But he could see that Kotsvili was nodding agreement, and then even Nicole, after a moment's reflection, said:

"Maybe you're the best choice to go with me at that, Airy, only your health—"

"I just had a transfusion," Kammer reminded her. "I'll be okay for a while, no matter what."

The captain glowered at them indecisively. It offended him that no one had bothered with even the formality of asking him to approve the mission. They would go ahead anyhow, of course, whatever he said. He knew that. But they should at least *ask*.

He stood up, unbuckling his harness. He reminded himself that he still had some rights of his own. "You've got one daylight and that's all," he said, listening with pleasure to the commanding tone of his voice. "Then I take the ship back to Genji orbit."

"But what if we need more time?" Kammer objected.

"You don't have it. That's final. Now come to bed, Nicole," he ordered his wife, triumphantly.

.   .   .

The landing on Chujo was uneventful. That didn't keep most of the people involved from having high emotional reactions. Captain Blow-Your-Horn glowered at the dwindling flare of rocket exhaust as though he wanted to kill. In the lander Aaron Kammer was grinning with pleasure as he guided the ship in. He wasn't the best choice for pilot, of course—hadn't had anything like the practice his ex-wife had. But Nicole let him take the controls. Partly because she had some private business to attend to in the lander's little sanitary room, mostly because she could see how desperately he wanted it . . . and because she knew how unlikely it was that Kammer's wants for the future would ever be satisfied.

3

Chujo was cold, because its thin air didn't trap much heat from Murasaki, whereas Genji had been hot because its murky miasma did. They landed on a mesa, just on the bright side of the dawn terminator. There were some really impressive mountains off to the east, and their landing site was on the shoulder of another one.

As soon as they were out of the ship they were both giggling. Chujo felt *good.* On Genji everyone weighed half again as much as Earth-normal; on Chujo only a fraction of that—good news for spacers. Or even for ex-Martians. On Genji you had to wear a pressure suit at low elevations, unless you wanted to wreck your metabolism and cough your lungs out, like poor, foolish Murqhad Fasbar. And on Chujo, at least at this elevation, all you needed was a nose mask to supplement the tiny partial pressure of oxygen, and then you could roam anywhere you liked. Almost.

"This is *fun!*" Aaron Kammer called to his ex-wife over the noise of the buggy as they rode it up to the formation that might, or might not, be ruins of some kind. Laughing, she agreed with him. It was so good to see Airy happy again!

Nicole was pleased with her landing, too. It had been a piece of cake, and all the time they were setting up to explore—deploying the plastic shelter, fitting each other's nose masks, reporting in to sullen Captain Washington up in orbit in the big ship—she was conscious of the way her onetime husband kept looking at her. She liked it. It was pleasurably exciting to be alone with this sweet, sad (and not at all disgustingly fat) man she had once been married to. Being alone together had rarely happened since the divorce. She wondered, not in the least apprehensively, if he would make any sort of sexual advances to her. She was pretty sure he might, and anyway she had resources of her own.

But there was business to attend to. Nicole had not forgotten that there was a world to explore, and that it was Airy's first. Everyone else on the ship had had some experience of that on Genji. Only Kammer had been left out, because Boulat Kotsvili's tests had warned that his damaged body couldn't take Genji's extra gravity. Nicole could see her ex-husband's excitement, and was only mildly disappointed to be aware that it had little to do with her. Mostly it was the thrill of at last doing the thing they had all come so far to do—doing it himself, in the flesh. Before they had gone a kilometer he could sit still no longer. "I can climb faster than this," he told her, and before she could stop him he was out of the buggy and trotting up the hill.

"Be careful!" she called, meaning, For God's sake, Airy, don't kill yourself this first time! But he only waved over his shoulder and kept on trotting.

The valley had broadened out into another broad meadow, twenty or thirty hectares of low yellow bushes. Nicole followed with the camera on Aaron as he ran over to touch them and came back with a handful of purplish berries the size of plums. Nicole wrinkled her nose under the mask. "What's that smell?"

"I guess it's the plants. They do smell pretty high," he admitted, "but I bet these are food for something."

"Something small and harmless, I hope," she said, but she was smiling as he dropped them in the buggy and turned to race ahead again.

They were following a nearly dry rivercourse up the mountain, with yellow-green forests on both sides. It wasn't much of a river, just an icy-cold trickle from the glaciers high on the peak, but it made the closest thing to a roadway for them. Unfortunately, it wasn't a very straight road. Nicole could only keep track of Kammer for a few minutes before he was out of sight on a bend of the stream.

She did what she was supposed to do, though. She guided the buggy with one hand and operated the camera with the other: pictures of the stream, pictures of the rocks it flowed through, pictures mostly of the curious trees—well, treelike things—that grew all around them. They would have to get samples of those trees, too—leaves, wood, fruit, and flowers if they had any. But she didn't want to stop now, because she didn't want to leave Kammer too long alone. On the way back would be plenty of time.

Peering ahead, she could make out glimpses of the odd formation they hoped might once have been a "city." If it was, it certainly didn't have any inhabitants any more. It had been visible enough to pick out from the orbital scans because it was exposed on a hillside. For the same reason, it was pretty well erased by time now. A thousand dust storms had eaten away most of the structure in Chujo's high winds; landslides from the slopes above had buried most of the rest of it.

Of course, there might still be some kinds of animals living in the ruins.

So she was relieved when the buggy nosed around a final bend and she could clearly see the oddly straight-lined rock formations they had picked out from space. She killed the motor and got out to join Aaron, lugging the camera. He was out of sight, but with the motor off she could track him by the crack of his geologist's hammer as he took samples of some rock or other.

It was all stone—several different kinds of stone. Nicole was not geologist enough to identify them at a glance, but one white stone was veined like marble, another a dull scarlet, another black as onyx.

There wasn't any doubt about it any more. Long before she reached Kammer she knew what he was going to say, because she had confirmed it for herself—the low walls, the unnaturally rectilinear bits of rubble—and, on the other side of that square-edged gap in the wall that might have been—no, really, surely was—a doorway, there was Aaron, turning around in delight to call to her: "Do you see, Nicky? These aren't just rocks. These were *buildings*! There was a time when people lived here!"

And, laughing, she called back, "Don't get so excited, Airy. But, yes, I think so, too."

In the three years they were married Nicole had really loved Aaron Kammer. She remembered positively that that was true—well, up to a point, anyway. There were different kinds of love, surely. There was the kind you dreamed of when you were fifteen and the teenage boys you knew, with their bruising kisses and clumsy hands, were simply an obstacle course you had to get through on the way to the Real Thing. The Real Thing was moonlit nights, warm breezes, you in a filmy dress with flowers in your hair and him tall and wise and tender. That was all fantasy, of course, especially for a spacer girl like Nicole—you didn't get moonlit nights in a habitat. But it was such a sweet and painful fantasy. Then there was the kind of love you hoped for when you were twenty, with a man who would put a child in your belly and share your work and your life, as well as your bed. How disappointing that that had turned out to be only fantasy, too, when you confronted the reality of the noisy, smelly, crowded little spaceship in midflight, with years behind you and years still to go.

It was a fact that when Nicole decided to switch husbands there was a lingering thought, in some part of her head, that Aaron's were the kind of genes she would like her kids to have.

But that was just another fantasy. Like every other woman on the ship, she had continued to wear her fertility blocker, because what were they going to do with a bunch of babies on a ship that was already too small for its grown-up crew? Reluctantly, Nicole had concluded that there wasn't any version of romantic love that could survive on a long-distance spaceship.

The thing about the present situation was that they weren't on the spaceship any more.

There was another significant fact, though, and that was that they weren't married any more, either. That fact troubled Nicole—some. The man she had divorced to marry Aaron Kammer was her husband again. The troubling part of that was that Nicole had a persistent conviction that married people should not love anybody but each other. To divorce a man was supposed to mean that you stopped loving him.

Yet here, on this cold, strange planet, it didn't seem to be working out that way.

Aaron was different here, for one thing. He was *alive* again. She had never seen him so happy and so excited. Certainly he still coughed and his hands still trembled, because he was still well into that process of dying. She knew that he was pushing his strength farther than it ought to go. But she couldn't stop him, because he was so completely absorbed in this exploration, chipping off bits of rock and throwing them on the buggy, scraping soil off what might have been flooring, shouting with joy as he picked up a thing like a potsherd or uncovered a thing like a rusted blade. So all that time she followed him around with the camera, watching him, and her heart was melting inside her.

It was Nicole who insisted that they stop and rest a moment. "And we have to eat something, too," she ordered.

Kammer looked at her in surprise. Then he reached out and touched her face—well, touched her mask, anyway; but it was a tender, tolerant kind of touch. "You know what you are, Nicky? You're blasé. This isn't exciting to you any more, is it?"

She said, grinning under the nose mask, "It's no big thrill. You've put your hands on me plenty of times before this."

He pulled his fingers back as though she had burned him. "No, I mean exploring. Coming to this *place*," he explained. "You've done it all already, haven't you? I mean, on Genji? But for me—"

He shook his head, delighted. Nicole said practically, "We still have to eat, you know."

"Oh, sure," he agreed, but his eyes were roving. He even tried to do what she ordered, but it was impossible. He couldn't make himself sit still. Long before she had finished chewing the last of the rations they had brought he was up again, circling the ruins, peering curiously into the stunted woods around them.

Nicole was not immune to the excitement of exploring Chujo, with its purply sky and the great crescent of Genji hanging off to one side. She was interested in what she saw, camera always busy, talking notes into her recorder about the sparseness of the birds (nothing like the flocks in Genji's soupy air; flying was hard work on Chujo) and the absolute absence of any detectable animal life (but of course they would have hidden from strangers, with all the noise they were making). But she could have called it a day a lot sooner if she had not been so pleased to indulge Kammer's delight. So she let her compassion outweigh her better judgment. They stayed a good deal longer than she had planned, but at last she called a halt. "Back to the lander," she ordered. "We have to report in next time the ship's overhead. Besides, you've got to rest."

"Just a little more—?"

"Now," she commanded.

He pouted at her, then grinned. "You drive," he said. "Slowly."

And while she was easing the buggy over the bumps and depressions on the way back down the hill, Kammer was loping around the margin of the forest, running back to the buggy with samples of leaves and fruits, never still, though she saw that his face was paling with fatigue.

In that reeking broad valley he dumped a load of the berry plants and she caught his hand. "Enough, Airy! We'll come back here if you like—but I want you alive when we do it."

He pulled free, trotting alongside the buggy, panting a little. "Well," he said, "I suppose you're right. Look, I've got something for you."

Carefully he pulled a little purple-blue flower out of his pouch and handed it to her. She looked at it and sniffed. It certainly didn't smell like any flower she'd ever seen from Earth; if it had any scent at all, it was more like ancient mold than rosebuds. "It's pretty," she said, guiding the buggy with one hand while she turned it in her fingers.

"It's the prettiest one I've seen," he told her. "I'm the discoverer, so I'm naming it after you. *Kammeria nicolensia,* or something like that."

She stared at him, suddenly embarrassed. He grinned and said, "Hang on to it, Nicky. Now just let me go back and get a couple of other things from the woods there. I saw some shrubs—"

"Airy!" she called peremptorily. But he was already on his way, halfway to the forest edge.

Nicole cursed to herself, and then out loud as the buggy hit a tuft of tangled vegetation and jolted alarmingly. By the time she got it straightened out and looked back, she was startled to see that Kammer was sprawled on the ground in the middle of the field.

"Airy!" she shouted again, panic this time. She stopped the buggy and ran over to him. He was trying to stand up, hand pressed to his forehead. There was blood on his fingers. "What *happened*?" she demanded, helping him up.

He stared at her dazedly. "I—I don't know. Something hit me on the head."

"What could hit you on the head?" she snapped—foolishly. Angrily. And then she heard something whiz through the thin air by them only centimeters away. "Oh, shit," she snarled. "Let's get out of here! Somebody's throwing rocks at us!"

Once they were in the lander Nicole felt safer—a little bit, anyway. With the port closed and the cut on Kammer's head bandaged, she began to breathe more easily. It was a deep cut, and it bled a lot, but the bone wasn't broken.

Then Aaron insisted on opening the port again so he could check the hold-downs on the external shelter, for fear of one of Chujo's sudden windstorms—he explained that he knew better than Nicole what they might be like, being Martian. Then at last he was willing to lie down and rest while she reported in to the ship. Yes, she informed the captain, there was definitely life on Chujo—animal life. "Those trolls in the picture?" the captain asked.

Nicole shuddered, remembering the noseless, apelike face and the teeth. "I don't know. I couldn't see them," she said, "but Airy claims he did."

"Well, almost," he called from the berth beside her. "I just saw shadows, really."

"Intelligent?" Nicole said, returning to Captain Washington's ques-

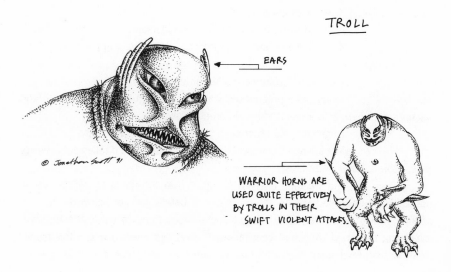

TROLL

EARS

© Jonathan Scott 91

WARRIOR HORNS ARE
USED QUITE EFFECTIVELY
BY TROLLS IN THEIR
SWIFT VIOLENT ATTACKS.

tions. "How do I know if they're intelligent? They throw rocks, but so do apes. No, I think we're safe enough here. I've got the sensors up, and there's nothing moving within half a kilometer."

"The trolls won't come out of the forest," Aaron put in.

She turned and frowned at him. "You don't know that."

"They didn't follow me," he pointed out.

She shook her head, but the captain was still speaking. "Well," he said, "if you say there are buildings there I'll take your word for it."

"Ruins, really," Nicole corrected.

"Of course they're just ruins. We know that much, don't we? And the scans from your landing orbit—?"

Of course, they had left the external cameras on as they looped in for their landing. "Have you analyzed the data? Any good pictures?"

"Boring," her husband told her. "Well, there are definitely buildings. More on starside than here, but all abandoned."

"Well, then!" Nicole said. "We ought to have at least one more landing on starside, right?"

"Wrong. We're going. I've already notified all the parties on Genji to stand by for pickup."

"But at least look at the starside buildings—"

"No." Nicole sighed. When Darryl Washington had made up his mind there was no changing him, right or wrong. *Especially* when he was wrong.

"Then at least let us see if we can find some animal life to bag."

"Only if you can do it before local dark," he said firmly. "Why bother? Animals are animals. If there ever was anyone civilized enough to build things on Chujo, they're all dead now."

"Except for the rock throwers," Nicole said.

The radio was silent for a moment. "If you're in any danger—" the captain began.

"We aren't!" Kammer called emphatically.

"—just as a precaution, you have enough fuel to jump and land again somewhere else a few hundred kilometers away."

"Negative!" Kammer said. "I want to see what's here."

More silence from the radio. Then, "I wish you'd taken some weapons," the captain fretted.

"But we didn't," said Nicole. "Now I'm going to switch over to data transmission so you can see our pictures before you get below the horizon again. Talk to you later, after we get some—something to eat," she finished, changing her mind. She had been about to say, "get some sleep." But to say that, to her very jealous husband, had suddenly seemed tactless.

. . .

They hadn't taken a food machine for just the two of them, so all there was in the larder was dehydrates and radiation-stabilized fruits. Well, almost all. Nicole had at the last moment packed some precious, hoarded wine as a little surprise.

Aaron had been drowsing off and on while she was on the radio, and now he was sound asleep. She watched him carefully. He looked so *tired.* She tried to remember what he had looked like when she had come to the conclusion she was more in love with Aaron Kammer than the man she was married to. He'd been good-looking then, before he let himself get burned refitting the drive. Even now, she thought, Aaron had a good, strong, solid body, without all that disgusting blubber Darryl Washington had allowed himself to grow. Not to mention a lot better disposition. Not to mention his—

Well, his sweetness. Aaron Kammer had enough of that for export. Who else would make clothes for a cat?

Sweetness hadn't been enough. And anyway, she thought, you can get really tired of sweetness.

When she woke him to say that dinner was ready, he blinked up at her contentedly. "How's your head?" she asked.

"Fine," he said, dismissing the subject. Lying about it, of course. "What's this?" he asked, looking curiously at the pouch of wine, but amused because he knew the answer. "I didn't know you had any wine left."

"This is the last. I thought we might celebrate," she said.

"Celebrate what?"

"Celebrate this, dummy! You know, this is the first time we've ever been really alone together?"

He gave her a thoughtful look as he sipped from the cup, but all he said was, "I guess I was sleeping while you were talking to the ship. How's Blow-Your-Horn?"

She looked at him. "He's fine," she said shortly. "You shouldn't call him that."

"And you shouldn't have—" He cut himself off, not wanting to say what was coming next.

"Go on," she prodded. "What shouldn't I have?"

"I don't have any right to tell you what you should do," he said.

"Oh, damn you, Airy, quit being so goddamned *understanding.* What's on your stupid mind?"

He grinned at her, feeling better. "I just can't help wondering why you went back to him, after."

"After you got hurt and I dumped you, you mean."

"No, Nicole," he said earnestly, "that's not what I mean. At least, not that way. I know why you didn't want to be married to me any more. I was sick. You thought I was going to die, and I was—still am. I was a real drag; I know that. But why *him*?"

Nicole hesitated, wondering how much truth to tell him. She tried a little, experimentally. "Darryl wasn't so bad in the old days. Before he got fat. Before he was captain. And anyway—" She shrugged and took the plunge. "Anyway, I owed him."

Kammer was startled at last. "You *owed* Darryl?"

She toyed with her food. "It goes back a long way," she said slowly. "When I was nineteen years old, I got raped. See, Airy, it never happened to you, so you don't know what that's like. After it's over you feel like—Christ—I can't tell you what you feel like. You feel like a toilet that's just been pissed in, and you keep on feeling that way."

He looked startled and puzzled at once. "You don't mean *Darryl* was the one who raped you?"

"Oh, hell, no. Just a guy. A date."

"Well, did the police—"

She stopped him. "I didn't report it. Maybe I should have, I think now I should, but I didn't. Anyway, then Darryl was there, and he was so strong, and he seemed to know what he was going to do with his life, and he liked me and wanted me to volunteer along with him for this—and most of all," she said, grimacing, "he could *protect* me, Airy. Or I thought he could. And anyway we'd be a million kilometers away from everybody if we signed up." She stopped and grinned sadly at him. "I guess that was why I ditched you, Airy. When you were sick you couldn't protect me any more."

"But going back to Darryl . . . "

"A woman doesn't have that many choices out here, does she? And he was the captain. And, damn it, Airy," she flared, "why did you start that Blow-Your-Horn stuff? It makes it really hard on him, and I *trusted* you, Airy!"

He shrugged. "I guess a woman should never repeat one husband's pillow talk to the next guy. Well, that doesn't excuse me, does it? I'm sorry. I was—well, not happy, after you dumped me."

"It was my fault," she said, reflecting that she didn't seem to understand just how a man felt when he got dumped. "I'm sorry, too. We should've worked things out better. If it was up to me we'd forget about all this pairing-off business and just make love when we felt like it with whom we felt like doing it with," she declared, watching him.

He grinned. "A lot of you came close enough to that, the last year or so before we reached Murasaki."

She smiled back. "Darryl raised hell about the fistfights that came out of it," she said reminiscently. "Me—"

"You what?" he challenged.

"Me, I thought those days were exciting," she said.

It was strange to be preparing for sleep in broad daylight—hardly even noon, by Chujo's long day. "Did I miss anything from the ship?" Kammer asked.

"Well," she said, hesitantly, "there is one thing. It's kind of like repeating pillow talk again, but I guess you ought to know. Darryl's evacuating Genji. He wants to head for home before the Jap ship gets here."

"I'm not surprised," Aaron said, and yawned. "I guess it's the wine," he apologized, grinning. "And maybe just being here, you know? It's such a nice break. Don't you get tired of being in a ship?"

"I haven't been stuck in one as long as you have," she told him. "Don't forget I did a tour on Genji."

He nodded, then looked across the bedding at her. "And what's the captain going to think about the two of us sleeping so close together?"

She shrugged, tugging the sleeping sacks nearer. "What do you think about it?" she asked.

Kammer didn't answer, just watched her closely. She was very conscious of that. It was disconcerting, in an unexpected way. She said over her shoulder, "When that troll hit you I thought you were dead."

"Sorry," he said, grinning again.

"Don't be a fool," she said. Then, "Airy? I never thanked you for Bandit's hat. It was nice of you to make it for her."

"It wasn't really finished. Did you try it on?"

"She loved it. Come here," she said, and gave him a kiss. "You're a nice man," she told him, pulling back breathlessly, looking at him with humor and fondness. She was not at all surprised when they kissed again, and kept on kissing.

When she woke up the ship was still and she was curled up with a sleeping sack over her. Nicole stretched comfortably before opening her eyes.

She wasn't surprised to be alone. No doubt Kammer had retired to his own place after they'd made love and she had fallen asleep. She thought drowsily about her absent husband for a moment, wondering whether she would tell him about this or not, and what he would say if she did. It didn't seem important. It was all too far in the future to worry about.

"Airy," she called, "it's your turn to make breakfast." And listened for a response.

But there wasn't any. He wasn't there.

He wasn't in the ship at all. The exit port was unlocked. It had been pushed shut from the outside, and Aaron Kammer was gone.

4

By Richard Feynman's criteria, Kammer decided, his state was no longer stable. All sorts of fast things were happening, and that special slow change of his own body from "life" to "death" wasn't really slow any more. It was definitely picking up speed.

For some reason, that knowledge didn't frighten him. He wasn't even in real pain. His head still hurt, but that didn't matter. And as to his mood he had, after all, had plenty of time to get used to the death sentence.

Although it was never hot on Chujo, Kammer felt himself sweating as he drove the buggy down and away from the lander. The buggy wasn't designed for such work as pushing through groves of trees as densely matted as these. The things were like cypress in a swamp, clustering around the place where the river once had been, perhaps sucking up water from what was underground. The twisting and bumping of the buggy made his head throb, but he was happy. The only thing he really regretted was not answering Nicole's voice when she called after him on the radio—demanding, pleading, hurting his conscience. She was still doing it, off and on. The sound was tiny, almost drowned out by the whine of the buggy's motor and the crackling of the slenderer tree trunks as he forced his way through them, because he had turned it down. But he knew what she was saying.

He was two or three hundred vertical meters below the plain where they had landed the shuttle now, and the riverbed was opening up into a grander plain than anything above. Kammer paused, making sure the camera was going. He had turned the transmitter off, but everything was being stored. The pictures would not be wasted, he told himself, but he didn't want Nicole tracking his transmissions. Not just now . . .

He did not face the question of whether he wanted that *ever*.

Experimentally, Kammer took the nose mask off for a moment, inhaling the thin Chujoan air. He could, he decided, get by without the mask—for a while, at any rate; especially now that he was going down the hill rather than up. It helped that he was Martian born, used to the standard 800-millibar air of the Martian domes. It made him feel almost at home. He looked around, feeling excited and pleased.

What he saw looked very like a valley in, say, one of the western American states on Earth. It looked *planted.* There were three big plots, separated by clumps of woods. The plots bore scars that might once have been streams winding through them, two of a single yellow-orangey kind of spiky vegetation, the other of a different kind, more like vines. The wind brought him the same faintly repellent smell that he had noticed in the field with the berries. It was not a smell he had found in, say, the forest.

The fields seemed to have a lot in common, not least that each one of them was composed entirely of a single species of plant.

Monoculture wasn't natural. Monoculture was something *people* did. And it was an interesting fact that, on this gently sloping mountainside, these fields were all quite level.

Kammer thought about that for a moment, listening to the silence, with only the faint purr of the camera motor and the distant noise of wind in the woods. There was only one word that fit the situation. *Farms.* These plots looked very much like farms.

Then, buoyed and excited, he started the buggy again and crossed one of the plantings, the stink strong around him as the vegetation was crushed under the buggy wheels. He did not stop until he was at the verge of the next wooded area. . . .

And might not have stopped then if he hadn't heard the screaming.

Aaron Kammer didn't merely stop the buggy. He stopped the motor, stopped moving, almost stopped breathing. The screams were both loud and terrible. Some living thing was being hurt very badly and with murderous violence; there was a thrashing in the forest as saplings were being knocked about in a ferocious struggle.

Kammer stood up in his driver's seat, craning his neck to peer through the yellow-brown tendrils. It sounded like a catfight—but had to be huge cats!—and there was a flurry of fast-moving large shapes—and it was moving.

It was coming in his direction.

There were four animals involved. One was a quadruped the size of a bear; it was skull-faced, and it was bleeding and bleating as it tried to escape from its attackers.

Who were trolls.

They were clear to see this time, and there was no doubt of their identity. Kammer recognized them at once from the handful of frames in the reconnaissance scans. They were half again as tall as a man—even a Spacer. Two-legged, like a man, with the same noseless face as the animal they were killing. They had the built-in weaponry any predator had to possess for murder: long blue talons, a shark's mouthful of teeth.

Kammer bent hastily to detach the camera from its mount so he could capture this scene for the archives. As quickly as he could he stood up again, eye to the finder, aiming at the death scene. When he had the animal in sight he zoomed the lens to bring it into sharp focus, right up front. It was a sickening spectacle. Kammer was revolted to see the details of its awfully lacerated hide, covered with a feathery sort of coating, not hair, not real feathers, perhaps rudimentary scales.

It took him a moment to realize that he was not getting the attackers in the shot, and then another to discover that the sounds of screaming had stopped.

The trolls were not slashing at their prey any more.

Belatedly Kammer took his eye away from the finder. When he saw the trolls, all three of them were loping silently through the trees—toward him.

If Kammer was resigned to his approaching death, he still could not help the shock of terror that drove him back into his seat. Frantically he was starting the buggy, wheeling it at top speed in a great arc, back out of the woods and across the planted field. A rock whizzed past his head and struck the wind-screen; the screen did not shatter, but his vision through it was distorted by the crazed star design the missile had left. He ducked down, foot pressed with all his strength to the accelerator pedal. He did not think the buggy could travel as fast as the trolls. He expected at any moment to have one of them scrabble up over the back of the buggy on top of him, clawing and biting. He risked lifting his head and turning around—

He had an unexpected reprieve.

All three of the trolls had stopped at the edge of the planted field. They were throwing rocks, but they weren't following; and he was nearly across the field, farther than even their pitching arms could reach—

Almost into the woods on the other side, in fact; but Kammer did not realize that until the buggy struck head-on against a giant of the forest, catapulting him into the windscreen.

If Kammer had been sitting in the normal driver's position behind the tiller he would have struck the screen headfirst. Certainly he would have knocked himself out at least, even if he hadn't fractured his skull. He wasn't; he didn't; he struck sidewise, with his arm and shoulder taking the brunt of the impact, his legs caught and twisted under him. That was a pity. Unconsciousness would have been preferable to the shock of agony that went through his body. He couldn't move. He lay there, hurting—hurting worse than ever before in his life—and didn't realize for some time that he was screaming. When he did notice it it made no difference. He couldn't stop until sheer exhaustion reduced the volume of sound to an agonized moaning as he lay there with his eyes closed.

When he opened them, a face was looking down at him.

A troll? But it wasn't leaping at him. And, if a troll, it was a small one—not much taller than Kammer himself; definitely much shorter and more delicately built than the ones that had brought down the bearlike thing. It had the same noseless face (but without that terrifying array of teeth), and he was quite sure that it couldn't possibly be one of the trolls, since it didn't rip his belly open with its long, blue nails.

No, whatever it was, it was definitely not a troll.

Kammer almost forgot to moan as he stared up at the thing; and then it did something incredible. It touched him gently. It whistled softly a few times, clear notes and trilled, like birdsong. It seemed to be expecting him to reply. When he didn't it gave one last faint, disappointed trill. And then it clambered up on top of the buggy and stood bent over, legs spread, holding to the top of the windscreen, looking down on him while a—a *something,* a penis perhaps, an organ of some kind at least—extruded itself from flaps of flesh at its groin.

The thing urinated on him. It did so methodically. Lavishly. Copiously. Covering every part of his body with the stream—strong-smelling, foul, almost like the stench of the plantings he had driven through—while regarding him gravely all the while.

Kammer, dazed, managed to whisper through bruised lips, "Why are you doing that to me?"

Of course, the thing didn't answer. It whistled softly again for a moment. Then it reached down and touched him again, and clambered down off the buggy and was gone, leaving Kammer with the agony of his broken body.

If he was going to die, Kammer thought, he had never, ever, thought it would be like this. He gazed up into the tree overhead, with bright Murasaki shining through the purple-dark sky, near the dimmer, almost hidden disk of Genji. He craned his neck, trying to see over the door of the buggy. No, the thing that had used him for a latrine was gone, or at least not in sight.

He lay there dazed, while the pain of his fractures and crushed flesh—no, did not dwindle; no, did not become more bearable; simply became more familiar. He knew that he was close to fainting from loss of blood as much as the pain.

Then a flicker of motion caught his attention.

He dragged his head around to see what it was. It was not good news. One of the trolls was standing there, regarding him with fury. There was no doubt that it was one of the three he had seen in the forest on the other side of the field. Its noseless face was still stained with the chocolaty-red blood of the animal it had attacked.

It did not, however, attack Aaron Kammer.

It simply stood there, watching. And when it was joined by another of its kind, and minutes later by the third, all three simply stood there, chittering softly to each other and watching.

How nice of you trolls, Kammer thought with gratitude, *to wait until I pass out before you kill me.*

And then the ruddy canopy of leaves overhead seemed to stir, and shrink, and fall in on him, and indeed he did pass out.

To Aaron Kammer's surprise, he woke up.

That was something he had not expected at all; it was an unexpected gift from fate, and he allowed himself to relish it for a moment before he addressed the other new surprises. Astonishingly, they were all good. He catalogued them one by one: He didn't hurt much; he was warm; and, most of all, he definitely was *alive.*

That was such an unexpected gift that it took a while for him to notice the other surprise. Quite a lot of time must have passed, for it was night. He was lying on his back on the ground, among trees. Through them he could see the purply-dark Chujo sky, with immense Genji hanging in it, brighter than a thousand moons.

Night meant that he had been unconscious for quite a long time— at least the equivalent of a day or two Terran, for it had been hardly noon by Chujo's long standards when he left the sleeping Nicole for his venture.

It also meant something else. They had planned to reorbit in daylight. It was very unlikely that Nicole was still where he had left her.

That was a sobering thought, but, he was sure, a true one. She might have wanted to search for him, but how could she when he had taken the buggy? The lander wasn't a helicopter, to search the woods from the air—if it had been, how would she have known where to search? And all the way, surely, Captain Blow-Your-Horn would have been ordering her to give it up and come back, insisting, probably even threatening— No. She was gone. It was very unlikely that any other human being was anywhere at all on the surface of this planet.

For what it was worth, Aaron Kammer had an entire world to himself.

He tried to sit up, and could not.

That was another surprise. Not a pleasant one. He lifted his head to look down at his supine body and saw that he was covered with something like a huge leaf—like an electric blanket, too, because he could feel with the heat on his face that it was radiating gentle warmth. But it wasn't electric. As he pressed against it with his chin it squeaked a faint protest and shuddered before relaxing to cover him again, like a disturbed kitten sleeping at the foot of its master's bed. The thing was alive.

He could not pause to wonder at that, though, because he was preoccupied with the bad news. He could not move his body at all. Not any part of it below the neck; not arms or fingers or legs or torso. The good part of that was that none of them was drowning him in pain, as they had been before. They felt nothing at all. His head still hurt—to be sure; a bearable pain, after all the worse ones from his crash. And his senses had not deserted him. Even his sense of smell was still working. He recognized the stench of the urine the creature had drenched him with. More than that, there was another stink, more familiar, a lot less pleasant. Was it, perhaps, the rot of his own damaged body? He could not answer that; yet he was still alive. His eyes could look around; his ears could hear.

There wasn't much to hear. The sighing of the thin wind in the trees; some minor, unalarming sounds of animals, perhaps, that might have been stirring, sighing, snuffling in their sleep. He couldn't see them.

He did see some little creatures hopping about in the trees—almost like squirrels, he thought, though their tails seemed to be flat and tapering to a point, like a dagger, rather than long and furred. It was interesting to see them, silhouetted against the disk of Genji, as they silently frolicked from limb to limb. Kammer watched them with pleasure until they moved out of sight.

Then there was nothing much to look at for a while. Kammer could see that he was deep in the forest, and wondered how he had got there. He wondered, too, what had happened to his body, and why he was not racked with the pain of his broken limbs. He wondered what the blanketlike thing was that was keeping him warm, and who had put it there. He wondered what was going to happen to him next . . . but he did not enjoy wondering about that, and dismissed it from his mind.

He even wondered, for quite a while, why he was calm enough to lie there wondering, when he should have been in a panic, or in pain—or, more likely, dead.

There wasn't any point in raising questions like that, though. Whatever had been done to him had at least left him conscious and not in pain. It was pleasant enough simply to be lying there, with no problems to face because there was nothing he could do about them.

He wondered, too, why he felt at home. It was a fact, though a puzzling one, that everything about him looked both strange and familiar at the same time.

Then he realized why.

What he was looking at was his own home, or at least his home the way he wished his own home was. Chujo was really another Mars—a Mars blessed with air (though not much) and water (even less), but a Mars with trees and living things moving about freely on its surface. In short, the Mars he had dreamed of as a child.

He laughed out loud at that—and quickly gasped with pain; because the motion had somehow twisted his neck, and something very painful made itself known at the back of the neck, just under his skull.

Then he became aware of a stronger smell, pungent as the urine that had drenched him. He heard a sound of movement. And a great skull-like face was looking down on him.

It was one of the creatures.

With the leisure he had now (nothing *but* leisure left to him!), Kammer could see that this creature was not a troll. It was not like a troll at all, not even a gracile version of them. It was no more like a troll than Kammer himself was like a mountain gorilla.

"Hello, there," he said, gasping a little. That was when he realized he had lost his nose mask somewhere along the way; but it seemed he could get by as long as he didn't overexert himself.

And, in his present condition, there seemed no chance of that.

The creature listened attentively. Then it whistled softly, as though trying to reassure him. It leaned toward him, reaching toward the back of his neck with its ill-shaped hands—did they have the right number of fingers?

"Watch it," Kammer gasped in alarm. "What are you trying to do to me?"

The creature chirruped gently, and stroked his head. The long claws did not touch his skin; it was only the pads that he felt, and they were more soothing than not. But the thing was persistent. It lifted his head carefully, and he could feel it doing something to his spine. Kammer could feel very little, though. The sensation was very strange; it felt as though thorns or needles had been stuck into him. They didn't hurt. It was almost like a hypodermic going into nerve-blocked flesh. It took a while for the creature to get the—the whatever they were—adjusted to its satisfaction, and Kammer could feel them moving as they were coaxed this way and that—

It was all strangely relaxing; and then, without warning, he was asleep again.

The stable system that was Aaron Kammer's life was at last moving toward the last of those slow changes that ended it.

Of that he was more certain each time he woke. He never stayed awake very long, because sooner or later something would begin to hurt. Then one of the things would come chirruping toward him and readjust whatever it was

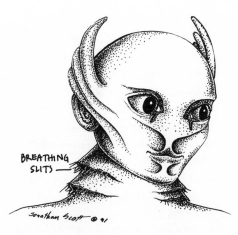

BREATHING
SLITS —

Jonathan Scott © 91

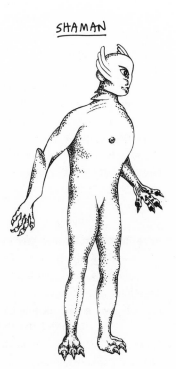

THUMBS

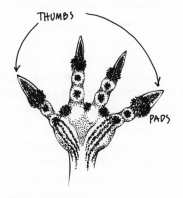

PADS

FUR-LO-SISER-CON

INDIGENOUS TO CHUJO. GIANT
"LEAVES" GROW IN THE MIDDLE OF
THE TREE. AS THE TWO BRANCHES
GROW AND WIDEN, THE LEAVES
MIGRATE UPWARD. HOLES IN THE
LEAVES ALLOW LOWER LEAVES TO
RECEIVE THE LIGHT NECESSARY
FOR PHOTOSYNTHESIS. ALSO
REFERRED TO AS "HAMMOCK
TREE."

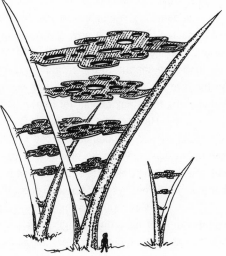

that they had done to his spinal cord. He was grateful for that. Less grateful, once, when one of them lifted the living rug off his body to inspect it and low in his field of vision Kammer caught a glimpse of his own body. His legs were bent in the wrong way. His naked belly was oozing slow trickles of pussy blood. He stank.

"Sorry about that," he said, apologetically joking as he stared up into the noseless face. It wasn't much of a joke. The Chujoan didn't laugh, of course, but it did something better than that. It offered him cool, clean water out of something like a wineskin—but it seemed to be made of a kind of fabric, with embroidery on its side—and when Kammer had swallowed a little it reached behind him and put him back to sleep.

In the little bit of life Aaron Kammer had left it seemed he had more time than he had ever had before. That was very strange, and he enjoyed pondering over the paradox. The thing was, he *only* had time. There was nothing he could *do.* Look around, as best he could, in those short periods when he was conscious. Maybe accept a few sips of water (but even that began to be tiring; just swallowing had become hard work). Watch what he could see—

Some of the things he saw were quite interesting. It was worth noting, for instance, that for reasons of their own it seemed the Chujoans had systematically dismantled his buggy. Parts of it lay spread under the trees, and he spent a pleasurable few waking minutes once watching a tall one and a little one (a child?) soberly rolling one of the great wheels back and forth to each other, while large four-legged animals grazed on the lower tree branches nearby. The Chujoans were playing a kind of game, Kammer realized. It pleased him to find out that his rescuers had pet animals (or work animals?) and played games, though he was saddened for a moment to see that his camera and transmitter had also been dissected. That was a pity. But, looking on the bright side (which was the only side Kammer had left to look on), it meant that even if Nicole had managed to persuade the captain to try to mount a rescue party there would be nothing to lead them to his position. And that was good, because he was quite sure there was not going to be any benefit for him in being found.

He saw, too, the way the Chujoans cooked a meal. One cut fruits and roots into a pot, while another stood whistling softly into the trees. One of the creatures he had seen in the branches hopped into the Chujoan's outstretched hand; the Chujoan stroked it gently, then wrang its neck and tossed it to the cook. What a very efficient system, Kammer thought, approvingly.

It was a pity that he couldn't eat any of the stew that resulted, but he simply did not have the strength. Apart from the fact that it might well have killed him at once . . . but of course, things like that didn't matter any more.

What might have mattered—at least, for a moment Kammer

thought it might—was the sudden apparition of those three great trolls in the shadows of the forest. It was night again (how many times had it been night? Kammer couldn't tell), and his hosts seemed to be asleep. Kammer was nearly certain that the trolls were stealthily approaching one of the four-legged animals, asleep as it leaned against a tree. He tried his best to yell. It wasn't a very good attempt. It wasn't much more than a harsh gasp, but one of the Chujoans looked up from sleep and saw them; whistled commandingly at them. The trolls retreated grudgingly; the Chujoan strolled over to the draft animals, leaped on the back of the nearest of them, and urinated on each, in turn. (Kammer was interested to see that this Chujoan was perhaps female.)

Then she came over to him, and gently put him to sleep again, and that was the end of another period for Aaron Kammer. It was, he thought interestedly when he was awake again, in some ways quite a lot like the interstellar trip. These short intervals of consciousness were a species of time dilation; Murasaki rising and setting in its long day and night, but himself experiencing only a few minutes of wakefulness at a time. That was worth mentioning to someone, he thought, if only he had someone to mention it to.

He thought, without regret, of all the someones he had left behind on the ship. Most of them had mattered to him lately only as unavoidable pains in the ass, but it hadn't always been that way. When the ship started out the crew had seemed like well-balanced, easygoing people. A decade and change of living in each other's pockets had soured all that, but still—

It was easy to forgive them everything, Kammer thought, now that he was sure he would never see any of them again.

He did miss Nicole—a little. At least, he thought of her with fondness, though not much regret. But that didn't matter. He knew that he was growing weaker and that, finally, the last thing he had left to do was to die.

His last thought was that this was a good and friendly place to do it; and perhaps a gentle death was the greatest of the treasures Chujo had to offer.

5

When the ship was five months along on its long voyage home, Captain Blow-Your-Horn made love to his wife. It was an occasion for him. It had not happened very often, because she blamed him for Kammer's loss. There had been a week of raging at him as they collected the crews from Genji, made all the worse because she was hopelessly outvoted. Unanimously, the rest of the crew supported his decision to go home, agreed there was no point in trying to find Aaron Kammer (or his body), accepted (or pretended to accept) the captain's assertion that Kammer was certainly dead, in that unwelcoming place, among all those savage trolls; and of course Nicole put all the guilt for that on her husband. Then there had been a month and more of cold and silent anger, when she would not sleep in the same harnessed bed with him. Ultimately, she did return to his bed. Sometimes now they did make love, more frequently they did not, but always, however much she shuddered and gasped, she seldom spoke to him.

Captain Washington did his best with his temperamental wife. He spoke of the lost man seldom, and only very kindly. In bed he deferred his own pleasure to her satisfaction, even when it became boring work; but there were certain things on his mind.

Then, five months after departure, on one morning, having waked her from sleep with caresses and certain that he had given her as many orgasms as ever in their life together, he pushed himself kneeling over her, swaying a little with the resilience of the harness. He looked down at her naked body, and could no longer ignore the contour of his wife's belly.

"You are pregnant, aren't you?" he asked.

She laced her fingers over her navel and thought for a moment before saying, "Yes, of course I am."

"Well, why didn't you tell me?" he asked, speaking softly in order to keep the anger out of his voice. "Having a baby on the ship—it's going to be a damned nuisance," he pointed out. She just closed her eyes without answering. "What if the other women decide to get pregnant, too?"

She didn't answer that, either, but began to unhook the bedstraps to lift herself out of it. The captain watched her, thinking sentences he didn't want to say to her. There were a lot of things on his mind. He had plenty of questions, all of which reflected on her irresponsible behavior. What if the baby turns out wrong because of some virus or something from Genji? What if Boulat Kotsvili turns out to be no good as an obstetrician? What if—

She was pulling on her boiler suit without looking at him, turned away as though to hide the embryo in her belly from him. But he knew it was there.

He tried to look at the more attractive aspects of the situation. He knew there were some. In a way, the captain told himself, it could be kind of interesting to arrive at a Spacer dock, bowing to the hurrahs of the welcoming crowd, leading a—what would it be?—a strong young son, or even daughter, of nine or ten. He decided to forgive, so he grinned at her. "I guess," he said, patting her belly, "that women are women, after all, aren't you? And it's kind of flattering, I guess."

"Flattering?" she said, her back still to him, her tone perplexed.

"I mean," he explained, "for me to know in spite of everything you wanted to have my child—"

But then she turned and looked at him, and the captain saw the unexpected information that was in his wife's face.

"Oh, I see," he said, no longer flattered at all.

GENJI

BY DAVID BRIN

It is, fundamentally, a question of balance, Minoru reminded himself as he stepped out of the lander, keeping his stance wide and footsteps close to the ground. *Balance is important when exploring a new world.*

During the ten-year journey out to Murasaki System, starship *Yamato*'s antimatter drives had been cranked up gradually to nearly one and a half gravities, so that all three hundred and five expedition members would have time to adapt in advance to conditions on Genji. Seldom mentioned during all that time had been the other motive for pushing the engines—to try to catch up with the Spacer expedition and make it to Murasaki first.

Yamato arrived just a few weeks too late. The upstarts from the asteroid colonies had already visited the twin habitable worlds of Genji and Chujo, taken samples of alien life, and usurped the privilege of first contact that should have been Japan's. Then, as if shamed by their impertinence, the Spacers hadn't even waited around to hold conference, but fled Earthward again on the flimsy excuse that their life-support systems were strained. Perhaps, in fact, they sensed it would not be wise to hang around and test the self-restraint of the larger, better-equipped crew.

The letdown after such a long chase told on *Yamato*'s complement. All that hurrying to get out here . . . then not be the first to set foot, to plant a flag, or to gaze into strange eyes on a new world? Japan could still claim prior discovery, of course. Its robot probes had sent back first word on this magnificent double-planet system. But that wasn't the same. Not the same at all.

Minoru stepped carefully along the blackened trail laid down by the lander when it alighted on this hilltop airstrip by the sea. Behind him, the flyer hissed as it cooled—touched by drifting fingers of sea fog. The pilot continued unloading crates of supplies Minoru and his partner would need during the months ahead. That included, to Minoru's resignation, many kilograms of nutritionally adequate but monotonous algae paste. One more reason to make friends with the natives, who were now spilling out of their hilltop hamlets to cross swampy farms on their way toward the landing field.

Minoru glanced up toward Genji's sister world—dry, little Tō no Chujo—which filled an entire octant of the sky. Chujo was so close you could make out wispy cloud formations, the dun color of its dry uplands, and the glitter of its midget seas. Here on this part of Genji, where Chujo permanently hovered at the zenith, you could tell time by watching shadows move across its constant face as the paired planets spun around a common center—their "day" a composite of their linked momenta. The glow given off by Murasaki might be pallid compared with Sol's remembered flame, but it nurtured life on both of these worlds. And as night's terminator flowed across Chujo's scarred face it was easy to see one likely reason why the natives of Genji had never invented clocks.

A neat explanation, Minoru told himself. *Except for the fact that fair days like today are the exception. It's usually overcast this close to the sea. And Genjians live nowhere else.*

Probably much of his life would consist, from now on, of coming up with interesting hypotheses only to find later evidence pointing elsewhere. On a new world it wouldn't pay to grow too fond of one's favorite theories. Yet another reason to cultivate balance.

He stopped at the edge of the landing field and laid down his bag of trade goods. Only then did Minoru turn around to make sure Emile was following him from the lander. Encumbered by his heavy pressure suit, Minoru swiveled a bit too fast in the fierce gravity. He had to tighten his abdominal muscles to compensate. The rapid jerk sent painful throbs ripping through stretched tendons, reminding him that, after a decade of subjective time aboard ship, he wasn't the same youngster who once upon a time set forth so eagerly toward the stars.

The weight here isn't so bad if you're careful. You can't ever forget, though. Not for a minute.

And there's the paradox, of course. For who can promise to re-member every minute of every day, for a lifetime?

Long-term effects of the planet's pull could be seen in the thick trunks and low profiles of the nearby trees, forming slope-hugging forests just beyond the ragged dirt landing field. Gravity was also manifest in the squat, wide-limbed gait of the natives, who used paths made of wooden planks to cross paddies and fern-lined fens on their way to the landing site. No matter how vivid the holoscreen images were, nothing short of the real thing brought you face-to-face with the strangeness of an alien world. The tug of gravity, the cries of this planet's myriad of flying creatures, the sluggish shove of heavy, moisture-laden air . . . Minoru wished he could feel it against his skin, but full environment suits were mandatory until the bioassay was complete, and probably for a long time after that.

He suppressed a temptation to rebel. One of the foolish Spacers had ruined his lungs by exposing them to Genji's intense sea-level pressure. And yet, Minoru half envied that act of defiance.

"Well, they look peaceful enough," said Emile Esperanza, his contact-team partner, who came up alongside Minoru to watch the Genjians waddle toward them. "I guess the Spacers didn't alienate the locals. Or infect them."

Despite his name, Emile's features were as pure-blooded Japanese as Minoru's, and much more so than the twenty or so men and women in the token "international contingent" that had shipped out aboard *Yamato*. Emile's grandparents had managed a Fuji Works plant in Paraguay, then retired there for the climate, elbow room, and lifestyle. Although his family kept faith with the Purity Rules, and so maintained Nihonese citizenship, they nevertheless had picked up many *gaijin* ways. For instance, Minoru saw with some envy that Emile had taken off his bulky gloves and armlets, sealing his suit above the elbows but leaving his hands and forearms free to feel the wind and air. *I wish I had the nerve.*

"We don't know for sure cross-infection isn't possible. There are many similarities between Genjian life and ours."

"And even more differences," the other man answered, his voice rich with Latin accents. "Genji-life uses more amino acids than we could get away with on Earth, because there's never been much ultraviolet in this system." Emile gestured toward Murasaki's Star, whose yellowish tinge was misleading. The eye adapted to reduced light levels, and so you forgot the poor dwarf put out only two percent of Sol's luminosity.

"So?"

"So any of their pathogens who tried to eat human cells would probably starve of some necessary ingredient. And *our* bugs would be poisoned by some complex chemical never known on Earth."

Minoru knew what that implied. If Earth germs could find nothing to eat here, what hope had human beings of doing so? He clung obstinately to hope, however. "There may be something here that's edible."

Emile shrugged, as if he was indifferent to the subject. Unlike many in the crew, he showed little outward frustration at the limited range of ship-grown fare. Emile never speculated, as others did incessantly, what new delicacies might await discovery on this new world.

"Anyway, none of the Spacers came down with weird plagues. And apparently they didn't loose any on the locals, either. Do you see natives rolling around in agony?"

Minoru did not. From the nearest hilltop hamlet, a kilometer away, the Genjians approached without apparent hurry, carrying only a couple of those trident-spear things the locals used as weapon-tools. From orbital scans—and data grudgingly shared by the departing Spacers—Minoru knew the creatures could move a lot faster if they had to. But as nonhomeotherms—lacking the sort of heat-balancing system Earth mammals possessed—they would naturally avoid temperature swings whenever possible.

At first glance, the natives looked like fat salamanders, whose long front legs gave them a reared, semi-upright stance. Yet, even at a distance, Minoru felt a chill of alienness. For even a salamander has a *face.*

No, he stopped and chided himself. *In all honesty, so do these creatures.*

But such a face! Instead of bilateral symmetry—two eyes atop and mouth below—the Genjians had four bulging vision organs spaced at the corners of a square, centered on their impressive, gaping jaws. Above all that, a waving snorkel tube gave vent to the amphibians' excited cries, audible even in the distance since sound carries so well in dense air. Opposite the snorkel tube, hanging below each Genjian's throat, were two slender, tentaclelike "hands" that served them for fine manipulation.

So strange. And yet, these clearly were intelligent beings. Here on this isolated mountain island, they lived a modest, agrarian-and-fishing existence, tending algal mats and pens of captive, iridescent-finned ichthyoids. But elsewhere the expedition had catalogued from space several widespread cultures possessing metallurgy, and even electricity.

"Anyway," Emile went on. "At least the Spacers had the sense to make their first contact on remote locales like this one, so any unforeseen infection would be self-limiting."

"Such courtesy," Minoru said acidly. But Emile seemed genuinely glad.

"Indeed. I'm grateful the Spacers jumped in ahead of us. Now the karma of any harm done rests on their backs, not ours."

Emile's blithe attitude was rare among *Yamato's* crew, most of whom still seethed at the Spacers' effrontery. Still, he had a point. Cultural contamination by the asteroidists spared Minoru a degree of tension that would have otherwise thickly overlain the approaching meeting. Now he worried much less about perpetrating some irretrievable faux pas that might bring with it a death-bond of shame.

Hissing and rattling, the translator apparatus made a broad range of sounds as Emile tested its sparse store of Genjian words, donated by the Spacers and augmented recently by two other Japanese contact teams already operating along this archipelago. Theirs wasn't even the primary group opening talks with Genjian settlements. That, too, lifted some tension off Minoru's shoulders.

"Hey! Are you fellows okay now? Do you want me to hang around, just in case?"

Remembering just in time to move slowly, Minoru turned carefully to look back at the lander, where their pilot had finished unloading supplies for their extended stay. "I could help you fellows erect your shelter," Don Byrne offered. As one of the few Occidentals on the expedition, his Japanese was thickly accented and much too formal. It made him the butt of jokes by some of the less tolerant crewfolk. Still, he never seemed to mind, and the cheerful Australian had won Minoru's undying gratitude during the seventh year of the voyage, by discovering three new recipes for preparing the same old hydroponic ship-fare.

Minoru liked Don. Nevertheless, he wished this assignment had been drawn by a different pilot—Yukiko Arama. There might have been a chance to get a moment alone with her. . . .

Ah, karma. Maybe next time.

"It isn't necessary," Emile told the pilot. "We can manage. You should return to Okuma Base."

Byrne shifted his weight. "Well . . . I figure I'll just hang around a few minutes, anyway." He began opening containers to lay out the storage dome, but Minoru noticed Don never strayed far from the rifle he had lain by one leg of the lander. And he kept glancing toward the approaching natives.

He's staying to watch over us, Minoru realized. And to his surprise he felt no resentment over this presumption. In fact, it came as something of a relief. Emile, on the other hand, sounded mildly irritated. "All right. But stay out of the way. And give us warning when you're about to take off! We don't want to frighten the Genjians."

Emile turned away again and spread a tarp on the ground. He began laying out objects to help identify the Genjian equivalent of nouns and adjectives, to establish a more orderly dictionary. Some of the objects would also be offered as gifts at the end of each session. Minoru opened his own satchel and started doing the same. Only, as he drew a hammer from the bag, its claw snagged on the material. Caught off balance, he was forced to lean over to compensate.

Gravity seized the momentary lapse. Minoru flailed, and hit the tarp before he could even get his hands out. Impact was sudden and also harder than instinct led him to expect. The blow stung.

Fortunately, despite his brash, *gaijin*-influenced ways, Emile had the decency to neither laugh nor even seem to notice. Overcoming embarrassment, Minoru moved with careful deliberation to push back into sitting position.

Balance, Minoru thought. *I may live the rest of my life on this planet. And it certainly isn't going to change to adapt to me!*

Starship *Yamato* Crew Database: General News

With phases One and Two accomplished, the following teams are now active—

Genji Expedition: Okuma Base on Genji-moonside established atop Mount Korobachi—4,500 meters altitude—Senior Scientist Matsuhiro Komatsu, commanding. Five domes. Three landers. Three power units. One compute facility. One hydrox fuel-processing unit. One hydroponics unit. All operational. * Two hydroponics units and four planetology laboratories nearing completion. * Preliminary survey parties detached to remote islands for early, minimum-contamination contact sessions. * Total crew on Genji—eighty-five personnel. Nineteen additional personnel designated for landing upon return of *Yamato* from belt mission.

Tō no Chujo Expedition: Capt. Koremasa Tamura has decided to lead a small-scale expedition to the smaller world personally. In addition to archaeological explorations, and attempts to make contact with the local inhabitants, this team shall determine feasibility of establishing a hydrogen-oxygen plant at the shore of one of Chujo's small seas.

Infrastructure Team: Following Captain Tamura's departure for Chujo, Senior Lieutenant Hideo Ishikawa will take the *Yamato*, plus two scout boats, on a brief survey of nearby space in search of candidate small bodies for use in infrastructure-manufacturing processes.

Casualty figures: Added to the twelve crew mulched or cryo-stored en route . . . One death at Okuma Base due to a fall. Eight gravity-related injuries, all minor. Dr. Komatsu reminds all expedition members to remember their drills and observe safety procedures at all times.

Minoru slogged through the boggy fields of Green Tower Village, taking samples and supervising as his native assistants labored on a treadmill linked to a scaffold of massive wooden gearing. That clanking, rattling assemblage, in turn, rotated a machine that projected a cylinder of force into the ground, digging ever deeper into the rich sedimentary layers below.

It had taken several days, working in conjunction with teams on other islands, to acquire enough of the local dialect to get across the idea that humans wanted to "hire" the natives. But once they understood, the Genjians became eager helpers, not only with the coring but also scurrying through the shallows and across the hillsides to snare and bring back countless wriggling things of all shapes and colors—from underground burrowers to multilegged insectoids to flyers with one, two, even three pairs of wings—the myriad of pieces Minoru needed to start putting together his own picture of this island's ecosystem.

Minoru stank from hour after hour in his biosuit. He itched from low-level rashes as his immune system adapted to new allergic irritants. On two occasions, valuable instruments had broken down, with no way of knowing yet if craftsmen back at Okuma Base could repair the parts or if they might have to send "home" for replacements—then wait forty years for them to arrive.

And yet, he could hardly complain about lack of progress. He had tools, and a good work force willing to labor long and hard for lumps of iron. Metal was precious on these remote islands, where Genji's continental industrial revolution was still no more than a rumor. Despite temptation, Minoru was careful not to overpay his workers, which would only disrupt their local economy.

Anyway, deferred gratification was an important lesson. You learned it early in Japan. Failure to understand the importance of patience and hard work had brought down great powers that once towered over Minoru's homeland.

The work was going so well, Minoru had even trained some of the small male Genjians to dissect and prepare animal specimens under recording cameras. The natives' coordination with their tiny feeler-arms, and ability to bring their eyes exceptionally close, enabled them to parse minute details, a pastime they obviously found amusing. One, a venerable brood-father named Phs'n'kah, seemed fascinated and enthusiastic to learn more.

It was Phs'n'kah who nudged Minoru out of a meditative state listening to the slow, steady drone of the treadmill. Minoru started at the sudden tug on his arm. With their broad peripheral vision, Genjians never seemed to grasp human entreaties "not to sneak up on us from behind."

"*I have brought more samples for study,*" the translator announced primly. Minoru glanced down and saw that Phs'n'kah had laid out a reed mat across the mud, whereupon he arrayed several score tiny animals, all with their necks neatly wrung.

"These were gathered within a single patch, one meter on a side?" Minoru asked, incredulously. Phs'n'kah made an assent gesture with his snorkel tube.

"*Yes. The very *** you marked off. I made sure to ***"

The last part dissolved in static as the translator tried guessing, then gave up. No matter. Minoru thought he got the gist.

This was a new phase. After taking samples randomly from all over the island, letting the natives bring in whatever was easiest to catch, it was time to start studying in depth. But he and Emile were stretched so thinly that Minoru had begun delegating some jobs.

"You sealed off the area as I showed you?"

"As you showed me . . . I *** down to one meter depth. I am sure nothing *** escaped. Nothing that *** larger than the holes in your *** sieve screen."

Minoru bent to peer at the samples. You could learn a lot just by seeing how the Genjian had sorted them. Not by size or color. Nor, apparently, by species relatedness. At first guess it seemed Phs'n'kah had put all the obligate carnivores together on one side, all leave-cutters in another corner, and so on. You are what you eat, Minoru thought. I should report this to the Xeno-Psychology group.

He made a note to that effect, and his auto secretary beeped acknowledgment. One problem with accomplishing so much so fast was that you absolutely relied on the semisentient computer devices to outline and send (and read!) a great many memos.

"Good work," he told Phs'n'kah.

"Time to dissect and record?"

"No. Not yet. Let me look over the samples first. Then we'll do another test dig together to make sure we haven't missed a trick."

He was confident the translator would get the meaning across. Phs'n'kah's snorkel waved, then he gathered up the samples and the reed mat. But, before turning to head back to the science dome, the little male stopped and asked one more question.

"Have we found any *** yet that the *** humans can honorably eat?"

Minoru started. How did Phs'n'kah know? That ulterior motive for Minoru's fevered sampling of flora and fauna went beyond the principal focus—of understanding this island's complex ecosystem.

But of course, he realized. That would be the first thing to occur to a native. . . . They have no real conception of science. But eating, cooking, the search for something new and good . . . he probably thinks that's the main purpose of all this collecting!

Perhaps this explained why it was males, the gatherers and tenders of the hearths and cook-pots, who were most enthusiastic about helping Minoru, while the females seemed to prefer gathering around Emile, with his endless appetite for words.

"No, my friend. Nothing good to eat, yet. But we can still hope."

"Hope is ***. Hope can even be ***."

Phs'n'kah turned away and waddled up the path leading to the science dome. Minoru wondered what piece of wisdom he had imparted. It sounded like an aphorism. He would store it, and play it back for Emile later.

"That's enough," he told the workers turning the corer. The translator wheezed something in the native language that must have been approximately correct, because they stopped working and squatted back, panting. Occasionally, one of them would open its mouth to pick its teeth with one of the slender tentacle arms. Only at times like that was Minoru able to tell for absolute certain which was male and which female. Besides being generally smaller, the males had tongues that were longer and raspier for some reason, ending in a sort of bulbous fixture. Curiously, it did not seem to affect their speech—at least to his untutored ears. Back at Okuma Base they were still trying to figure out what the apparatus was for. It was one topic the locals kept decidedly closemouthed about.

The latest core sample came up slickly . . . a tube of past history sheathed in electro-stiffened plastic. His helpers were by now well-rehearsed in this procedure. They detached and then loaded the five-meter tube onto the ingestion tray of a portable disassembler-reader. As the core passed into the machine, layer after sedimentary layer was atomized. A dust of ages came out the other end, while all the information content that had been locked in ordered patterns of mud and ancient fossils flowed as data into the capacious memory of the computer back at the dome.

Gradually, a database was forming. It would take years, probably decades, to comprehend more than a cursory view of life on Genji—its detailed chemistry and complex, interlaced ecologies. Nevertheless, some pieces were already falling into place.

For one thing, life was at least as old here as on Earth. Evolution had apparently progressed at almost the same pace, despite a lower incidence of ultraviolet irradiation to cause mutations. Here, instead, a built-in driver toward diversity came about because of half a dozen extra, unconventional amino acids that were added to the protein code. With that increase came a higher chance of replicative error, and so Darwin's grinding-mill had as much to work with as back home, producing a profusion of winners and losers to make up a broad-branched tree of life.

Broader than Earth's, in certain respects. Murasaki System was emptier of comets and asteroids than Sol's, and apparently there had been fewer big impacts to shake up the Genjian biosphere. Few mass extinctions meant many ancient, ancestral families and phyla that might have gone extinct still co-inhabited the planet. It was as if some of the wild experiments tried on Earth during the pre-Cambrian, recorded in half-billion-year-old formations like the Burgess Shale, had never died out but gone on to share the seas with shark and squid and whales. In addition to multicelled creatures built from segmented tubes—like Phs'n'kah's people and all metazoans on Earth—there were also distantly related branches that specialized in growing as flat sheets, or as radial stems. Orbital scans of the other hemisphere appeared to show creatures so eerie that Genjians themselves could be thought almost human.

One of his workers performed something akin to a yawn, and Minoru blinked, stepping backward suddenly. Apparently some of the other natives were as put back as he was by the gesture, since several hissed and one even tried to take a nip at the offender's tail. She snarled back.

Then, quite suddenly, the altercation was forgotten. Almost as one, the natives lifted their heads and turned. Minoru carefully shuffled around to look, and saw that a darkness had begun approaching from the east. The deck of low-lying clouds dimmed along a sharp border that approached rapidly, laying a rapidly nearing shadow across the hillsides and the fog-draped sea. A low moan rose from the Genjians as they reared to gape in the direction of Chujo—even though the sister world was covered from view by clouds. The translucence of sunlight vanished as Genji's twin passed in front of Murasaki, signaling commencement of the noon eclipse.

Time to down tools. This was—at least for this culture, on this archipelago—a holy interval, lasting about twenty minutes, during which it was permissible to speak and rest, but never to work or fight.

Minoru stood in what he hoped the natives took as an attitude of respect. After all, on shipboard—and even in their tiny habitation domes—many human crewmembers kept little Shinto or Buddhist or Christian or Gaian shrines. He was proud of the Japanese attitude toward religion, which said, essentially— *whatever works.*

As soon as the Genjians' keening song of greeting was finished, one of the largest females turned and approached Minoru in a slow, tail-swishing undulation. He recognized Ta'azsh'da by several scars along her left flank, which she had told Emile she'd acquired in a raid by another village, during her youth on another island. Females were the wanderers and warriors in this species, a fact that still had some sociobiologists at Okuma Base puzzled. Minoru, at least, thought he was beginning to see why.

"You *** our Rites of *** and Shadow," the translator said, struggling with her words. It had more trouble with some topics than others. *"If we are *** will you convey our *** to ***?"*

"I'm sorry ... I ... " Minoru gave up. "Connect to Emile," he said, and almost without a pause, his partner's face lit up the left quadrant of his visor.

"Minoru. I'm kind of busy."

Minoru could see Emile with three of his language helpers, squatting in the shirt-sleeve environment of the halfway dome ... set to an atmospheric pressure midway between that of Genji's surface and what was comfortable for humans. Emile's skin pallor didn't look good, and his eyes were droopy, but at least he didn't have to wear a stinking suit all the time. Minoru envied him.

"Just a quick one. Give me a read on this, will you?" And Minoru squirted over Ta'azsh'da's question. Emile puzzled for a moment, then he laughed. "Oh, she's just asking to hitch a ride to Chujo."

"To Chujo!"

Emile lifted one eyebrow. "You hadn't heard? It seems, according to their mythology, Chujo is the home of the angels. Many of them think that's where we came from."

"No wonder they're so cooperative! But what will happen when they find out—"

"Relax. There's no religious hysteria about it. At least not among this group . . . though the boys over at Purple Cliffs Island seem to have had a rough moment when the truth came out. Anyway, I've already explained the entire situation to several of their traveling monks, or rabbis, or holy whatever you call them—and say, did you know they're nearly all females? Anyway, I told the priests we're not from Chujo but another star. They don't seem to mind.

"Here, let me give you a nice, soothing, diplomatic answer for Ta'azsh'da."

Emile muttered a command and Minoru's translator conveyed a string of Genjian words directly from Minoru's helmet speaker. Ta'azsh'da took a couple of steps back at one point, rocking her head in an expression Minoru thought might mean perplexity.

But then she seemed satisfied. Or at least she turned and wandered away. Emile's picture disappeared without a sign-off, and Minoru tried not to be offended. He himself must sound just as curt when experts from other teams called him, demanding quick biological answers while he was still flailing around, looking for the big picture.

Sometimes, it seemed almost too much, and he longed for crowded but comfortable Osaka.

I am doing my life's work, Minoru reminded himself at those moments. *No one could be happier.*

That was true, as far as it went. Only occasionally Minoru wished he were a different sort of person altogether . . . one born with simpler tastes and more mundane interests, who was not the type to volunteer at age fifteen to be sent hurtling toward such a heavy world. Weren't there less exhausting roads to happiness?

Alas, those roads were not in his dharma to tread.

Genji Expedition Database:

SUMMARY ON GENJIAN SAPIENTS
by Shigei Owari, Chief Xenologist

The intelligent beings we call Genjians bear some resemblance to Earth's amphibian life-forms. Such comparisons can be misleading, however, since there is nothing at all primitive about this planet's autochthons. It is true that they have not spread to as many ecological niches as humans had, at similar levels of technological development. (By the Iron Age, human beings occupied even mountaintops and arctic wastes, while the natives of this world seem almost exclusively to inhabit coastlines and alluvial basins.) Nevertheless, it should be noted that in most other indicators we seem to have met peers. Preliminary studies by Komiko Takashita reveal an emotional range as vivid and finely textured as our own. Komiko's preliminary intelligence profiles demonstrate considerable overlap in cognitive ability with precomputer human societies. . . .

. . . the Linguistic Group has decided to adopt as generic the species self-name used in this archipelago by the autochthones. In all future documents, therefore, sentient Genjians shall be referred to as *Ihrdizu*. This has been deemed acceptable by natives at all contact sites. . . .

. . . their strong tails, with two horizontal flukes, appear to propel the torpedo-shaped Ihrdizu efficiently through the water. On shore, they use their tails for support and to assist locomotion. The heavily muscled appendages also serve as formidable weapons. . . .

. . . Adult females measure about two meters in length and mass nearly 100 kilograms. The slender male seldom exceeds a meter and a half in length. . . .

. . . only capable of poor directionality with their flap-and-tympani hearing apparatus, although we expect the system probably works quite well underwater. Their vision system is capable of extreme dark-adaptation, and can focus under a wide variety of conditions. . . .

Another word for balance was *equilibrium.* Minoru contemplated this as he sat naked under a sunlamp, in padmasama position, on a reed mat that had been donated by the village elders. The little habitation dome hissed as it fed the produce of his respiration—and from his previous meals—into wall panels that used sunlight and algae to recycle human wastes. At the output end, there accumulated an all-too-familiar green paste that, despite its blandness, would keep his body going, enabling him and Emile to extend their visit here at least an extra month.

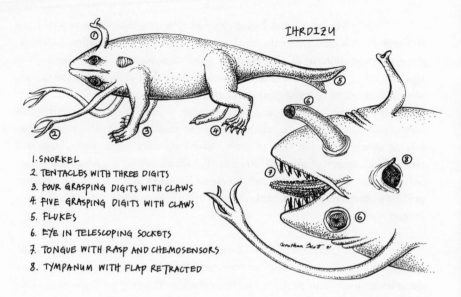

IHRDIZU

1. SNORKEL
2. TENTACLES WITH THREE DIGITS
3. FOUR GRASPING DIGITS WITH CLAWS
4. FIVE GRASPING DIGITS WITH CLAWS
5. FLUKES
6. EYE IN TELESCOPING SOCKETS
7. TONGUE WITH RASP AND CHEMOSENSORS
8. TYMPANUM WITH FLAP RETRACTED

The dome-recycler seemed a perfect example to contemplate. At first sight, it appeared to be a balanced system. But it wasn't in equilibrium, not really. The pallid glow of Murasaki was barely adequate to drive the process, for one thing. And anyway, even at best the return was less than thirty percent efficient.

Minoru often dreamed he was back aboard the *Yamato,* where, despite the ennui of ten years' subsistence on hydroponics, there was at least *some* variety. And, once a month the chef would prepare delicacies from that exclusive, locked chamber where fish were kept in special tanks, where licentious amounts of power and resources were spent nurturing rare herbs.

Tomorrow the supply boat would come with provisions for the two of them. Even if it failed to arrive, the clever recycling devices would certainly keep Minoru and Emile alive for some time. But not in equilibrium. Without replenishment, they would waste away on a narrow diet of ever-declining value.

There was a parallel in his mission here. His purpose on this island was only partly to help Emile and the main xenology team on Purple Cliffs Island make contact with the Ihrdizu. Over the months and years ahead, Minoru's principal job would be to figure out what kept this world from toppling over into catastrophe.

Catastrophe like the kind we experienced on Earth so recently, he thought. Only in his parents' lifetime had the chain of ecological crises back home abated enough for nations to contemplate deep-space exploration again. And although heroic efforts had finally stopped the spreading deserts, Minoru knew that those gleeful, rosy-eyed propagandists in the press were wrong. Earth would never be "just as good as before."

The timer on the sunlamp rattled to a stop. The warm, brilliant glow from the UV panels tapered off gradually to let his eyes readapt. These daily sessions were welcome, as well as necessary to stave off Sunlight Deficiency Disorder. But they also reinforced his sense of being on an alien world. The most luminous day on Genji wasn't bright enough to satisfy a human's biological hunger for light.

Nor was this a particularly shiny day even for Genji. Wrapping a robe around himself, Minoru went to the east-facing window and watched high tide finish inundating the natives' broad expanse of trapping ponds, depositing the sea's bounty there to be left high and dry when the waters receded again. Tending these carefully designed basins took up the time of half the labor force, and their ownership was subject to fierce inheritance tradition . . . sometimes enforced by nasty local feuds among the natives.

Minoru went to his computer deck and surveyed his latest composite of this island's biological history. Slowly, out of all his deep core samples, soil siftings, and animal dissections, a picture was resolving. The family tree he had already traced out—of land and shore species indigenous to the region—was probably no more than two percent filled in. And yet, the *shape* of that tree was taking form. From the fossil record, he was beginning to suspect all was not as it appeared here on Genji.

My supervisor may not like this report, he thought as he popped a macro-cube into the memory slot and copied onto it his monograph, to be sent back to Okuma Base.

Nevertheless, he looked forward to tomorrow's lander. Perhaps Yukiko would be the pilot.

If only I had something to offer her.

Starship *Yamato* Crew Database: General News

Infrastructure Team: Sr. Lt. Hideo Ishikawa, in temporary command of the *Yamato*, reports finding an unfortunate lack of carbonaceous chondrite asteroids in convenient orbits near Genji-Chujo space. It appears we will have to set up a purification plant on Chujo, after all, to provide water for our orbital facilities.

Tō no Chujo Expedition: Capt. Koremasa Tamura commands from Lander Four. Exploration dome established near the Area Fifty-one Anomaly—a purported "archaeological" site according to surveys by the Spacer party. Twenty-five total personnel. Fifteen assigned to the forthcoming attempt to contact purported sentients. Ten to examine Spacer landing area for evidence of contamination.

Genji Expedition: With deployment of the big antenna in high orbit, a report has been prepared for beaming back to Earth. Unlike prior data-clusters, this one shall be designed specifically for public consumption. It has been decided to focus this first show on the harmonious, cooperative nature of Ihrdizu society. Although violence does play a small role in life among the inhabitants, their traditions of serenity appear to have much in common with those which we have managed to maintain in Japanese society. The value of this message to the people of Earth as a whole should be exemplary.

The Ihrdizu children were engaged in one of their frequent games of hide-and-find-the-object. Among the younger ones, this apparently involved a lot of sniffing and nosing around to find some concealed item—usually an overripe piece of fruit. But as the game involved older participants, teams formed and elaborate rituals of clue and deception seemed to come into play. According to Emile, understanding the game ought to reveal a lot about the natives' psychology, and so Minoru's partner became a fixture in the village green just before sunset, when the competitions were most frequent. He could be seen quite often clumsily but enthusiastically following the players about in his clunking pressure suit, breathlessly speaking into his portable recorder and panning with his camera.

Minoru, meanwhile, had taken an interest in the village pets, and pests.

"So you say the Kaw Kaw were brought to the island by your ancestors?" he inquired of Ta'azsh'da late one afternoon, pointing to a pair of snuffling, six-legged animals that prowled the fringes of the hamlet's garbage midden.

*"It is true. ***. It is said that Ish'n'Po herself took the *** Kaw Kaw on her very own raft, lest the *** families on other rafts throw the *** things overboard during the long voyage."*

"You mean your ancestors actually had a use for those things?" he asked dubiously. The Ihrdizu had symbiotic relationships with quite a few other creatures, which appeared to serve roughly the same roles dogs, cats, donkeys, and falcons used to play for humans back on Earth. But this disgusting creature rooting around below them hardly seemed promising. From the natives' name for it—which translated as something like "bad stink"—Minoru gathered it was considered vermin.

"Oh, yes . . ." Ta'azsh'da's snorkel waved clockwise. *"It is said*

they were useful keeping the *** under control . . . and for locating nests of ***. Of course, there are no *** any longer, except on a few outlying islands."

Minoru quashed his impatience with the translation. This conversation would presumably have more meaning later, after Emile's next linguistic update. For now, it was important to keep the momentum going.

"It is said your people came to these islands eighty-two generations ago—"

"So very ***. Do you want me to recite my genealogy?"

"I'd be honored to hear it," Minoru said, politely. "Might we put that off for a more convenient time?" He did not want to offend Ta'azsh'da, but listening to long lists of ancestors was a daunting prospect right now.

"That would be fine. I come from a very *** line of mothers."

"Of that I'm certain. But what I'm most interested in is what your legends say about the plants and animals your ancestors found here. Especially those no one has seen for a long time."

Starship *Yamato* Crew Database: General News

Genji Expedition: The results of preliminary contacts at several island sites seem wonderfully encouraging. There is a growing consensus that nothing stands in the way of proceeding to direct encounters with the more cosmopolitan and technologically advanced Ihrdizu cultures on the mainland. . . .

. . . Chief Ecologist Seigi Sato reports—"This solar system is a less dynamic place than our own, less subject to stellar perturbations or asteroidal impacts. In this more stable environment, which has not gone through the frequent fluctuations of our home system, we find none of the signs of spreading wasteland and desertification that have inflicted so much pain at home.

"From orbit we see clear evidence that the Ihrdizu have been industrialized in some locales for much longer periods than humans were on Earth—although at a lower technological level—and yet, they appear to live without significant environmental degradation, such as erosion or desertification. I am now convinced we have found here proof of what Japan has contended all along, that the environmental disturbances suffered by Earth during recent generations were the product of natural forces, and not the result of so-called human mistreatment of our home world. For astronomical reasons, Genji is a luckier planet than Earth. It is as simple as that."

Dust rose around the jets of the lander as its engines turned over on idle. Near the ramp, Emile Esperanza went over an inventory list next to a stack of fresh supplies, just delivered from Okuma Base. Minoru, on the other hand, insisted on escorting the pilot back to her craft personally. When they reached the bottom of the ramp, he handed her the data cube containing his report, which she pushed into a pocket of her provocatively snug pressure suit.

"You're sure you can't stay?" he asked Yukiko, unable to keep disappointment out of his voice. She shook her head. "I can't, Minoru-san. I promised to drop in at Purple Cliffs Station for dinner this evening." Then, with a light in her eyes, she leaned toward him and whispered, almost conspiratorially. "They say they have found a local berry with low toxicity levels, and what they call a 'tart but pleasant' taste."

"Lucky bastards," Minoru commented, and meant the remark in more ways than one. He knew full well what Todo and Shimura were trying to accomplish, by inviting Yukiko to stay for a "feast."

Yukiko smiled—dimples under her brown eyes made him want to reach out and touch her smooth skin. Only propriety, and her helmet faceplate, prevented him. "I'll let you know how it tastes, Minoru-san," she said. "Really. If it's any good, I'll bring you some next time I drop by."

"Just so." Minoru looked away. He sometimes wished this expedition had been run in a somewhat less Japanese way. On the trip out there might have been more liberal sexuality, as practiced by the Spacers. But the Japanese response to intense pressures—especially those of long, confined spaceflight—was instead to *tighten* social strictures. There had been ten women, all of them of foreign extraction, whose berths on the *Yamato* had been won only partly by virtue of their technical skills. They had also promised to "adopt" several unmarried male crewmembers each. But Minoru had seldom opted to take on that release. As for unmarried women, chastity had been the rule for ten years.

Now that they had landed, though, and people had occasional moments of privacy, something had changed in the social climate. Soon, larger living quarters would be available in the high, altiplano freshness of Okuma Base. Room for new couples to set up house, and even start families.

He and Yukiko, like many others, had set out from Earth as teenagers. And yet he was still looked on as an awkward youth, while she was considered the most beautiful and desirable woman among those left unattached. Clearly she was in the process of looking, sampling, making up her mind. Underneath his outwardly impassive shell, Minoru felt helpless and, to a growing degree, desperate.

"Oh, I almost forgot," she said, turning at the top of the ramp. She reached inside the ship and brought down a slim, lacquered box, crafted delicately out of hard wood. This she handed to Minoru. "A present, since you miss the cooking we get at Okuma."

He looked down at the gift. Under the veneer of wood, a refrigeration unit purred delicately. His mouth watered. "Is it . . . ?"

"Sushi. Yes. Hamachi and Uni. I hope you like it."

Her smile filled Minoru with wonder, encouraging imagined possibilities he had all but given up on only moments before. "Will I see you again soon?"

"Maybe." Then, impulsively, she touched her helmet to his for just an instant. "Take care, Minoru."

Soon the lander rose on its column of heated steam . . . watched, as usual, by a crowd of Ihrdizu gaping from behind a safety line scratched in the sand. Minoru watched the flying machine peel away, and followed its progress across the sky until it disappeared. Then he went to help Emile move the supplies.

"You've got hopes," Emile commented succinctly, perhaps dubiously.

"Come on," Minoru grumbled. "I still have the east slope cliffs to cover before nightfall. And haven't you got work to do, too?"

He hoisted a crate that should have called for two in this gravity, and moved awkwardly but happily toward the storage dome, away from Emile's knowing smile.

The laser played across the cliff face in double waves. First a gentle scan lit up every millimeter of the sheer sedimentary surface, while widely spaced recording devices read its reflections, noting every microscopic contour and color variation. Then, when that first scan was finished, the machine sent forth a much more powerful second beam, which seared away a thin layer wherever it touched. The monitors now recorded glowing spectra from these vapors, taking down elemental compositions in minute detail.

Minoru always made certain only a few Ihrdizu were present to watch this process. He did not want superstitious awe of humans spreading even faster than at present. A certain minimal amount was good, since it meant he and Emile would probably be safe from receiving the pointy end of a trident in some future tiff or labor-management dispute. On the other hand, he had no wish to be mistaken for a god.

I might have been tempted, were the natives more attractive, Minoru admitted wryly. Adolescence was not so far in the past that he didn't recall fantasies of old. The comic books he used to read in Japan had been filled with seraglios and other imaginative scenarios to titillate bored teenagers and suppressed businessmen alike. Even on shipboard—*especially* on shipboard—fantasy had been a way to swim against the tide of ennui. He recalled one mural, painted on the lower decks by frustrated engineers, that depicted green-skinned but nubile alien princesses, catering to the desires of noble Earthling demigods.

Minoru had thought the notion childish, and unlikely, given the reports on Genji from the robot probe. Now, all he could conjure in his mind was one face. One person. His job forced him to spend too much time exploring sterile cliffs, when what he really needed to impress Yukiko might be waiting in some nearby meadow, some underground burrow, or a tidal shoal.

Well, at least Phs'n'kah is out there looking on my behalf. I'm sure he'll come up with something.

Minoru focused attention onto the business at hand. What grew in the computer display was a slice-by-thin-slice representation of the cliff. Each horizontal lamina layer had been laid down along this ancient coast long ago, when the vagaries of a slowly shifting archipelago pushed lapping tidal waters over the place where he now stood. Amid the slowly growing images in his holo screen lay speckles of bright color where the semi-intelligent device discovered the outlines of fossils . . . the remains of dead Genjian creatures in the mud so very long ago, only to have their hard tissues replaced gradually by a process of mineralization and preservation quite similar to what occurred countless times on Earth.

Playing with the controls, Minoru zoomed among these discoveries, linking and correlating each one with his database of currently living animal types. Tentative identifications could be made in real time, by phylum, family, genus . . . and sometimes even by species. This, too, was just a sampling at the edges of the island's complex history. Still, what emerged was a picture that—added to what the other teams were determining elsewhere—would eventually tell the story of life here on Genji.

Already it was clear that here, just as on Earth, the epic began in the sea. Quite early, some Genjian life-form discovered a chemical similar to chlorophyll. Using sunlight as an energy source, it used this "xanthochlorophyll" to split water, manufacturing its own carbohydrates and proteins. This had a side effect—spilling a waste product, oxygen, into the atmosphere. Eventually a crisis developed as that corrosive substance built up in the air. As on Earth, Genji's early, microscopic creatures had to adapt to changing conditions or die.

Eventually, they not only adapted, but learned to thrive on the stuff. Higher-energy chemistry enabled experiments in faster, more complex modes of living.

Over the course of time, some one-celled animals fell on the knack of combining and sharing roles just as the eukaryotes did on Earth, 700 million years before Minoru was born.

The complex of biochemical interactions specific to Genji had already been worked out before the *Yamato* arrived, by one of the scientists aboard the Spacer vessel. That genius among a crew of idiots had described how the typical Genjian metazoan cell operated . . . a picture of symmetry and molecular cooperation—just like the machinery grinding away in Minoru's own body.

Amazing similarities. Amazing differences. As the cliff face dissolved, micron by micron, Minoru fell into a zenlike work trance, absorbed by the beauty of the story unfolding before his eyes. His hands flew across the controls, eyes darting from discovery to discovery.

In his youth, he had pictured exploring alien worlds as a matter of striding forth, ray gun in hand, to rescue (and be rewarded by) beautiful alien maidens. He had envisioned himself the hero of space battles, planting the flag, beating off hordes of monsters in order to uphold the right.

The fantasies of childhood were vivid, barbaric. Minoru recalled them with affection but, all in all, much preferred being grown up.

Starship *Yamato* Crew Database: General News

Tō no Chujo Expedition: ... News! News! News! ... While Captain Tamura and most of his team prepare for their first encounter with the migratory Chujoans, those investigating the former Spacer landing site have made an important discovery. A human being, abandoned for dead by the Spacer landing party, has been found alive on Chujo! He has been identified as Engineer Kammer, reported missing shortly before the Spacers' abrupt departure from Murasaki System.

This will surely present a major embarrassment to the Spacers. But even more important will be to learn how Kammer survived. Lacking ship-produced provenance for several months, he can only have subsisted on local materials, possibly provided by the Chujoans themselves.

At present, the man appears incoherent, slipping into consciousness only briefly. But from what little we have learned, it seems he has benefited from care by the natives. Captain Tamura's party hopes that this will bode well for the upcoming moment of contact. More as things develop.

More transients had arrived to set up camp in the shantytown over by the funnel-weed swamp. They were young adult females mostly, just past their First Blush and into their wandering, home-finding phase. They had been drifting in for days, from distant parts of the island, and even nearby isles, attracted by the sudden wealth of circulating metal provided by the Earthmen. The newcomers' shelters were rude, makeshift affairs, built on high stilts to rise just over the average daily tides.

The hovels looked quite miserable in the shadow of finely carved and dressed hilltop farmsteads. Established villagers glared down from their family compounds. Some were seen sharpening "decorative" wooden stakes, arranged in close, neat rows around their grounds. Guards were posted to prevent pilfering from the Terran domes, when Minoru and Emile were away. Recently, there had been incidents between locals and newcomers in the village common areas—scrapes and jostlings for the few jobs on Minoru's work crews. Tail blows exchanged as young females preened and competed for the attention of the bewildered local bachelors.

Yesterday, at Minoru's urging, Emile took a break from interviewing his personal coterie of "wise women" and began questioning some of the transients instead. On his return to the habitation dome, the young linguist had expressed dismay. "We've disrupted the economy of the entire island! Everything is in an uproar, and it's all because of us."

Minoru had not been surprised. "That's one reason contact teams were spread widely—to lessen the impact. Anyway, what you're seeing is just an exaggeration of what went on all the time, even before we came."

"But the fighting! The violence!"

"You've been listening to Dr. Sato's romantic notions about our Peaceful Ihrdizu Friends, who don't even know the meaning of war. Well, that's true up to a point, but don't you ever listen to the folk tales you yourself recorded? How about the story of Rish'ong'nu and the Town That Refused?"

"I remember. It's a morality tale about the importance of hospitality—"

Minoru interrupted, laughing. "Oh, it's much simpler than that. Rish'ong'nu really existed, did you know that? And the village she conquered did not burn once, but at least forty times, over centuries both before and after her adventure."

Emile blinked. "How do you know that?"

"Simple archaeology. I've taken cores of the site where Rish'ong'nu supposedly lived, and found carbon layers that give very specific dates for each rise and fall.

"Anyway, it makes perfect sense. These beings exercise female-mobile exogamy accompanied by partial polyandry based on male-intensive nesting. It's not quite like anything seen among higher animals on Earth, but the pattern's pretty familiar among some types of birds and amphibians back home. Young females have to set out and win a place for themselves in the world—and find a husband who will take primary care of the offspring. She does this either by wooing a mate from a strong, well-established line, or by pioneering new territory, or by taking a place from someone else."

"You make it sound so savage."

Minoru shook his head. "It's right and proper to love and admire Nature, Emile, but never to idealize it. The process of survival is a competitive one. Always has been, in every species ever known.

"For instance, it didn't take us long to confirm that the most fundamental rule of biology on Earth applies just as universally here, on Genji and on Chujo."

"What rule is that?"

"It was known even before Darwin, and it goes like this—*in all species, the average breeding pair usually tries to have more offspring than is required to replace themselves.* In hard times, that extra effort helps keep the population stable, making up for those that die without reproducing at all. And during good times, or when opportunity knocks, it results in the spreading of genes—"

"But if that's the rule, what keeps animals from overpopulating?"

"Good question. And the answer is—natural controls. Predation by carnivores higher on the food chain, for instance. Or, for the top predators, competition among themselves for a limited supply of food and shelter. I know it doesn't sound nice. It's just nature's way."

"But humans, on Earth . . . "

"Again, good point. We're an exception, indeed. We learned to control our numbers voluntarily. But after how long a struggle? At what price? And by what force of will? I assure you, no other Earthly species even makes the effort.

"So, it's only natural I was curious about the sentient creatures we found here. I don't know about the Chujo natives yet—"

"Who does?"

"—but on Genji I set out to learn, did the rule hold here as well? And if so, what about the sapient natives? The Ihrdizu? That's why I asked you to inquire about their use of birth control."

"They do have some means," Emile said eagerly.

"Yes, though practiced only sporadically. And so the question remains: what else controls the Ihrdizu population?"

Emile looked at Minoru glumly. "I suppose you're going to tell me."

But Minoru only shrugged. "I'm still not sure myself. It seems a little bit of everything is involved. Some deliberate birth control, to be sure. Some predation by sea carnivores, whenever Ihrdizu venture out too far, foraging. There is definitely a portion of the death rate that is attributable to low-level internecine fighting over the better fens, farmlands, and housing sites. At intervals, there has clearly been starvation.

"And then there's the environment."

"How do you mean?" Emile asked.

"Have you noticed the way Ihrdizu houses are shaped like boats, even though they're built mostly on hilltops?"

"Of course. It's a holdover from their ancestor-legends, from when they were seafaring . . . " Emile trailed off when Minoru shook his head. "No?"

"I'm afraid not. They build them that way for much less romantic, more pragmatic reasons. Because, every once in a while, the tides sweep up that high."

Emile gasped at the mental image that evoked, but Minoru went on. "That's why the shantytown looks so out of place. On Earth most cities used to have poor areas, even slums, which played major, long-lasting roles in community life. Here, though, everybody knows such areas can only be temporary. For the newcomers it's win a place on high ground, or die. And not all high ground will do. Only slopes overlooking water are really suitable."

As the implications soaked in, Emile muttered a Buddhist prayer for mercy. At the same time, he crossed himself in the Latin manner. "No wonder the level of tension is rising so!"

"No wonder. Obviously, you and I will have to leave soon."

"But—you said this sort of thing was going on anyway, even without our presence."

"We are setting off a local intensification, though," Minoru said. "I don't want the consequences on my karma. Besides, conditions here are no longer natural. We must try to finish soon, before there's nothing left here to learn any more."

Starship *Yamato* Crew Database: General News

Infrastructure Expedition: Sr. Lt. Hideo Ishikawa reports that smelting has begun on asteroid M27852. It is hoped that within three months we may be able to establish a minimal, phase-one solar array in orbit above the combined Genji-Chujo epicenter. Even at best, however, it will take several years to create enough infrastructure to be certain of human survival in this alien system. . . .

A picture was beginning to take form. From his sampling of sedimentary layers, from his survey of the island's flora and fauna, and from the natives' own legends and traditions, Minoru felt he was beginning to see an outline of Genji's recent geological history. Only a sketch as yet, but a startling one nonetheless.

Dr. Sato and the others weren't going to like his report at all.

There were some things he hadn't told even Emile, about what happened when the ancestors of Ta'azsh'da and Phs'n'kah arrived on this isle, eighty or so Ihrdizu generations ago. The paleontological record was clear, though. Within four of those generations, *half* of the species native to this isolated ecosphere were extinct, or driven across the waters.

This was no intentional genocide, of course. Human migrants had done the same thing just as inadvertently, back on ancient Earth—as on Hawaii, where countless bird species vanished soon after men and women arrived in Polynesian canoes. Far more of the harm was actually done by the creatures arriving *with* men—rats and dogs—than by human hunters themselves.

Destruction of habitat was another major cause, both on Earth and in this part of Genji, where nearly every shallow area near the tidal zone had been carved into terraces for algae farms and collection traps.

The history of species die-offs was right there to be seen, in the uppermost layers of soil and rock. Phs'n'kah and a few other bright Ihrdizu had been astonished when Minoru gave them lessons how to read that record. It was not the stuff of legends, just a long list of animals and plants that weren't around any more.

But that wasn't the biggest surprise. No, not the biggest one at all.

Starship *Yamato* Crew Database: General News

Genji Expedition:

. . . one of the most curious things about our discovery of Genji is the incredible temporal coincidence—that we should have happened upon this world at the very time when mainland cultures are amidst their burgeoning industrial revolution, spreading both physically and in their confident grasp of their technology.

What a fluke of timing! Consider. Had we on Earth been slower, and the Ihrdizu faster by a few millennia—a mere flicker as time goes by in this vast galaxy—it might have been *they* who discovered *us*.

Let this realization teach us humility as we seek to learn from our new neighbors.

She stepped down the lander's ramp with a grace that was pleasurable to watch. It was so much like the way she flew machines across the sky, somehow both demure and erotic at the same time. He doubted any Occidental woman could ever manage it.

Minoru's heart leapt at the sight of her; nevertheless, he kept his greeting properly reserved. They exchanged bows. To his delight, he saw she carried an overnight bag.

"So, what is this surprise you promised me?" Yukiko asked. Did something in her voice imply possibilities?

Ah, but what are possibilities? To become real, they must be earned.

"You'll see," he told her, and gestured toward the village, where smoke curled up from smoldering cook fires. "This way. Unless you want to freshen up first?"

She laughed. "Wriggling out of this suit so soon after I just put it on? No, I 'freshened' in the lander. Come on, I'm hungry."

So, she's guessed what this is about. Minoru was only slightly disappointed. After all, her insight showed an aspect of compatibility. They thought alike.

Or, at least we share one obsession.

It hardly seemed very intimate, walking slowly side by side in clunking, ground-hugging steps, carefully maintaining balance on the sloping path. Gravity was like a treacherous octopus, always waiting to grab you. Swaddled inside their suits—even with their arms and lower legs now free by decree of Okuma Base doctors—it felt as if they were performing a long, slow promenade.

Minoru hoped to dance a different dance with Yukiko, later. One in which gravity would play a friendlier role. But he kept a tight reign on such thoughts.

"Where is Emile?" she asked as they passed several hilltop citadels and finally approached the plateau where village center lay.

"He's observing an Ihrdizu folk moot, over there in the civic arena." Minoru gestured toward where several close hills formed a bowl, from which the low hum of several hundred voices could be heard, rising and falling in a moaning melody. Minoru had witnessed moots before, though none this large. They struck him as somewhat like a Greek play—with chorus, actors, and all—crossed with Nō theater, and interrupted at odd moments by bouts of something that seemed vaguely reminiscent of sumo wrestling.

"Emile persuaded the Village Mothers to hold a special event for the transients, to relieve tensions and maybe give them a stake in the community."

"Sounds pretty daring, an alien making suggestions like that."

Minoru shrugged. "Well, we had to try something. The poor kid was wracked with guilt feelings, even though the situation isn't really our fault. Anyway, it seems to be working. I'd have been expected to attend as an honored guest, only I'm one of the cooks for the feast afterward, so I'm excused."

"Ah, so." She said it calmly. But had he picked up just a trace of excitement in her voice? Minoru hoped so.

Phs'n'kah had been tending to the preliminaries for Minoru, carefully removing the external carapaces of thirty recently snared, inch-long *zu'unutsus,* and one by one laying the nude insectoids on a wooden cutting board near the cooking fire. Before being cut up, the *zu'unutsus* looked like Earth caterpillars, and fit a similar niche in this ecosystem, though nowadays they were very rare.

"Thank you," he told his assistant, then explained to Yukiko, "In my routine bioassay I finally struck it rich. Two plants and this insectoid, all of whom practice chemical segregation of just the kind we need."

"What does that mean?"

"It means that in all three cases, every chemical that might be toxic to humans happens to be segregated—isolated—to specific parts or organs. A lot better than those berries the Purple Cliffs team fed you—"

Yukiko frowned. "I was ill for a week."

"—which were considered 'edible' only because the poison levels were low and 'tolerable.' In this case, all you have to do is carefully remove the bad parts...." With a dissecting scalpel he deftly excised portions that served functions similar to kidneys and livers for the *zu'unutsus,* flicking them in high arcs to sizzle on the coals. "You might say it's a lot like preparing Fugu, back home—"

"Really?" She grabbed his arm so tightly that he felt it through the suit fabric. "You devil, you!"

She seemed impressed, even thrilled, when he compared this delicacy to Fugu—to Oriental blowfish—which was considered one of Japan's paramount delicacies, commanding titanic prices back home. Fugu chefs were respected more than surgeons, and yet mistakes still killed hundreds of customers each year. The appetite for Fugu never slackened. Indeed, risk seemed part of the excitement. Minoru had been about to assure her that he had taken precautions. Even in the event of a mistake, the poisons found in the forbidden organs of *zu'unutsu* weren't so bad they couldn't be dealt with by vomiting and some antitoxin, which he had at hand.

But Yukiko's expression stopped Minoru. From the look in her eyes, either she had great faith in his skill, or this was a girl who relished a thrill now and then.

Even after the joyful discovery of something edible out of the countless field samples, it had still taken considerable trial and error to reach this point. The recipe had come about after many tests, of which the last involved himself and Emile as guinea pigs. Nevertheless, the culmination had been saved for tonight. It was to be the first complete, all-Genjian meal served for humans, ever. That is, if all went as planned.

Carefully he slit open several *yer'tani* roots and slipped the flayed filets of *zu'unutsus* inside, along with chopped *qui'n'mathi.*

"They should bake for an hour," he said, wrapping each combi-

ZU'UNUTSU

ONE OF THE ONLY CREATURES FOUND ON GENJI
THAT IS EDIBLE BY HUMANS. RAPID GROWTH
OF SIDE PLATES REQUIRES NEARLY CONSTANT
MOTION TO WEAR DOWN "NAILS." AS A
RESULT, THE ZU'UNUTSU'S BORE HOLES ARE
FOUND IN SUN-BAKED SOIL CAPABLE OF
WEARING OUT EVEN HIGH-TECH EQUIPMENT.

Jonathan Scott © 91

KAW KAW

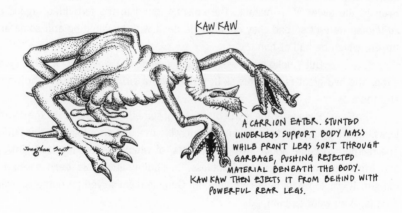

Jonathan Scott © 91

A CARRION EATER. STUNTED
UNDERLEGS SUPPORT BODY MASS
WHILE FRONT LEGS SORT THROUGH
GARBAGE, PUSHING REJECTED
MATERIAL BENEATH THE BODY.
KAW KAW THEN EJECTS IT FROM BEHIND WITH
POWERFUL REAR LEGS.

nation in funnel-weed fronds and putting them directly on the coals. "Why don't we go for a walk in the meantime?"

The other cooks, most of them males with infants riding on their tails, hissed amiably as Minoru led Yukiko through the press toward a steep embankment overlooking the tidal basins. There the two humans sat down, dangling their legs over a hand-wrought stone wall, looking up as low clouds parted to show the broad, desert-brown face of Chujo. It was a little eerie to realize that up there, right now, some of their crewmates were attempting to make contact with aliens more enigmatic than even the Ihrdizu.

"You know, your latest report almost got you recalled to Okuma Base," she told him.

"I know. How is Dr. Sato taking it?"

"He's hopping mad. And Dr. O'Leary feels hurt you made these revelations without consulting him first."

"That might have gotten my report buried in the database. This is something that must be known by all, before we decide how to make our homes on this world."

"Our principal purpose is study."

"Indeed. But we'll also live, as men and women. Have homes. Perhaps children. We should know the implications, and not take such steps unconsidered, like animals."

She looked at him, obviously feeling his intensity. Minoru sensed somehow that she approved. "Tell me about the cycles, then," she asked.

Minoru sighed. He had gone through it all so many times, first over and over in his head and in the database, then in his report, and finally in interviews for Team Yamato News. But this audience could be refused nothing.

"There is no coincidence," he began. "Or not as great a one as Sato thought. It's still surprising that two stars so near each other developed technological cultures so close in time. But we didn't just happen on Genji's solitary industrial revolution. It's occurred on this planet before, at least six or seven times."

From a pouch at his belt, he withdrew a corroded lump of metal. "This may be a coin, or a medallion. I found it locally, only a little ways underground, but none of the natives can identify the writing. And I doubt they'll be able to on the mainland, either.

"The present culture settled this island eighty generations ago. Before that, it was deserted. But earlier still, other Ihrdizu lived here. Those occupations came in multiple waves. And several times they had metallurgy."

"Did they . . . was each fall because of war?" Yukiko asked in a hushed voice.

"Who can say? Oh, there's no sign of nuclear combat, if that's what you mean. No war-induced endless winter. You might think there was such a holocaust, though, from the way species died out in waves, then recovered after Ihrdizu disappeared again. And every decline seemed to occur at the same pace as environmental degradation."

"No wonder Dr. Sato's mad at you! You agree with the Americans and Spacers—that technology can harm a world!"

Minoru shrugged. "There was a time when that was a central dogma of ecology. Perhaps we abandoned such a view too quickly, for reasons more political than scientific."

"I don't know what you mean."

"No matter." He shook his head. "Anyway, the Genjians appear to have been lucky; one of the limitations of their race actually led to its survival. Since they were—and are—constrained to living in areas near the shore, none of their past civilizations could ever do much harm to the *interiors* of the continents. Those and the great oceans served as genetic reservoirs, so that each time Ihrdizu civilization fell, and the natives' numbers plummeted, there were lots of species that could drift into the emptied niches and fill them again. In fact, it's rather startling how quick some recovery times were. As little as ten thousand years in one case."

Yukiko frowned, looking down at the ground. "I'm beginning to see what you mean. Back at Okuma Base, there was talk among some of the engineers—about some of the advantages we'll be able to offer Ihrdizu civilization. With the right tools, they could exploit much more territory than they now have available—"

Then she blinked. "Oh . . . and humans. We'll eventually make our homes on the highlands and mountaintops, where we can breathe without machines. But anything we do up there will affect whole watersheds. . . ."

Minoru shrugged. "Just so."

They sat together in silence then. Minoru regretted having spoiled the mood in this way, and was at a loss how to recover their previous high spirits. *Idiot,* he thought. *Can't you ever leave business at the shop?*

But he shouldn't have worried. Yukiko nudged him. "Well, we humans haven't done any harm *yet,* have we? Never borrow karma from next week, I always say."

He grinned in response. "A wise woman is a treasure beyond price."

"And it's a wise man who realizes what outlasts beauty." She answered his smile. "So, it should be almost time now. Let's eat!"

The moot was still in its last phases when they returned to the cook area. But stragglers were already slithering into the clearing to line up in winding queues with clay and wicker utensils. Newcomer females mixed with the locals with apparent conviviality, and Minoru could tell Emile's plan must have worked. For now at least, all thought of strife had been put aside. Good.

He fished the *zu'unutsus* from the coals and gingerly unwrapped the steaming leaves. Balancing their meals on native crockery, he and Yukiko claimed jars of a yeasty native brew that had been deemed only marginally poisonous by Okuma Base doctors . . . certainly no more dangerous than some of the concoctions whipped up aboard the *Yamato* during the long voyage out.

When Yukiko inhaled the aroma, then bit into her first roll, the expression on her face was Minoru's reward. Tears streamed down her cheeks, and he heard a soft sob of joy. The ridiculousness of such emotion—to be spent on a mere meal—did not escape her, and she burst out laughing, demurely hiding her mouth behind one hand. Minoru, too, alternately laughed and cried as he savored the rich, delicious flavors.

Together, silently, they ate and watched Murasaki settle toward the horizon, igniting the western cloud banks with streamers of golden fire.

At last, wiping his mouth through his helmet's chow-baffle, Minoru commented. "Stupid Spacers. They hurried home with a few chemical samples. So what? If they'd stayed another few months, we could have sent *zu'unutsus* home with them, and we'd all be rich, Spacer and *Yamato* crew alike."

"I'm just as glad that never happened." Yukiko sighed. "For the first time . . . I think I can picture *this* as my home. I don't even want to share this with Earthlings."

She grinned at the irony of her remark.

It felt good, stretched out in the twilight, laughing together and sharing the very first moment two humans drew a full measure of sustenance from Genji and only Genji. "Of course we'll have to plant Earth crops on the highlands, and make orbital farms, and do lots of other things. But it's good to know we can partake of this world, too."

She agreed in silence, but set his heart beating faster by slipping her hand into his.

The noisy clamor of Ihrdizu banqueting rose behind them, followed by a round of their strange, atonal singing. Minoru and Yukiko lay contentedly, watching Chujo head slowly from crescent to quarter phase. They barely turned to look when Phs'n'kah waddled up to ask if there was anything more Minoru needed. It seemed several of the newcomer females wanted to serenade Phs'n'kah, tonight, and he had gotten a baby-sitter for the kids. . . .

"No, I don't need anything more. You've already earned a bonus, today," Minoru assured Phs'n'kah. "Tomorrow, though, I want to get together some of our best foragers and go after some more *zu'unutsus*! We must learn how to breed them in captivity. Send samples to Okuma Base . . . "

Minoru was already thinking how well this might serve as a peace offering to Dr. Sato, and so he rambled on for a while before noticing the stance of the Ihrdizu male, whose snorkel drooped disconsolately.

"What's the matter?" Minoru asked through the translator.

"No more zu'unutsus. *All* ✳✳✳. *This was the* ✳✳✳.*"*

Yukiko gasped. But Minoru squeezed her hand and laughed, a little nervously.

"Oh, come on, I know they weren't plentiful. But surely there must be some hives left in the hills. Or on other islands..."

His voice trailed off as he wished he did not know this Genjian so well. Or that Phs'n'kah weren't so well known for utter reliability and truthfulness.

"That is where we had to go to find these," Phs'n'kah answered simply.

"But..." Minoru swallowed. "Are you absolutely sure?"

Phs'n'kah whirled his snorkel clockwise. *"All the best* ✳✳✳ *foragers took part. We knew it would bond you to us... if only you could* ✳✳✳ *eat of Genji. So we made a vow of* ✳✳✳. *We did not fail. Now it is done."*

Minoru sat back against the stone wall with a sigh.

This was a blow.

It was inconceivable.

It was...

Yukiko suddenly giggled. And Minoru could not prevent a flicker of a smile from twitching the corner of his mouth.

It was... horribly hilarious!

He laughed, saw the shared understanding in Yukiko's eyes, and broke up, shaking with guffaws.

Of course, he realized as his sides began to hurt. *Of course it had to be this way. In order to make this our home, we had to do more than just partake of its substance... we must also share its karma.*

And what better way to do that than to sacrifice the one thing on Genji we might have come to treasure above all others? Above—may the gods forgive us—even the Ihrdizu?

What better way to demonstrate what we have to lose?

Oh, he would do his best to persuade his fellow colonists to establish rules and traditions that would keep the Earthling share of ecological shame to a minimum. Perhaps they might even help the Ihrdizu escape the cyclic trap that had them ensnared for so long.

On the other hand, perhaps humans would prove a bane to this world, helping the Genjians complete a job of destruction their own limitations had prevented them from finishing before. He would fight to prevent that, but who could predict the future?

All of that lies ahead, though, Minoru thought. *All that and much more. For well or ill, we are part of this world now. Phs'n'kah was right. This is now our home.*

Yukiko held up the last pair of *zu'unutsu* rolls, now cold, but still aromatic with a flavor to make the eyes water with delight . . . and irony. "One we save for Emile, of course. Shall we seal and refrigerate the other one for Sato?"

He took the tender object from her, tore off a morsel, and tossed it into the bay far below. She met his eyes, and reached out to do the same. Then, with his free hand, he helped her stand.

"Let's save it, all right," he said. "But for a special occasion."

"Like tonight?" Yukiko smiled. "I know just the thing."

She took his arm and led him past the singing natives, down through a reed-lined valley, across glistening fens, and then up to a plateau where a white dome shone in the glow of a lantern hung over the door.

Minoru glanced back to see Emile dashing to and fro, joyously recording every aspect of the native celebration. He probably wouldn't be back for hours.

LANGUAGE

BY POUL ANDERSON

"**H**e's crazy," they warned her at Okuma Base. "Buried his wife ten years ago and been a hermit since." They meant Earth years, of course. Under the guise of practicality, did they cling to each possible reminder of the world that few among them would see again, or ever? "Ask any of the pilots who've flown there. Don't go there alone." You, a woman, they implied.

"I'm supposed to find out whether support for his research should be continued," Rita Byrne reminded them. "That involves staying a while. You can't spare two people that long. Also, I'll do better without a third party cluttering the scene."

As shorthanded as the scientific enterprise was, and the damned mystics claiming more and more of its scanty resources, nobody argued much with her. Besides, Malchiel Holden was, at the very least, eccentric and irascible; but he'd scarcely get violent, would he? Nonetheless, Byrne felt glad that a flyer's outfit included a pistol, against the occasional carnivore that didn't know it couldn't digest human flesh. The caliber was only .22, but the slugs were explosive.

Wishing to reach Farland fairly early in the morning, she took off about midnight. The mountain bleakness, little relieved by scrub growth and huddled buildings, turned into grandeur as she rose above it, crags, peaks, gorges dappled white by snowfields and glaciers. Nearly full, like a huge tawny moon mysteriously emblazoned, Chujo turned the cloud deck over the lowlands into a sea of milk washed with pale gold.

After she leveled off, however, it was just to purr along on robot for almost thirty hours, nearly halfway around the globe. She ate a meal and sought her bunk. Always grab a chance to rest. Born and raised on Genji, she handled herself readily enough, but her kind had evolved to weigh two-thirds what it did here.

Murasaki rose, broad and fulvous. Chujo, already waning, seemed abruptly dim against the sunlight. The companion planet fell beneath the horizon. Still the aircraft flew, under a plum-dusky day sky, over the ocean that covered starside. When the hemisphere's single continent appeared, multitudinously yellow, through rifts in the overcast, Byrne had been through a full circadian cycle. She had occupied her waking hours by accessing data on her goal for review, together with background music, and felt entirely fresh.

Taking the pilot's seat, she switched to manual control and slanted downward. Once below the clouds, she compared the map display with what she saw. Gray, green, purple, foam-streaked, the waters marched from the west to break in monstrous cascades and geysers on land that hereabouts reared granite cliffs against it. Flying on throttled engines, she caught a murmur that was the roar of yonder surf. A canyon, cleaving the shore, made a fjord, protected by outlying skerries. Magnifying in a viewscreen, she spied houses on the heights and vessels tied at a floating dock. Yes, that would be the Gash. Given all the uncertainties still plaguing navigation, her robot had done well. Then Rockridge lay about ninety kilometers south. She swung in its direction.

Most names on the map had been bestowed by Holden over the years—some, Byrne supposed, by his wife before she died. Who better, indeed who else at all, when a handful of people were trying to know an entire world? Certain names were obvious attempts at rendering Ihrdizuan ones; others were probably translations into the man's native English; others might be personal creations, bearing what freight of memories? Suddenly, more sharply than before, Byrne realized how ignorant she was, even of this small and detached undertaking that she was to pass judgment on.

Ringed by sheer hills, Gunnunggung Bay glimmered sixty kilometers from north to south, forty from west to east. Islands dotted it. There were more in the sea outside, and countless rocks and reefs. White fury churned among them. That, and the narrow strait that was its opening, kept the bay reasonably calm, at least in fair weather. Turbulence did roil about its holms, and at the north end where a great brown river emptied. The tide appeared to be just past high, ebbing rapidly. Rock and mud, down which water foamed, made a rim of darkness under the xanthous vegetation that covered the upper slopes. Wildlife was abundant, wings storming in their thousands above swimmers that grazed mats of pelagic weed.

Rockridge Thorp clustered atop the highest hillcrest at the eastern shore. A windbreak of squat trees surrounded a dozen beehive-shaped homes and as many hemicylindrical utility structures. Building materials were stone, brick, tile. Perhaps no fire-resistant wood grew in this part of oxygen-rich Genji; Byrne recognized yet another gap in her information. The human dwelling was unmistakable, a boxy metal T-shape equipped with air locks and glass ports. Steam vented from the power plant in one crossarm. It stood about a hundred meters outside the settlement. A tar-and-gravel spot nearby must be the landing place.

As she descended, Byrne glanced west. The coastal range fell away in rolling valleys. She glimpsed roads that connected other communities, plowland, pasture, lakes and marshes devoted to the more important aquaculture, mills and smithies gathered smoky near a minehead. How many centuries since the first Ihrdizuan explorers discovered Farland, the first colonists followed? They were still rather isolated and primitive here.

She came down vertically. The engines hummed to a silence through which beat the noises of the water, a kilometer or more distant but carried loud. She unharnessed, fetched her mask, donned it and snugged it tight. This was the newest model. A headband formed the casing of the little motor and contained both pressure-reduction intake and forced-draft exhaler. A retractable rocker arm enabled her to run the unit by hand, should its battery give out and no replacement be available. Air at three bars is inadvisable for humans to breathe. Molecular adhesion along the edges held a self-cleaning blinkie visor and the stiff fabric beneath to her skin, while allowing enough play to leave her mouth free. There she could insert a stopcocked drinking tube or push solid food through a slit whose cling prevented any significant amount of gas from entering.

Ihrdizu scuttled from the thorp toward the jetplane. Their big, torpedo-shaped, sleekly blue-gray bodies lent a touch of familiarity to the foreignness encompassing her. The four eye sockets around each mouth were telescoped outward and the snorkel trunks pointed straight ahead, as if reaching for maximum sensory input. Both three-digited tentacles waved to and fro. Tail flukes flapped. Excitement, oh, yes.

A servomotor opened the door for her. Outside air gushed in. Her ears twinged for a moment before adapting to the higher volume of sounds. Heat and damp enveloped her. They weren't too bad, here beside the ocean, and she was used to odors that newcomers found rank. In fact, a clean tang blew off the bay.

She climbed out. The Ihrdizu arrived. They stopped a short way off and stared. A female waddled forward, to sit upright on hind legs and tail while offering a forepaw. "Welcome." She coughed. Byrne could barely understand the dialect. "I am (harsh noise). But to him I am—" Did she really say "Wilhelmina"? She added, "You call us what you want. How can we help?"

Touched, Byrne shook hands. Clumsy though it felt to her, the paw had enough dexterity to work effectively in conjunction with the tentacles. "I am Rita," she replied. They could come closer to voicing that than her surname. She wondered if they perceived any individuality in her. Already she saw their differences from each other, but she had known many Ihrdizu. These were familiar with no human but Holden. The supply pilots came seldom and briefly. Did the Rock-ridgers identify her as a slender young woman with black hair and blue eyes, or were all her kind alike to them, except the one?

She forced forth the best, crude approximation of Genjian sounds she could make. "Where is the male who lives here?"

Wilhelmina followed her better than she had anticipated. "You are female? Do you seek a mate? That would be good. His is long dead." A tentacle pointed. Byrne saw a crudely chiseled slab behind the house, doubtless the wife's headstone. "He has gone to his (whistling noise; must mean "himatids") as he always does, most days more than once and often at night. You wait."

Byrne needed a while to work out what that had meant. Then she couldn't help laughing. "Is it a matchmaker you'd be?" she asked in English. Wilhelmina and the rest stiffened a bit. Maybe they thought she made fun of them. Byrne hastened to stumble on in their language. "No. I do have business with him, I will stay a while, but then I go back."

Mate . . . She'd avoided any real ties so far. For a moment she wished Carlos Villareal were at her side.

Somebody in the group hooted. "Och-h'ng, he comes," Wilhelmina exclaimed. "He must have seen your boat and turned back." It seemed the locals referred to Holden exclusively by the pronoun. In northeastern Nighland that was a mark of respect, but farther south it implied coolness, emotional distance. Which, if either, was it here?

Holden had evidently been on a trail downhill to the water. The strides were long and quick that bore him up to the ridge. They wasted energy; but they gave outlet to anger, Byrne thought. She braced muscles and spirit. If he tried to browbeat her, he'd make a bad mistake.

When he reached her, he loomed. Shabby coverall and worn deck shoes covered a rawboned height. His pressure container was outmoded, a transparent globe on a collar gasketed to chest, shoulders, upper back. Fitted with wipers, defogger, and sound amplifiers, it had provision for a water tube but none for eating. On the other hand, a long snorkel, now coiled around the rear-mounted pump, allowed him to stay submerged. Gray hair and beard bristled on the head within. The nose was bladelike, eyes bullet-colored, skin furrowed, leathery, but even more mushroom-white than that of most Nordics, Celts, and Slavs on Genji.

Byrne reached out her hand. "How do you do, Dr. Holden," she said. "I am—"

He ignored the gesture and snapped her greeting across. "I know. They phoned me you'd arrive this evening. Why didn't you? I'm not ready."

Byrne told herself that she shouldn't let him anger her. "I'm sorry. It happened I completed another mission unexpectedly early. Rather than stay idle forty or fifty hours, I thought you, too, would like me to begin here at once."

She couldn't refrain from adding, "My services are much in demand, you know. We've a great deal to do on moonside, and not many people to do it."

"Well, the result is, you'll cool your heels till sundown or later. I'm not about to stop and talk. The research opportunity today comes once in ten or fifteen years." Doubtless he meant swings of the planets around Murasaki: in other words, about two or three Terrestrial. "All right, get yourself settled in the house. The croakers will unload and store the supplies. You did bring what I ordered, didn't you?"

"Yes." She was sorely tempted to point out that further shipments might well depend on his conduct toward her. But no. If he'd forgotten what common courtesy was, that ought to be his problem alone. "What are your immediate plans . . . may I ask?"

"To observe, inquire, and not stand here chattering any longer." Holden glanced at the Ihrdizu. "Karl, Otto, Friedrich, see to my goods." He barked it in English. "This person will take care of her things."

Impulse burst up and congealed into decision. "One moment," Byrne said. "Why don't I come with you?"

Surprise became scorn. "You're not prepared, that's why. I tell you, this is an important day. I can't waste it dragging your weight around. And if you drown or something stupid like that, it's my ass will be in the teeth."

Byrne rejoiced at having reason to put a whipcrack in her voice. "For your information, Holden, I've retrieved everything you ever put in the main database, I've talked with the pilots who've flown this route, and my whole career has been in the Exploration Corps. Did you think they'd send a schoolgirl to evaluate your work? Let me grab some rations for myself, and the two of us can commence our mutual business. The sooner begun, the sooner done, correct?"

For a second he glared. Then, shrugging: "We'll try it. Bring food for forty-eight hours; we may not get back till after dark. Life jacket. Sleeping bag. Warmer clothes than you're wearing, and several changes. It's cold on the water, and you'll be drenched repeatedly. You'll have to separate out your stuff when we return. The croakers will put everything in the storerooms. Quick, now!"

She sought the aircraft and did what was needful in a few minutes. Show that bastard. Strap the pistol back on over the new outfit; opposite it hang a Sony audiovisual recorder the size of her hand. Lash bag to packframe, stuff everything else inside, slip arms through straps, secure the bellyband, step forth again. "Quick enough?"

Holden stopped pacing. Most of the Ihrdizu were gone. They had work of their own. Three males lingered. "Get busy," he told them, and set off.

Byrne took pleasure in matching his pace, burdened as she was. She could spare breath for speech, too. "Aren't you pretty arrogant with them? And that word 'croaker'—we don't consider it polite."

"You're not at Okuma Base, and those aren't your hangers-on."
He didn't look at her. Admittedly, you'd better watch your step on a downslope.
Carelessness broke a lot of bones. "Here they respect power."

Beneath the mask and the tropical air, she felt her cheeks heat.
"The power belongs to our administration and council, sir. We do not use it for
bullying. A few thousand people on an entire planet, two decades from Earth,
can't afford to antagonize the inhabitants."

"Did I ever scream for help? I'll protect myself."

"I'm here, among other things, to find out what kind of relationship
you maintain. If nothing else, future generations of us will be dealing with the
Farlanders."

"God damn it, I don't abuse them! Did they seem terrified? You
don't know how often I've forced myself to stay my hand—But not against the
Rockridgers. I tell you, we have a perfectly reasonable arrangement. They've come
to count on the tools and materials I requisition for them. In exchange, they assist
me when I need it. But they are slobs. I have to make it quite clear to them, in
as few and simple words as possible, what I want, else nothing would get done
right."

"English words?"

"They've learned. Why should I ruin my throat mangling their language? Besides, it's hopelessly vague and long-winded."

"You'd come to know them better."

"That isn't what I'm here for. My purpose is to discover something
about the himatids, remember?"

"You could at least show the Ihrdizu the respect to address them
by their proper names."

"They don't mind. My wife bestowed them. She was German. Those
were pet names she gave them, and they knew it. She . . . liked them."

As you don't, Byrne thought.

"We named individual himatids, too, according to a different system, and I've continued that," Holden went on. "Sheer necessity there. How could
a human keep a set of clicks and twangs straight in his mind? Not that I believe
they have any concept corresponding to anything we'd recognize as nomenclature."

"So you've reported. But have you considered the possibility that
an individual may use a variety of different names according to circumstances,
and frequently drop some or adopt new ones? It was the practice in Japan of the
Heian period."

He gave her a brief regard. "You really have studied my work," he
said slowly, "and thought about it."

"How else could I judge what you're doing?"

His voice hardened. "Yes, I tried to analyze my data on the theory you mentioned. Failure. You think the . . . Ihrdizu are unlike us. Compared to the himatids, they—and those Chupchup vags—are our kissing cousins. Look sharp, now!"

Byrne obeyed. They had reached steepness. For a while the trail switchbacked among stiff yellow bushes that rattled in the wind. At high-water mark, the hillside turned into what was nearly a cliff. Only bare rock remained, under a blackly gleaming layer of ooze. Seaweed, dead ichthyoids, shells, less identifiable debris littered it. Flying creatures strange to her wheeled and whistled in their hundreds, landed to feast, flapped off again in alarm. Water ran down every channel. Close to receding sea level, it made a stream, centimeters deep, of the path the Ihrdizu had carved. Unhampered, they could climb freely about, but here they generally carried loads. It was well that they had corrugated the surface. Holden went ahead, often halting, ready to help Byrne. She picked her way cautiously. Despite the breeze, sweat soon dripped off her skin. Several times she almost fell. Damn if she'd give him the satisfaction, though.

Waves hacked, foam leaped, but there was no surf on the bight. Like the colonists of the Gash, the Rockridgers kept a pontoon dock moored some distance off. They swam to and fro, or used lighters to transfer freight. Several boats were tied up, together with a pair of ships about forty meters long. Their rigs were fore-and-aft, gaff-headed; on Genji, you'd best keep your center of action low. Holden's craft lay closer in, a twelve-meter turbo cruiser with a crane and capstan forward of the deckhouse. When he spoke into a radiophone he took from his pocket, the vessel heaved its anchor, drew close, and extended a gangplank.

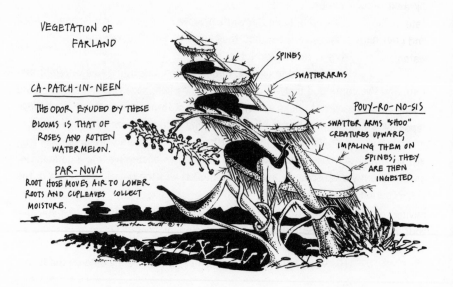

VEGETATION OF
FARLAND

SPINES

SWATTERARMS

CA-PATCH-IN-NEEN

THE ODOR EXUDED BY THESE
BLOOMS IS THAT OF
ROSES AND ROTTEN
WATERMELON.

POUY-RO-NO-SIS

SWATTER ARMS "SHOO"
CREATURES UPWARD,
IMPALING THEM ON
SPINES; THEY
ARE THEN
INGESTED.

PAR-NOVA
ROOT HOSE MOVES AIR TO LOWER
ROOTS AND CUPLEAVES COLLECT
MOISTURE.

Jonathan Scott © 91

As she boarded, Byrne noticed corroded bronze letters on the bow: EMMA. She nodded at them. "Your wife's name?" A possible approach through his hostility.

"Daughter," he said. "Died in infancy."

"Oh. I'm sorry."

"It happens."

Too often among humans on Genji, even where medical care was available. Sometimes Byrne wondered why they were on the planet, what sense it made. Yes, yes, the historical reasons, science, prestige, politics, superstition; quite a few people came voluntarily, though they knew it would be a one-way trip, hoping for freedom or challenging work or whatever they hoped for; the old reproductive instinct whispered, "Under these conditions, children = the fastest means of increasing our numbers = improved chances for bettering our lot"—yes, yes. But were they actually just building new pyramids, waging a new Crusade, investing their dreams in a new cargo cult? Suppose they beamed Home a petition for an end. Suppose Earth was willing to pay the cost of bringing them back.

What the hell was there for her on Earth?

Only one grave behind yonder house. May the small coffin still have been sound when Holden opened the soil for his wife. Genji lacked the right bacteria and worms to reduce a human corpse to clean bones.

Byrne stowed her gear in the cabin, which was crammed full of apparatus. A locked cabinet held pistol, automatic rifle, and grenade gun. Were there large, dangerous animals in this vicinity?

She joined Holden in the ample cockpit. He had taken manual control. The cruiser growled swiftly outward. It rocked and bucked in the chop. Spray flew over the bows. Gunmetal whitecaps ran to the western steeps and the gate between them. Wind skirled, as chilly as he had warned. Clouds swept low and gray upon it. Occasionally a sunbeam struck through and flared off a patch of water. In this weather it was red.

"You did remember to put on your life jacket," he grunted.

She sat down on the starboard bench beside the wheel and drew a long breath. "Why do you act like this?" she demanded. "I'll try to enter a fair report in spite of your insults, but you could make things easier for both of us."

He peered straight ahead. "Should I pretend I'm overjoyed? I've lost the knack of pretending. But no, I didn't mean any insult. I'm only trying to speak frankly and clearly. Don't be so thin-skinned."

She clung to her patience. "I can understand if you're piqued at having the value of your work questioned. Well, nobody denies that what you and your wife accomplished was extraordinary. You pioneered whole new fields of science."

He barked a laugh. "Indeed? When you don't recall her name?"

"Jesus Christ!—Uh, I'm sorry. It escaped me. Can't you see what a shipload of information I had to acquire in a short time, if I was to do my job right? They thought about sending a fellow scientist who might better talk your language. But as you yourself remarked, the himatids are so different from the Ihrdizu. Nobody was professionally qualified except maybe Li Yuan, who's old and frail. All the others have their hands full, anyway. And then, we're concerned about more than just the science. Relationships with the autochthons, for instance. In the end, they settled on me. I'm . . . a kind of generalist." She waited a little before adding, "We're stuck with each other. Let's make the best of it."

"Why must they send anybody? What's the complaint been?"

"You know perfectly well. No complaint. Certain disturbing hints the pilots brought back. A couple of them speak fluent Ihrdizu and managed some conversation with the Rockridgers. Your overbearing attitude. Your outright threats against the community to the north, in the Gash. We want to forestall any possible trouble."

"I told you," he rasped, "I get along with the Rockridgers. I don't fawn on them, as apparently a lot of you moonsiders do on your croakers, but we get along. As for the Gashers, don't you realize that they still hunt himatids? They gave up enslaving calves two or three generations ago simply because it no longer paid. Instead, they ate them. Not a one left there. They go after wild calves along uncolonized shores and carpet whales at sea."

"Is it that important? Oh, I know the arrival of the Ihrdizu was catastrophic for the himatids, but the horrors were phasing out already before humans reached Murasaki."

"Not because of any goodness in croaker hearts. Enslavement became uneconomic. It's easier for the Rockridgers to get their local himatids to do odd diving jobs in exchange for cheap iron knives that soon rust away and need replacement. As for whaling, the Rockridgers never were real seafarers; they just trade up and down this coast. The Gashers, they are bold sailors. They *like* hunting, and the meat."

"I know. You've described it often and bitterly in your reports. But you admit it isn't a real Gasher industry. They take opportunities, which aren't common enough to threaten the species. They never hunt in this bay, do they?"

"No. I'd blow them out of the water if they tried."

"I'll agree the situation is deplorable. However, we can't impose our will on beings who do us no harm and outnumber us a millionfold and in this case live half a planet away. Besides, Rockridge and the Gash belong to the same society. How would you like it if a foreigner attacked neighbors of yours? How well would you cooperate with him afterward?"

"The Rockridgers would, for the sake of my trade goods. Croakers have rudimentary consciences, if any."

Indignation snatched at Byrne. "So you say! I don't. And certainly humans care. Especially when we know the Ihrdizu are intelligent beings, and it's far from proven that the himatids are."

"I haven't done anything," Holden said sullenly. "Unless you'd forbid me to express outrage."

Byrne calmed somewhat. "I'm not accusing you, sir. You asked if there were complaints against you. I listed certain matters that headquarters feels should be cleared up. I'm sure you can do that. Don't be so thin-skinned."

His short-lived grin surprised her. "Ha!"

"The major question—" Byrne broke off.

"Yes?" he prompted.

She sighed. "I was searching for words. But if you want a moratorium on tact, all right. You know quite well what the problem is. You receive messages as well as send them. Your replies have been . . . unsatisfactory. Resources for scientific research on Genji are more tight than ever, what with Chujo studies competing. Your station is a significant drain on them. A single man, true—but he needs food, clothes, medicines, spare parts, new equipment, everything, first produced, then flown around the globe. Plus the hazard. You remember, I hope, how Antonio Simonetti lost his aircraft and barely escaped with his life on a flight to you. You may not have stopped to think what the rescue operation cost."

"Do you mean that what we do should be cost-free?" he gibed. "If so, I have news for you."

"Oh, of course the outlays were justified earlier"—she paused for half a second—"when your work was epoch-making. But what has it become, these last several Earth years? Your reports have grown more and more perfunctory, repetitious, concerned with trivial details. Identification of another kind of weed the himatids make rope from. Isolation of another combination of sounds, with clues to suggest it *might* mean a specific rock at a certain point of ebb tide. Is that sort of thing worth maintaining you, when we could perhaps unravel that wonderful system of kinship among the Flowery Mountain Ihrdizu?"

"Which you claim matters more than getting to understand an entire different race?" he snapped. "Or is it simply easier?"

Abrupt, unexpected sympathy touched Byrne. "I realize this has been your lifework," she said. "But you are growing old, Dr. Holden. And maybe you're at the limits of what one man, even a young man, can discover alone. Maybe your himatids will have to wait for a proper xenological team, someday, that'll build on what you've discovered. You needn't rusticate on moonside, you know. There's never a dearth of problems to tackle.

"I don't claim, right now, that that is the case. I'm here to find out what is, and make recommendations, that's all. Won't you please help? You'll find me wide open to whatever you want to say or show."

"Then pay attention," he answered.

She bit her lip and fell silent, gazing about her. Afar she spied a schooner, if that was the right term, that had rounded the northern headland and was bound in the gate. Tiny at their distance, sails spread like wings before the sea wind. Its deep whittering was well-nigh lost in the rush and boom of water close ahead. There a reef lay near a sparsely begrown islet. Waves broke on both, riptides churned and spouted between. And, yes, two himatids were present. One swam in the channel, visible to her as a ribbon that occasionally reared up out of the foam. The other was picking berries on the holm. Byrne's look sought it eagerly. Hitherto she had seen the creatures only in visuals.

This calf must be rather young; perhaps ten Earth years had passed since it came here from ashore and ceased to be a tad. She gauged by size. The body, a few centimeters thick, was about two meters long and half a meter wide, a sinuous wet obsidian shading to gray-white on the belly where the many tiny mouths were, each with its claw-tooth. Between the fifteen pairs of flexible arms she made out glints off the eyes. The two arms flanking the blunt point to which the ribbon came remained idle; they could grasp things if necessary, but were specialized for making sounds. Farther back, digits held fast to the slippery surface. The last third was submerged, taking up moisture and dissolved oxygen. That didn't matter to Byrne; the ends were exactly alike.

The swimmer lifted itself again and—stared?—in her direction. It was older, twice the size of its companion. After a moment it oscillated toward the boat.

Holden had set the engine to idle and taken an optical from its case beside the wheel. He peered. "Japheth," he said. "And, hmm, that's Ishmael ashore."

Byrne recollected that he had his own names for them. "How can you tell?" she asked.

He cast her a disdainful glance. "Markings, proportions, style of motion and body language. It takes experience, patience, time that can't be accounted for in any properly academic report." After a moment he added, "I think that more than half of himatid communication is by signs. The most important half, at that—emotion, art, what'd give us a little insight into their psychology. How am I supposed to learn it from them, let alone talk it with them? If Okuma would send the equipment for decent simulations— But no, they'd rather bitch at me for not producing more reports."

"They've explained that both the hardware and the program would have to be developed practically from scratch," Byrne retorted. "If you refuse to believe— Never mind." Conciliate him. "Yes, you are handicapped. We all are, on Genji. Just the same, you've done a remarkable job of getting to know these beings." Well, it was his obsession, his reason for remaining alive. "Seems like that fellow has something to say to you. Or is it simply curious, or what?"

She saw how the man tensed. "I hope to find out. Get a hint, anyway. They often wait for me here. At least, I often find some here. I told you this is a special time."

Her pulse quickened. "How?"

"A pod of carpet whale are passing offshore, bound north after budding. That's always a great occasion, like a holy day." Holden made a mouth. "Except that it isn't superstitious. This epiphany is real."

"But how do the calves know? I thought juveniles and adults had nothing to do with each other."

Contempt flared. "Carpet whales mate, hermaphroditically, when they've built up adequate tissue reserves. There's no fixed time for that, but after they've reached these waters and budded off, the young swim ashore to take up life on land. The calves notice the tads coming in. They're not stupid, whatever the croakers claim."

Byrne flushed hot. She barely controlled her reply. "I'm not stupid either, sir. If you were dumped down in a totally new environment, a fact or two might fail to pop out of your memory at once. Or do you deny that?"

Was he a trifle mollified? He didn't apologize, but did say, rather quietly, "I suspect the cues are more chemical than visual. The new-budded tads are so small, and come in randomly. Himatids give off their wastes through the skin, as liquids and gases, you know; and they appear to sense with their entire bodies. It's nothing like what you and I experience."

No, she thought, absolutely not. The whole cycle— Mindless little thing like a caterpillar, prey for every larger animal, but adding neuronal tissue as well as size till it was too big for existence on land. The tough, wary, lucky, minuscule minority that survived, seeking out tidewater regions where calves dwelt and coming under their tutelage. No concept of family; but the little ones could hunt and gather in crannies where larger, older individuals could not. In exchange they got protection, training, education in whatever passed for tradition among himatids— It wasn't anything a human would ever really comprehend. Did the effort to do so make him, in the end, unhuman? Byrne thought of a mystic striving to know God. But Holden spat on any such ideas.

He pointed. "See that trident Japheth's carrying?" he remarked. "Pure native work, shell, bone, wooden shaft, rawhide lashing. I've never seen a calf with metal when the whales are passing by. Ritual, or what?"

The great form drew alongside and rose above the port rail. Feet braced wide on the swaying cockpit floor, Holden tilted his head back, looking up toward the foremost hands. Byrne had a fleeting fantasy of an ancient savage before

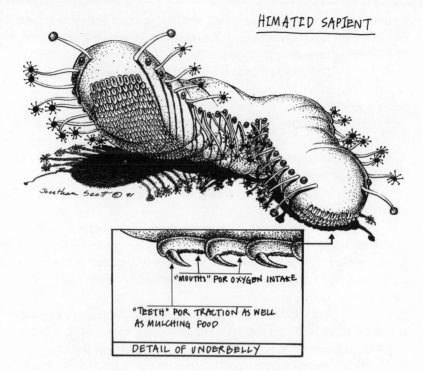

Jonathan Scott © 91

"MOUTHS" FOR OXYGEN INTAKE

"TEETH" FOR TRACTION AS WELL
AS MULCHING FOOD

DETAIL OF UNDERBELLY

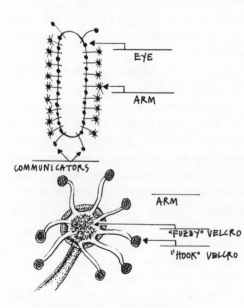

EYE

ARM

COMMUNICATORS

ARM

"FUZZY" VELCRO

"HOOK" VELCRO

NOTE ON RESPIRATION:
THE STOMALIKE MOUTHS CAN TAKE
IN OXYGEN EITHER DIRECTLY
FROM THE AIR OR OUT OF WATER.
THE INTAKE SEEMS MINIMAL,
BUT EACH MOUTH HAS
COMPARATIVELY FEW CELLS TO
PROVIDE FOR.

some idol, about to make sacrifice. Digits rubbed over textured palms and against each other. Stridulations went loud through wind and water noises. Holden uttered harsh sounds—meant to imitate?—and made gestures. Byrne reached for her recorder.

Odors welled from the himatid. They weren't offensive, they were pungent, bittersweet. Dizziness swooped. Byrne gasped. There'd been something buried in the mass of briefing material, yes, narcotic effect on humans; and here she was, less than two meters downwind.

Holden saw. "Get below!" he yelled. "Quick, before you're so looped you walk overboard!"

She scrambled. Having closed the cabin hatch, she stumbled to the bow port, opened it, and breathed deep. Her head cleared. The dose had been slight.

But she was stuck here till the himatid left. Holden's air intake held a chemical filter. He must take it for granted after these many years. His visitor's need didn't occur to him. Well, now he'd better not sneer at her for being forgetful. *He* didn't have to cram everything into his head in a couple of Genjian days. No, he'd been told to expect her, if not quite this soon, and make things ready. He couldn't be bothered. The wretch.

Huddled in racketing gloom, Byrne waited. It seemed long before his voice reached her, faint and dull through the hatch. Nonetheless, she heard the excitement.

"I'm going off with Japheth. It has...invited me...to witness something, I think. Sit tight. Don't fool with the boat. It'll keep station by itself."

She let fury flare, though she spoke the words under her breath. When she had finished and emerged, she was alone. The berrypicker had filled a woven basket and departed. Byrne settled onto a bench and glowered across the whitecaps. The schooner had drawn nearer.

Time dragged by. The murkiness under the hills grew higher as the enormous tide receded. When the mud flats were exposed, they'd be full of stranded sea life and the Ihrdizu would come down to scavenge. Doubtless they had long since wiped out competing animals. In many respects they resembled humans. Was that why Holden disliked them? He couldn't reasonably blame them for what their ancestors did to his beloved himatids—to the himatids on which he was fixated.

Not that the creatures weren't fascinating. What did they think, feel, dream, create? Had such questions any meaning?

Once Byrne had read about a flurry of enthusiasm on Earth a few centuries ago, for a notion that the cetaceans, the big aquatic mammals, possessed intelligence comparable to the human. Facts soon killed it. Was Holden similarly deluding himself? Most Ihrdizu who thought about the subject at all maintained to this day that the himatids were merely clever animals. True, they made simple tools; but other beasts made nests, burrows, traps, artifacts often intricate, designs cunningly adapted to ambience. Need the himatids be more sentient than, say, *Australopithecus* was? That would explain why Ihrdizu who tried—whether as slavers or otherwise—never managed to communicate beyond the most elementary signals, never got more performance than a skilled trainer could get out of a dog.

Certainly the himatids had nothing like a brain. How much thinking was possible in that diffuse a nervous system?

Some Ihrdizu did believe the carpet whales, the sexually mature stage, attained mystical insights during their long lives at sea. (How long? Unknown.) What was Holden's opinion? Byrne smiled. She could well imagine. On the other hand, could he plausibly claim that the adults kept anything of calf culture, even of calf sapience? Pasturing on equivalents of krill and plankton, too huge for natural enemies except hypothetical disease germs, synapse paths grown fifty or more meters long, wouldn't they placidly lose whatever consciousness they once had? In truth, they showed scant wits when Ihrdizuan hunting ships came upon them. Harpooned, held fast, they were cut to pieces. Occasionally a seine trapped one in shoal water till the tide went out; then the Ihrdizu began eating it while it was alive.

Byrne grimaced. She had seen visuals taken from aloft by early explorers. If Holden hated the cruelty, she agreed, and regretted the infeasibility of putting a stop to it. However, she suspected his resentment was of interference with his research. The more himatids for him to study, the better; and their numbers were shrunken.

Lightning flared among the clouds. A line squall swallowed vision as it swept up from the south bay. Byrne retreated to the cabin. Humans didn't have Ihrdizuan skins. That rain would be downright painful, striking her. Let Holden endure it, since he chose. It roared on the overhead. The boat pitched and rolled. She was immune to seasickness, but dank chill gnawed through her clothes. How had Holden's wife enjoyed living, existing, in this environment, year upon year upon year? The record showed the couple seldom taking a vacation among what amenities moonside offered. Well, maybe he wasn't such a grouch in those days. But he should have seen how Farland was wearing her down. Although no autopsy was done, it was obvious from the laconic statement he entered that her heart gave out. Why hadn't she quit in time? Didn't she notice? Did she choose to stay regardless? What for? She'd already lost her child. Did she love Malchiel that much? In God's name, why?

When the storm had passed and Byrne went back topside, the sky was half clear. Murasaki light blazed and shattered on waves still high. The wind had lessened and warmed, shifting easterly; now the ship yonder must tack across it. Given a thick atmosphere with a steep density gradient, a large bowl among hills often bred its own weather. Byrne was hungry. She assembled a sandwich from her rations while she spent a little charge on a bottle battery to make some coffee. Just a little; Genjian wildernesses taught frugality. The trick was to flash a small amount of water to its boiling point under this pressure, then use that to extract the essence and heat the rest.

No sign of Holden yet. Damn him for a lead-plated boor. She squinted against the brilliance around her. Something in the west, an extra turmoil, a dark movement— Decision. She appropriated a length of line, rigged a safety harness, and climbed the crane. Doing that alone wasn't the best idea in the universe, when the launch reeled through a good fifteen degrees of arc and the acceleration downward was almost as many meters per square second. The hell with it. If Holden caught her, she'd point out that he habitually went partnerless. She had slung his optical around her neck. Raising it to her eyes, she magnified and amplified.

Yes, a whole school of calves, all sizes up to the one about which the others writhed, dived, made spyhopping leaps . . . danced? It was much the biggest. Estimating distance as seven klicks, she deemed its length five meters. That was about as large as they got during their thirty-some Earth years of calfhood, she remembered.

Hold on. Wasn't a black shape bound away from them, toward her? A wake roiled behind its swiftness. That wouldn't ordinarily happen, as smoothly as himatids moved. A metallic gleam. Uh-huh. The great Dr. Holden deigned to return. Byrne clambered back down and waited for him. Her back felt stiff enough to ache between the shoulder blades.

The swimmer, half again the man's length, gripped his belt with six rear arms and towed him. For the most part he was submerged, but his snorkel stuck erect. Thus equipped, he could stay under more deeply than an Ihrdizu. His time must be limited by heat loss, if nothing else, but as he neared she saw that he had changed into a wet suit while she was below. He probably kept it in a locker under a bench, wanting to be prepared for a dive on short notice, and had left his coverall there. Byrne had seen scuba gear in the cabin. With this kind of help, he'd rarely need it. His reports never mentioned such details. They were altogether impersonal. "It was observed that—"

At the hull, the himatid let go. Treading water, Holden raised an arm. "Thanks, Joshua," she heard. So he was capable of gestures toward that species, if not his own. A ripple passed through the broad thinness; a response? Byrne noticed spots of somewhat lighter black scattered along it. By such marks, among other tokens, Holden told his individuals apart. Joshua didn't turn around. Double-ended, it headed straight back toward the commotion among its kind.

Holden came up the Jacob's ladder amidships. Water ran off him into the cockpit. The launch absorbed it in the pores of its fabric and spewed it off. Byrne tried for politeness. "How did your excursion go?"

"It's just begun," he said, no less brusquely than before. "Now, I have to peel this thing off me."

Byrne grinned. "I'm not shy. If you prefer, I'll turn my back."

He acted indifferent. That might well mean he'd rather not display an aging, knobbly frame to a young woman who had no sexual interest in him. Byrne looked outward. Sunlight and cloud shadows swept over the whitecaps. "Would you like me to heat you some soup?" she ventured. It was all the food he could take in that helmet of his.

"No. No time. I'll lose too much as is, letting you off."

Her fingers closed on the coaming. "What?"

"I'll transfer you to yonder ship. I know it, a coastwise packet, it'll take you ashore. I need to speak with the captain anyway."

Almost, Byrne swung around and glared. She curbed herself. "Why? Where are you bound?"

"To sea. A piece of serious work ahead. Can't have an outsider underfoot."

Byrne clenched her jaws before she said, "For your information, I've been on eleven xenological expeditions, four of them to littorals. You know who Elena Sarbiewski is, I trust. She recommended me for this job. In fact, she talked me into it. I will not get in your way. I may well be of help. Do you want me to enter an honest, complete report on your activities and what they're worth, or don't you?"

For the first time, she caught hesitation in his tone. "I didn't fore-see . . . what this situation would prove to be. Things may get . . . a bit dangerous. No, I don't question your courage or competence." Was that reluctance, or was she being unfair? The wet suit smacked on the floor. She heard a locker opened and brisk toweling. "But I am the only man alive who's got any fractional familiarity with what's here. Would you want me along in the jungles of Southland when you knew things were about to go critical?"

"Will you explain to me what you mean?"

"It's . . . complicated. I've learned that this is a special occasion indeed. Call it sacred if you choose. I, well, I'll have trouble enough avoiding, uh, faux pas. You know nothing about their, their mores."

Byrne relaxed very slightly. "A point. I can stay well inboard, though."

"No, no. It's . . . too subtle. That's part of the reason my reports have grown, uh, brief. What I'm beginning to discover—the language of science doesn't reach to that sort of thing."

Byrne nodded. "I can empathize. Among the Ihrdizu, too, we get into areas where all we have is intuition, for whatever little it is worth."

"Yes," he said eagerly. "That's what I meant. You wait ashore. When I get back we can talk at leisure."

She couldn't argue. Somehow she didn't feel he was quite sincere. Hermits got scant practice in lying. However, what could she do? She stared west, marshaling her thoughts.

"I'm ready," Holden said. She joined him at the wheel. Again he was coveralled. He opened the engine up and steered for the ship. Athwart wild silvery clouds his head, inside the helmet, lifted like a brush-bristling crag. Wind skirled, sharp with salt. Waves crashed.

"Can you tell me anything of what this is about?" Byrne asked.

He scowled forward awhile. When he answered, each word was chosen beforehand. "I suppose you've met Christians. But do you know what their faith really is—originally was? Not milksop goodwill and vague self-delusions about some pink-and-white hereafter. It was as stern a religion as Earth ever saw. What it dealt with was death, judgment, and transfiguration." The majestic phrases rolled off his tongue: *"For if the dead rise not, then is not Christ raised: And if Christ be not raised, your faith is vain; ye are yet in your sins."*

A hand chopped air. "Men lived and died by that for centuries before they learned better. Now what if it were true?"

He glanced at her. "I don't say the himatids have anything we'd call a religion. What do we mean by that noise, anyway? But they do know transfiguration, not as something a preacher tells them, not as metaphysical gabble, but a fact. The calf becomes a whale and moves from the tidewater to the deep sea. It is never heard from again, seldom and barely glimpsed. But from it arises the new, blind life, which gains awareness among the calves. What further comes, once the creature swims beyond the horizon? We've read our anthropology, you and I. Can you imagine how it must be not to need myths, because life itself is the myth?"

Her skin tingled. "Rite of passage," she whispered.

He nodded. Once more his voice came hoarse and dry. "Solomon, the oldest of them, is going out. It's not quite so big yet that it can no longer live in the bay, but it soon will be. And today the carpet whales are passing by, bound for the arctic—which the calves know only is a mystery somewhere northward. Solomon will join them. It is dying as a calf, being born as a whale. Because that is happening right after the tads came ashore, Solomon is—especially blessed. I doubt we have any concept that fits.

"They'll let me escort him to the pod."

The wind shrilled.

Byrne's mind leaped. "Your chance to make contact with the whales?"

"You do catch on fast," he granted. "Not that I haven't tried before."

"I know. You'd go out and signal them according to what you'd learned from the calves. They ignored you."

"Correct. My guess is that the personality, the language, changes even more than the body. They . . . put childish things behind. My attempts at communication mean nothing to them. If I could find one or two that used to live in Gunnunggung Bay, individuals who actually knew me—that may not be too many years ago for them to remember and be interested. But I never have. A pod keeps moving, and it's widely dispersed over an enormous area. Long before I get close to more than a few, my fuel runs low and I've got to turn back. Today I'll be with Solomon. I don't know what difference that will make. Maybe none. But at least I'll see something I never did before, and, and Solomon may come . . . say hello to me in my boat, when it returns here."

"Revelations aren't common in science," Byrne said. "I envy you this possibility." She wished she meant that a hundred percent. It wasn't his unpleasant character, she told herself. Well, it shouldn't be. But he was hiding something from her.

The cruiser met the schooner and matched speed, three meters off. Holden shouted. An Ihrdizu who must be the skipper pushed through several crewfolk at the rail and replied. The cries went back and forth. Byrne saw Holden's fingers whiten on the wheel spokes. What news had he received? What reply did he give? She realized that he could form those sounds better than she when he cared to. Between her own unfamiliarity with the dialect and the noise from sea, wind, creaking tackle, she caught no more than fragments.

He turned to her. "All right," he said. "They'll take you. Can you get aboard in a sling?" Grimly, she declined to resent that. "Fetch your pack. I'll transfer it first. Settle yourself in ashore."

Power-operated, the crane lowered her to the other deck. Nonetheless, she needed agility when everything swung and jerked under Genjian weight. She waved at Holden. He sheered off without response. Maybe he hadn't noticed. His propeller left a white tumult aft as he made for the himatids.

The Rockridge sailors were friendly, excitedly curious. In the three hours that followed, Byrne struggled toward communication with them. Those pilots who had talked more easily in the past knew the patois from which this derived. She did not. Near the end, she had acquired sufficient vocabulary that she could ask questions. "What did you tell the male of my kind?" The captain broke in, belching and gobbling words strange to her. Slang? The crew hesitated a moment. Then, oh, yes, they would be delighted to show her around.

She didn't believe they had misunderstood her. But what was the use? Holden had ordered them to keep mum. They probably didn't know why. That the trade goods came through him gave him ample authority. Besides, otherwise humans were essentially an unknown quantity. Discretion was the better part of valor.

The differences from moonside vessels made her tour interesting, though the cargo of salt ichthyoid smelled like a sewage processor in Okuma. Meanwhile, Holden's craft disappeared out the gate.

The ship lay to at the dock. Two sailors brought her ashore in a dinghy. Well, not quite. Twin outriggers stabilized it against waves that traveled faster and struck harder than on Earth. Ihrdizu were ill-suited to rowing; one took the helm, the other walked a treadmill that drove small paddlewheels.

The climb to the heights was long, stiff, wet below and hot above. She reached the house very ready to put her feet up near a cup of coffee with a shot of whiskey in it. Later she'd find her things among the shipment boxes. Bringing them into the living quarters would require several tedious depressurizations in the lock.

To take off her mask and breathe cool, odorless, Earth-type air was like a benediction. She spent a minute savoring it before she rummaged about. While the coffee brewed she investigated further. Snooping? No, she'd be here a while, she needed to scout the territory.

Nothing private came to light. The main room included the kitchenette. Behind it were a lesser chamber with a double bed, a bath cubicle that promised her a shower, and a laboratory equipped for basic biological, chemical, and geological work. She could spread her pad and sleeping bag there. Holden wouldn't likely offer her the bed. She'd decline if he did. His wife had shared it, and a crib must once have stood close by.

Should he make a pass, he'd be sorry. Byrne held a black belt. She felt certain he had no such intention. If nothing else, he'd never willingly reveal that much vulnerability to her.

She reentered the main room. It was as impersonal as a cell. Whatever decoration his wife put in, he had removed. Maybe he didn't care to watch it gather dust and decay, year by year. His desk stood equally devoid of everything nonfunctional. Audiovisuals of people and past scenes must be in his database, along with recreational reading, shows, music, and, to be sure, his references and files. Yielding to an impulse, she keyed the computer. It required a password. She suspected it was programmed to wipe its entire contents in case of any other entry mode.

She lingered at the phone. How about calling HQ? No. They knew she'd arrived safely, and she had no hard information for them. When might she? When Holden gave her some cooperation, damn it. Couldn't he see how he damaged his cause? He was no fool. Could they be right and he actually cracked?

The reason he gave for not taking her along to sea was . . . paranoid. He had no cause to suppose her incapable of discretion, tact—assuming he knew what the words meant! If somehow she did jeopardize his mission, he was the captain, he could order her below and she was legally bound to obey. Instead, he left her on that ship, after getting some news from its crew and laying silence about it on them.

Byrne frowned. The fortified coffee comforted her mouth and cleared weariness from her mind. Let her think.

She'd taken him more or less unawares. That he carried on as planned, on this special day for his himatids, was understandable. But did the invitation to accompany Solomon out catch him quite by surprise? Hardly. Again and again and again, his reports had dwelt on the difficulty of communication. He believed the whole basis of language—not the kind of signals, but their semantics, their structure—was unlike the human, the Ihrdizuan, or, probably, the Chujoan. That was plausible, as alien as the himatids were. In fact, it was grounds for closing down the project. If he couldn't really talk after all this time, if he couldn't even prove the creatures were fully intelligent, then hadn't he gone past the point of diminishing returns?

A sideline question. Byrne hauled her attention back to the main issue. Supposing that Holden was not merely reading into their behavior what he wanted to find and that the himatids did possess minds, then they could *not* suddenly have sprung their proposal on him. He must have angled a long while for something of the kind, they striving to grasp what it was he meant. Probably there was never any breakthrough of comprehension. This simply became the day when the plan was finally agreed on.

What was in it for the calves? Could the original request have been theirs? They might see an opportunity to learn something about those beings whom they only knew were their elders and parents—like Christians given a chance to send a living emissary to the afterworld—

What if he came back and told them the ancient Romans had been right and the departed were feeble-minded shades? What if the carpet whales lost sapience? Another sideline question.

It still didn't make sense that Holden dismissed Byrne. She would in fact have been a genuine, perhaps vital help, as crew, assistant, independent observer. Did he want to hog the entire credit? No, that was crazy; everybody would know how subordinate her role had been, and he could well hope for a glowing encomium from her. Was he crazier yet, unable to see plain logic? In either case, he had no business out there.

Or perhaps—

Byrne snatched a breath. A spurt of coffee flew along. She dropped the cup in her lap, choked, sputtered, dabbled futilely at the mess.

Somehow that became a sign unto her. Nobody is perfectly competent, completely sane. We need to watch over each other. She had the capability; therefore, she had the duty.

Hours had passed. Holden had traveled far. Nevertheless, Byrne went through the drill step by conscious step. The least failure of preparation might kill her, or more than her.

When she went forth, Murasaki burned close to noonday height. Windless heat baked acrid odors from the soil. Leaves on shrubs and low trees hung as if cut from brass. Few clouds remained overhead, but in the west, above the ocean, they raised a darkling rampart where lightning flickered and, faintly across distance, thunder mumbled. Near the thorp, half a dozen Ihrdizu stared her way. She knew by their stance how uneasy they were. Well, she too. She crawled into her aircraft, sealed it, depressurized the cabin, slipped her mask off, strapped in. Her fingers roved the controls. Engines droned. She lifted.

Gain altitude. If nothing untoward was going on, she didn't wish to disturb Holden's subjects, his work. Get invisibly high.

The bay dwindled to a mercury pool between golden and dun contours. Outside it stretched arrays of rock and white chaos, a dangerous passage for a man to dare. Beyond, the planet curved vastly westward, sea gleaming wrinkled, until the storm front raised its wall. Byrne saw it white above, blue-black and flameful below.

Close by—yes! Byrne set the robot to fly slowly in a circle and activated her main viewscreen. Magnified, the scene leaped at her.

A score of carpet whales swam within a reach of several square kilometers. The titanic black forms—the largest easily a hundred meters long, twenty-five broad—flowed on the waves; she saw how each billowed up and back down, in different sectors, as the surges passed beneath. Windblown scud hazed the sight, but she also made out their own long undulations, which drove them ever northward. The pace was as slow, a few knots. It never slackened, though, it went on and on, it would march like the tides or the days and nights or a Bach fugue until the giants were home in their waters around the pole. Abrupt tears stung her eyes. She had seen visuals, but here she met the elemental reality.

And Holden was down there amidst it. She thought that now she might begin to comprehend him.

Holden. Where was he? She reduced magnification, broadening the field. Yonder? She redirected the instrument and magnified afresh. *"No!"* ripped out of her.

Blood made a spreading inkblot across the gray, green, white stampede that was the sea. A whale writhed to and fro at the middle. In her mind she heard wind-hoot, wave-rush, the crash when that body heaved and fell back. Through the cold she tasted salt and blood in spindrift, smelled agony in the air. A ship lay by. Its sails were furled except for a jib and a main reefed to the last point. Masts swayed wildly. They slammed to a halt at one end of their arc, as the harpoon lines binding hull to prey drew taut.

Humans would be mad to make thus fast in such weather. Ihrdizu could swim ashore, come worse to worst. Holden had called the Gash folk bold sailors.

Holden, Holden. She turned the dials in frantic search. A second ship appeared. Its mainmast floated in a tangle of rigging, to batter at planks already chewed. Flames licked over the deck, smoke blew off in rags. The ship listed ever more heavily to starboard. The sea must be pouring in through some hole such as a launched high-explosive grenade would blast.

Holden's cruiser roiled water, bound for the first whaler she had seen. It was tiny in the viewfield, a horrible toy. Stop it, stop it.

Byrne drew breath after breath. She willed steadiness. Slow the pulse, cool the heart, sharpen the eyes, quicken the brain. After a minute she took over control and dived.

No use radioing. He was on deck, the murderous lunatic, at the wheel, at his guns. Put the fear of the Lord into him. Her engines drummed, louder than the nearing thunders. Ocean swelled till she could have counted every maned crest and cavernous trough.

The screen had locked onto the cruiser. Beneath her Holden turned into a human figure. And there came an Ihrdizu. He (?) must have jumped from the doomed ship while Holden lay close and fired on it. Behind him swam two more. Their tentacles held knife, ax, boat hook—weapons. Oh, the brave idiots! The leader intercepted the boat. As it rolled to port, he reached up a forepaw, caught the rail, started to pull himself aboard.

Holden saw. He drew his pistol and shot. The Ihrdizu fell back into the sea. Holden left the others in his wake.

The aircraft raged toward him. He looked aloft. Byrne stabbed touch pads. Sight dimmed when acceleration dragged blood downward. A hundred meters high, the flyer swung back heavenward.

Panting, she leveled off at one klick, circled about, and peered. He was still clear in the screen. His left hand gripped the wheel. He raised his right fist and shook it.

"You son of a bitch!" she screamed uselessly into the transmitter. "Get away! Return! Next time my jets will make a cinder of you!"

He increased power. The launch skimmed over wave tops, tore through their masses, onward. A fountain spouted at either bow.

Vomit rose bitter in Byrne's gullet. She swallowed it but could not altogether quell tears. Her threat was not only unheard, it was empty. Safe herself, she couldn't loose her sole weapon, because it was lethal. She'd go on trial for manslaughter at least. Not that her hands would obey, did she command them to attack. And Holden knew it. Did he laugh aloud, into the oncoming storm?

"All right," she gulped. "For your information, sir, in case you've forgotten, the law makes killing of any sapient, human or nonhuman, the same. It's got to, or we'd soon be hated and overwhelmed. We have no jurisdiction over what aliens do to each other, but we have over our own kind. You've committed murder, Holden."

A faint hope fluttered. She kept her altitude and circled, waiting. Back and forth she swept the viewfield.

The cruiser lanced toward the first ship. Byrne found its deck and magnified. "Thanks, thanks," she gasped. She must, though there be nobody to say it to. That crew was casting loose from the whale. A second jib and the mizzen were going up.

Clouds had boiled eastward across the sky. Rain cataracted from them. Byrne tossed about in blind, lightning-riven gray. Hailstones banged on metal.

When the squall had passed, the main storm hulked very near. Byrne saw the Gasher ship close-hauled, beating north. Holden trailed at a distance. So he didn't intend to sink it. He'd just make sure it went home, bearing its story. His fanaticism recognized some limit. But how many sailors from the foundered vessel would reach land alive?

Byrne focused on the wounded whale. Two of its fellows had swum to its side. She wondered what passed around the herd—those sounds traveled tens of kilometers—and what it meant. Pledge of help? Consolation for the dying? She didn't know whether the creature was mortally hurt or not. Nor did she know whether the clicks and thrums and boomings were aught but animal noises. Silverbucks, fenrises, skyrangers, and more rallied to their distressed kindred. Documentaries from Earth told of apes, wolves, dolphins, and their big cousins. Instinct. Some consciousness, too, yes, but dim, unreasoning.

"I hope you survive," she whispered.

The storm was almost upon her. She must either run from it or rise above it; else it might break her wings and dash her into the sea. A well-found watercraft could better ride it out. Nevertheless, Holden was crazy reckless to keep dogging the ship.

Maybe best would be if he sank. Byrne winced. She brought her aircraft about and fled east.

Land. Make the vehicle secure. Genjian winds were usually slow, but density gave monstrous momentum. Get inside.

While the weather brawled around, she paced, lashed by her

thoughts. What to tell them at Okuma? A police squad couldn't arrive till well after Holden had probably returned here. Of course, she could leave before then.

She wouldn't. She'd come to do a job. Too much was unexplained, unfinished. Holden should keep sense enough not to menace her, unless he had turned into a homicidal maniac. If he had, she expected she could cope.

In any event, the information needn't perish with her. She didn't want to divulge it, not yet. That would take matters out of her hands. The authorities themselves would have little choice. There were depths and subtleties here, and maybe a hermit's stubborn pride to placate. There were issues larger than one man's fate, or one woman's. She needed to explore them.

In the end, she made a satellite relay call to Carlos Villareal. He was out; she got his machine, which was a disappointment. Some talk, private jokes, pet names would have been welcome in this wanly lit, chilly room where walls trembled under the wind. However, she would have concluded regardless by logging an encrypted message, putting him on his honor not to decode for fifty hours and to wipe it if she called back sooner.

Thereafter it was a matter of waiting. She helped herself from the cupboards and cooked a meal. Holden ate adequately but dully. She napped. When the storm had passed, she went out, brought her things from the storerooms, and arranged them in the house. She had another meal. She resumed her mask and strolled to the thorp, where she talked with the natives, bit by bit mastering their dialect.

Either they shied from saying much about Holden or they didn't know much, after these many years. His concern was with the himatids, they said. A himatid could catch tasty ichthyoids, reap useful sea vines, search for glowpearls, if you gave it a knife or something like that; but it was stupid. Making clear to it what you wanted was hard work, and possible only for simple tasks. No wonder the forebears had quit catching and training them. Why *he* cared, well, who knew what goes on in the bellies of you *io-hyumanai*? Yes, he often ranted against the Gashers. Might he want the carpet whales to multiply freely for eventual harvesting by his own kind? No? Well, doubtless you fathom him. We are content to give him help now and then in exchange for rotproof cloth, rustproof steel, such things . . . That was as far as Byrne got before exhaustion overwhelmed her.

She slept. She made breakfast. She prowled. Murasaki stood about twenty degrees above the western ocean when Holden returned.

She glimpsed his cruiser through a port. Externally, her preparations were scarcely more than securing her pistol to her hip before she masked and went out. Most were within herself.

The tide was flowing, the bay rising. It glared steely beneath a cloudless slate-colored sky. Shadows were long in the yellow of the hills, bringing forth their folded and scarred intricacy. Air steamed. As if they sensed something amiss, the Rockridgers had withdrawn from sight. Byrne stood on the path where the hillside bent sharply downward, so he would see her from afar. She kept her hands clear of her weapon. As he trudged upward, she saw he wasn't armed.

He reached her and stopped. The features inside the helmet were hueless, sunken, a mesh of lines and creases; his eyes laired in dark hollows. Shoulders slumped. His coverall hung stiff with salt.

Pity smote. "Come inside," she said gently. "I've got a pot of coffee on. Or there's your whiskey, and I can rustle some food if you like."

He nodded. She stepped aside. A slight, crawling caution told her to let him go first.

They cycled through and removed their headgear. "Sit down," she proposed. He sagged onto a threadbare lounger. She poured the coffee and set it on a table beside him, adding the bottle and a shot glass. He picked up the mug and sipped noisily. She smelled the old sweat on him.

Standing in front, she asked, "Would you rather sleep first?"

"Oh, no." The gray head lifted. A bit of life entered the words. "I let the cruiser take me back while I bunked down. We should settle what's between us right away."

"As you wish. I've entered a report, but under seal unless I don't call in again. Talk as freely as you want. Be warned, though, I'll decide what I pass on to headquarters."

He nodded. "Fair enough. You're honest." Stillness, until: "And maybe you aren't the officious bungler I supposed. To me, headquarters is mostly complaints, demands, and begrudging me my necessities."

"Your isolation has cost you your perspective. We have two planets to think about. Three, if you count Earth."

"Therefore you wonder whether my work is still worth supporting." He sighed. "I would need long to explain why. Quite likely I can't. I'm not a poet."

"What you shall have to show," she told him, "is that your work is important enough to justify murder."

His visage went empty. For a moment he seemed helpless. Resolution welled into him. His voice stayed low, but the tone strengthened. "No, you saw me preventing murder. Doesn't the law permit that?"

Memory whetted her reply. "I saw you'd started a ship to the bottom. I saw you shoot a crewbeing who tried to climb aboard your boat."

"Self-defense. They would have killed me."

"For cause," she clipped. "What about Ihrdizu that didn't live through the storm and the surf, to get ashore?"

"They brought it on themselves. You must have seen. They were out to slaughter sapient creatures."

"Indeed? They surely didn't think so. What proof have you?"

A fist knotted on his thigh. Blue veins bulged among white hairs. "Were you an intelligent being as a child," he grated, "and are you a dumb animal now?"

"The calves are . . . controversial."

"Because of the language problem. Entirely because of it. Civilized humans on Earth, in the age of discovery, they found other humans who were in the Stone Age, but they could soon talk together. Look at the himatid tools. Think how in the water they can't have fire, houses— Think how remarkable it is they make as much as they do. If we could talk with them, there'd be no doubt.

"I can't teach you what little I've learned of their language. You'd need years of the same experience. I myself, I haven't gotten much further than the fact that it *is* a language, and this is something I know more in my guts than my brain, the way I know how to walk.

"Byrne, have you never read the linguists, the school of linguists who trace back to Chomsky? Our ways of perceiving and describing the world are hard-wired into us. We were led astray by the accident that the croakers are wired pretty similarly. Maybe the Chupchups are, too; we don't know yet. But the himatids certainly are not. That's the barrier between them and us."

He was harmless now, save perhaps to himself. Byrne felt the physical alertness unwind in her. A deeper tension took its place. She poured a shot, drew a chair opposite him, and sat down. The whiskey smoked warm across her tongue. Into the haggardness she said: "Maybe. As far as the calves are concerned. Did they want you to go halt the whaling? If so, how did they know about it?"

Startled, he took a moment to answer, slowly, "They may well not have. There was a . . . a feeling that it'd be good if I accompanied Solomon out. More than that I can't say. Give me another ten Earth years, and maybe I can."

Keep him on the defensive. "Your motives for going, then?"

"Why, to see what Solomon did yonder, and the pod did, and take advantage of any opportunity that might come up."

"But you already suspected Gashers were in the vicinity," she flung at him. "You'd have caught word, a rumor, from the Rockridgers. In spite of your threats, you'd never taken action against whalers; they wouldn't expect you to. That's why you got rid of me. You thought you might do so. The ship you unloaded me on, its crew confirmed the rumor."

He stared at his feet. "True. I . . . preferred no witnesses. All I meant to do was escort Solomon, keep it safe till it had joined its fellows, and . . . and possibly start making friends at last. But if I had to fire a shot or two for that, well—"

"You were ready to kill sapients—you did, it turned out—for the benefit of what?"

He looked up, almost bewildered. "Why, other sapients. I told you. The carpet whales."

"Whose intelligence is even less proven than the calves'. If they're smart, why don't they protect themselves against the hunters?"

"I can't say for sure. I can guess. Given their size, they aren't able to go far below the surface. Cross-currents would ripple them out of control, and pressure derange the whole thin body. Also, they can't swim as fast as a ship can sail with a fair wind. And they're naive. They're gentle philosophers who haven't realized the world is full of predators. The calves know it is, but the adults forget. They have no natural enemies any more, and they have their contemplation to do."

"Ha! I thought you despised mysticism."

Holden bridled. "I didn't call them mystics. I said the carpet whales spend their long, peaceful lives thinking. Compared to their oldest and wisest, those Chupchups that everybody slavers over nowadays are morons or— Aargh!" His mouth contorted.

"So you believe," Byrne said. "Can you prove it?"

The response was bleak as his dwelling. "Of course not. Can you prove to me that you have consciousness? It's the hypothesis that best fits the facts. Give me a chance to learn more."

"What about the hypothesis that the whales gradually lose whatever intelligence they may have had as calves?" There passed through the back of Byrne's mind: An interesting moral question. How human is a brain-decayed *Homo sapiens*? What rights has he? Why shouldn't an alert animal have the same?

The unkempt head shook. "Doesn't make sense. The whales beget the young. How could the species stay sapient if there weren't selection for sapience among the breeders? Nature puts no more pressure on them, as big as they are. The selection must be internal to the species, sexual, whatever. The poets, musicians, storytellers, philosophers get the mates. Look, *Australopithecus* or *Homo erectus* on Earth were already pretty successful. They had no serious natural enemies left. What do you suppose pushed their brains onward?"

She had seen the argument among his reports. She had never before heard it uttered. The force of it rang.

Yet— "You took the law into your own hands, on the basis of your pet theory," Byrne said. "Whaling has gone on for centuries. You hated it, but this was the first time you actually did anything about it. Why?" She raised a hand as lips parted in the beard. "Yes, you were escorting Solomon. The Gashers wouldn't have come near you, would they? They must have known how you felt and what weapons you commanded. There was no threat to Solomon."

"There was," Holden declared. "My fuel was limited. I'd soon have to turn back, unless one or more of the whales stopped to . . . have an exchange with me. That would not happen if the rest were being pursued."

"Which they often were, when their migration took them by." Byrne leaned forward. "The only difference this time was that you companioned a single calf, something you might very well do again in the future when conditions were more favorable. How, then—since you have not proved the carpet whales, or even the calves, are sapient,"—*have souls?* gibed a childhood half-memory—"how do you justify attacking those poor sailors?"

He rose. His shadow fell huge between her and the light. The gray mane was a cloud around a half-seen face. "Joseph," he said.

She must needs also rise. They stood confronted. "Joseph?"

"What I called it in its calfhood. A distinctive marking on the back identifies it. Solomon led me straight there. Scent? Suddenly, here were two of them I knew. And Joseph remembered. It curled its front end over my deck and made the old music we'd worked out together. I had my opening, my foothold I'd always hoped for. But yonder came the Gasher ships and commenced their butchery.

"I had to stop it. Fuel wouldn't let me follow the second ship far, but the crew wouldn't know that. I lay out till the pod must be well past their fjord. With luck, the hunters will accept that this stretch of coast is interdicted to them; and Solomon and Joseph and I can meet again. Otherwise I'll do whatever is necessary, as often as necessary, till the sanctuary is established. If your damned smug politicians and bureaucrats will allow."

Byrne's throat tightened until she could barely get out, "That, for the sake of research?"

"For the sake of humanity," he growled.

She blinked. "What?"

A rusty clang of defiance: "Or philosophy, or the next stage of civilization, or whatever you choose to call it. Grandiose? Well, ask yourself what kind of megalomaniac it would take to seriously claim our species is in no need of improvement. But for that we'll have to understand ourselves, and we never will till we can get outside ourselves.

"What are we, besides animals? Our language. Symbols, arts, sciences, hopes, fears, everything that makes us human is in language. And it isn't a set of arbitrary conventions. The basis of it is biological.

"Gödel's theorem. Nothing can completely describe or account for itself. We can't reason about the basis of language except in a metalanguage. For that, we've first got to compare at least one other language totally different from ours, different right down in the genes, and see what our own built-in premises are. Between us and the himatids—"

Holden's fist struck the table. The sound went small through stillness. "Oh, hell," he said. She heard how he could no longer fight off the weariness. "Let my advocate make the fine speeches in court." Seeking her eyes: "But could we spend a while together before then, you and me, while I try to show you what I mean? Maybe you'll put in a good word afterward. Maybe they'll let me continue here. Or else somebody new."

For a space she heard only, remotely, the wind and the sea. At last he muttered, "You look puzzled. Well, I guess I didn't make myself clear."

Byrne shook herself. The chill that had gathered while he talked still stirred beneath her skin. It wasn't from fear or shock or even pity. She had felt it before, a few times, when a bugle blew at sunset in memoriam, when understanding of the cosmological equation opened up to her, when— "No, I think I followed you," she breathed. "And yes, I think I will argue for . . . for leniency. You did wrong today, but your cause is . . . tremendous."

The dulled voice and drained countenance became earnest. "Do you really see, already?" he asked. "You agree I couldn't abandon it?"

The deaths came back to crowd the future out of her. "*We* can't," she corrected him. "We humans, that is. You were too impatient. We've got generations ahead of us to pursue this."

"You won't, unless I nail your attention fast to it," he replied. "And I will, whatever the cost."

She wondered how sane he in truth was. She wondered what sanity was.

He went to the computer on the desk. A big, knuckly hand worked its keyboard. Byrne saw just his back, like a stooping darkness. He accessed a visual. The woman had been plain, middle-aged, but she kept a young smile.

"This was her idea," Holden said. "What she lived for."

He switched off, turned around, and spoke curtly of practical matters.

WORLD VAST, WORLD VARIOUS

BY GREGORY BENFORD

1
THE CUSP MOMENT

The vortex wind roiled stronger, howled across the jagged peaks to the south, and provoked strange wails as it rushed toward the small band of humans.

The sounds seemed to Miyuki like a chorus of shrill, dry voices. Three hundred kilometers to the south these winds were born, churned up by the tidal surges of the brother planet overhead. Across vacant plains they came singing, over rock sculpted into sleek submission by the raw winds. Gusts tore at the twenty-three Japanese in their air masks and thick jackets. A dusty swirl bedeviled them with its grit, then raced on.

"They're coming," Tatsuhiko said tensely.

Miyuki squinted into the cutting cold. She could barely see dots wavering amid the billows of dust. In her rising excitement she checked again her autocam, belt holdings, even her air hoses. Nothing must go wrong, nothing should steal one moment from this fresh contact between races. The events of the next hour would be studied by future generations, hallowed and portentous. As a geophysicist, her own role was minor. Their drills had taught her to keep Tatsuhiko and the other culture specialists in good view of her autocam, without being herself conspicuous. Or so they hoped. What if beings born of this austere place found smell, not sight, conspicuous?

"They're spreading out," Tatsuhiko said, standing stick-straight. "A sign of hostility? Maneuver?"

Opinions flowed over their suit comm. Tatsuhiko brushed aside most of them. Though she could not see his face well, she knew well the lean contours of concern that would crease his otherwise smooth, yellowish complexion. Miyuki kept silent, as did all those not versed in the consummate guesswork that its practitioners called Exo-Analysis.

The contact team decided that the Chujoans might have separated in their perpetual quest for small game. This theory seemed to gain confirmation as out of the billowing dust came a peri and two burrowbunnys, scampering before the advancing line. The nomads doggedly pursued, driving game before them, snaring some they took by surprise.

I hope they don't mind an interrupted hunt, Miyuki thought. They seemed stolid, as if resigned to the unrelenting hardship of this cruelly thin world. Then she caught herself: *Don't assume.* That was the first rule here.

She had seen the videos, the scans from orbit, the analytical studies of their movements—and still the aliens startled her.

Their humanoid features struck her first: thin-shanked legs; calves muscled and quick; deep chests broad with fat; arms that tapered to four-fingered hands. But the rest . . .

Scalloped ears perched nearly atop the large, oval head. Eyes were consumed by their pupils. A slitted mouth like a shark's, the rictus grin of an uncaring carnivore. Yet she knew they were omnivores—had to be, to survive in this bleak biosphere. The hands looked *wrong*—blue fingernails, ribbed calluses, and the first and last fingers both were double-jointed thumbs.

These features she took in as the aliens strode forward in their odd, graceful way. Three hundred and twenty-seven of them, one of the largest bands yet seen. The wind brought their talk to her from half a kilometer away. Trills, twitterings, lacings of growls. Were they warning each other?

"Showing signs of regrouping," Tatsuhiko called edgily.

As leader of the contact team, he had to anticipate trouble of any sort. The aliens were turning to bring the vector of their march directly into the center of the humans. Miyuki edged into a low gully, following the team's directives. Swiftly the Japanese formed a triangular pattern, Tatsuhiko at the point. To him went the honor of the cusp moment.

The pale morning light outlined the rumpled peaks to the west, turning the lacy brushwork of high fretted clouds into a rosy curtain, and their light cast shadows into the faces of the approaching aliens.

Miyuki was visible only to a few of the tall, swaying shapes as they made their wary way. She thought at first that they were being cautious, perhaps were fearful, but then she remembered the videos of similar bands. They perpetually strode with an open gait, ready to bound after game if it should appear, eyes roving in a slow search pattern. These were no different.

With gravity fifteen percent less than Earth's, these creatures had a graceful, liquid stride on their two curiously hooflike feet. They held lances and clubs and slingshots casually, seemingly certain that whatever these waiting strangers might be, weaponry could keep them at bay. They were only a few hundred meters away now, and she felt her breathing tighten.

Chujo's thin, chilly air plucked at her. She wondered if it affected her eyes, because now she could see the aliens' clothing—and it was moving.

They wore a kind of living skin that adjusted to each change in the cant of their arms, each step. The moving brown stuff tucked closely at neck and armpits and groin, where heat loss would be great, yet left free the long arms and muscled thighs. Could such primitives master biotech capable of this? Or had they domesticated some carpetlike animal?

No time left for speculations. Her comm murmured with apprehension as the nearest alien stolidly advanced to within a hundred meters.

"Remember Kammer," one of the crew observed laconically.

"Remember your duty!" Tatsuhiko countered sharply.

Miyuki's vision sharpened to an unnatural edge. She had a rising intuition of something strange, something none of them had—

"Tatsuhiko," she called. "Do not step in front of them."

"What?" Tatsuhiko answered sharply as the leading alien bore down upon him. "Who said that? I—"

And the moment had arrived.

Tatsuhiko stood frozen.

The face of the truly alien. Crusty-skinned. Hairless. Scaly slabs of flesh showing age and wear. The alien turned its head as it made its long, loping way by Tatsuhiko. Its skin was fretted, suggesting feathers, with veins beneath the rough hide making a lacework of pink, as in the feet of some earthly birds. And the eyes—swollen pupils giving the impression of intense concentration, swiveling across the landscape in smooth unconcern.

The alien rotated its torso—a flickering of interest?—as it passed. Tatsuhiko raised a bare hand in a sign they had all agreed had the best chance of being read as a nonhostile greeting, Tatsuhiko smiled, careful to not reveal white teeth, in case that implied eating or anger among beings who shared a rich lore of lipped mouths.

To this simple but elaborately rehearsed greeting the alien gave Tatsuhiko a second's further gaze—and then strode on, head turning to scan the ground beyond.

And so they all came on. No sounds, no trace of the talk the Japanese had recorded from directional mikes. The second alien drew abreast Captain Koremasa Tamura, the expedition leader. This one did not register Koremasa with even the slightest hesitation in the regular, smooth pivot of its head.

So came the next. And the next.

The Chujoans pressed forward, nomads in search of their next meal.

Miyuki remembered the videos taken from orbit of just this remorseless sweeping hunt. Only the first of them had permitted its gaze to hesitate for even a moment.

"I . . . I do not . . ." Tatsuhiko whispered over comm.

The aliens swept by the humans, their eyes neither avoiding recognition nor acknowledging it.

"Do not move," Koremasa ordered.

Even so, one woman named Akiko was standing nearly directly in front of an approaching Chujoan—and she lifted a palm in a gesture that might have meant greeting but Miyuki saw as simple confusion. It brushed the passing alien. Akiko clutched suddenly at the Chujoan hand, seeking plaintively. The creature gave no notice, allowing its momentum to carry it forward, freeing its hand.

Koremasa sharply reprimanded Akiko, but Miyuki took little notice of that, or of the buzzing talk on her comm. She hugged herself against the growing chill, turned away from the cutting winds, and watched the aliens continue on, unhurried. Hundreds of evenly spaced, oblivious hunters. Some carried heavy packs while others—thin, wiry, carrying both slings and lances—had little. But they all ignored the humans.

"Anyone registering eye contact?" Tatsuhiko asked tersely.

The replies trickled in reluctantly. No. No one.

"How do they *know*?" Tatsuhiko asked savagely. "The first, it looked at me. Then the rest, they just—just—"

Faintly someone said, "They won't even piss on us."

Another whisper answered, "Yes, the ultimate insult."

Chuckles echoed, weak and indecisive against the strong, unending alien wind.

The humans stood in place, automatically awaiting orders, as endless drill had fashioned them to do. Dust devils played among them. A crusty-skinned thing the first expedition had unaccountably named a snakehound on the basis of a few glimpses on their video records—though it showed no signs of liking the fat worms that resembled Earthly snakes—came bounding by, eluding the hunters. Likewise, it took no apparent notice of the humans frozen in their carefully planned deployment of greeting, of contact, of the cusp moment.

In their calm exit Miyuki saw her error, the mistake of the entire crew. These Chujoans had two hands, two feet, binocular eyes—primatelike, city-builders, weapon-users. Too close to human, far too close.

For they were still alien. Not some pseudo-Navajos. Not more shambling near-apes who had meandered out of the forest, patching and adding to their cerebral architecture, climbing up the staircase of evolution toward a self-proclaimed, seemingly ordained success.

These beings shared no genes, nor assumptions, nor desires, with the seemingly similar humans. Their easy sway, their craftily designed slingshots and arrows—all came from unseen anvils of necessity that humans might not share at all.

She leaned back, smothering an impulse to laugh. The release of tension brought a mad hilarity to her thoughts, but she immediately suppressed the urge to shout, to gesture, to stamp her boots into the dusty certainties of this bleak plain. After all, Tatsuhiko had not given the order to disperse the pattern— he was stiff with shock.

Perhaps this sky gave a clue. How different from Earth! Genji loomed, a great mottled ball fixed at the top of the sky.

How well she knew the stories of the *Genji Monogatari,* by the great Murasaki. Yet the imposition of a millennium-old tale on these hard, huge places was perhaps another sign of their underlying arrogance.

The whirl of worlds, she thought. Spheres stuck at the ends of an invisible shaft, balls twin-spinning about each other. Tidal stresses forced them to eternal mutual regard, rapt, like estranged lovers unable to entertain the warmer affections of the swollen, brooding sun that even now sought to come onstage, brimming above the horizon, casting slanting exaggerated shadows. The aliens headed into this ruddy dawnlight, leaving the humans without a backward glance.

2
ARRESTED ATHENS

They took refuge in the abandoned cities. Not for physical shelter, for that was provided by the transparent, millimeter-thin, yet rugged bubbles they inflated among the ruins. They came here to gain some psychological consolation, for reasons no one could quite express.

Miyuki sat in one of the largest bubbles, sipping on aromatic Indian tea and cracking seeds between her teeth. So far these small, tough, oddly sweet kernels were the only bounty of this dry planet. Miyuki had been the first to master them, cracking them precisely and then separating the meat from the pungent shell with her tongue. Gathering them from the low, gnarled trees was simple. They hung in opulent, unpicked bunches; apparently the Chujoans did not like them. Still, it would be interesting to see if anyone without other food could eat the seeds quickly enough to avoid starvation.

The subject never came up, she realized, because no one liked to jest about real possibilities. The entire expedition was still living off the growing tanks on the mother ship. Every kilogram of protein and carbohydrate had to be brought down with many more kilos of liquid hydrogen fuel. That in turn had to be separated from water on Genji, where their main base sprawled beside a rough sea.

Such weighty practicalities suppressed humor. Not that this crew was necessarily a madcap bunch, of course. Miyuki spat her cheekful of shells into her hand, tossed them into the trash, and started listening to Tatsuhiko again. He had never been a mirthful man, and had not responded well to her suggestion that perhaps the Chujoans had played a sort of joke.

"—so I remain astonished by even the suggestion that their behavior was rooted in anything so obvious," Tatsuhiko concluded.

"As obvious as a joke?" Captain Koremasa asked blandly. He sat while the others stood, a remnant of shipboard discipline. The posture was probably unnecessary, for the captain was already the tallest and most physically commanding figure in the expedition. Standard primate hierarchy rules, Miyuki thought distantly. Koremasa had a broad forehead and strong features, a look of never being surprised. All quite useful in instilling confidence.

"A joke requires context," Tatsuhiko said, his mouth contracting into tight reserve. He was lean and angular, muscles bunching along his long jawline. She knew the energies that lurked there. She had had a brief, passionate affair with him and could still remember his flurries of anxious attention.

Partly out of mischief, she said, "They may have had enough 'context' for their purposes."

Tatsuhiko's severe mouth turned down in scorn. "That band knew nothing of prior contact—that was why we selected them!"

"How do you know?" Miyuki asked mildly.

Tatsuhiko crossed his arms, energies bundled in. "First contact was with a band over three thousand kilometers from here. We tracked them."

Miyuki said, "Stories fly fast."

"Across a mountain range?"

"In months, yes."

"These are primitives, remember. No signs of writing, of metallurgy, of plowing. Thus, almost certainly no information technology. No semaphore stations, no roads, not even smoke signals."

"Gossip is speedy," Miyuki said. The incredible, irrational, and cowardly withdrawal of the first expedition had left Chujo for the Japanese, a slate virtually unblemished. But in the time since, the Chujoans might have turned that first contact into legend.

"We must go by what we know, not what we invent." Tatsuhiko kept his tone civil, but the words did his work for him.

"And I am a geophysicist and you are the culture specialist." Miyuki looked at him squarely, an unusual act among a crew trained for decades to suppress dissension.

"I believe no one should proceed to theory without more experience," Koremasa said evenly. His calm eyes seemed to look through them and out, into the reaches beyond. She caught a sense of what it was like to have more responsibility than others, but to be just as puzzled. Koremasa's years of quiet, stolid leadership on the starship had not prepared him well for ambiguity.

Still, his sign of remote displeasure made both Miyuki and Tatsuhiko hesitate, their faces going blank. After a moment Tatsuhiko nodded abruptly and said, "Very much so."

They automatically shifted to routine matters to defuse any tensions. Familiar worries about food, air, illness, and fatigue surfaced, found at least partial solutions. Miyuki played her part as supplies officer, but she let her mind wander as Tatsuhiko and Koremasa got into a long discussion of problems with their pressure masks.

They had retreated into studying artifacts; after all, that is what archaeologists were trained to do, and artifacts could not ignore you. Two women had trailed the Chujoans for several kilometers, and found what appeared to be a discarded or forgotten garment, a frayed legging. The biologists and Exo-Analysis people had fallen upon it with glad cries.

Quite quickly they showed that the snug-rug, as some called it, was in fact a sophisticated life-form that seemed bioengineered to parasitic perfection, for the sole purpose of helping the Chujoans fend off the elements. It lived on excrement and sweat—"biological exudates," the specialists' jargon said. The mat was in fact a sort of biological corduroy, mutually dependent species like small grasses, moss, and algal filaments. They gave back to their host warmth and even a slow, steady massage. They even cleaned the skin they rode—"dermal scavenging," the specialists termed it. Useful traits—and better than any Earthly gadget.

The specialists in Low Genji Orbit had labored to duplicate the snug-rug in their laboratories. The expedition depended on powerful biotech resources, for everything from meals to machine repair. But the snug-rug proved a puzzle. The specialists were, of course, quite sure they could crack the secret . . . but it would require a bit of time. They seemed equally divided on the issue of whether the snug-rug was a remnant from an earlier biotech civilization, or another example of evolution's incredible diplomacy among species.

Appetites whetted by one artifact, the team turned to the province of archaeology. The abandoned cities that dotted Chujo were mostly rubble, but some like this—Miyuki glanced out through the transparent bubble wall—still soared, their creamy massive walls blurred by winds until they resembled partly melted ice-cream sculptures. Little metal had gone into them, apparently not needed because of the milder gravity. Perhaps that was why later ages had not plundered these canyonlike streets for all the threads of decorative tin and copper.

Sand, frost, storm, invading desert brush—all had conspired to rub away most of the stone sheaths on the grander buildings, so little art remained. Koremasa and Tatsuhiko went on discussing matters, but Miyuki had heard the same debates before; one of the mild irritations of the expedition was that Koremasa still sought consensus, as though they were still packed into a starship, mindful of every frown. No, here they needed daring, leadership, dash and verve.

At the right moment she conspicuously bowed, exaggerating her leave-taking just enough for a slight ironic effect, and slipped through the pressure lock.

She slipped her pressure mask on, checked seals, tasted the slightly oily compressed air. This was the one huge freedom they had missed so much on the long voyage out: to slam the door on exasperation. There had been many elaborate ways to defuse stresses, such as playing smashball; the object was to keep the ball aloft as long as possible, not to better your opponent. Long rallies, cooperation, learning to compensate for inability or momentary fault, deploring extravagant impulse and grandstanding—all good principles, when you are going lonely to the stars. They had similarly lasted through their predicted season of sexual cookbook athletics. The entire team was like an old married couple by now—wise and weathered.

The chilly bite of even noonday never failed to take her by surprise. She set off quickly, still enjoying the spring that low gravity gave to her step, and within minutes was deep among the maze of purple-gray colonnades. Orbital radar had deepscanned the sandy wastes and found this buried city. Diggers and wind machines had revealed elegant, airy buildings preserved far better than the weathered hovels found on the exposed surface. Had the city been deliberately buried? The street-filling sands had been conspicuously uniform and free of pebbles, not the residue of eons of runoff from nearby hills. Buried for what?

The moody, shadowed paths gave abruptly into hexagonal spaces of pink flagstones. Above, high-pitched roofs and soaring towers poked into a thin blue sky that sported small, quickly scudding clouds like strands of wool. To her eye the styles here, when they struck any human resonance at all, were deliberate blends, elements of artful slope and balanced mass that made the city seem like an anthology of ages. Could this be the last great gathering place of the ancient natives, erected to pay tribute to their passing greatness? Did they know that the ebbing currents of moisture and dusty ice storms were behind the ceaseless slow drying that was trimming their numbers, narrowing the pyramid of life upon which all large omnivores stood? They must have, she concluded.

In this brooding place of arched stone and airy recesses there came to her a silky sense of melancholy, of stately recessional. They had built this elaborately carved and fretted stonework on the edge of what must have then been a large lake. Now the diminished waters were briny, hemmed in by marshes prickly with bamboolike grasses. Satellites had found larger ruined cities among the slopes of the many mountain ranges, ones displaying large public areas, perhaps stadiums and theaters—but humans could not bear those altitudes without bulky pressure suits. She coughed, and remembered to turn up the burbling humidifier in her air feed. There was enough oxygen here, five hundred meters above what passed for sea level on a world where the largest sea was smaller than many of Earth's lakes. But the air stole moisture from sinuses and throat, making her skin prickly and raw.

Miyuki peered up, past the steepled roofs and their caved-in promise, at the perpetual presence of Genji. Geometry told her that at noon the brother world should be dark, but the face of milky swirls and clumpy browns glowed, reflecting Chujo's own radiance. Even the mottlings in the shadowed and strangely sinister face of Chujo's brother seemed to have a shifting, elusive character as she watched. Genji loomed twelve times larger than the moon she had known as a child in Kyoto, and at night it gave hundreds of times as much light, enough to read by, enough to pick out colors in the plains of Chujo. Now high cirrus of glittery powdered ice momentarily veiled it in the purpling sky, but that somber face would never budge from its hovering point at the top of the sky. A moist, warm, murky sphere. How had that richness overhead affected the Chujoans, through the long millennia when they felt the thieving dryness creeping into their forests, their fields, their lives?

She turned down a rutted path beside a crumbled wall, picking her way, and before her a shadowy form moved. She froze. They all wore the smell-dispersers that supposedly drove off even large predators, but this shape—

"We should not be alone here," Tatsuhiko said, his eyes hooded behind his pressure mask.

"You frightened me!"

"Perhaps a little fear would be wise."

"Fear is disabling," she said disdainfully.

"Fear kindles caution. This world is too Earthlike—it lulls us."

"*Lulls?* I have to fight for oxygen when I trot, we *all* scratch from the aridity, the cold seeps in, I—"

"It deceives us, still."

"You were the one maintaining that the natives couldn't possibly be joking with us, or—"

"I apologize for my seeming opposition." Tatsuhiko bowed from the waist.

She started to reply, but his gesture reminded her suddenly of moments long ago—times when the reserve between them had broken in a sudden flood, when everything important had not seemed to require words at all, when hands and mouths and the simple slide of skin on welcoming skin had seemed to convey more meaning than all the categories and grammars of their alert, managerial minds. Times long gone.

She wondered whether Koremasa had delicately implied that Tatsuhiko should follow her, mend fences. Perhaps—but this perpetual wondering whether people truly spoke their minds, or merely what solidarity of effort required—it provoked her! Still . . . she took the space of a heartbeat to let the spurt of irritation evaporate into the chilly air.

She sighed and allowed herself only a sardonic "You merely *seemed* to differ?"

"I merely expressed the point of view of my profession." Tatsuhiko gave her a direct, professional smile.

Despite herself, Miyuki grinned. "You were an enthusiastic advocate of sociobiology, weren't you?"

"Still am." His heavy-lidded eyes studied her. The age-old male gaze, straying casually away for a quite unconscious study of what the contours of her work suit implied, a subtle tang of the matters between men and women that would never be settled . . . not that anyone wished them to be.

She nodded briskly, suddenly wanting to keep their discussion businesslike. "I suppose we are all at the forefront of our fields, simply by being here. Even though we haven't kept up with Earthside literature."

Communicating with Earth had proved to be even more difficult than they had imagined. In flight the hot plasma exhaust tail had blurred and refracted transmissions. Further, the Doppler shift had reduced the bit rate from Earth by half. Few dry academic journals had made it through.

Tatsuhiko's blunt jaw shifted slightly sidewise, which she knew promised a slightly patronizing remark. He said, "Of course, you are on firmer ground."

"Oh? How?"

"Planetary geology cannot falsify so easily, I take it."

"I don't understand." *Or are we both sending mixed signals?* Then, to shake him a little, she asked liltingly, "Would you like a drink?"

"I wished to walk the city a bit, as you were."

"Oh, this is in the city. We don't have to return to camp. Come."

She deliberately took him through galleries of stone that seemed feather-light, suspended from thick walls by small wedges of pale rock; the sight was still unsettling, to one born to greater gravity. She padded quickly along precarious walkways teetering above brackish ponds, and then, with no time for eyes to adjust, through murky tunnels. A grove of spindly trees surrounded a round building of burnt-orange rock, breezes stirring from them a sound like fat sizzling on a stove. She stopped among them, looking for damp but firm sand. Without saying a word in answer to his puzzled expression, she dug with her hands a hole a palm wide and elbow-deep.

"Wet gravel," she said, displaying a handful. He looked puzzled. Did he know that this made him boyish and vulnerable? She would not put that past him; he was an instinctive analyzer. Once he had tried with her all the positions made possible by the short period when the starship had glided under low deceleration—penetrating her in mechanical poses of cartoonish angles, making her laugh and then, in short order, come hard and swiftly against him. Where was that playful man now?

On alien ground, she knew. Preoccupied by the central moment of his life. And she could not reach out to touch him here, any more than she had the last few years on board.

The stand of pale-yellow reeds she had noticed the day before nearly blocked the building's ample arched doorway. She broke off two, one fat and the other thin. Using the smaller as a ramrod, she punched the pith from the larger. Except for some sticking at the joints it worked, and she thanked her memory of this trick.

"A siphon," she said, plunging the larger reed into the sand hole and formally offering it to Tatsuhiko. A bit uncertainly Tatsuhiko sucked on this natural straw, his frown turning to surprised pleasure.

"It works. Ground water—not salty."

"I tire of the processed taste in our water. I learned this on one of our desert classes." Pre-expedition training had been a blizzard of facts, techniques, gadgets, lore—all predicated on the earliest data from the probes, most of it therefore only marginally relevant; planets proved to be even more complex systems than they had suspected.

He watched her carefully draw the cool, smelly, oddly pleasant water up and drink long and steadily. The very air here robbed the skin of moisture, and their dry throats were feasting grounds for the head colds that circulated among the crew.

"This unfiltered water should be harmless, I suppose," he said hesitantly, his face turning wary too late.

She laughed. "You've already got a bellyful of any microbe that can feast off us."

"I thought there weren't any such."

"So it seems."

Indeed, this was the most convincing proof that panspermia, the seeding of the galaxy by spores from a single planet, had never happened. Chujo and Genji shared a basic reproducing chain, helical like DNA but differing in elemental details. Somehow the two worlds had shared biological information.

The most likely explanation lay in debris thrown out by meteorite bombardment through geological time scales, which then peppered the other planet. She saw his familiar self-involved expression and added, "But, of course, we've only covered a tiny fraction of Chujo yet."

His look of dismay made her suppress another laugh. Specialization was so intense among them! Tatsuhiko did not realize that biospheres were thoroughly mixed, and that the deep, underlying incompatibility of Chujoan microbes with Earthly biochemistry was a planetwide feature. "I'm just fooling, Tatsuhiko-san," she said, putting stress on the more friendly form of address.

"Ah." Abrupt nod of head, tight jaw, a few seconds to recover his sense of dignity. There had been a time when he reacted with amusement to her jibes. Or rolled her over and pinned her and made her confess to some imaginary slight, laughing.

They walked on, unspoken elements keeping them at a polite distance. She fetched forth a knife and cut a few notches in the soft length of the reed. As they walked she slipped the tip of the reed under her mask and blew through this crude recorder, making notes oddly reminiscent of the stern, plaintive call of the ancient Japanese country flute, the *shakuhachi.* She had played on such hastily made instruments while a young girl, and these bleak, thin-textured sounds took her back to a life that now seemed inconceivably, achingly remote—and was, of course. Probably few of them would ever walk the soil of the Home Islands again. Perhaps none.

They wandered among the tumbled-down lofts and deeply cut alcoves, Miyuki's music echoing from ruined walls. Here they passed through "streets" that were in fact pathways divided by thin partitions of gray-green stone, smoothed by wind and yet still showing the serpentine elaboration of colors—maroon, rose, aqua—inlaid by hands over ten thousand years ago. The dating was very imprecise, of course. Weaker planetary magnetic shielding, a different sun, an unknown climate history—all made the standard tables of carbon dating irrelevant.

Tatsuhiko raised his hand, and they stopped before a worn granite wall. Deeply carved into it was one of the few artworks remaining in the city, perhaps because it could not be carried away. She estimated it was at least a full Chujoan's height on each of its square sides.

She followed the immense curves of the dune tiger. Only twice had any human glimpsed this beast in the flesh. The single photograph they had showed a muscular, canvas-colored, four-legged killing machine. Its head was squat, eyes enormous, mouth an efficient V design. Yet the beast had a long, sensuous tail thickly covered with gray-green scales. Intricate, barbed, its delicate scales almost seemed like feathers.

The ancient artist had taken this striking feature and stretched it to provide the frame and the substance of his work. The dune tiger's tail flowed out of the beast—which glowered at the viewer, showing teeth—into a wraparound wreath that grew gnarled branches, sprouted ample flowers, and then twisted about itself to form the unmistakable profile of an alert Chujoan native.

The strange face also looked at the viewer, eyes even larger than the reality Miyuki had seen, mouth agape, head cocked at an angle. Miyuki would never know if this was a comic effect, but it certainly *looked* that way. And the sinuous tail, having made this head, wriggled around the design—to be eaten by the tiger itself.

"Writhing at the pain of biting itself?" she whispered.

"That could be. But wouldn't the whole tiger struggle, not just the tail?"

"Unless the tiger has just this instant bitten itself."

"Ummm, I hadn't thought of that. A snapshot, an instant frozen in time."

She fingered her reed. "But then why does its tail make that face?"

"Why indeed? I feel so *empty* before this work. We can bring so little to it!" He gestured angrily.

"The archaeologists, they must have some idea."

"Oh, they suppose much. But they know little."

She followed the tiger's tail with her eyes, looking fruitlessly for some clue. "This city had so many things ours do."

"But were they used the same way? The digging team hasn't found a single grave. Most of what we know about ancient Earth comes from burial of the dead."

She touched the stone, found its cool strength oddly reassuring. "This has outlasted the pyramids."

"Maybe it was cut very deep?"

"No . . . How long it has been buried we cannot tell. And Chujo's lighter gravity should lead to less erosion, generally. But I would have expected the winds to rub this out."

Tatsuhiko shrugged. "Our dating could be wrong, of course."

"Not this far wrong." Miyuki frowned. "I wonder if this place was more like an arrested Athens."

He looked at her speculatively. "A city-state? Difficult to tell, from a ruin."

"But the Chujoans still camp here—you found their old embers yourself."

"Until we scared them away, I suppose."

Miyuki studied the great wall. "You suspect they linger here, to view the ruins of what they were?"

"They may not be even the same species that built all this." Tatsuhiko looked around, as if trying to imagine the streets populated, to envision what forms would have ambled here.

She gestured at small circles that appeared above the carving. "What are these?"

Tatsuhiko frowned. "Symbols?"

"No, they look like a depiction of real objects. See, here's one that's a teardrop."

He stooped to examine the wall. "Yes, the lowest of them is. And higher up, see, another teardrop, only not so pronounced."

Miyuki tried to fathom some sense to the round gouges. If the piece had perspective, the circles could be of any true size. "Teardrop at the bottom . . . and as they rise, they round out?"

Tatsuhiko shrugged. "Rain droplets form round in the air, I believe, then make teardrops as they fall."

"Something the tiger gives off?"

"How?"

His questions were insightful, but there was something more here, she was sure of it. Her mother had once told her that art could touch secret places. She had described it in terms of simple events of childhood. When the summer rain had passed and the air was cool, when your affairs were few and your mind was at ease, you listened to the lingering notes of some neighbor's flute chasing after the clear clouds and the receding rain, and every note seemed to drop and sink into your soul. That was how it was now, this moment, without explanations.

Miyuki let the moment pass. Tatsuhiko gave up in exasperation. "Come—let's walk."

She wanted to move through the city as though she had once been a citizen of it, to catch some fleeting fragrance of lives once lived.

They walked on. She blew into her crude recorder again.

To her the atonal, clear, crude tones seemed to mirror the strangely solid feel of this place, not merely the veiled city of opaque purpose but as well the wind-carved desert wastes surrounding it. Motionless and emotionless, at one moment both agonized and deeply still.

"Perhaps that would be better to send back," Tatsuhiko said suddenly.

"What?"

"Better than our precious reports. Instead, transmit to Earth such music. It conveys more than our data, our measurements, our . . . speculations."

She saw through his guarded expression—tight jawline, pensive lips, veiled eyes—how threatened Tatsuhiko felt. The long voyage out had not made every member of the 482 crew familiar to her, and she and Tatsuhiko had always worked in different chore details, but still she knew the character-indices of them all. Crew had to fit within the narrow avenue that had allowed them to withstand the grand, epic voyage, and not decay into the instabilities that the sociometricians had so tellingly predicted.

Tatsuhiko had lost great face in that abortive first encounter, and three other attempts by his team to provoke even a flicker of recognition from the Chujoans had failed just as miserably.

Yet it would not do to address Tatsuhiko directly on this issue, to probe in obvious fashion his deepest insecurities. "You have illuminated a principal feature of their character, after all. That is data."

He snorted derisively. "Feature? That they do not think us worth noticing?"

"But to take no notice—that is a recognition that says much."

Suspiciously: "What?"

"That they know our strangeness. Respect it."

"Or hold it in contempt."

"That is possible."

His face suddenly opened, the tight lines around his eyes lightening. "I fear I have been bound in my own discipline too much."

"Sociobiology?"

"Yes. We attempt to explain social behavior as arising from a species' genetic heritage. But here—the categories we ourselves bring are based on a narrowing of definitions, all accomplished by our own brains—wads of gray matter themselves naturally selected for. We *cannot* use words like 'respect' or 'contempt.' They are illusions here."

She frowned. "In principle, of course. But these natives, they are so like ourselves. . . ."

Tatsuhiko chuckled. "Oh? Come tomorrow, we'll go into the field. I'll show you the proud Chujoans."

3
SO-SO BIOLOGY

They squatted in a blind, peering through a gauzy, dim dawn.

Recently cut branches hid them from the roaming animals beyond. "I can't see anything." Miyuki shifted to get a better view of the plain. Scraggly gray trees dotted it and low, powder-blue brush clung to the gullies.

Tatsuhiko gestured. "Look on the infra monitor." He fiddled, sharpening the image.

She saw a diffuse glow about half a kilometer away. It was near a snaky stream that had cut deeply into the broad, flat valley. "Something killed a kobold last night?"

Tatsuhiko nodded. "Probably a ripper. Our sensors gave us an audio signature. Picked it up on omni and then focused automatically with a directional mike."

"Could it have been a dune tiger?"

"Don't know." He studied her face. "You're still thinking about the carving."

"It is beautiful," she said quickly, embarrassed for reasons she could not fathom.

"Indeed." His quick eyes gave nothing away. "The kobold kill is scenting in the air, and this breeze will carry it. We now wait to see what the Chupchups do."

"They call each other Chupchups?"

"We have analyzed their voice patterns. No clear syntax yet, of course. We aren't even sure of many words. We noticed that they make namelike sounds—*preess-chupchup,* for example—they always end in that phrase."

"Perhaps it means 'Mister.' Or 'Honorable.' "

He shrugged. "Better than calling them 'apes,' as some crew have started to do."

She sat back, thighs already aching from squatting, and breathed in the dry aroma of the hunting ground. It was like Africa, she thought, with its U-shaped valleys cut by meandering rivers, the far ramparts of fault blocks being worn down by windblown sand. Only this world was far more bleak, cold, eerie in its shadows cast by the great sun now rising.

This star always made her uneasy when it ponderously rose or set, for the air's refraction flattened it. Filling four times as much of the sky as the sun she knew, it was nonetheless a midget, with a third the mass of Sol. Though the astronomers persisted in calling Murasaki a red dwarf, it was no dull crimson ember.

In the exalted hierarchy of solar specialists, stars like this one, with surface temperature greater than a carbon-filament incandescent lamp, were nonetheless minor lukewarm bores. Had they been rare, astronomers might have studied them more before the discovery of life here. Though Murasaki sported sunspots and vibrant orange flares, its glow did not seem reddish to her, but rather yellow.

The difference from Sol became apparent as she squinted at the carrion awaiting the dawn's attentions. Detail faded in the distance, despite the thin air, because there was no more illumination than in a well-lit Earthly living room after dark. Only as this swollen sun rose did it steal some of the attention from Genji, which perched always directly above, splitting the sky with its sardonic half-moon grin.

"Here come the first," Tatsuhiko whispered tensely. His eyes danced with anticipation. When she saw him like this it was as if his formal skin had dissolved, giving her the man she had known.

A fevered giggling came over the chilly plain. Distant forms scampered: small tricorns, running from a snakehound. Their excited cries seemed nearly human. As they outdistanced the snakehound, which had sprung from concealment too soon, they sounded as though they laughed in derision. A hellbat flapped into view, drawn by the noise, and scooped up a burrowbunny that appeared to be just waking up as it stood at the entrance of its hole.

Then she saw the band of low shapes gathering where the kobold carcass lay. They were hangmouths—ugly hyenalike beasts that drooled constantly, fought each other over their food, and never hunted. These scavengers dismembered the kobold as she watched, hunching forward with the rest of the survey team. Short, snarling squabbles came over the audios.

"Vicious," she whispered, despite her resolution to say nothing about others' specialties.

"Of course," one of the team said analytically. "This is an ecology being slowly ground down by its biosphere. Hard times make hard species."

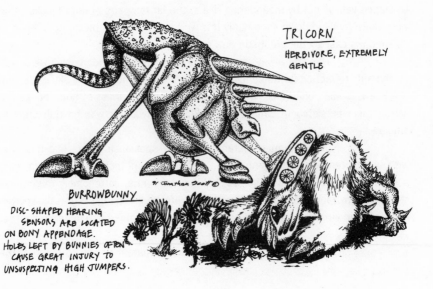

TRICORN

HERBIVORE, EXTREMELY GENTLE

BURROWBUNNY

DISC-SHAPED HEARING SENSORS ARE LOCATED ON BONY APPENDAGE. HOLES LEFT BY BUNNIES OFTEN CAUSE GREAT INJURY TO UNSUSPECTING HIGH JUMPERS.

She shivered, not entirely from the dawn chill.

As they watched, other teams reported that a party of Chujoans was headed this way. Tatsuhiko's team had tracked these Chujoans, noted the kobold kill, and now awaited their collision with the squinting intensity of an author first watching his play performed.

Miyuki could not see the Chupchups at all. The gradual warming of the valley brought tangy suggestions of straw-flavored vegetation, pungent meat rotting, the reek of fresh feces.

Tatsuhiko asked over comm, "Team C—have you counted them yet?"

The reply came crisply. "Eight. Three female adult, three male, two children."

"Any displays that show parental investment?"

"Males carry the children."

Tatsuhiko nodded. "It's that way in all groups smaller than a hundred. Interesting."

"What do those groups do?" Miyuki asked.

"Food gathering."

One of the team, Hayaiko, said, "You should look at that data on incest avoidance. Very convincing. Female children are separated from the male in an elaborate ceremony, given special necklaces, the entire panoply of effects."

Tatsuhiko pursed his lips. "Don't deduce too much too soon. They might have been marrying them off, for all we know."

Hayaiko blinked. "At age four?"

"Check our own history. We've done about the same not that long ago," Tatsuhiko said with a grin. He seemed relaxed, affable, a natural leader, but undercurrents played in his face.

She saw that he was no longer beset by doubt, as he had been in pensive moments in the ancient city. He would redouble his efforts, she saw, summon up more *gaman,* the famed dogged persistence that had made Japan the leader of the world. Or did he aspire higher, to *gaman-zuyoi,* heroic effort?

"The Chupchups are creeping up on the carrion," came a comm message.

"They'll fight the hangmouths?" Miyuki asked.

"We'll see," Tatsuhiko said.

She caught sight of the aliens then, moving in a squat-walk as they left a gully and quickly crossed to another. Their zigzag progress over the next half hour was wary, tediously careful as they took advantage of every tuft of grass, every slope, for concealment. She began to look forward to a fight with the hangmouths as their continuing snarls and lip-smacking over the audio told of the slow devouring of the carcass. It was, of course, quite unprofessional to be revolted by the behavior of species they had come so far to study, but she could not help letting her own delicate personal habits bring a curl of disgust to her lips.

"They're leaving," comm called.

The hangmouths began to stray from the carcass. "Picked it clean," Tatsuhiko said.

The Chupchups ventured closer. The two children darted in to the kill, dodged rebuffs from the larger hangmouths, and snatched away some carelessly dropped sliver—like pauper children at a land baron's picnic, Miyuki thought, in the days of the Shogunate. This intrusion seemed to be allowed, but when the adults crept closer a hangmouth turned and rushed at the leading Chupchup. It scampered back to safety, despite the fact that it carried a long pointed stick. It held the stick up as if to show the hangmouth, but the drooling beast still snarled and paced, kicking up curtains of dust, holding the band of Chupchups at bay for long minutes.

"Why don't they attack it?" she asked.

"I have no idea." Tatsuhiko studied the scene with binoculars. "Could the stick be a religious implement, not a weapon at all?"

"I do not think it is trying to convert the hangmouth," Miyuki said severely.

"Along with semantic language, religion is the one accomplishment of humans that has no analogy in the animal world," Tatsuhiko said stiffly. "I wish to know whether it is a biological property here, as it is for us."

"You believe we *genetically* evolved religion?"

"Plainly."

"Oh, come now."

A flicker of the other man: a quick smile and "Religion is the opiate of the mortal."

How could he still surprise her, after many years? "You believe we've had religion so long that it's buried in our genes?"

"It is not merely a cultural manifestation, or else it would not be universal among us. Incest avoidance is another such."

She blinked. "And morals?"

"Moral pronouncements are statements about genetic-fitness strategies."

All she could say was, "A severe view."

"A necessary one. Look there!"

Two hellbats had roosted in trees near the kill site. "Note how they roost halfway down the canopy, rather than in the top. They wish to be close to the game."

The hangmouth had turned and now, with aloof disdain, padded away from the Chupchup and its raised stick. Trotting easily, the hangmouths

HANGMOUTH

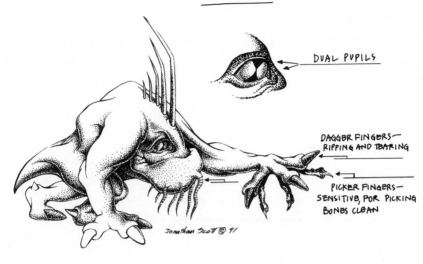

DUAL PUPILS

DAGGER FINGERS—
RIPPING AND TEARING

PICKER FINGERS—
SENSITIVE, FOR PICKING
BONES CLEAN

Jonathan Scott © 91

HELLBAT

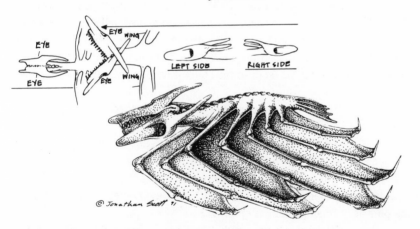

EYE

EYE

EYE WING

EYE WING

LEFT SIDE

RIGHT SIDE

© *Jonathan Scott 91*

BECAUSE OF THE LOW GRAVITATIONAL PULL, FLIGHT
IS EXCEPTIONALLY EASY FOR THE HELLBAT. WITH ITS STRANGE
VERTICAL MOUTH, AN EYE ON THE SIDE OF EACH JAW, AND
DANGEROUS-LOOKING HORNS, IT IS NO WONDER THAT EARLY
SETTLERS DUBBED THE CREATURE "HELLBAT." ONLY HELL
COULD HAVE CREATED SUCH A MONSTER. . . .

Jonathan Scott —Field Artist

SIDE VIEW
OF FOOT,
CONTRACTED

SIDE VIEW
OF FOOT,
RELAXED

departed. The Chupchup band ventured forward to the kobold body and began to root among the remains.

Miyuki said, "The hellbats—"

"See what the Chupchups are doing? Breaking open the big thigh bones." Tatsuhiko pointed to the vision screen, where a full-color picture showed Chupchups greedily sucking at the cracked yellow bones.

Miyuki was shocked. "But why, when there's meat left?"

"The marrow, I suspect. It is rich in calories among the larger species here."

"But still—"

"The Chupchups *prefer* the marrow. They have given up on finding fresh meat, for they have given up hunting." Tatsuhiko said this dispassionately, but his face wore an expression of abstracted scorn.

With screeches they could hear even at this range, two hellbats launched themselves upon the knot of stooping Chupchups. The large, leathery birds dove together at a Chupchup child that had wandered a few meters from the band. Miyuki watched their glittery, jewellike eyes and bony wings as they slid down the sky.

The first hellbat sank claws into the child and flapped strongly. A male Chupchup threw itself forward, but the second hellbat deflected it. A female Chupchup ran around the male and snatched at the child. The hellbat bit the female deeply as it tried to gain the air, but she clubbed it solidly twice with the flat of her hand. The hellbat dropped the child. It flapped awkwardly away, joined by its partner.

"They nearly got that little one!" Miyuki cried.

"They go for the weaker game."

"Weaker?" Miyuki felt irritated at Tatsuhiko's cool analysis. "The Chupchups are armed."

"But they do not use them to hunt the larger game. Or even, it seems, to defend themselves. The only use we have observed for those weapons is the pursuit of small game. Easy prey."

Miyuki shook her head. "That seems impossible. Why not use them?"

Somehow this direct question shattered Tatsuhiko's stony scientific distance. "Because they have adapted—downward."

"Maybe just sideways."

"A once-proud race of creators, now driven down to *this*."

"We ourselves, early man, we hunted in places like this. We could be forced back to it if—"

"No. We were hunters, like the lion. We did not scavenge."

Miyuki said quietly, "I thought lions scavenged."

Tatsuhiko glared at her but acknowledged this uncomfortable fact with a curt nod of his head. "Man the hunter did not. These Chupchups—they have let themselves be driven down to this lowly state."

She saw his vexed position. Traits derived from genes had led humans upward in ability. It had been a grand, swift leap, from wily ape to sovereign of the Earth. That tended to salt the truths of sociobiology with the promise of progress. Here, though, the same logic led to devolution of the once-great city-builders.

She said lightly, "We are merely talking wildly. Making guesses." She switched to English. "Doing so-so biology." Perhaps the pun would lift their discussion away from the remorselessly reductionist.

He gave her a cold smile. "Thank you, Miyuki-san, for your humor." He turned to regard the distant feeding, where the Chupchups now nuzzled among the bones. "Those cannot be the breed that built the cities. We have come so very slightly late."

"Perhaps elsewhere on Chujo—"

"We will look, certainly. Still . . . "

She said evenly, hoping to snap him out of this mood, "For four billion years, Earth supported only microbes. Oxygen and land plants are only comparatively recent additions. If those proportions hold everywhere, we are very lucky to find *two* planets that have more than algae!"

His angular features caught the dawn glow, giving him a sardonic look even in his pressure mask.

"You are trying to deflect my dark temper."

"Of course."

Each crewmember was responsible for maintaining cohesion. They kept intact the old ship disciplines. In solidarity meetings, one never scratched one's head or even crossed legs or arms before a superior, and always concluded even the briefest encounter with a polite bow—fifteen degrees to peers, forty-five degrees to superiors. Every week they repeated the old rituals, even the patient writing of Buddhist sutras with wooden pens. The officers polished the boots of the lower ranks, and soon after the ranks reciprocated. Each was bound to the others.

And she felt bound to him, though they had not been lovers for years, and she had passed through many liaisons since. Her longing to know him now was not carnal, though that element would never be banished, and she did not want it to be. She felt a need to *reach* him, to bring out the best that she knew lay within him. It was a form of love, though not one that songwriters knew. Perhaps in some obscure way it knitted into the cohesion of the greater expedition, but it felt intensely personal and incommunicable. Especially to the object of it all, standing obliviously a meter away. She snorted with frustration.

Not noticing her mood, Tatsuhiko smacked his fist into his palm. "But so close! If we had come fifty thousand years ago! Seen those great ancestors of these . . . these cowards."

Miyuki blinked, sniffed, chuckled. "Then we would have been Neanderthals."

4
THE LIBRARY

Their flyer came down smoothly beside the spreading forest. The waving fields of dark grain beckoned, but Miyuki knew already that the stuff was inedible.

Nearly everything on Chujo was. Only the sugar groups were digestible. Their dextro-rotary sense was the same as that of Earthly ones, a simple fact that led to deep mystery. Genji's sugars had that identical helical sense, though with myriad different patterns. And the intelligent, automated probes that now had scanned a dozen worlds around farther stars reported back the same result: where life appeared at all, anything resembling a sugar chain had the same sense of rotation. Some said this proved a limited form of molecular panspermia, with a primordial cloud seeding the region with simple organic precursors.

But there still were deeper similarities between Genji and Chujo: in protein structures, enzymes, details of energy processing. Had the two worlds once interacted? They were now 156,000 kilometers apart, less than two-thirds the Earth-moon separation, but tidal forces were driving them farther away. Their locked rotation minimized the stress from each others' tides. Even so, great surges swept even the small lakes as the mother-sun, Murasaki, raised its own tides on both her worlds. Miyuki stood beside a shallow, steel-gray lake and watched the waters rush across a pebbled beach. The rasp and rattle of stones came like the long, indrawn breath of the entire planet.

"Regroup!" Koremasa ordered over comm.

Miyuki had been idling, turning over in her mind the accumulating mysteries. She studied the orderly grain fields with their regimental rows and irrigation slits, as the expeditionary group met. Their reports were orderly, precise: discipline was even more crisp amid these great stretches of alien ground. Close observation showed that this great field was self-managing.

She watched as one of the bio group displayed a cage of rodents, each with prehensile, clawed fingers. "They cultivate the stalks, keep off pests," the woman said. "I believe this field can prune and perhaps even harvest itself."

Murmurs of dissent gradually ebbed as evidence accumulated.

Remains of irrigation channels still cut the valley. Brick-brown ruins of large buildings stood beside the restless lake. Small stone cairns dotted the landscape. It was easy for Miyuki to believe the rough scenario that the anthropologists and archaeologists proposed: that the slow waning of Chujo had driven the ancient natives to perfect crops that needed little labor, an astounding feat of biotech. That this field was a fragment of a great grain belt that had fed the cities. That as life suited to cold and aridity moved south, the ancients retreated into a pastoral, nomadic life. That—

"Chupchups!" someone called.

And here they came, already spreading out from the tree line a kilometer away. Miyuki clicked her vision to remote and surveyed them as she moved to her encounter position. This tribe had a herd. Domesticated snakehounds adroitly kept the short, bulky, red-haired beasts tightly bunched. A plume of dust pointed at the baggage train—pole arrangements drawn behind thin, flat-headed animals. An arrowfowl came flapping from over a distant hillside and settled onto the shoulder of the largest Chupchup—bringing a message from another tribe, she now knew enough to guess. The races met again.

The leading Chupchup performed as before—a long, lingering looking straight at the first human it met, then ignoring the rest. Miyuki stood still as the smelly, puffing aliens marched obliviously through the human formation.

Nomads had always been a fringe element in human civilization, she reflected. Even ancient Nippon had supported some. But here the nomads *were* the civilization. The latest survey from satellites had just finished counting the

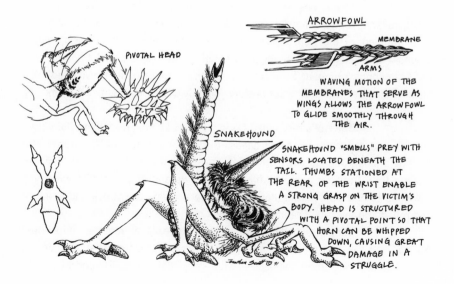

ARROWFOWL

MEMBRANE

PIVOTAL HEAD

ARMS

WAVING MOTION OF THE MEMBRANES THAT SERVE AS WINGS ALLOWS THE ARROWFOWL TO GLIDE SMOOTHLY THROUGH THE AIR.

SNAKEHOUND

SNAKEHOUND "SMELLS" PREY WITH SENSORS LOCATED BENEATH THE TAIL. THUMBS STATIONED AT THE REAR OF THE WRIST ENABLE A STRONG GRASP ON THE VICTIM'S BODY. HEAD IS STRUCTURED WITH A PIVOTAL POINT SO THAT HORN CAN BE WHIPPED DOWN, CAUSING GREAT DAMAGE IN A STRUGGLE.

Chupchups; there were around a million, covering a world with more land area than Earth. The head of Exo-Analysis thought that the number was in fact exactly 1,048,576—1,024 tribes of 1,024 individuals apiece. He even maintained that each tribe held 32 families of 32 members each. Even if he was right, she thought, and the musky bodies passing stolidly by her now were units in some grandly ordained arithmetic, had it always been that way? How did they maintain it?

She caught an excited murmur on comm. To her left a crewmember was pointing toward a few stacked stones where three Chupchups had stopped.

Slowly, gingerly, they pried up the biggest slab of blue-gray granite. One Chupchup drew something forth, held it to the light—a small, square thing—and then put it in a pocket of its shabby brown waistcoat. Then the Chupchups walked on, talking in that warbling way of theirs, still ignoring the humans who stood absolutely still, aching for contact, receiving none. She almost laughed at the forlorn expressions of the crew as the last of the Chupchups marched off, leaving only a fragrant odor of musty sweat. They did not inspect the fields or even glance at the ruins.

"It's a library!" someone called.

Miyuki turned back to see that a crewman, Akihiro, had lifted the granite slab. Inside rested a few cubes, each ornately decorated. "I think this is a library. They were picking up a book."

Koremasa appeared as if he had materialized from the air. "Put it back!" he ordered tersely.

Akihiro said, "But I—look, it's—"

"Back!"

But by then it was too late. From the trees came the trolls.

Miyuki was not a first-line combat officer. She thus had a moment, as others ran to form a defensive line, to observe the seemingly accidental geometry that unfolded as the troll attack began. The Chupchups had stopped, turned around—and watched impassively as the trolls burst from the thick tree line. Had the Chupchups summoned the trolls, once they saw their library violated? She could not guess from their erect posture, blandly expressionless faces, unmoving mouths.

The trolls resembled Chupchups as chimps resembled humans—shorter, wider, long arms, small heads. But they ran with the fluid speed of a hunting animal, and caught the nearest crewmember before she could fetch her weapon forth from her pack. A troll picked her up and threw her like something it wished to discard—hurling her twenty meters, where she struck and bounced and rolled and lay still. The other trolls took no notice.

They hesitated. Had they gotten some signal from the Chupchups? But no—she saw that the wind had shifted. The odorous extract that the biotechs had made everyone smear themselves with—yes, that was it. The cutting reek of it, carried on the breeze, had confused the trolls for a moment. But then their rage came again, their teeth flashed with mad hunting passion, and they fell upon the next crewmembers.

She would remember the next few instants for all her life. The weapons carriers liked to fire from a single line, to minimize accidents. Trolls struck that still-forming line. When he saw that the smell defense had failed, Koremasa blinked, raised his hand with a sad, slow gravity—and the rifles barked, a thin sharp sound in the chilly air.

The sudden hard slaps were inundated by the snarls and howls of trolls as they slammed aside their puny opponents. The aliens were swift, sure, moving with enormous power and sudden, almost balletlike agility. In their single-footed swerves, their quick ducks to avoid a rifle shot, their flicked blows that struck with devastating power, Miyuki saw how a billion years of evolution had engineered reflexes intricately suited to the lesser gravity.

But then the concerted splatting violence took them down. Their elegant, intelligent attack had not counted on a volley of automatic fire. The great, bright-eyed beasts fell even as they surged on, oblivious of danger.

The last few reached Miyuki and she saw, in slow-motion surrealism, the flushed, heady expression on a troll that stumbled as it took a round in its massive right arm. *It's ecstatic,* she thought.

But it would not be stopped by one shot. It staggered, looking for another enemy to take, and saw her. Red eyes filled with purple pupils widened. It swung its left arm, claws arcing out—and she ducked.

The swipe whistled over her ear, caught her with a *thunk* in the scalp. It was more a sound, a booming, than a felt blow. She flew through the air, turning, suddenly and abstractly registering the pale-blue, cloud-quilted sky, and then she landed on her left shoulder and rolled. A quick rasping *brrrt* cut through a strange hollow silence that had settled around her. She looked up into the sky, and the troll eclipsed this view like a red-brown thundercloud. It was not looking at her, but instead seemed to be gazing off into a world it could not comprehend. Then it felt the tug of mortality and orbited down into the acrid clouds of dust stirred by the battle, landing solidly beside her, not rolling, its sour breath coughing out for the last time.

5

I-WITNESSING

They devoted three days to studying the fields and burying the bodies. A pall spread among them, the radio crackled with questions, and mission command wrung from each fact a symphony of meaning, of blame, of outrage.

Miyuki was doubly glad that she had not sought a higher post in this exploration party. Koremasa had to feed the appetite of his superiors, safely orbiting Genji, with data, photos, transcripts, explanations, analysis. Luckily, two cameras had recorded most of the battle. Watching these images again and again, Miyuki felt a chill at the speed and intelligence of the troll assault. Her own head wound was nothing compared to the bloody cuts and gougings many others had received.

Koremasa would probably not be court-martialed—but Akihiro Saito, the crewman who had opened the cairn in a moment of excited curiosity, would have been tried and humiliated, had he survived.

It was something of a relief that Akihiro had died. They would have had to watch him for signs of potential suicide, never leaving him alone or assigning him dangerous tasks. No one could be squandered here, no matter how they violated the expedition's standards.

No one ever said this, of course. Instead, they held a full, formal ceremony to mark the passing of their companions, including Akihiro. The meal was specially synthesized on the mother ship and sent down in a drop package. The team sat in a precise formation, backs to the wild alien landscape outside the bubble, and within their circle Old Nippon lived still. The captain produced a bowl for each, in which reposed a sweetened smoked sardine, its spine curved to represent a fish in the water. It had been carefully placed against two slices of raw yellowtail, set off by a delicately preserved peeled plum and two berrylike ovals, one crisp and one soft, both dipped in an amber coating. A second bowl held a paper-thin slice of raw Spanish mackerel, cut to catch the silver stripe down its back, underpinned in turn by a sliver of seaweed to quietly stress the stripe, all resting on molded rice. A small half-lobster, garnished with sweet preserved chestnuts, sent its aroma into the close, incense-scented air. Thin-sliced, curled onions came next, sharp and melting in the mouth. A rosette of red pickled onion heart came wrapped in a rosy cabbage leaf. Finally, tea.

And all this came from the processors aboard the mother ship, fashioned finally by the master chef who everyone agreed—in the polite, formal conversation that followed around their circle—was the most important member of the entire expedition.

The beautiful meal and a day of contemplation did their silent work. Calamity reminded one to remain centered, to rely on others, to remember that all humanity witnessed the events here. So as the numbness and anxiety left them they returned to their studies. Five crew kept watch at all times while the rest tried to comprehend why four humans and six trolls had died.

In the end, the simplest explanation seemed best: the trolls guarded the ancient, self-managing fields, and this task included the library cairn.

The biologists found rodentlike creatures that pruned and selected the grain plants, others that gathered them into bunches, and further species that stored them among the caved-in brick-brown buildings. Subtle forces worked the fields: ground cover that repelled weeds, fungoids that made otherwise defenseless leaves distasteful or poisonous to browsers, small burrowers that loosened the soil for roots. The trolls assisted these tasks and made sure that only passing bands of Chupchups ate the grain. They tended fruit-bearing trees in the next valley as well, where two more library cairns stood.

The cube from the cairn yielded nothing intelligible immediately, but would doubtless be studied in infinitesimal detail when they got it to the mother ship. The sciences were biased toward studying hard evidence, and the oddly marked stone cube was ideal for this. Miyuki doubted whether it could ever yield very much.

"It could be a religious talisman, after all," she remarked one evening as they gathered for a meager supper.

"Then it would probably be displayed in a shrine," Koremasa said reasonably.

"They have no churches," Miyuki answered.

"We think," Tatsuhiko said sourly. "We have not searched enough yet to say."

Miyuki said, "You believe the cities at the rim may tell us more?"

Tatsuhiko hesitated. He plainly felt besieged, having failed to anticipate well the danger here, a continuing humiliation to him. "There might be much less erosion at high altitudes," he said warily.

Koremasa nodded. "Satellite recon shows that. High winds, but less air to work with."

Miyuki smiled. Seen from above, planets seemed vastly simple. The yellowish flora and fauna of Chujo tricked the eyes of even orbiting robot scanners. The molecule that best harvested Murasaki's wan glow was activated by red-orange light, not by the skimpy greens that chlorophyll favored. That simple consequence of living beside a lukewarm star muddied the resolution of their data-reduction programs.

"We had better leave such high sites for later work," she ventured.

Koremasa's eyebrows showed mild surprise, but he kept his mouth relaxed, quizzical. "You truly feel so?"

Though she did not wish to admit it, the thought of wearing the added pressure gear needed among the raw mountains of Chujo's rim grated upon her. She itched from dryness, her sleeping cycle veered in response to Chujo's ninety-one-hour day, her sinuses clogged perpetually from constant colds—and everyone else suffered the same, largely without complaint. But she decided to keep her objections professional. "Our error here suggests that we leave more difficult tasks to others." There. Diffident but cutting.

Koremasa let a silence stretch, and no one else in the circle ventured into it. A cold wind moaned against the plastic of their pressure dome. Their incandescents' blues and violets apparently irritated the local night-hunters and pests, keeping them at bay, one of the few favorable accidents they had found. Still, she felt the strangeness of the dark outside pressing against them all.

She saw Koremasa's talent as a leader; he simply sat, finally provoking Tatsuhiko to say, "I must object. We need to understand those who build the cities, for they plainly are not these Chupchups. Then—"

"Why is that so clear?" Miyuki cut in.

Tatsuhiko let a small trace of inner tension twist his mouth momentarily. "You saw the scavenging. That is not the behavior of a dominant, intelligent race."

"What's intelligent is what survives," she answered.

Tatsuhiko flared. "No, that is an utter misunderstanding of evolutionary theory. Intelligence is not always adaptive—that is the terrible lesson we have learned here."

"That is a hasty conclusion," Miyuki said mildly.

"*Hasty?* We know far more than you may realize about these Chupchups. We have picked over their campsites, studied their mating through infra-distant imaging, picked apart their turds to study their diet. We patched together their broken pots. Their few metal implements are probably stolen from the ruined cities and reworked down through many generations; they certainly look it."

"It is difficult to read meaning in artifacts," Koremasa said.

"Not so!" Tatsuhiko stood and began to pace, walking jerkily around the outside of the circle. He made each of his points with the edge of his right hand, cutting the air in a karate chop. "The Chupchups wander perpetually. They cook in bark pots and leather bags using heated stones—stew with dumplings, usually. They like starchy sweets and swallow berries whole. They pick their teeth with a bristly fungus that they then eat a day later—"

"They must be civilized, then," Miyuki broke in. "They floss!"

Tatsuhiko blinked, allowed himself a momentary smile in answer to the round of laughter. "Perhaps so, though I differ." He gave her a quick significant glance, and she felt that somehow she had momentarily broken through to the man she knew.

Then he took a breath, lifted his narrow chin high, put his hands behind his back in a curiously schoolboyish pose, and went on doggedly. "You will have noticed that Chupchup males and females look nearly alike. There are no signs of homosexual behavior—which is hard to understand. After all, humans have genetically selected for it through the shared-kinship mechanism and inclusive fitness, in which the homosexuals further the survival of genes they share with heterosexuals. They're not permanently rutty, the way we are, and perhaps an explanation lies there—but how? The female does the courting, singing and dancing like Earthside birds. No musical instruments used. They do it more often than reproduction requires, though, just like us. Some pair-bonding, maybe even monogamy. Approximate equality of the sexes in social matters and labor, with perhaps some slight female dominance. They carry out some sex-separate rites, but we don't know what those mean. Hunter-gatherer routines are—"

"Quite so," Koremasa said softly. "We take your points."

Somehow this ended the spontaneous lecture. Tatsuhiko fell silent, his lips twitching. She felt sympathy for his frustration, mingling with his restless desire to fathom this world in terms he could understand.

Yet she could not let matters rest here. She set her face resolutely. If he wished a professional contest, so be it.

"You read much into your observations," Miyuki said. She looked around the circle to see if anyone nodded, but they were all impassive, letting her take the lead.

"We must," Tatsuhiko said testily.

"But surely we can no more portray a society by recording facts, filtered through our preconceptions, than a literary critic can get the essence of Murasaki's great *Genji Monogatari* by summarizing the plot," she said. "I think perhaps we are doing 'I-witnessing' here."

Tatsuhiko smiled grimly. "You have a case of what we call in sociobiology 'epistemological hypochondria'—the fear of interpretation."

Koremasa let the wind speak to them all again, sighing, muttering, rubbing at their monolayer defense against it.

"We appreciate your views, Tatsuhiko-san, but there are fresh facts before us now," Koremasa said in calm, measured tones. "The satellites report that the Chupchup tribes are no longer wandering in a random pattern."

Tatsuhiko brightened. "Oh? Where are they going?"

"They are all moving away from us."

Surprise registered in a low, questioning mutter around their circle. "All of them?" the communications engineer asked.

Koremasa nodded. "They are moving toward the ridge-rim. Journeying from the moonside to the starside, perhaps." He stood, smiling at Tatsuhiko. "In a way, I suppose we have at last received a tribute from them. They have acknowledged our presence."

Tatsuhiko blinked and then snorted derisively. Such a rude show would be remarkable, except that Miyuki understood that the contempt was directed by Tatsuhiko at himself.

"And I suggest," Koremasa continued with a quiet air of authority, "that we study this planetwide activity."

"Of course," Tatsuhiko said enthusiastically. "This could be a seasonal migration. Many animal species have elaborate—"

"These are *not* animals!" Miyuki surprised herself with the vehemence in her voice.

Miyuki opened her mouth to reply, but saw Captain Koremasa raise one finger slightly. He said casually, "Enough theory. We must look—and quickly. The first bands are already striving to cross the rim mountain ranges."

6

PARADIGM LOST

Chujo and Genji pulled at each other incessantly, working through their tides, and Murasaki's more distant stresses added to the geological turmoil. This powered a zone of incessant mountain-building along the circumference of Chujo. Seen from Genji, this ring rimmed Chujo with a crust of peaks, sheer faults, and deep, shadowed gorges. Lakes and small, pale seas dotted Chujo's lowlands, where the thin air already seemed chilly to humans, even in this summer season. Matters worsened for fragile humans toward the highlands.

The muscled movement of great geologic forces lifted the rock, allowing water to carve its many-layered canyons. As they flew over the great stretching plains Miyuki feasted on the passing panorama, insisting that their craft fly at the lowest safe altitude, though that cost fuel. She saw the promise of green summer, lagoons of bright water, grazing beasts with white hoofs stained with the juice of wildflowers.

This was a place of violent contrasts. In an hour they saw the land below parched by drought, beaten by hail, sogged by rain, burnt by grass fires. But soon, as their engines labored to suck in more of the skimpy air, the plains became ceramic-gray, blistered, cracked. From orbit she had seen the yellow splashes of erupting lava from myriad small peaks, and now they came marching from the girdling belt of the world. Black rock sliced across the buff colors of windblown sand. Glacial moraines cupped frozen lakes, fault blocks poked above eroded plains, valleys testified to the recent invasion of the great ice.

Yet this world-wracking had perhaps made life possible here. Chujo was much like a fortunate Mars—small, cold, huddled beneath a scant scarf of sheltering gas. Mars had suffered swerves in its polar inclination and eccentricity, and this may have doomed the fossilized, fledgling spores humans had found there. But Genji-Chujo's whirling waltz had much more angular momentum than a sole spinning planet could, and this had fended off the tilting perturbations of Murasaki and the outer, gas giant planets. Thus neither of the brothers had to endure wobbling poles, shifting seasons, the rasp of cruel change.

Small bushes clung to the escarpments of a marble mountain. Compressional scarps cut the mountain as though a great knife had tried to kill it. These were signs of internal cooling, she knew, Chujo shrinking as its core cooled, wrinkling with age, a world in retreat from its warmer eras. Twisted spires of pumice reared, light as air, splashed with stains of cobalt, putty, scarlet. Miyuki watched this brutal beauty unfold uneasily. Smoke hazed the snowcapped range ahead. The Genjians must have wondered for ages, she thought, at the continual flame and black clouds of their brother's perimeter. They probably did not realize that a similar wracked ridge girdled their own world. Perhaps the Genjians had seen the great Chujoan cities at their prime—it was optically possible, with the naked Genjian eye—but could legends of that have survived the thousands of generations since? Did either intelligent race know of the other—and did they still? Certainly—she glanced up at the crescent of Genji, mottled and muggy, like a watercolor artwork tossed off by a hasty child—the present Chupchups could gain no hint from that sultry atmosphere. Still, there were hints, all the way down into the molecular chemistry, that the worlds were linked.

Koremasa rapped on the hard Plexiglas. "See? All that green?"

Miyuki peered ahead and saw on the flank of a jutting mountain a smooth, tea-green growth. "Summer—and we're near the equator."

Koremasa nodded. "This terrain looks too barren to support plants year-round."

Tatsuhiko put in, over the low rumble of their flyer, "Seasonal migration. More evidence."

"Of what?" Miyuki asked.

"Of their devolution. They've picked up the patterns of migrating fowl. Seasonal animals didn't build those cities."

Koremasa said, "That makes sense."

Tatsuhiko pressed his point. "So you no longer believe they are fleeing from us?"

Koremasa smiled, and Miyuki saw that his announcement two days before had all been a subtle ruse. "It was a useful temporary hypothesis."

Useful for what? she wanted to ask, but discipline and simple politeness restrained her. Instead she said, "So they migrate to the mountain chain to—what? Eat that grass, or whatever it is?"

Tatsuhiko nodded enthusiastically. "Of course."

She remarked dryly, "A long way to walk for such sparse stuff."

"I mention it only as a working hypothesis," Tatsuhiko said stiffly.

"Did you ever see an animal wearing clothes?" Miyuki let a tinge of sarcasm slip into her voice.

"Simple crabs carry their shell homes on their backs."

"Animals that cook? Carry weapons?"

"All that is immaterial." Tatsuhiko regarded her with something like fondness for a long moment. Then his face returned to the cool, lean cast she had seen so much of these last few years. "I grant that the Chupchups have vestigial artifacts of their ancestors. Those mat-clothes of theirs—marvelous biological engineering, but plainly inherited. The Chupchups are plainly degenerated."

"Because they won't talk to us?"

"Because they have abandoned their cities, lost their birthright."

"The Mayans did that well over a thousand years ago."

Tatsuhiko shook his head, his amused smile telling the others that here an amateur was venturing into his territory. "They did not revert to Neanderthals."

Miyuki asked with restrained venom, "You would prefer any explanation that made the Chupchups into degenerated pseudo-animals, wouldn't you?"

"That is an unfair—"

"Well, wouldn't you?"

"—and unprofessional, unscientific attitude."

"You didn't answer me."

"There is no need to dignify an obvious personal—"

"Oh, please spare me—"

"Prepare for descent," Koremasa said, looking significantly at both of them in turn.

"Huh!" Miyuki sat back and glowered out at the view. How had she ever thought that she could reach this man?

They landed heavily, the jet's engines whining, swiveling to lower them vertically into a boulder-strewn valley, just short of the green expanses. Deep crevasses cut the stony ground. Miyuki climbed out gingerly, her pressure suit awkwardly bunching and pinching. The medical people back in Low Genji Orbit had given them only ten hours to accomplish this mission, and allowed only six of them to go at all. The cold already bit into her hands and feet.

A white-water stream muttered nearby and they headed along it, toward the brown and green growth that filled the upper valley. Broken walls of the ancient Chujoans lay in the narrow box canyon at the top of the valley, near a spectacular roaring waterfall. It had been a respectable-sized town, she judged.

Why did those ancients build anything at all here? Most of the year this austere place had no vegetation at all, the satellite records said.

She stumbled. The ground was shaking. Slow, grave oscillations came up through her boots. She looked up, her helmet feeling more bulky all the time, and studied the mountain peak that jutted above them. Streamers of black smoke fretted away in the perpetual winds. Crashes echoed in the valley, reflected off the neighboring peaks from the flanks of the mountain—landslides, adding their kettledrum rolls as punctuation to the mountain's bass notes.

Fretful comments filled the comm. She marched on grimly. Tatsuhiko and Koremasa seemed to have already decided how to interpret whatever they would find; what was the point of this? Sitting back in camp, this quick sortie to the highlands—a "sprint mission," in the jargon—had seemed a great adventure.

She studied the bare cliff faces that framed the valley. Volcanic ash layers like slices in an infinite sandwich, interspersed with more interesting lines of pink clay, of pebbled sand, of gray conglomerates. So they would have to do what they did at so many sites—sample quickly, thinking little, hoping that they had gotten the kernel of the place by dint of judgment and luck. So much! A whole world, vast and various—and another, hanging overhead like a taunt.

The biologist reached the broad, flat field of green and knelt down to poke at it. He looked up in surprise. "It's algae! Sort of."

Miyuki stepped on the stuff. It was so thin she could feel pebbles crunch beneath it. She bent to examine it, her suit gathering and bunching uncomfortably at her knees. The mat was finely textured, green threads weaving among brown splashes.

The biologist dug his sample knife into it. "Tough," he said. "Very tough." With effort he punctured the mat and with visible exertion cut out a patch. His portable chemlab shot back an answer as soon as he inserted the patch. "Ummm. Distinct resemblance to . . . oh, yes, that Chupchup clothing. Same species, I'd say."

Tatsuhiko's voice was tight and precise over comm. "This proves how long ago the original form was developed. Here it's assumed a natural role in the environment. Unless the Chupchups simply adapted it themselves from this original species. I—"

"Funny biochem going on here," the biologist said. "It's excreting some kind of metabolic inhibitor. And—say, there's a lot of hydrogen around it, too."

Tatsuhiko nodded. "That agrees with the tests on the Chupchup living cloth. It interacts with the Chupchup body, we believe."

"No, this is different." The biologist moved on, tugging at the surface, taking readings. "This stuff is interconnected algae and fibers with a lot of energy stored in chemical bonds."

"Look at these," Miyuki said. She lifted a flap of the thin but tough material. There was a pocket several meters long, open at one end.

"Double-layered, I guess. Wonder why?" The biologist frowned. "This thing is a great photosynthetic processor. Guess that's why it flourishes here only in summer. Now, I—"

The ground rolled. Miyuki staggered. The biologist fell, throwing his knife aside to avoid a cut in his suit. Miyuki saw a dark mass fly up from the mountain's peak. A sudden thunderclap hammered down on them. The valley floor shook. Dust rose in filmy curtains.

"Sample taken?" Koremasa asked on comm. "Good. Let us—"

"But the ruins!" Miyuki said. "They'll want at least a few photos."

"Oh. Yes." Koremasa looked unhappy but nodded.

Miyuki could scarcely believe she had blurted out such a rash suggestion. Not only was it quite unlike her, she thought, but it contradicted her better judgment. She did want to have a look at the ruins, yes, but—

A temblor rocked her like an ocean wave. More smoke spat from the peak, unfurling across a troubled sky. The other five had already started running uphill across the mat.

She followed, turning every hundred meters to glance behind, memorizing the way back in case they had to retreat in a hurry. She heard Tatsuhiko's shout and saw him pointing just as another slow, deep ripple worked through the valley.

"Chups!"

They were in a single file, winding out of the ruins. They did not turn to look at the humans, simply proceeded downhill.

Miyuki's perspectives shifted and danced as she watched them, the world seemed to be tilting—and then she realized that again it was not her, but the valley floor that was moving. What she felt was not the wrenching of an earthquake.

It was the mat itself. The entire floor of the valley wrinkled, stretched, slid.

The Chupchups seemed to glide across the wrestling surface of the mat, uphill from the humans. They were headed for a crevasse that billowed steam. Streamers of sulfurous yellow swirled across the mat. Yet the Chupchups gave none of the gathering chaos any notice.

"Back!" Koremasa called on comm. "Back into the flyer."

They had nearly reached the ruins. Miyuki took a moment to snap quick pictures of the crumbled structures. The slumped stoneworks did not look at all like housing. In fact, they seemed to be immense vats, caved in and filled with rubble. Vats for what?

She turned away, and the ground slid out from under her. She rolled. The others were farther downhill, but the jerking of the tawny-green growth under them had sent them tumbling pell-mell downward, rolling like dolls. They shouted, cried out, swore.

Miyuki stopped herself by digging in her heels and grabbing at the tough, writhing mat. It was durable material, and she could not rip it for a better hold. In a moment the convulsions stopped. She sat up.

Pearly fog now rose from the mat all around her. She felt a trembling and then realized that she was moving—slowly, in irregular little jerks, but yes—the mat was tugging itself across the pebbles beneath it. She scrambled for footing—and fell. She got to her knees. Somewhere near here the Chupchups—

There. They were standing, looking toward the chasm a hundred meters away. Miyuki followed their intent, calm gaze.

The mat was alive, powerful, muscular—and climbing up the sky.

No, it merely reared, like the living flesh of a wounded thing. It buckled and writhed, a nightmare living carpet.

It jerked itself higher than a human, forming a long sheet that flexed like an ocean wave—and leaped.

The wave struck the far side of the crevasse. It met there another shelf of rising mat. The two waves stuck, clung. All along the chasm the two edges slapped together, melted into one another, formed a seamless whole.

And rose. As though some chemical reaction were kindling under it, the living carpet bulged like a blister. Miyuki clung to the shifting, sliding mat—and then realized that if she let go, she could roll downhill, where she wanted to go.

She watched the mat all along the vent as it billowed upward. The Chupchups made waving motions, as if urging the mat to leave the ground. She thought suddenly, *They came here for this. Not fleeing from us at all.*

Then she was slipping, rolling, the world whirling as she felt the mat accelerate. Her breath rasped and she curled up into a ball, tumbling and bouncing down the hillside. Knocks, jolts, a dull gathering roar—and then she slammed painfully against a boulder. A bare boulder, free of the mat.

She got up, feeling a sharp pain in her left ankle. "Koremasa-san!"

"Here! Help me with Tatsuhiko!"

Tatsuhiko had broken his leg. His dark face contorted with agony. She peered down into his constricted eyes and he said, speaking very precisely between pants, "Matters are complex."

She blinked. "What?"

"Clearly something more is going on here," he said tightly, holding the pain back behind his thin smile.

"Never mind that, you're hurt. We'll—"

He waved the issue away. "A temporary intrusion. Concentrate on what is happening here."

"Look, we'll get you safely—"

"I have missed something." Tatsuhiko grimaced, then gave a short, barking laugh. "Maybe everything."

She felt the need to comfort him, beyond placing compresses, and said, "You may have been right. This—"

"No, the Chupchups are . . . something different. Outside the paradigms."

. "Quiet now. We'll get you out of here."

Tatsuhiko lifted his eyebrows weakly. "Keep your lovely eyes open. Watch what the Chupchups are doing. Record."

Something in his tone made her hesitate. "I . . . still love you."

His lips trembled. "I . . . also. Why can we not talk?"

"Perhaps . . . perhaps it means too much."

He twisted his lips wryly. "Exactly. That hypothesis accounts for the difficulty."

"Too much . . . " She saw ruefully that she had thought him stiff and uncompromising, and perhaps he was—but that did not mean she did not share those elements. Perhaps they were part of the personality constellations chosen long ago on Earth, the partitioning of traits that ensured the expedition would get through at all.

He said, "I am sorry. I will do better."

"But you . . . " She did not know what to say and her mouth was dry, and then the others came.

They lifted him and started toward the flyer. The others had rolled onto the rocky ground below as the mat moved. Miyuki stumbled, this time from a volcanic tremor. She got to the flyer and looked back. The entire party paused then, fear draining from them momentarily, and watched.

The mat was lifting itself. Alive with purpose, rippling, its center axis bulged, pulling the rest of it along the ground with a hiss like a wave sliding up a beach. It shed pebbles, making itself lighter, letting go of its birthplace.

"Some . . . some reaction is going on in the vent under it," the biologist panted over comm. "Making gases—that hydrogen I detected, I'll bet. That's a by-product of this mat. Maybe it's been growing some culture in the volcanic vents around here. Maybe . . . " His voice trailed away in stunned disbelief.

She remembered the strange vatlike openings among the Chupchup buildings. Some ancient chemical works? A way to augment this process? After all, the Chupchups had clothing made of material much like this crawling carpet.

They got Tatsuhiko into the bay of the flyer. Koremasa ordered the pilot to ready the flyer for lift-off. He turned back to the others and then pointed at the sky. Miyuki turned. From valleys beyond, large green teardrops drifted up the sky. They wobbled and flexed, as though shaping themselves into the proper form for a fresh inhabitant of the air.

Organic balloons were launching themselves from all the valleys of the volcanic ridge. Dozens rose into the winds. In concert, somehow, Miyuki saw. Perhaps triggered by the spurt of vulcanism. Perhaps responding to some deeply imprinted command, some collision of chemicals.

"Living balloons . . . " she said.

The biologist said, "The vulcanism, maybe it triggers the process. After the mat has grown to a certain size. Methane, maybe anaerobic fermentation—"

"The carving," Miyuki said.

Koremasa said quietly, "The Chupchups."

The frail, distant figures clung to the side of the mat as the center of it rose, fattening. Some found the pockets that the humans had noticed, and slipped inside. Others simply grabbed a handful of the tough green hide and hung on.

"They are going up with it," Koremasa said.

She recalled the carving in the ancient city, with its puzzling circles hanging in the backdrop of the tiger eating its tail, nature feeding on itself, with the Chujoan face arising from the writhing pain of the twisting tail. "The circles—they were balloons. Rising."

The last edge of the mat sped toward the ascending bulge with a sound like the rushing of rapids over pebbles. The accelerating clatter seemed to hasten the living, self-making balloon. Frayed lips of the mat slapped together below the fattening, uprushing dome. These edges sealed, tightened, made the lower tip of a green teardrop.

On the grainy skin of the swelling dome the Chupchup passengers now settled themselves in the pockets Miyuki had noted before. Most made it. Some dangled helplessly, lost their grip, fell with a strange silence to their deaths. Those already in pockets helped others to clamber aboard.

And buoyantly, quietly, they soared into a blue-black sky. "Toward Genji," Miyuki whispered. She felt a pressing sense of presence, as though a momentous event had occurred.

"In hydrogen-filled bags?" Koremasa asked.

"They can reach fairly far up in the atmosphere that way," Tatsuhiko said weakly. He was lying on the cushioned deck of the flyer, pale and solemn. The injury had drained him, but his eyes flashed with the same quick, assessing intelligence.

Miyuki climbed into the flyer and put a cushion under his helmet. The crew began sealing the craft. "I don't think they mean to just fly around," she said.

"Oh?" Tatsuhiko asked wanly. "You think they imagine they're going to Genji?"

"I don't think we can understand this." She hesitated. "It may even be suicide."

Tatsuhiko scowled. "A race devoted to a suicide ritual? They wouldn't have lasted long."

She gestured at the upper end of the valley. "Most of them didn't go. See? They're standing in long lines up there, watching the balloon leave."

"More inheritance?" Tatsuhiko whispered. "Is this all they remember of the technology the earlier race had mastered?"

Miyuki thought. "I wonder."

Tatsuhiko said wanly, taking her hand, "Perhaps they have held on to the biomats, used them. Maybe they don't understand what they were for, really. A piece of biotech like that—a beautiful solution to the problem of transport, in an energy-scarce environment. Are the Chupchups just . . . just joyriding?"

Miyuki smiled. "Perhaps . . ."

They lifted off vertically just as another rolling jolt came. The flyer veered in the gathering winds, and Miyuki watched the teardrop shapes scudding across the purpling sky. Soon enough they would be the object of scrutiny, measurement, with the full armament of scientific dispassion marshaled to fathom them. She would probably even do some of the job herself, she thought wryly.

But for this single crystalline moment she wished to simply enjoy them. Not analyze, but feel the odd, hushed quality their ascent brought.

They were probably neither Tatsuhiko's vestigial technology nor some arcane tribal ceremony. Perhaps this entire drama was purely a way for the Chupchups to tell humans something. She bit her lip in concentration. Tell what? Indeed, satellite observations, dating back to the first robot probe, had never shown any sign of a Chupchup migration here. It might be unique—a response to humans themselves.

She sighed. Cabin pressure hissed on again as the flyer leveled off for its long flight back. She popped her helmet and wrestled Tatsuhiko's off. He smiled, thanked her—and all the while behind his tired eyes she saw the glitter, the unquelled pursuit of his own vision of the world, which Tatsuhiko would never abandon. As he should not.

The biologist was saying something about the balloons, details—

that they seemed to be photosynthetic processors, making more hydrogen to keep themselves aloft, to offset losses through their own skin. He even had a term for them, *bioloons*. . . .

So the unpeeling of the onion skins was already beginning. And what fun it would be.

But what did it *mean*? The first stage of science atomizes, dissects, fragments. Only much later do the Bohrs, the Darwins, the Einsteins knit it all together again—and nobody knew what the final weave would be, silk or sackcloth.

So both Tatsuhiko and herself and all the others—they were all needed. There would be no end of explanations. Did the Chupchups think humans were in fact from that great promise in the sky, Genji? Or were they trying to signal something with the mat-balloons—while still holding to their silence? An arcane ceremony? Some joke?

The Chupchups would never fit the narrow rules of sociobiology, she guessed, but just as clearly they would not be merely Zen aliens, or curators of some ashram in the sky. They were themselves, and the fathoming of that would be a larger task than Miyuki, or Tatsuhiko, or Koremasa could comprehend.

The flyer purred steadily. The still-rising emerald teardrops dwindled behind. Their humming technology was taking them back to base, its pilot already fretting about fuel.

Miyuki felt a sudden, unaccountable burst of joy. Hard mystery remained here, shadowed mystery would call them back, and mystery was far better than the cool ceramic surfaces of certainty.

A PLAGUE OF CONSCIENCE

BY GREG BEAR

Kammer looked worse than any corpse Philby had seen; much worse, for he was alive and shouldn't have been. This short wizened man with limbs like gnarled tree branches and skin like leather—what could be seen of his skin beneath the encrustations of brown and green snug—had survived ten Earthly years on Chujo without human contact. He could hardly speak English any more.

Kammer regarded Philby through eyes paled by some Chujoan biological adaptation—the impossible that had happened to him first and then had spread so disastrously to the Quantist settlers and the Japanese stationed here. Three hundred dead, and it had certainly begun on Kammer's broken, dying body, pissed on by a Chujoan shaman.

They stood four meters from each other, Chujo's sky darkling to squid's-ink purple in the gloaming. Philby was unused to feeling nervous before any human. Kammer, not wholly human any more, coughed, and his snug wrinkled and crawled in obscene patches, revealing yet more leather. "Not many people let to see me," he said. "Why do you?"

"I come from Genji," Philby said, "with a message from the Ihrdizu to the Chujoan shamans. Talking to you seems to be a bonus." His voice was somewhat muffled by the isolation suit's helmet; they were taking no chances with Kammer, or with the Chujoans.

"Ah, Christ," Kammer said roughly, and spat a thin stream of green and red saliva on the rocky ground between them. The stream lapped onto Philby's plastic boot covers. "Pardon. No offense. I still hate the . . . taste. Keeps me alive, I think, my human thoughts think, but tastes like essence of crap profane."

"You've heard what happened to the Quantist crew?" Philby asked.

"Bloody *criaock* and *oonshlr#hack*."

The translator could not work with this humanized pronunciation; so little was known of Chujoan language anyway, the Masters being spare with their communications. Philby jotted the words on his notepad in the Chujoan phonetic devised by the Japanese, who had dropped transmitters into a number of encampments and farm centers four years before Philby's ship arrived in the Murasaki System. The Chujoans had tolerated the transmitters, and what few phrases they uttered had been fed into the All Nihon shipboard supercomputers. The Japanese had been kind enough to share their knowledge with Philby.

They knew Philby would be useful. He was, after all, rational—unlike the members of the God the Physicist Church, the Quantists.

"I've come to talk about Carnot," Philby said. Kammer hummed briefly and leaned on his thick, snug-encrusted stick. Dusk was settling quickly, and Genji was a huge rotten orange high above, its own sunset line green and purple and yellow. "He's using your name. Claims to have been blessed by you. He's spreading a religion, if you can call it that, around the Ihrdizu associations, the families...."

"I know little about the Ihrdizu," Kammer said, voice cracking. "Never been there." The leathery face seemed to half smile.

"He met with you, talked about his version of Jesus with you. He says you have seen visions of Chujo and Genji united under the rule of Jesus, who will come to these planets when the time is right."

The moss-covered mummy shrugged. "We didn't talk much, doing the first," Kammer said.

Philby tried to riddle what he meant, and decided to let context be his guide. The notepad was recording all—perhaps meaning could be found later.

"Doing the second, he was already ill. Could see that."

"You met with him twice?" Philby asked.

Kammer nodded. "Sick the second time. He was doing the wind."

"He was ill with the plague," Philby paraphrased hopefully, his skin crawling even beneath the protective suit at the thought that Kammer had probably been the source of that plague.

"He was doing the wind," Kammer said. "Pardon me. He was almost dead. He was looking for signs. I did what I could."

"What was that?"

Kammer shook his head slowly and lifted his stick. "I hit him." He brought the stick down on the ground with a sharp crack. Philby noticed there was snug on the stick as well. Some of the snug on the stick fell away in patches. "He made away before I could hit him again."

"Do you know where Carnot has set up his base?" Philby asked, hoping that Kammer's use of his stick had reflected an extreme personal distaste.

"Wonderful man," Kammer said, hawking again—his entire chest patch of snug heaving like a sewage-befouled sea—but not spitting. "I don't. Where he is. On Chujo or Genji. Who are you? Beg pardon. That means . . . What will you be doing here?"

General clean-up. Triage. Sanitizing. After four years of intermittent dialogue with the Quantist ship, between the stars, pondering imponderables, watching their quasi—New Age religion grow to an obsession in the rainbow-belted times, the times of funhouse stars, in the dark profundities of loneliness every ship knows . . .

"I'm here to investigate the plague," Philby said, adjusting his hydrator. "And to find Carnot."

Kammer laughed. "Thinks I'm something."

"I'm sorry, I don't understand."

"Risked doing martyr to the bullyboys. The trolls. They dislike anything new. Do the thorn fence." Kammer made a disgusting excretory sound in his throat and rasped, "Knew. Knew."

Philby glanced at the line of Chujoans standing mute, motionless, six human paces east of them, and the trolls—good name that, and original with Kammer, apparently—standing with mindless patience at the edge of the village waiting for some false move, some physical or biochemical sign of his alienness, his undesirability.

"He survived the plague," Philby said offhandedly, as if conveying sad news.

"Know that," Kammer said. He snorted, looked directly at Philby, and Philby saw for a moment the remaining humanity, as one might see the shadow of a former man in the face of one who has walked the streets too long, cut away from social graces. "Vector of the cultural disease."

"Yes," Philby said, surprised that Kammer was so in tune with his own thoughts. "Then you agree with me, that he—that his people are a danger?"

"You try to block him?"

"Yes," Philby said. "We . . . communicated with them on the way to Murasaki. They're from the American Southwest. Fifty million New Age believers in the Southwest commissioned a starship from orbiting—"

"How?"

"I beg your pardon?"

"How will you do the stopping?"

"By going from village to village among the Ihrdizu, and telling them the truth. Not mystical nonsense."

Kammer smiled, his teeth a ruin encrusted with gray. "Doing the good. I mean, that's good of you. What will you make of Carnot . . . doing with him when you find him?"

"Make him stop polluting these worlds," Philby said.

"Ah. A service to us all."

"You tried to stop him as well, didn't you? With your stick?"

"He's alive, isn't he? You'd better go now," Kammer said, turning his head and poking his raw-looking chin at their Chupchup observers. "They'll make you do martyr soon. Best pass on your message from Heaven and do a . . . be a trotter. Trot off. You're beginning to *bore* them, you silly wretch."

"Do I bore you as well, Kammer?" Philby said sharply. He trusted the trolls would not detect or react to his human irritation.

Kammer said nothing, the whited eyes with their pastel-green irises and pinhole pupils moving back and forth independently, like a lizard's hunting for a flying insect.

"No, old fellow," Kammer said. "I'd really like to sit and do the talk some more. But my skin tells me I'm not up to it. I always listen to my skin. Without it, I'm an indigestible memory."

Philby nodded, the gesture almost invisible inside his helmet. "Thank you, Mr. Kammer," he said.

Kammer had already turned and begun his limping retreat to the safety of the village. "Nothing, old folks," Kammer said. Lurching on his beggar's rearranged limbs, S-curved back hunched like a ridge of iron-rich mountains, without looking back he added, "Hope you know what the lo-Ihrdizu *fchix * are saying to these." He waved a thin, crooked hand at the shaman and his attendants.

Philby didn't. He had to take that risk.

The flat-faced, large-eyed shaman approached, ears swung forward like tiny sails, and without looking at him, as if direct eye contact was either unknown or an unspeakable breach, snatched the Ihrdizu package from Philby's grasp and walked away, quietly erecting his genitalia and pissing all over the sacred himatid pelt wrapper.

Philby, hair on his neck rising with fear of blue troll claws and shark teeth, walked away from the village to rejoin the transport crew on the cliff ledge a kilometer outside the village. The Japanese escort, a small, attractive, middle-aged woman named Tatsumi, bowed on his return. Sheldrake and Thompson, pilots from his own crew, stiffened perceptibly. He lifted his arms and they sprayed him down, just as a precaution. *Our own pissing ceremony.*

Kammer's spit had landed on the toes of his disposable boots.

"He's become the Old Man of the Mountain," Philby said, doffing the boot covers and tossing them into the transport's external waste-hopper. Removing the helmet, he was left with only a hydrator and supplemental tank. Doffing these, he climbed into the transport. Tatsumi, Sheldrake, and Thompson followed. "He knows what I'm here for. I think he approves."

Dream journey above the pastel land, dreary dry old Chujo, yellow husk of a world with a thin cloak of dry air and an illustrious past, if what the Japanese had witnessed years ago—that incredible ceremony of bioloons carrying Chupchups high into the atmosphere—was any indication . . . And of that, Philby was doubtful.

Edward Philby, First Planetfall Coordinator of the multinational starship *Lorentz,* who answered only to the captains and First Manager, tried to sleep and found himself opening his eyes to stare over the mountains and once, briefly, a small pale-green lake with ancient shores like lids around a diseased eye. *We have come so far and suffered so much to be here.*

He concentrated on the crooked shape of Kammer in his thoughts, broken and mummified, smelling like an unwashed tramp and yet also like something else: flowers. An odor of sanctity. Eyes like that lake.

The Quantists had come here to find something transcendental, their ragged poor ship surviving the voyage just barely, their faith strengthening in the great Betweens, knowing they could not return if they could not find It here, and they had been lucky. They had found It, and then It had killed them as mercilessly as the unthinking void. . . . *Listening to the tales of their shipboard problems, the technical problems with a ship not well made, the social problems with a crew chosen haphazardly, on principles of ignorance. Coming to truly despise Robert Carnot as it became obvious the New Agers were falling into the grip of an even more radical revelation, receiving truth . . . The bitter debates coming to an end, mutual silence . . . And realizing the New Ager ship would reach Murasaki first, a year ahead of the British ship. Arriving first, and eager to spread their revelation. And before the* Lorentz *had gone into orbit, hearing the news, that ninety percent of the* Benevolent's *crew had died of an unknown plague, and several dozen Japanese, as well. Relief at the decimation of a foe? Sadness? Triage . . .*

But Carnot and twenty of his shipmates had survived, and their faith had strengthened, as Carnot integrated Kammer into his new religion: a glory of Chujoan biology, the truly transcendental; that which takes a man and transforms him into a survivor and a symbol. Carnot had said: "He is resurrected. The old Kammer died, just as we thought. They resurrected him, cured him of his radiation disease and his wounds, and imbued him with their spirit of Christ." *A dirty, ragged, smelly sort of Christ.*

Tatsumi saw that he was not asleep. "You are worried about the settlers on Genji," she said. "Your countrymen."

"They're not my countrymen," Philby said. "I'm English. They're bloody Southwesterners from the U.S.A."

"I beg your pardon."

"Easy mistake, we might as well be a state of the U.S.," he said. "Europe won't have us now. And the Spacers won't have the Earth now. Or rather, *then* . . ." He waved a hand over his shoulder and the seat back; time dilated by decades. He had not bothered to catch up on the thin messages from distant Sol, slender lifelines to far-flung children.

She smiled and nodded: Earth history, all past for her as well.

"You believe they will do great damage," she offered cautiously, as if Philby might be offended to have a Japanese commenting upon people at least of his language and broad culture, if not his nationality.

"You know they will, Tatsumi-san," he said. "Kammer knows they will. He says he tried to kill Carnot and failed."

Tatsumi pressed her lips together and frowned. She did not appear shocked. "Carnot thinks Kammer is a . . . Jesus?"

"An avatar of the ancient spirituality of Chujo," Philby said. This he had picked up from conversations with several Quantists during welcoming ceremonies on Genji. *Welcome to the world we have already made our home, and the peoples we are already trying to convert. Pity you couldn't get here sooner.* "Cognate to Jesus. Jesus can be found in the universal ground state, where all our redemptions lie. God the Physicist shows us the way through physics. Just what the Ihrdizu need—visitors from the sky able to take messages to Heaven."

"So you take messages in his stead."

"They know I'm not a spirit. I'm a man of solid matter. I don't feed them Physicist nonsense."

"And what will you do next?"

"Talk to Carnot, if I can find him."

Tatsumi frowned again, shaking her head. "He is not on Chujo? Our information was that he had left the mountains of Nighland to come here. . . ."

"I've been looking for him for the past three weeks."

"Then he must be back on Genji. If he is there, I can find out where he is, and take you to him."

Philby hid his surprise. "I thought your people wanted to stay out of this."

"We thought all the cultists would die," Tatsumi said, lowering her eyes. "They did not."

Philby looked at her intently. *Did you offer them your cure? No; they had already found their own, somehow. Would you have offered them your cure?*

"Pardon my inquisitiveness—" Philby began.

"Your *inquisition*?" Tatsumi interrupted with a faint smile. He returned her smile, but with slitted eyes and an ironic nod.

"Believe me, I represent no religious authority on Earth. We are England's last vanguard, but England is hardly a religious state."

"Of course not," Tatsumi said.

"I'm wondering just what your position is on these settlers."

"Earth will keep sending them," Tatsumi said sadly. "There is nothing we can do. Dialogue takes decades. The people back home have apparently made the Murasaki System into a symbol of . . . manliness? National prestige? Earth in particular. They purchase broken-down starships, and they flee the solar system to die in darkness. Some survive. We cannot fight such a thing."

"There are two more ships nearby," Philby said. "They'll be here in a year or so."

Tatsumi nodded. "We hope they are as enlightened as your own expedition."

Irony? "Thank you," he said.

"But since dialogue with the solar system is so difficult, we wonder where you derive your authority. You represent no church, and any government is too far away to instruct you. Who gives you orders to quell the Quantists?"

Philby shook his head. "Nobody outside of the Murasaki System."

"Then you perform your duty autonomously?"

"Yes."

"Self-appointed."

He flinched, and his face reddened. "Your people should remember the nastiness of a cultural plague. The nineteenth century . . . Admiral Perry?"

"Nobody forces the Ihrdizu to accept our commercial products. There are none yet to force upon them. And the West came to Nihon before Perry. We had had Christians in our midst for centuries before Perry. They were persecuted, tortured, murdered by their own people . . . yet fifty thousand still lived in Japan when Perry arrived."

"What Carnot wants to force upon the Ihrdizu could lead to war, death, and destruction on a colossal scale."

"Carnot seems to want to reestablish the ancient links between Chujo and Genji, to teach them to build great cities once again, and recognize their brotherhood," Tatsumi said. "A kind of interplanetary nationalism, no?"

Thompson, who had listened attentively and quietly in the seat behind Tatsumi, leaned forward. "We're here to preserve Ihrdizu self-rule. Carnot is a missionary. We can't allow the kind of violation of native cultures that happened on Earth."

"Oh, yes, that is true," Tatsumi said. She appeared mildly flustered. "I do not wish to be flippant, Mr. Philby, Mr. Thompson."

"They're out of their minds," Philby said, grimacing. Listening to Thompson, though, he realized how much his people sounded as if *they* were mouthing a party line, rehearsed across years in space; how much it sounded as if they might be the persecutors, the inquisitors, as Tatsumi had so pointedly punned. "They really are."

"A cultural plague," Tatsumi said, attempting to mollify when in fact no umbrage had been taken.

"Precisely," Philby said. *What Kammer said. Have the Japanese spoken to Kammer?*

Sheldrake had kept his silence, as always, a young man with a young face, born on the journey and accelerated to manhood, but still looking boyish.

"What do you think, Mr. Sheldrake?" Tatsumi asked him.

Sheldrake gave a sudden, sunny smile. "I'm enjoying the landscape," he said in his pleasant tenor. "This is very like Mars. But I've never been to Mars. . . . "

"Please be open with us," Tatsumi pursued, very uncharacteristically for a Japanese, Philby thought.

"It's not their war," Sheldrake said, glancing at Philby. "It's ours. No matter what we do, we're imposing. I think we just have to reduce that imposition to a minimum."

"I see," Tatsumi said. "Do you know the story of a man named Joseph Caiaphas?" she asked him.

"No," Philby said. She queried the others with a look as they seated themselves in the tiny cockpit. None of them did.

Across the channel between the two worlds, on heavy, storm-racked Genji, Robert Carnot walked around the temenos, watching the Ihrdizu workers stalk on strong reptilian legs through the sporadic pounding rain, carrying bricks and mortar and covered buckets of paste-thick paint. He rubbed his neck beneath the seal, wondering how much longer this shift before he could take a rest, lie down. He disliked Genji's gravity and climate intensely. His back ached, his legs ached, his neck and *shoulders* ached from the simple weight of his arms. The pressure produced shooting pains in his skull. The hydrogen-helium mixture in his tanks hissed; twice now the valves had allowed in more oxygen from Genji's thick atmosphere than was strictly healthy at this pressure, and his throat was raw. With the Ihrdizu, he deliberately turned off the electronic modulator that brought his helium-shrill voice back to normal human tones; they seemed to prefer the shrillness.

He looked longingly up at the point in the sky where Chujo would be, if they could see it through the rapidly scudding gloom. Compared to Genji, Chujo was heaven . . . and even the Genjians thought so. Strangely, there were strong hints that the Chujoan Masters—so called by the Japanese who had witnessed Chupchup bioloons—regarded Genji as a kind of heaven, or at least a symbol of ascendancy.

The boss of the temple construction crew, a sturdy female named Tsmishfak, approached him with a pronounced swagger of pride. It was good that they should feel proud of what they had accomplished; their pride was good, not the civilized, stately antithesis of resentment that had so often brought Carnot's kind low.

"Tzhe in spatch endED," Tsmishfak told him, four red-brown eyes glancing back and forth on her sloping fish head, facial tentacles curled in satisfaction. The Ihrdizu had adapted quickly to this kind of pidgin, much more merciful to their manner of speech than to the humans'. The Japanese had never thought of creating a pidgin; the rationals would despise Carnot for doing so.

"Tzhe in spatch finitchED?" he asked, using an Ihrdizu inquisitive inflection.

"FinitchED," Tsmishfak confirmed.

"Then let me see, and if it matches the Chujoan dimensions—which I'm sure it does—we'll begin the consecration, and I can move on to the next temenos." Tsmishfak understood most of this high-pitched, ducksquawk unpidgined speech.

She guided him through the fresh rain—each drop like a strike of hail—to the site he had laid out two weeks before. The temple's exterior was still under construction; when completed, the walls would be smooth and white and square, sloping to the broad foundations to withstand the tidal inundations Tsmishfak's region experienced every few Genjian years. Muddy rain fell along the unplastered bricks in gray runnels; clay scoured by clouds from the high mountains above the village's plateau. He would be a Golem-like mess before this day was over.

The in spatch—inner space, interior—was indeed finitchED. Within the temple, out of the sting of clayed rain, the walls were painted a dreadful seasick green, the paint pigments mixed from carpet-whale slime and algoid dyes. Tsmishfak had assured him this was a most desirable and sacred color to the Ihrdizu. Carnot pretended to admire the effect, then noticed he was dripping mud on the clean green floor. Tsmishfak was as well.

"Lengd it," Carnot said, which meant simply, "I will length it," or "I will measure it." Tsmishfak backed away, awed by this moment.

Carnot wiped mud from his faceplate and produced a spool from his pocket. String unwound from the two halves of the spool into two equal lengths; he had made up this device several months before, aware that the temples were nearing completion and some sort of masonic service would be useful.

By lifting the spool toward the ceiling, Carnot indicated that it came from Chujo. That was a lie. No matter. What was important was the spiritual import.

He laid one string along the north wall, found it matched precisely, then laid the second string along the east wall. The second wall was the same length as the first. He then produced a simple metal protractor and measured the angles of each corner. Ninety degrees. A fine square box painted sick green. Perfect.

He raised his hands. "In the name of the Great Ground of all Existence, that which is called Continuum, which breathes with the life of all potential, which creates all and sees all, in the name of the human Kammer who has survived the bonding of human and Chujoan, in the name of the Ihrdizu Christ called Dsimista, who tells us that all worlds shall be one, I consecrate this temple, which is well-built and square and essential. May no one who does not believe in the Ground, in Kammer, and in Dsimista enter into this place. May a new community start here, that the Io-Ihrdizu will gather in villages, and then cities, and gather in strength, as well."

Tsmishfak found this eminently satisfactory, particularly as she understood only about a third of what Carnot had said. She echoed, in pidgin, his last commandment, stalked around the walls, then clacked her jaws to summon workers. The workers cleaned up the mud and the in spatch smelled of Ihrdizu, a not-unpleasant smell to Carnot, though pungent.

"Ny mer dert," Tsmishfak promised him as they returned to the exterior. The clayed rain had let up; now there was only drizzle. *Like living at the bottom of a fishbowl.*

"No more dirt, that's fine," Carnot said. "You've din guud, *akkxsha hikfarinkx.*"

Tsmishfak accepted this with a slight swagger.

Good, good, all is well.

"Must move on now," he said in plain English, walking to the edge of the plateau and trying to find his wife and the ship's second officer in the crowded beach area below. "Ah. There are my people." He nodded cordially to the solicitous Tsmishfak. "Must go."

"Dthang u," Tsmishfak said. "Dum Argado."

She was using both English and the Japanese she had acquired.

"You're most welcome," Carnot said. He felt he would die if he could not soon rest his leaden arms and relieve the weight on his back.

Tsmishfak bounced off on spring-steel legs to her workers near the temple, swagger lessened but tentacles waving enthusiastically. *Big lumbering thing. Something out of Bosch; fish with legs, but eyes above and below the jawline... anatomically improbable. Not easy to love them, but I do, Jesus, I do.*

Carnot switched on his modulator and found his wife by the ichthyoid pens, standing with the second officer on a wicker frame, nodding to some point of technicality being explained by a small male Ihrdizu. Not much call for the kind of work she was skilled in, helping poor natives feed themselves. The Ihrdizu did well enough at that. But scratch beneath their quiet strength and you found a well of anguish; paradise lost and set high in the sky. Connections broken with their distant relations, the Chujoans, millennia past... Desire to rise to Heaven and be one with another race. Another species. Or so he interpreted their stories.

What if his theories were correct? The rationalists would never accept that intelligent cultures—technological cultures—could rise and fall like fields of wheat coming in and out of season. Perhaps that was why they were looking for him, why he was finding it necessary—through the inner suspicion of aching instinct—to hide from Philby, his persistent, annoying, and finally infuriating debater between the stars.

Madeline saw his wave and gently broke off their conversation with the pen manager. It seemed eternities as they made their way back to the ship along the beach. The transport's struts were awash with thick swells of water— no spray under these conditions, only a fine mist like smoke around the sharp rocks. They waded through the swell, more eternities, then the second officer lifted the transport from the beach, its name becoming visible as it rose to a level with him: *2T Benevolent.* Second transport of the starship *Benevolent.* These transports—and the large lander that waited for them in the mountains—were among the few things on the *Benevolent* that had proven trustworthy. Blessings of small favors.

They touched down again near the lip of the plateau overlooking the beach, and he climbed through the door, wheezing. "Enough," he said. "They'll do fine without us. Let's move on."

Madeline touched him solicitously. "You're hurting, poor dear."

"I'm fine," he said, but her touch and sympathy helped. Madeline, thin small strong Madeline, so perfectly adapted to life aboard the *Benevolent,* could crawl into cubbies where large, lumbering Carnot could not hope to find comfort. Cramped starship, crowded with pilgrims. Madeline who had married him en route and did not share in the sexual-spiritual profligacy, even when her new husband did. Madeline of the bright intense gaze and extraordinary sympathetic intelligence; his main crutch, his main critic. Why did he not love her more? He smiled upon her, and she smiled back like a tough-minded little girl.

"I'd enjoy studying their fish farming," she said. "We *might* be able to give them benefit of our own experiences on Earth."

The second officer, a thin African-Asian, Lin-Fa Chee by name, did not share Madeline's interest. "They don't farm *fish,* madam," he observed. "And these people have farmed the ichthyoids for who knows how many thousands of years."

"Tens of thousands, perhaps," Carnot said. "Lin-Fa is right, Madeline."

"Still, they need us in many ways," Madeline said, staring through the window as the transport lifted and flew out across the oily rain-dappled sea. "They need *you,* Robert." She smiled at him, and he could read the unfinished message: *Why shouldn't they need me, as well?*

"Look," Lin-Fa said, pointing from his pilot's seat. "Carpet whales."

Carnot looked down upon the huge multicolored leviathans with little interest. *Carpet whales. Himatids, hih-MAH-tids, some called them, from the Greek* himation, *a kind of cloak. Great flat mindless brutes. Not even Madeline would wish to help them.*

■   ■   ■

ICHTHYOID

CONVEYOR-BELT ARMS SIFT THROUGH MUD AND MOVE NUTRIENTS TO A CHAMBER WHERE THEY ARE RECEIVED AND PROCESSED.

FEEDER TENTACLES

FEELER SPINES— ALSO THOUGHT TO PROVIDE TRACTION IN THE MUD

UNDERWATER PROPULSION SYSTEM SUCKS IN WATER, SHOOTING IT OUT IN THE REAR.

Suzy Tatsumi watched the distance lessen between the orbital shuttle and Genji. Tō no Chujo grew as small as a basketball held at arm's length, visible through the shuttle's starboard windows. She pushed her covered plate of food—sticky rice and bonito flakes topped with thick algal paste—down the aisle between the twenty seats, plucked it deftly from the air, and sat beside Thompson, who had already eaten from a refillable paste tube.

"Fruit yogurt," he said, lifting the empty tube disconsolately. "Supplemented. All we brought with us."

"I would gladly share..." Tatsumi said, but that was forbidden. They were still not sure of all the vectors a new wineskin plague might follow. Intimate contact between those who had lived long on Chujo, partaking of its few edibles—or the transfer of food possibly grown on Chujo—was against the rules.

Casual contact had not yet shown itself to be dangerous among those protected against the plague, but even so...

"I know how your people conquered the plague," Philby said to her. "A remarkable piece of work. But how did Carnot and the last of his people survive?"

Tatsumi shook her head. "We doubt they had any native ability to resist. We still do not know.... They were already cured by the time our doctors went among them. But they had suffered terrible losses, on the planet and on their ship.... There are only twenty of the original two hundred left alive."

"Could they have found the same substances you did?" Thompson asked.

"They did not have our expertise. Nor did they equip themselves with the sophisticated biological equipment we carried... the food synthesizers, large molecule analyzers, and the computer programs to run such devices. They arrived here in a weakened state, their ship crippled. We do not know how they survived."

"They get along with the Ihrdizu," Philby mused. "Maybe the Ihrdizu helped them."

"The Ihrdizu have not the biological mastery of the Chujoans," Tatsumi said. "And the plague originated on Chujo."

"Still, there might have been a folk remedy, something serendipitous."

Tatsumi was not familiar with that word. Her translator quickly explained it to her: fortunate, unexpected. "Perhaps," she said. "It was *serendipitous* that we found our own remedy in Chujo's deep lake muds. An antibiotic grown by anaerobic microbes, used to defend their territories against other microbes, and not poisonous to human tissues... Most unexpected. We thought we would all die."

Philby smiled. "Luck favors those who are prepared. . . . Which is why all of Carnot's people should have died. They're as innocent as children."

Tatsumi raised her eyebrows. "You admire their strength and their luck?"

Philby lifted an eyebrow dubiously. "What I admire has nothing to do with what damage they can do here."

"No, indeed," Tatsumi said, dreadfully aware that she had irritated this strange man yet again. She had met Carnot only once, when the *Benevolent* first arrived in orbit around Genji, a year and a half past, but she thought these two were well-matched as opponents. Determined, opinionated, they might be brothers in some strange Western tale of Cain and Abel, or *East of Eden,* which she had read as a girl back on Earth.

"Do you believe Genji and Chujo are so closely connected, biologically?" Thompson asked.

"They must be," quiet Sheldrake said from behind them all.

"What circumstance would bring organisms from Chujo to Genji?" Philby challenged with professorial glee. Tatsumi had noted that these people enjoyed debating, and seemed not to understand boundaries of politeness in such discussions. She had heard them argue violently among themselves without anyone losing face or apologizing, even when ranks were greatly disparate.

"Besides the rocket balloons from Chujo . . ." Thompson said.

"I don't yet accept those as fact," Philby said. He glanced at Tatsumi. "Your people didn't actually see rockets . . . just balloons. Bioloons. And those could have been a natural phenomenon."

"It seems pretty certain the elder Chujo civilizations were capable of some kinds of rockets," Sheldrake said. Tatsumi was attracted by the young tenor's calm, confident reserve. A child quickly, artificially raised to manhood in space . . . What strange wisdoms might he have acquired in those years? "But I was thinking of cometary activity—"

"Rare in the Murasaki System," Thompson noted.

"Or even extreme volcanic events. Chujo's ejecta might have carried spores into the upper atmosphere . . . and beyond."

"Not likely," Philby snorted. "Such a journey would almost certainly kill any living thing, or any spores. There's no easy mechanism, none that doesn't stretch credibility."

"Nevertheless," Tatsumi said, perversely enjoying the spirit of this debate, "the genetic material is closely related in many primitive organisms on Chujo and Genji."

"There's no denying that," Philby said. "I wish your people had solved this riddle before we arrived . . . there are too many other problems to take care of."

"You did not come here to find and solve such problems?"

"I did," Sheldrake said. "I'm not sure Edward did. . . ."

"Essence of crap profane," Philby said, not unpleasantly.

"What's that?" Thompson asked. Philby was not usually so expressive.

"Something Kammer said. He said his mouth tasted like essence of crap profane. After he expectorated red and green saliva."

Tatsumi wrinkled her nose despite herself. "Our biologists would love to be allowed to study him," she said. "His use of the snug-rug. How he managed to survive radiation-induced leukemia. What he eats, if he eats . . . We might have saved lives, had we been allowed to."

"I don't think anybody's going to study him without killing a lot of Chujoans," Philby said. "And that we will not allow."

A planetary consciousness . . . Something that united both worlds, something only vaguely felt by either the Ihrdizu or the Chujoans. If he could prove its existence, as one might prove the psychic link between two twins, then all of his beliefs would fall into place. . . .

Carnot tossed in his weightless bed within the *Benevolent,* drifting slowly between the cylindrical wall of the elastic net. He felt it was important to return to the starship every couple of weeks, important that he maintain direct contact with the ship's captain, who had suffered horribly from the plague, and might even now be insane.

When Carnot thought of what they had lost, of the price paid by 183 of the *Benevolent*'s crew, he felt a sick darkness rise inside him. Not all the faith, not all the conviction of his service to Jesus the Ground of All Being could erase his sense of loss. From here on, his life would be a scarred, dedicated emptiness; he knew he would be little more than an efficient shell; the old Carnot had been burned out, leaving fire-hardened wood.

He could not even find the fierce love he had once felt for his wife. He rotated to view her sleeping form beside him. He needed her, admired her enormously, but they paid each other the minimum due of affection, all each seemed to require now. She, too, had been burned hollow. Sex between them was at an end. Sex had always been a kind of play, and this close to the truth, this close to the death and disfigurement of their people, no play could be allowed.

And now to be hunted . . .

He closed his eyes tighter, hoping to squeeze a tear or some other sign of his humanity between the lids, but he could not. The shooting pains in his skull had subsided; his backaches and strained muscles had improved in the two days in orbit, breathing shipboard air.

He thought of the Earth and his young adulthood and the simple miseries that had filled him then. Had his people suffered any more than others had suffered for their faiths? Was he being pressed any harder than any other leader of peoples who believed in pattern and justice and order? These events had been enough to drain him of the pleasures of simply existing; was that the sure sign of his ultimate weakness, that he could no longer take satisfaction in serving Jesus? That he could no longer take satisfaction in having a wife, in breathing in and out, in not being hungry or in having survived that which had turned so many of his people into corpses or pain-racked monsters?

Now he found his one tear, and he let it bead beneath his left eye, then break free to float before his face, a true luxury. Deep inside, a younger voice said, *You're goddamned right you've had it hard. Space was supposed to be clean and clear-cut, with sharp dividing lines between life and death, a beauty of pin-sharp stars and mystic nebulae. It wasn't supposed to be this way, tending this horrible leaky tub across nine shipboard years, and then arriving on the inconceivably far shore and finding disease and hideous death. Not supposed to be that way at all. You've been pushed. Don't expect joy when you've been pushed this hard; do not be so demanding as to expect joy after what you've experienced.*

Carnot opened his eyes and saw Captain Plaissix floating in the open hatchway. Beyond Plaissix, through the transparent blister of the central alley's cap, Carnot saw Genji's blue-gray surface fall perpetually beneath them. "The Japanese have sent a message," Plaissix said. "They wish to speak directly to you."

Half of the captain's face had crumpled inward. The wineskin plague had been made up of Chujoan bacterioids particularly well-adapted to living on minerals; they had devoured much of the calcium in his bones, and in his nerves, as well.

"All right," Carnot said, giving up yet another attempt at sleep. He slipped from the net, glanced at Madeline, sleeping soundly, and floated past Plaissix, who tracked him with off-center haunted eyes.

The ship's communications center was in a constant state of repair. George Winston, the last remaining engineer, moved to one side to give Carnot room. The image of a young Japanese woman floated a few hands away from its expected position. Winston shrugged in apology: best he could do with what they had. Her voice was distant but clear.

"Carnot here."

"My name is Suzy Tatsumi," the woman said. "I've just traveled to Chujo and back with Edward Philby. We would like to arrange a meeting between your group and his. . . . To settle your disputes."

Carnot smiled. "I don't believe we've met, Tatsumi-san. I've been working with Hiroki-san of Station Hokkaido on Genji."

"He has transferred his responsibilities to me."

Apparently the conflict between Carnot's expedition and the rationalists was beginning to worry the Japanese. Until now, they had been content not to intervene in any disputes. Had this Tatsumi woman already been poisoned by Philby and his representatives?

"I have no time to meet with the rationalists," Carnot said quietly. "They are physically stronger than we are. They would have attacked us by now, if it weren't for their lack of offensive weapons. . . . They cannot harm our ship in orbit." Actually, he was not sure of that.

"Your problems do not seem nearly so . . . unsolvable," Tatsumi said. "Nor violence so near. I think it would be good for you to begin speaking to each other."

"You have remained neutral until now," Carnot said through tight lips. "I can only trust you will not join up with them, against us."

"There are many problems we can resolve, Mr. Carnot. We are very far from home, and it is ridiculous to fight among ourselves, when we have faced so many common dangers."

"Tatsumi-san, you underestimate the depth of divisions between our kind. I have already had my dialogues with Edward Philby. We spoke while still traveling here . . . in deep space. We talked to each other like students in a philosophy class, sharing opinions, until he accused me of wanting to destroy Murasaki's natural systems. He became intransigent. We know where we stand. If you will not take sides—" *And damn you if you stay neutral!* "—then please leave us to our histories," he fumbled for what he wanted to say, "our destinies. For what lies ahead."

Tatsumi regarded him with sad, serious eyes. "Mr. Carnot, Edward Philby has spoken with Kammer. He says that Kammer tried to kill you. If the man you consider so vital a link, if he himself believes you are wrong . . ."

Carnot laughed sharply. "Please do not argue my faith with me, Tatsumi-san. He struck me with his stick. He did not kill me."

Tatsumi said nothing, puzzled into silence, trying to riddle this human mystery.

"His stick, Tatsumi-san," Carnot repeated, surprised they had not guessed by now. "He blessed me with his greatest gift. Because of that blow, some of my people are alive now." He was too weary to waste his time with her any longer. "Good-bye, Tatsumi-san. If you wish to offer us help, we are not too proud to accept."

He ordered Winston to end the transmission. The engineer did so and stared at him as if awaiting more instructions. Captain Plaissix had come into the communications room and simply floated there, his deformity an accusation.

Carnot had applied the crushed and writhing balm of a patch of

Kammer's symbiotic snug, embedded by the stick in his own skin, first upon his wife, and then upon the others. By circumstance Plaissix had been last. Surely by circumstance and not by Carnot's own subconscious planning. Plaissix had been the most doubtful of his revelation regarding Kammer. The one most likely to frustrate their designs, after they had come so far . . .

Casual contact with the avatar was death; the Japanese had learned that much. But to arouse the avatar's passion, and be struck by him, was *to live.*

"Who is the fanatic, then?" Eiji Yoshimura asked. "And who is the aggressor?" The director of Hokkaido Station rose from his squat stone desk, cut from Genji's endless supply of slate, and stood by a rack of laboratory equipment. By trade Yoshimura was an agricultural biologist; he had never wished to be a politician, but deaths at the station during the plague had forced this circumstance upon him.

Tatsumi tried to say something, but Yoshimura was angry and raised his hand. "They are all fools. This Englishman Philby, by what right does he dictate his philosophies?"

"I regret Philby's determination—" Tatsumi began.

"They are all troublemakers!" Yoshimura ranted.

"Director, please hear me out," Tatsumi said, her own voice rising the necessary fraction of a decibel to break through her superior's indignation.

"My apologies," Yoshimura said, glancing at her from the corner of his eye. "I am not angry with you, nor critical of the work you have done."

"I understand, sir. Philby's fears are well-founded. Already Carnot has spread his religious beliefs to nine Genji associations. Already nine temples to their version of Jesus, and to Kammer, have been built, and villages established. Carnot will soon have a broad enough base of support to endanger our own mission, should he so choose—using Ihrdizu as his soldiers. His success is quite remarkable, and I would not put it past him, at some point . . . " She paused, wondering how much of Philby's attitude had penetrated her. "He might do so," she concluded, dropping her gaze.

Yoshimura considered this with deep solemnity. "Do you truly believe Carnot will go that far?"

"He has been pushed very hard," Tatsumi said. "By the plague, and now by the rationalists."

"I once would have counted myself among the rationalists," Yoshimura said. "But I have never tried to impose my will upon those who disagreed. Has Carnot made any converts in our camp?"

Tatsumi reacted with some surprise to this question, which had not occurred to her. "Not to my knowledge," she replied.

"I will inquire discreetly. You look shocked, Suzy."

"I find it hard to believe any of our people would believe such drivel." She spoke with more heat than she had intended.

Yoshimura smiled sagely. "We are human, too. We are in a strange land, far from home, and we can lose our bearings as quickly as anyone else. We do have some Christians among us—Aoki, for example."

"Aoki is very circumspect," Tatsumi said. "Besides, traditional Christians would hardly recognize the beliefs of the God the Physicist Church, as preached by Carnot."

"Such an awkward name," Yoshimura said, making a monkey face. "Still, I would hate to fight an army of Ihrdizu—led by the females, no doubt." His expression slumped into solemnity again, and he seemed very old and tired. "Try to reason with Carnot again. If he is still unwilling to meet with Philby, then ask him if he will meet with our people—with you."

"I do not believe he will. He is exhausted and depressed, sir."

"Do you know that for certain?"

"It's obvious."

"Then he's even more dangerous," Yoshimura said. "But we will try anyway."

Tatsumi sighed.

Six kilometers above sea level, perched on Mount Niitake, the first Genji station of starship *Descartes* overlooked a vast, broken deck of clouds, a muddy blue-gray horizon spotted with deep thunderheads, and to the north, a magnificent vista of ragged hogback ridges.

In the gymnasium, Philby stood up under Genji's excessive affection, muscles aching from the hour of acclimatizing exercise. With most of his time spent on kinder, simpler Chujo, the storms and thickness and pull of Genji was like being immersed in heavy sleep; but here was the core of their problem, among the apparently gullible Ihrdizu, who were building temples to Kammer— and to Carnot's Jesus. And who were changing thousands of years of tradition by banding together into makeshift villages.

Theresa O'Brien joined him in the gymnasium, dressed in exercise tights, short hair frizzed with the inevitable moisture. Theresa was the *Lorentz*'s female captain, nominally in charge of shipboard activities only, but still highly regarded, and still Philby's superior. "How's the tummy, Edward?" she asked.

"Ah, tight as a drum," Philby responded, thwupping his abdomen with a thumb-released finger. "I've never been in better shape."

O'Brien shook her head dubiously. "You've always inclined to more muscle than you needed, then neglected, then to gut. I watched you put on and take off at least three crewmember's masses during the journey."

"Brutal Theresa," Philby said dryly, continuing his leg-lifts.

"When are you leaving for the Showa Bay temple site?"

"In four hours," Philby said.

"I've come from Diana's bungalow," O'Brien said. Diana Cicconi was the expedition's First Director, directly above Philby in the chain of command. O'Brien squatted carefully beside him. Exercise on Genji seemed ridiculously slow; anything faster and they might injure themselves. She sat and watched his red face. "Don't overdo it."

"The exercise, or . . . ?" Philby didn't finish.

"We don't like what Carnot's doing any more than you," O'Brien said. "But the Japanese concern us, too. We're making an impression here, not just with the Ihrdizu and the Chujoans—with our fellow humans, as well."

"They seem to be on our side, certainly more than on Carnot's side," Philby said, stopping to devote his full attention to their conversation. "I hope Diana's not rethinking our plans."

"It seems to some of us that you're the one doing the rethinking."

"Diana put me in charge of relations with the *Benevolent*. We've all agreed they're dangerous; I'm following through."

O'Brien nodded. "Edward, it sometimes seems you're the aggressor, not them. What will the Ihrdizu think if . . ." She shook her head and didn't finish.

"If Carnot's made such an impression on them, and we constrain him?" Philby finished for her. She raised her chin in the slightest nod, as if wary of him.

"I apologize, Theresa," Philby said. "You know my temperament better than anybody. I'm thorough, but I'm not a loose beam. Reassure Diana for me."

"She's arranging for a reception. The Japanese are coming—and she tells me they're trying to get Carnot to come, as well."

"I'm always a man for dialogue," Philby said. He replaced the padded bench and weights and wiped his face with a towel. "But Carnot . . . I think he is not."

"Will you listen to Carnot if the Japanese convince him to come?"

"What will he . . ." Philby realized he was being excessively contrary, and that more argument might tip the balance in O'Brien's eyes. "Of course. I'll listen."

She turned to leave, and he could not restrain himself from saying, "But, Theresa, there must be constraint on their part. That should be clear to all of us. We are *protecting* the Ihrdizu from the worst parts of ourselves."

"Are we?" O'Brien asked over her shoulder.

"Yes," Philby said after a pause. "Any doubts on that score and we might all be lost."

"I do not doubt Carnot is a danger," O'Brien said, and closed the door behind her.

That evening, as Philby checked in with the *Lorentz* for up-to-the-minute map upgrades, the communications manager told him they had received a signal from two light-years out, from the first expedition, and that among the messages was something extraordinary. Philby read the newest message again and again, feeling both exhilarated and sad, and the wheels began to turn in his mind.

If he must meet with Carnot, then he wanted to be able to shatter that little plaster prophet once and for all. Now, he might have the hammer to do so.

When traveling at close to lightspeed, our geometry is distorted, such that, to an outside observer, we reveal aspects of our shapes that are not usually seen . . . around curves, edges. We are warped in ways we cannot feel. . . . Is this also not true of our souls?

Carnot inspected the eleventh finished temple, his legs and feet aching abominably. He used two canes now to support his weight; to the Ihrdizu, he called them "Kammerstaffs."

He had long since spread the story of Kammer's striking him. He had found an interesting analogy to his contretemps with Kammer in Ihrdizu storytelling, a resonance he could take advantage of.

Indeed, this was the very association of Io-Ihrdizu, so said Ihrdizu legend, where the angelic Szikwshawmi had landed in ancient times and struck the female warriors with staffs of ice to give them superior strength. At the same time, the Szikwshawmi had frozen the tongue-penises of the males, making intercourse in both senses of the word impossible. The females had gone out in their frustration and gathered in new males from distant villages, leaving frustrated females in *those* villages to go forth and do likewise . . . and so on, a great wave of Sabine rapes.

It was hardly a precise analogy. In some respects it was embarrassingly inappropriate; but the Ihrdizu found it compelling, and when searching for mythic roots, one had to bend and to be bent.

The temple, constructed in a thick patch of beach forest like giant, thick-stumped manzanitas, deep in a shadowy hollow filled with drifting mist and sea spray and dark tidal pools, was certainly the gloomiest that had been built so far. The Ihrdizu in this association, which spread from the shore to over ten kilometers inland, were larger, more sullen, more suspicious than any they had encountered before. The females certainly seemed to be brusquer and more dominating. There was also less monogamy here than elsewhere; females took two males as mates about half the time, reflecting recent depredations because of warfare with another association to the east along the coast.

This region had been visited by the Japanese only once, years before. Yet still the stories of Jesus and Kammer and Carnot and the Chujo connection had spread into these shadows and taken root. In this Carnot took substantial satisfaction. He had hooked into the myth, and the shoots would spread of themselves. *Even if I die.*

The temple matched the necessary specifications. Carnot performed the ritual blessing and walked on the sticks to the lander. The females watched him closely, beautiful agate eyes totally open, all membranes removed. The males were hiding. Sight of him was not for the weak and small. He was powerful. He was their reawakening.

"You have done well," Carnot told the chief females, who bounced and swaggered solemnly on their large rear legs, horizontal bodies quivering. He cringed inside at this unseemly alienness, craving the company of humans, wishing to be relieved of this burden; ashamed of his prejudice, he retreated on his Kammerstaffs to the ship, where Madeline and Lin-Fa Chee waited.

He took his seat in the transport and lay down the crutches. Madeline massaged his arms and shoulders. He lost himself in thought, ignoring her ministrations.

There was a disturbing trend. Five associations had so far refused Carnot. All of these had been visited by Philby and his agents, spreading rationalist doctrine. Carnot had heard only bits and pieces of this antithesis to his thesis: Philby was apparently feeding them visions of a future when Genji and Chujo would be united, not in any mystical sense but politically, in league with human advisers.

A dry, deadly sort of myth, Carnot thought. To tell the truth, he wasn't sure *what* role humans would play in his own scheme; perhaps none at all. There were so few of his people left. They could find comfort in a small corner of Chujo, perhaps acting as spiritual advisers, setting up a center for pilgrims. They would certainly not stride hand-in-hand into a bright future with the rationally corrected and technologically equipped Ihrdizu and Chujoans....

And yet still the Japanese tried to arrange a meeting, and still Philby's people visited the Ihrdizu associations, creating territories where Carnot could not operate.

It was a war.

Carnot realized how reluctant he had been, until now, to accept that fact. He had always felt hunted, opposed; he had always pictured the conflict in terms of a personal vendetta by Philby or some other; he had never devised a strategy whereby he might counterstrike. But it was clearly becoming necessary.

"Another message from the Japanese," Madeline said quietly when they were settled and the transport had lifted off. The ship's engines made a high-pitched whickering noise and the starboard side settled as they rose; Lin-Fa Chee corrected, and the transport gained altitude, but more slowly. The transports were well-made, but they were aging; there were not enough people on the *Benevolent* to run the machines necessary to make parts to maintain all the equipment.

"Of course," Carnot said, his face pale, eyes shifting between the window and the pilot.

"The captain thinks we should talk to them."

Carnot lifted an eyebrow. "Yes?"

"We need to barter," Lin-Fa Chee added. "We need spare parts."

"The captain has spoken with the Japanese, with Suzy Tatsumi. She says they will manufacture spare parts for us, in trade. . . . " Madeline's voice trailed off, watching her husband's reaction.

"Generous," Carnot said, closing his eyes again. He hoped his authority was not being undercut. If he could be said to be responsible at all, Captain Plaissix was responsible only for the *Benevolent;* Carnot was in charge of making policy on the planets.

"They'll only trade if we meet with them, and with the rationalists," Madeline said.

Carnot pretended to sleep.

"Robert, we have to make a decision soon," Madeline said, a note of worry in her voice. "There's a lot at stake."

"We'll meet," he said softly. "How many more temples?"

"Three, I think . . . Perhaps more next week."

"I want to see the ceremonies completed." He could speculate on the dimensions of the human conflict—small and bitter, perhaps never escalating to violence, but deadly to his cause—their cause—all the same. But what would the dimensions of a conflict between the Ihrdizu be? If Ihrdizu could not encompass contradictions in human doctrine, how would they react? What alien catharsis would their unplumbed psychologies demand?

Suddenly he was feeling very mortal—with more than a suspicion that what lay beyond mortality was not what he most fervently desired.

Philby walked slowly toward the loose line of twelve trolls. His hydration suit reeked of Chupchup protective scent. The trolls lifted their heads, each standing over two and a third meters high. They sniffed the air casually, remained where they were. Surely they could see he was not Chujoan; surely they had minds enough to recognize that scent alone did not guarantee his belonging.

But they restrained themselves, and once again added to the mystery of how they functioned in Chujoan society.

He passed between two of them, barely a meter on each side from their claws, their razor fangs barely concealed behind slack lips.

The shamans formed the next loose line. Beyond them lay the edge of the cluster of yurts that had been erected for this temporary settlement. Between the shamans and the main cluster squatted the yurt that Kammer had taken, or had been assigned, who could say which. He was on the outskirts, rather than in the center; that might be significant. Perhaps he was not as important to the Chujoans as this peculiar reception ceremony implied; perhaps Chujoan ritual went beyond the simple analogy of enfolding and protection, and put their most valuable icons on the edge rather than the center of their loose and mobile village.

Perhaps he didn't understand Kammer's meaning at all.

A loose dry breeze blew dust between the spindly legs of the shamans. The line parted, as if Philby had ordered the breeze as a signal. He could feel the casual, unreacting presence of the bullyboys behind him. He was coming to prefer Kammer's name to "trolls." It was so much more descriptive, evocative.

The work he had done in the past week to make this meeting useful—to be able to ask the question he would now ask of Kammer—had taxed his patience to its limit.

Now he approached the shamans, wearing only a hydrator; taking his chances without the isolation suit.

He had asked five of his ship's biologists, and three of the Japanese doctors and biologists, how much of a risk Kammer might pose to crews if they were actually exposed to his physical presence. None had been willing to give a straight answer at first; fear of the wineskin plague had distorted simple rational judgments, leading to hedged bets, hems and haws, a reliance on very fuzzy statistics.

Finally Philby had been able to draw a consensus from the scientists and doctors: Kammer was not much of a threat now. If indeed the wineskin plague had begun on Kammer, which was almost universally accepted, then it was likely that they had protected themselves against all possible varieties he might have generated.

Kammer could walk among them, if he so chose.

Philby stood outside the plaited reed walls of the yurt. "Hello," he said. Nothing but silence within.

"Hello," he called out again, glancing over his shoulder at the shamans, shivering despite himself. Which was worse—to be ignored as if one didn't exist, or to be recognized by something so intrinsically alien? In some respects, now that he was familiar with the two species, the humanoid Chujoans seemed much more alien than the Boschian Ihrdizu. . . .

"Doing you here?"

Kammer came around the other side of the yurt. Philby started, turned slowly, trying to regain dignity, and faced Kammer.

"I've brought a message," he said. "From your starship, on its way back to Earth. They're about five light-years out now. They intercepted Japanese reports that you had been found alive. . . ."

Kammer glanced up at the sky speculatively with one pale eye, lips moving. "Must be about two years ship time," he said. "Doing fast by now. Bit-rate way down. Bandwidth doing the very narrow."

"A woman who held you in high regard sends a message to you," Philby said. This, he hoped, was the shock that would jolt Kammer back to some human sense of responsibility. "It's rather personal, and I regret springing it on you like this, but its reception by our ship—and the Japanese ship, simultaneously—was hardly private. I thought I should tell you first."

"Something to be read, or just spoken?" Kammer asked. Philby interpreted that question as a promising sign. Curiosity, plain English syntax, a tone of some concern.

"You can read it if you wish."

Kammer's mummy mask slanted, wrinkled in something between a smile and puzzlement. "I know her. I did life with her." He tapped his leathery pate. "In dreams."

"Her name is—"

"Nicole," Kammer said.

Philby said nothing for a few seconds, watching the brown, tortured face reflect some inner realization, some reawakening of old memories. "Right. Nicole."

"What does she say?"

Philby held out a slate. Nicole had convinced the powers that be— apparently her husband, Captain Darryl Washington—that a message of several hundred words was necessary. This had required considerable diversion of resources—turning antennas around, readjustment, expenditure of valuable communications time. Philby had read the message several times. He had no idea what Kammer would make of it. If he had been Kammer—a long shot of supposition—Philby would have been deeply saddened.

Dearest Airy,

I cannot believe what we have heard. That you are alive! By what miracle is not clear to us; we have only been able to receive about three-quarters of the transmissions from Murasaki, and only since we stopped accelerating, turned off our torch. We all feel incredibly guilty about leaving you behind. There was no chance of your survival—we knew that, you must believe we knew that! I grieved for you. I punished Darryl for years. This has been cruel to all of us, but especially I think to him. Whom I punish, I feel the most sympathy for. . . .

What are you now, after so many years with the Chujoans? Do you still think of us, or have they changed you so much you have forgotten? I cannot tell you all that has happened to us. . . . We feel like such cowards, such fools, having left Murasaki just when the rush from Earth was beginning. We should have stayed, but we did not have the heart. Darryl wanted the riches; we wanted the riches and fame before we were too old. So we didn't finish our job. What reception we will return home to, I cannot say. . . . Perhaps the reception reserved for (L.O.S. 2.4 kb?).

. . . were the better man. I chose you. Know that about me now, Aaron, that in the end, I chose you, my body chose you. Darryl has lived with this, and I think I admire him more now, despite my punishments and inward scorn, for having lived with it.

We have a son, Aaron. You and I. He is your boy. He was born five months ago. I have named him after your father, Kevin. He is healthy and will be a young man when we return to Earth.

He will be told that you are his father. Darryl insists, especially since we've learned you are alive.

That knowledge grinds Darryl down more each night. Who can understand the grief of strong men?

I love you, Aaron.

Nicole

Kammer let the slate drop to the ground, then swayed like an old tree in a slight breeze. "I am not that same person," he said throatily. "He did the dying."

"I think that person is still here," Philby persisted. "You remember Nicole. You remember who you were. And you knew that Carnot would cause great damage. You hit him to stop him."

"I hit him to save him," Kammer said with a sudden heat. "Could not see them all do the dying."

"I don't understand," Philby said, eyes narrowing.

"They gave me this," Kammer said, lifting the stick covered with patchy snug. "Long times past. Years, maybe. I thought I was going to die. I felt as if I had died. Then I recovered, and then I began to die again. I did the bloating, too, and the filling with liquids, skin turning wine red, the twisting of bones. This," he indicated his contorted trunk and limbs, "was not from breaking my back. I did the sickness myself. Body like a skin full of wine. They gave me the stick, and the snug took me over. It found what was making me sick, and it killed them, or tamed them. I got better."

Philby's eyes widened, and for the first time in Kammer's presence, he felt a shiver of awe. What did the Chujoans know—what could they do? He slowly turned to survey the shamans, uncaring and implacable in their loose line between the two humans and the bullyboys.

"Hit him to save him, if he had the brains to know what it was I gave," Kammer said. "I see he did." Kammer's gaze was intense, his eyes seeming darker, more human now. "Perhaps that was when he did the prophet. Bent body, bent mind. Saved from death. Knew, knew."

Softly, shivering slightly, Philby said, "He wanted to be a prophet before they reached Murasaki. But you . . . blessed him, I suppose is the word." Philby sighed. All of his errors, his misinterpretations; was it due to arrogance? How much of his arrogance had poisoned the debate between the stars? How much had he driven Carnot to his hard positions, his fanaticisms? "We're going to meet with the Quantists, with Carnot. I think it's important that you talk with him."

"Can't go back and do the human thing," Kammer said. "Being this. Knew, knew."

"If you believe his distortions are dangerous—and you must, Aaron, you must!—you cannot refuse us this. Talk with him, tell him what you know. Try to make him stop this insanity. He could destroy all the Genjians have in the way of—culture, language, independent thought."

"Never did them," Kammer said.

"Aaron . . ." Philby stepped forward, hands beseeching. He removed his hydrator, to speak directly with Kammer. The cool dry air felt like dust in his throat, and he coughed.

Two trolls shoved him roughly away and spilled him on the ground. His mask flew high into the air and came down six or seven meters away. A troll loomed over him, baring its teeth, seeming to grin, examining his form as if it might be a long diversion from the troll's normal mindless boredom.

Kammer stood back, stick lifted as if to defend himself as well against the trolls, and said nothing.

The shamans moved in around Philby. He tried to get up, but the troll casually kicked his arm out from under him and he fell back. He prepared himself to die, but first he triggered the emergency signal in his belt. That would bring Sheldrake and Thompson; they were armed. If he was dead, they would do nothing but try to retrieve his body; but if he was still alive, they would carve their way through trolls and shamans alike to save him.

He considered this for a moment, realized what an ugliness might spread from another such incident—realized that what the Japanese had done, years before, might still linger between Chujoans and humans—and shouted to Kammer, "For God's sake, Aaron, this is awful! Stop them!"

He saw part of Kammer's twisted leg between the legs of a troll. The leg moved, then the stick came down with a thud. More snug dropped away from the stick. Fascinated, anesthetized by his terror, Philby watched the fallen patches of growth twist about and crawl along the ground, back to the stick.

"There isn't much I can do," Kammer said. "Lie still."

"Damn it, you're sacred to them! Tell them to stop!"

"I'm hardly sacred," Kammer said. The troll stepped aside, and Philby saw Kammer clearly. He backed away from the trolls, who showed their teeth to him with as much apparent enthusiasm as they did to Philby. "I thought you were smart enough to see. I'm an experiment, and nothing more."

The trolls turned suddenly on Kammer and shoved him rudely, knocking him from his feet. He struck out with his stick, but they ignored him. Another group of trolls loped to his yurt and began to tear it apart, tossing sticks, mud, and thatch in the air. In minutes, as they both watched from the ground, trolls looming but not striking them any more, the yurt was demolished and the dirt beneath it kicked over.

Kammer seemed to be laughing weakly. The shamans shooed the surrounding trolls away from the men with wavings of wands and noisy expectorations. They surveyed Kammer intently, one shaman squatting beside him and lifting his right arm. Kammer accepted this with no apparent resentment, still chuckling.

"We're lucky we're not doing martyr," he said to Philby. Philby tried to get up, but a shaman kicked out with a foot, delivering a blow more informative than painful, and he remained on the ground. Sheldrake and Thompson stood a dozen meters away, calling to Philby.

"Stay where you are—don't do anything unless they set the trolls on us again!" Philby shouted.

"What's happening?" Thompson asked.

"I don't know!" The shaman kicked him again. "Son of a *bitch*," he exclaimed. Sheldrake raised his weapon but did not fire.

"Be still," Kammer called. "If you want me, you have the all of me. If I'm still alive, I'm yours."

"What are they doing?"

"Finishing, I think," Kammer said. The shamans turned him over on his stomach, prodded him with their own sticks, and finally pushed and kicked and rolled him until he was within a couple of feet of Philby. Kammer regained his breath, his entire bent body shuddering, and moaned, leathery lips still wreathed in a smile. "You've made a lot of nasty noise. I'm not worth it any more. I think the experiment is over."

"They are the *goddamnedest* most arrogant sons of bitches," Philby shouted, pounding the bulkhead behind the transport cockpit. Sheldrake grinned ruefully and edged past him. Their new passenger sat gingerly in a rear seat. Thompson stayed well clear of him as he closed the hatch and stowed the weapons.

All but Philby remained in their isolation suits. Lack of conviction in their science; rational thought giving in to fear. They had their prize, but hardly knew what to do with him.

Philby gradually controlled his rage, glanced back at Kammer, and edged down the aisle to sit in the seat across from him. Philby could hardly restrain his urge to retch, though Kammer's odor of flowers was stronger than his odor of unwashed humanity. Constrained within the transport, contrasted with the clean technological lines of seats and walls, Kammer seemed even more of a ruin.

The transport lifted away. They would take Kammer to the nearest Japanese station—Hokkaido—and leave him in quarantine there, if the Japanese gave permission, and they almost certainly would. There was hardly time enough to take Kammer up to the *Lorentz,* and not nearly enough of their own equipment on Genji to examine him. The Japanese would have to be the ones to benefit from this windfall.

Sheldrake was informing them of the circumstances now.

"Welcome back," Philby said to Kammer.

"Doing the anger bit," Kammer commented, nodding at the bulkhead and then at Philby, milky eyes blinking slowly. "Don't blame you."

"I hadn't expected this," Philby told him.

"Expected it for many times," Kammer said. "I don't sleep. I eat very little. But I'll die."

Philby stared at Kammer, wondering what he meant. "You need special nutrition . . . your snug needs something special?"

Kammer's head bobbed on his neck and the snug slithered about his body. "I'm not like you now. Test-tube specimen. Can you save me?"

"We'll certainly try."

"Not so profound. Not so . . . able to die happy. After all this. Christ, Philby, can I learn to speak again?"

"I hope so," Philby said, anger suddenly changed to sadness. Kammer seemed so subdued, in shock almost.

"I am an ugly thing," Kammer said. "I have a son. Nicole sends messages to me. She punishes him. Ah, the memories of that, Philby. I'm decompressing. Coming up from the depths again."

"Why did they reject you?"

"Learned what they needed to know," Kammer said. He began to choke or cough, then looked around with lips pursed. Philby promptly produced a specimen bag from his kit, and Kammer expectorated red and green saliva into it. "Crap profane."

Philby took the bag from him, sealed it, and marked it before stowing it in the transport biologicals box. Kammer looked through the port beside his seat at purple sky and wide pale-yellow desert.

"Did they send the plague?" Philby asked as he seated himself again.

"Not deliberately. I don't think," Kammer said. "Can you understand me? How's my grammar?"

"Good," Philby said.

"Good. I'm not human, Philby."

"Don't worry about that. The Japanese call them the Masters. They are, aren't they? Masters of biological engineering?"

"Not engineering. Farming. They farmed little things. Made spaceships out of organisms. Everything alive. We wondered about that long ago, in our youth; could such things be."

"And now?"

"Fallen, but still mighty. No more spaceships."

"Why are they so aloof?"

"Philosophy," Kammer said. When Philby pressed him, he seemed reluctant to explain further, but finally he said, "They're in the endgame. Doing the dying. They're meditating, I think. Want to go soon. Would have gone long ago."

"Chujo will stay livable for tens of thousands of years yet," Philby said. "Why are they so fatalistic? We can help them—give them the technology necessary to save their planet."

Kammer's torso shook. "Carnot would understand better," he said.

Philby wondered if he had just been laughed at. "But I'm serious. In a century, we'll be able to bring—" He caught himself. He had been about to say, "Bring ice from the asteroids," but there were no ice asteroids and few comets in the Murasaki System. He had lapsed back into Earth-think.

Kammer regarded him expectantly, saying nothing.

"We can bring water up from Genji, replenish Chujo."

"Maybe you can," Kammer said. "But they'll die anyway."

Philby slapped his fist on the seat arm. "Why, goddammit? Why such fatalism?"

"They're not you," Kammer said. "They do themselves only."

Sheldrake tapped Philby on the shoulder. Philby angled his torso around to peer through the helmet at him. "Suzy Tatsumi gives permission to bring Kammer to Hokkaido; seems quite excited by the prospect. And she says that Carnot will meet with all of us—our people and the Japanese."

"Good," Philby said. His original plan was not in ruins after all.

Through thick panes of glass, Suzy Tatsumi watched the doctors work on Kammer in the isolation room of the Hokkaido Station hospital. Kammer lay on a low table, stick clutched in one hand beside him, staring off into nothingness. His expression made her shudder. Dr. Nogura emerged after several hours of intensive examination and confronted her with weary but astonished eyes.

"He's a mess," Nogura said. "He shouldn't even be alive. The snug has worked its way into almost every part of his body. He's a symbiont now—with two different biologies cooperating. We have no idea what to feed him. He says he does not eat. He no longer has a urinary tract or an anus. He seems to excrete by spitting."

Philby entered the observation room. "What's the prognosis?" he asked in English. Tatsumi was irritated that he could not speak Japanese, did not even think to tune his translator to Japanese.

Tatsumi spoke English very well, but Dr. Nogura did not. Her eyes narrowed and she sighed. "Dr. Nogura is telling me now."

"Can Kammer attend the meeting?"

"I do not know, Mr. Philby. Please be patient."

Philby sat in a small chair, his big frame making it squeak in protest.

"Please continue, Doctor," Tatsumi said.

"He is adapted to conditions on Chujo, that much we know," Nogura said. "He could apparently survive in the open on Chujo indefinitely, if what he says is true—and I have no reason to doubt him."

Tatsumi passed this along to Philby, who nodded impatiently. "What about his psychological state?"

"He is calm, speaking clearly, though I do not personally speak English well. . . . My colleagues have been interpreting for me. They say he appears contented, but he is certain he will die soon. There is a possibility he will die if removed from Chujo. . . . Although . . . and here I hesitate, Tatsumi-san, because none of this is certain. But it appears that his body is adapted to high-pressure conditions as well."

Tatsumi asked what good that would be, on Chujo.

"None at all. On Genji, however, it would be very useful. Professor Hiraiwa is conducting tests now on specimens of Mr. Kammer's 'snug,' to discover their reaction to Genjian conditions."

Tatsumi translated for Philby, who wore a look of almost comic befuddlement. "Why would they do that? Give him abilities he'd never need?"

"Mr. Philby, you contemplate taking him to Genji, do you not?" Tatsumi asked.

"*They* wouldn't know that."

"I am much less certain about some things than you are."

"They'd have to expect us to take him there. . . . " Philby mused, crossing his arms. "They couldn't do it themselves."

"At one time, they could have gone to Genji. . . . Probably did go, and very often," Tatsumi said.

"That's a Japanese team conclusion we don't yet support," Philby said.

"Please do not be stubborn or devious with us, Mr. Philby," Tatsumi said sharply. "Kammer has told us his thoughts, and surely he has told you, as well. He says they could have once built spaceships, biological spaceships."

"He told me that," Philby admitted. "Do you believe him?"

"They might have used their bioengineering skills to adapt themselves to life on Genji," Nogura said, catching only part of the English conversation.

Philby looked at Kammer through the window, shaking his head and frowning. *Time to give in. Time to begin accepting the obvious.* "It's hard to be skeptical when I look at Kammer. But what about the plague?"

Dr. Nogura said, "The plague originated with Kammer, as we suspected. However, it appears that Kammer saved the remaining members of the *Benevolent* crew by striking Mr. Carnot with his stick. The snug contains chemicals that can regulate Chujoan bacteroids . . . or destroy them. These chemicals are similar to the chemicals we discovered ourselves, and used to protect our team members."

"But he only struck Carnot!"

"Mr. Carnot must have been a very intelligent man," Tatsumi said. "Perhaps he conferred protection upon his surviving colleagues. We must ask him when we all meet."

"How long before you can make a decision about Kammer?" Philby asked.

Tatsumi deferred to Dr. Nogura. "Two days," Nogura said. "There is a great deal more to study. We have an incredible opportunity. . . . "

"There may be a problem," Tatsumi told Philby as she escorted him out of the lab. "Kammer is insisting he be taken to Genji. He has been looking through our texts, on a notebook loaned to him by Dr. Hiraiwa. He wonders if you want him to meet with Carnot, and says he will only meet with Carnot on Genji."

"Why didn't you tell me this earlier?"

Tatsumi shrugged, slightly embarrassed. "I am not used to dealing with so many unreasonable people at once," she said, glancing at Philby as if expecting him to blow up.

"I see," Philby said. "Your doctors are sure he can survive there?"

"Perhaps better than we," Tatsumi said.

"You have trouble dealing with me. I have trouble dealing with all these ideas," Philby said, making an attempt at placation. Clearly Tatsumi was angry with him, with the entire situation; he did not want to antagonize her beyond her limits. He rather liked her; she would be an asset on any team.

"We must adjust quickly," Tatsumi said. "A crisis has been provoked. Carnot is establishing and sanctifying temples as fast as he can. Your people are trying to wall off his influence by going from association to association with their own stories. It is already a kind of war; the Ihrdizu are being changed by both sides."

Philby did not disagree. There was really nothing to say; it was true.

"I'd like this resolved soon," he told her. "It's very painful to all of us."

"I can arrange for a meeting," Tatsumi said. "I can set up a spot on Genji, near a large Ihrdizu whaling association that has not been touched by either of you. There you can meet with Carnot, and there Kammer can...do whatever it is he plans to do."

"He's on our side," Philby said.

"He saved Carnot," she reminded him. "He is hardly even human now. You cannot say whose side he is on."

Her anger had, if anything, increased. Philby inwardly saw himself as Tatsumi must have seen him. His neck muscles twitched, and he turned away. "I am not a zealot, Tatsumi-san," he said.

"You think you are antibody, don't you?" she asked, walking around to stand before him. "Antibody for all of the Murasaki System, to prevent contamination by human folly. Well, we are here also, and we are human also, Mr. Philby." Her face was stiff, eyes wide. "The meeting will be neutral, Mr. Philby. We will give you no advantage. Kammer will be in the care of our biologists and physicians. You will speak with him no more. No more prompting. We will not take part in a war, even if it is to be without weapons!"

Philby regarded her, face flushed. They were taking Kammer away from the *Lorentz*. There was nothing he could do about it. "All right," Philby said quietly. "You think you can afford neutrality. I understand that." He stepped around her and pushed open the door to the air lock.

Tatsumi raised her fists to the ceiling, felt the tears start in her eyes, and shook her head furiously, alone in the corridor where nobody could see her.

Chujo and Genji moved across the hours around each other, in Lady Murasaki's novel brothers-in-law, but in planetary terms husband and wife, gravitational lovers, condemned to never touch, growing farther apart centimeters each year. Yet they had touched, once tens of thousands of years ago, through the proxies of their children. Perhaps for a thousand years they had remained in communication. And then . . .

Tatsumi lay in her bunk, trying to sleep after the passage from dry lightness to wet and heavy darkness, from Chujo to Genji. Breathing the damp cool air of the highland base at Honshu Station, she had felt her sadness deepen, and wondered if perhaps, after so much time on Chujo, Genji was working a kind of seasonal depression on her, like a plunge into winter in Japan.

Absurdly, she was saddened by the image of worlds apart, like lovers. Her parents had been forced by their separate employers to live apart for years, in a strange and even feudal struggle to keep families loyal to one corporation, one *zaibatsu*. . . . Only after her father had attempted *seppuku* while on a business trip to United Korea had his corporate parents relented, and the family had become one. Ten years of such misery.

She had traveled so far to escape the injustices of Earth, only to find an analogy, a myth of her own making perhaps, that saddened her. She saw—perhaps irrationally—that Philby wished to prevent a reunification of Chujo and Genji, facilitated by humans, but reunifying nonetheless. She saw as clearly as Philby that reunification was merely a blind for Carnot, who was playing midwife, living a spiritual myth vicariously, but also conceiving and delivering a child whose shape no one could predict.

These disturbing thoughts echoing unity and apartness had plagued her for several hours already, but she refused to induce sleep. So much was artificial about her existence: the food she ate, the air she breathed, the daily round of her existence. Surely she could enjoy natural sleep!

In less than two hours, she would interview Kammer one last time, then escort him and the biologicals team to the fishing association on the coast below Honshu Station.

Carnot had agreed to come meet there.

Dr. Hiraiwa had agreed to provide spare parts and supplies to the Quantists.

Edward Philby, speaking for the male and female captains of his ship, had agreed to the ground rules for the meeting.

Now, to put the last piece of the puzzle together, she had to see what Kammer's state of mind would be. He had agreed tacitly to everything so far. *He looks upon me with those pale eyes, and he is sad as well. Philby was cruel to tell him about his son, to give him his lover's message. They are separated now, by circumstances neither can overcome.*

She felt the bunk shift beneath her, liquid-filled mattresses adjusting to prevent skin lesions.

What about my own separation? Can one be apart from somebody one has not yet chosen?

In time she did sleep, but only for an hour and a half. Genji's clouded night still lingered and snow fell around Honshu Station as she dressed in the crew lounge, preparing herself for the long sojourn in the planet's heavy deeps.

Two hundred kilometers from Honshu Station, the Ihrdizu fishing shelter of Kiariakchou!ck stood on an artificial rock plateau some twenty meters above the beach. Only fishing shelters for the seasonal whalers and fishers, boat launches, and wide racks draped with the skins of harvested carpet whales had been erected along the shore. Storm surges and tides could wipe out these structures at regular intervals. To protect their resources, the fishers and whalers had constructed a strong stone shelter on a plateau overlooking the shore, and given it an almost unpronounceable name.

Only fishing associations left large permanent structures on Genji. Fishers and whalers from associations hundreds of kilometers around gathered here to harvest the seas, as a kind of migrant community. Sometimes they chose mates here; sometimes fresh associations were born in the minds of various females, and they took their new mates outside the boundaries of the old associations to start new fishing centers.

A storm was brewing now to the south, and it looked to Tatsumi— observing from the window of her transport—that it might be a strong one, strong enough to make the Ihrdizu withdraw from the shore, dismantle their huts, roll their himatid skins and squirrel them away in the stone-walled shelter above. She pointed this out to Dr. Hiraiwa and Dr. Nogura. Hiraiwa consulted the transport's radar and a Japanese satellite picture.

"It's at least five hours away, which should allow plenty of time for the meeting," he concluded. He glanced at Aaron Kammer, who sat quietly in the rear of the transport. "If we have arranged things properly. Who knows how to handle such volatile people? They are alien to me. . . . And I used to live among English and Americans, before I volunteered for this journey."

Dr. Nogura smiled. "They are irritating, but they are not incomprehensible. Each has his motives, each his outlook . . . like ourselves."

"*We* strive for unity of purpose," Dr. Hiraiwa said testily.

"The role of a maker of compromises is not dishonorable," Nogura said, shrugging slightly.

Tatsumi checked her notebook for time. They were less than ten minutes away from the village. She unhooked her seat belt and walked back carefully to where Kammer sat.

"We'll be there soon," she said. "How are you?"

"Heavier," Kammer said. "Not uncomfortable."

Tatsumi looked on him with undisguised wonder. Kammer was the genuine mystery in the midst of all this sordid conflict. Dr. Hiraiwa's biologists had monitored him for three days, taken tissue and snug samples, analyzed him from gnarled toes to leathery bald snug-covered crown, but they had not been able to measure Kammer's mental state, or come to understand his reasoning. Why did he wish to venture onto the surface of Genji? He seemed to know his abilities, as a bird might know that it is built to fly; they could not constrain him in a helmet or suit—his snug would die if they did, and he would die with it—but the consensus among the biologists was, he could survive indefinitely without aid in Genji's thick lower atmosphere, the only human who could do so. And he knew it.

He had politely refused their offers to let him see the association and shelter in their vid and photo collections. He had used the notebook loaned to him, but only to access and read text novels from the twenty-first and twentieth century—romances, chiefly, in English and French. He had ignored the preparations, paid little attention during all the attempted briefings, answered few questions.

"Are you ready?" she asked him. The odor of flowers and stagnant moss—and an odor of wet dog—assaulted her nose. Kammer twisted his head back, the snug crawling around his neck, and gave her a gray-toothed, cracked-lip smile.

"You do the understanding, the standing between, don't you?" he asked in English.

It was the first question he had asked her directly. "I try," she said. She had no doubt about what he meant.

"Learned much myself on Chujo about understanding and standing between. Masters and slaves. Everybody's right, everybody's wrong."

This was much less clear. She sat, buckled herself in, said nothing, willing to just let Kammer talk even if he rambled. Nogura and Hiraiwa listened as well. No doubt recorders were on; Kammer had no private existence. He did not seem to notice or mind.

"Have there been any more messages?" he asked.

"From who?"

"From Nicole. From my . . ." He coughed. "Family."

"Mr. Philby hasn't mentioned any to us, and our ships haven't received any."

"When this is over, I'd like to send a message to them. Is that possible?"

"I think so," Tatsumi said.

"I'd like to tell them a few simple things, set their minds at ease." He smiled again, that ghastly, corpse-of-old-man grin. "That I think of them, even though everybody assumes . . . I'm doing the missing me."

Tatsumi frowned in puzzlement. "I beg your pardon?"

"Assumes I'm not here. Who would be here?" He tapped his head. "After all I've seen. Years among the Masters. Aloof sons of bitches. Good reason, too. Doing the endgame."

Tatsumi nodded.

"Carnot will be there?" he asked.

"He says he will be."

"This is a large village, near the shore?"

"Yes," she said. "Not a village, actually. An association of fishers and whalers. Whaling now, this season."

"We can take boats out on the water?"

This was something new. "I don't know about that," she said. "We've made no arrangements. We have no boats of our own there."

"All right," Kammer said. "Just curious."

The transport passed through a bumpy high-pressure ridge lying offshore on its curving path to approach the association from the sea. Kammer looked through his port intently, ignoring Tatsumi. She kept her seat, however, in case he should speak some more.

"Boats," Kammer said. "Fishing boats." He pointed through the window. A flotilla of Ihrdizu boats lay some ten kilometers offshore. Tatsumi saw that they were carpet whalers. There did not seem to be any of the himatids visible. Somehow, she was relieved; the whaling disturbed her on an instinctive level, never expressed. Japanese had savaged the very different whales of Earth's seas for decades longer than they should have; there was still controversy about that historical episode.

"Brave creatures, doing the sea," Kammer said softly.

They passed low and slow over the shore, and landed a hundred meters from the tide line.

"Carnot's ship is here," Dr. Hiraiwa observed. "At least this much is accomplished."

Tatsumi looked through the port and frowned. He was not supposed to arrive early; Philby might interpret that as a breach. *Perhaps it is a breach. What has he done? Has he spoken to the Ihrdizu here, proselytized? The culture team will have prevented that . . . I hope.*

All but Kammer donned helmets with helium/hydrogen mix tanks for the excursion. Hiraiwa and Nogura watched anxiously from within their helmets as the transport's air-lock pressure completed the slow equalization that had begun since they left Honshu Station. Kammer stood steady against the weight and the inrush of Genjian atmosphere, thick and moist. The air lock filled with steam, which vanished immediately as the outer door opened. Hiraiwa stepped out first, then Kammer, with Nogura and Tatsumi following.

Kammer stood on the flat slate stones of the upper beach, turning this way, then that, as if getting accustomed to a place he had been away from for a long time, but a place he knew nonetheless. He did not betray any distress.

The three Japanese stood around him anxiously awaiting an adverse reaction. Kammer reached out with a twisted arm and touched Tatsumi's shoulder, patting it as if in reassurance. His voice sounded softer but more resonant as he said, "They did their work well. I'm comfortable."

"Good," Tatsumi said. Her own voice sounded high and squeaky in her ears; the helmet modulator deepened its tone for the others.

"Where is Philby?" Nogura asked. "He should be here."

A group of four humans walked along the beach toward the Japanese transport, followed by a straggle of ten female Ihrdizu carrying ritual drapes of ocean weed. With some concern, Tatsumi realized these were members of Carnot's party, and no Japanese had served as mediators between them and the Ihrdizu. "How long have they been here?" she asked.

"Not long, I hope," Hiraiwa said. "Where is our culture team?"

Tatsumi felt a sudden chill. "Something's wrong," she said. She made connections through her helmet with the transport's communications system and sent a query to their ship in orbit. Kammer simply stood on the beach, rocking gently back and forth, waiting.

Carnot's party was barely a dozen meters away when she received her answer.

"Japanese culture team met Philby's party to arrange for rendezvous. Carnot's party was not there; they must have gone ahead to the village."

"Against our request?" Tatsumi said, face growing hot. She stared at the approaching group of four.

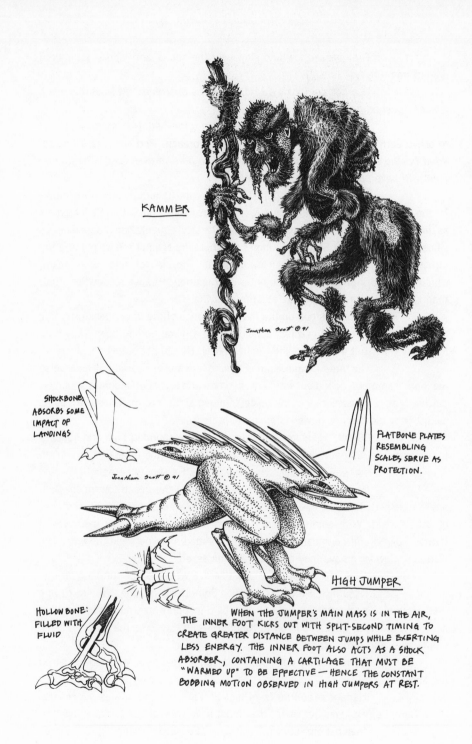

KAMMER

Jonathan Scott © 91

SHOCKBONE ABSORBS SOME IMPACT OF LANDINGS

Jonathan Scott © 91

FLATBONE PLATES RESEMBLING SCALES SERVE AS PROTECTION.

HIGH JUMPER

HOLLOW BONE: FILLED WITH FLUID

WHEN THE JUMPER'S MAIN MASS IS IN THE AIR, THE INNER FOOT KICKS OUT WITH SPLIT-SECOND TIMING TO CREATE GREATER DISTANCE BETWEEN JUMPS WHILE EXERTING LESS ENERGY. THE INNER FOOT ALSO ACTS AS A SHOCK ABSORBER, CONTAINING A CARTILAGE THAT MUST BE "WARMED UP" TO BE EFFECTIVE — HENCE THE CONSTANT BOBBING MOTION OBSERVED IN HIGH JUMPERS AT REST.

"Culture team reports they cannot advance to village now. There is a storm moving in rapidly. They are digging in for the next few hours; Philby's party cannot leave, either."

Tatsumi shut off the link in disgust. Not going at all well. She quickly explained to Nogura and Hiraiwa.

Kammer did not move forward to greet Carnot and his party. He leaned on his staff, still swaying back and forth.

"We could not land at the rendezvous," Carnot explained, coming forward, stopping two meters from Kammer, as if undecided where to go next. "There was a big storm coming in. . . . I believe your team and Mr. Philby are going to be there for some time."

How convenient, Tatsumi thought.

"We haven't spoken with the Ihrdizu here, other than to exchange greetings," Carnot continued. "We're trying to observe the terms of this meeting as much as possible."

The Ihrdizu, staring at Kammer, had withdrawn a dozen meters and stood on the shingles, bobbing back and forth. Nogura broke away from Tatsumi and Hiraiwa and walked up to them, stepping carefully on the rounded stones. He spoke to them through the translator.

"Excuse me," Kammer said. "There's something I need to see." He walked away from Tatsumi, toward the ocean and the racks covered with himatid skins. Tatsumi glanced at Hiraiwa and followed him.

"Please, Mr. Kammer, we need to stick together. We should return to the ship and wait for the others to join us. . . . "

"Big storm, Carnot said. Not for hours, maybe longer. I need to see something."

Tatsumi shuddered again at a sudden chill. *Keep him away from the beach.* But she could not simply grab him and hold him. Instead, she followed at his side, noting with fascination above her apprehension that his snug was actually getting *greener* the longer he stayed in the Genjian atmosphere. The snug was growing thicker; he seemed less like a mummy now and more like a vegetable man out of folklore, someone made of trees and moss.

With a start, Tatsumi realized that Carnot was walking on her right. He had left the rest of his party to stand in embarrassed silence with the Japanese. She looked back and saw three of the Ihrdizu also following, attention focused on Kammer. "We should go back, all of us, please," she said.

"Mr. Kammer," Carnot said. "I am most happy to see you again, and startled to see you *here.*"

"Doing the shock bit," Kammer said. "What are those things?" He raised a gnarled hand and pointed to the racked skins.

"Are you well? I did not know you could leave Chujo, or I would have—"

"Nobody knows what those are?" Kammer asked, turning to query Tatsumi. His pale eyes lingered on the Ihrdizu for a moment, then he faced forward again.

"They are skins, carpet-whale skins," Tatsumi said. "This is a fishing and whaling association."

Kammer stopped, seemed to breathe deeply, then continued, Tatsumi and Carnot tagging along.

"I would like to speak with you about what I've been doing, on your behalf," Carnot said.

Two of the Ihrdizu cut in front of Tatsumi, blocking her progress down the beach. They did not stop Carnot or Kammer. She tried to go around them, but they swiftly sidled to block her again.

"Please let me pass," she said, first in Japanese and then using the translator.

The Ihrdizu female who seemed to be senior in the party of three said, in Ihrdizu and very choppy Japanese, "We have heard of this human. Whalers bring stories from other regions. . . . You have told us nothing. Is he from Heaven?"

"He is human," Tatsumi said.

"He walks without a suit, and does not die."

So little time to explain. "Please, let me pass—"

"Has this one come to *judge* us?" The translator was struggling for the closest word. The other females gathered around Tatsumi, waiting for her answer.

"He isn't here to judge anybody," Tatsumi said, but it was obvious the translator did not express her meaning clearly.

"This one is from Heaven?" they repeated, three speaking at once. The translator squealed its inability to cope.

"Is this the human who bears messages from Heaven?" asked another female behind Tatsumi, speaking quite good Japanese. There were two males in her train, small and obsequious. "The other in the suit, who calls himself Carnot."

"I can't answer these questions," Tatsumi said, lifting her hands, spinning to face all the Ihrdizu in turn. "Please, let me bring them back to our ship."

The first three females blocked her when she tried to walk to the shoreline. "The judgment must come."

Horrified, Tatsumi switched on her link with the transport. Another team must come down, now; there was something wrong here, and her group was not sufficient to handle it.

Eyes wide, she watched Kammer and Carnot proceed alone down to the racks of skins. Beyond them, the gray-blue sky, thick with rain and clouds several kilometers beyond the shoreline, pulsed with thick oily lightning discharges. The sound arrived moments later, pushing at them. "Please!" she begged. The Ihrdizu bunched closer in front of her, a solid wall.

Kammer glanced over his shoulder, eyes narrowing at a burst of wind and sound. Carnot followed with pained diligence, hunched over slightly, eyes eager through the faceplate. "I've been spreading your story to the Ihrdizu, to tell them about their ancient past, about the return of Christ to these worlds. . . . "

Kammer ignored him.

"They've listened and built temples. There are temples all over Genji now, awaiting your sacrament, your signal, to become villages, and then cities. We can give them back all that they lost, thousands of years ago."

Kammer stopped three meters from the closest rack of skins. Three immature himatid skins—the upper portions of the whale, that is, less skins than flensed plates of tissue—lay draped over many crossbars mounted on sticks carefully thrust into the shingles. They were not so much drying as curing; rain had pooled in their hollows and folds. A rainbow sheen glowed around the highlights of the wrinkles.

"My God," Kammer said, raising his hands, dropping them.

"I beg your pardon?" Carnot said. He lifted his own arms tentatively, as if following some ritual gesture.

"What have they done? What are they doing?"

"Is there something wrong?" Carnot asked.

"These are the creatures in the sea. The brave beasts." Kammer fingered his snug, then ripped away a patch of it and offered it for Carnot's examination. Carnot stepped forward, saw the layering in the snug, the way it writhed in Carnot's fingers like something with its own independent life.

"I see it now," Kammer said. "I'm doing the understanding now, the standing between. There's real ignorance here, all forgotten, all abandoned. . . . Real evil here! Sadness!"

"Yes," Carnot said, enthused, bobbing his helmeted head. "You need to stay here and teach them, complete the link with Chujo."

"They were slaves!" Kammer screamed at him. "They don't want the Masters here! They were used like . . . They did the . . . " He could not finish. "And now they have their revenge. All the work of the Masters, all the planning, the genius . . . "

He shook his hands at the racked skins. "My God, my humanity!" Kammer reached up and tore a long strip of snug from his face. Blood trickled from raw pink skin beneath the thickest patches of snug.

Carnot turned, confused, and saw forty, fifty, sixty Ihrdizu coming in a broad line down the beach toward them. The other humans were pushed close to their ships by burly females armed with flensing knives and clubs. He saw Madeline and Lin-Fa making broad gestures, Madeline bowing and raising her arms in fear and frustration, to no avail. "Mr. Kammer," he said. "We must be careful. We should go back now."

Kammer threw the ripped snug onto the shingles and reached his hands out to caress the ragged edge of a skin. A dense cloud of scent rose from the skin, and he inhaled. "The small young, the mobile ones. I'm remembering now."

"They are trained by the Ihrdizu, they work with the Ihrdizu, some of them," Carnot said. "I think there's going to be trouble—"

"And the old . . . " He passed between the first few racked skins, to stand beside a huge skin, some fifty meters long and twenty across, like a mountain range in miniature: shiny black and green, dead. He touched this skin and more scent rose, and he screamed again. Up the beach, the Ihrdizu doubled their pace.

"Mr. Kammer," Carnot said. "Please . . . "

Kammer kicked out at the nearest pole and smashed his foot. Oblivious of the pain—if indeed he felt any pain—Kammer tried to pull the skin from the rack, but it was far too large, too tough, too heavy. Now the scent of the skins came through Carnot's helmet, through the oxygen-intake filter, and it was strong, and it made his eyes sting.

The horde was upon them, in a clearing surrounded on one side by immature skins, on the other by the single huge skin. They circled Kammer and Carnot, singing in their dreadful manner, feet pounding the shingles. Carnot's translator did not work well; it hummed and squealed alternately. Kammer ignored them, struck out with his staff at one close female, hit her on the crown between her upper eyes. The blow must have been slight, but she fell to the shingles nonetheless, and writhed there, foam pouring from her mouth.

"No!" Carnot screamed, horrified. "We must go back! Kammer, no!"

"You goddamned butchers!" Kammer shouted, striking again at another. The Ihrdizu went down, rolled over, kicked its legs in the air. "They're the ones! *They're* the ones, and you're killing them!"

Again and again he struck out, and more females fell to the stone beach, not dead, perhaps not even injured, but motionless. Carnot had a horrible realization that this was ritual and he did not know its purpose, or its end. He was seeing lights dance now, streamers of color surrounding the prostrate Ihrdizu, Kammer. He was having a revelation. He did not want a revelation now.

"Stop!" he cried, but his helmet muffled him. "Stop this, for the love of Christ!"

"We are judged!"

The Ihrdizu song reached a pitch, repeating this phrase again and again, and he heard the translation. He was on his knees, then on his hands and knees. Strong limbs grabbed his helmet and ripped it away, seals separating, baring his skin. His nose began to bleed. The residual hydrogen and helium in his lungs turned his screams into squeaks. He heard nothing now but a roaring. He saw Kammer with wings, the Ground of All Being a buzzing many-caverned hollowness behind, the face of Jesus rising from the clouds, approving, his nose bleeding.

"We are judged!" the Ihrdizu females cried, lifting Carnot above their heads. Naked, bruised and torn, blood dripping onto the shingles, he was carried around the giant himatid skin, and then propped against two poles erected in the shingles. His head lolled; he looked with pain-glazed eyes on the Boschian monsters dancing around him, his back a single-splintered lance of pain, his shoulders loose under the burden this world imposed, his hands scraping against the rocks. One arm was mobile; with it he picked up a flattened stone, tried to throw it at one of his tormentors, but his head lolled to the opposite side. He considered the death of Christ and the return to the Ground of All Things, which he could feel so clearly, his soul leaking below the Planck length, all things being equal there and fertile and unexisting. The stone rolled from his hand.

"Kill the judges!"

Tatsumi heard this cry, and wept; she knew this ritual. She knew its finish. Expiation for the act of hunting the himatids. Cleansing and renewal; rejection of the ultimate judgment, for the whalers were whalers, and must continue, but they must feel shame, they must face judgment. She could not see Kammer or Carnot, but she saw the stones filling the air like a cloud.

After just a few minutes, the Ihrdizu around her straggled away, leaving her on her knees, unharmed. All the Ihrdizu, females and males, returned to the high shelter plateau, mounted the steep stairways, and were gone from the beach. All that remained were the skins; she still could not see Carnot or Kammer.

Dr. Hiraiwa helped her to her feet. He could not wipe the tears from his eyes, behind his faceplate. Dr. Nogura stood a few paces away, repeatedly striking his hip with one hand and cursing in Japanese and English, a continuous, meaningless stream, interlaced with "Not again. Not again."

Tatsumi knew he was remembering the deaths on Chujo, years past.

It was not fair, but she could not keep the thought from her head: now damned English rational Philby had what he wanted all along.

. . .

Edward Philby walked along the beach, between the soaked and ruined skins, in the presence of mystery. A Genjian night had passed, with rare clear skies and Chujo high in the murky heavens, and this was the middle of the next day.

They had broken free of the storm, flying out in a sudden calm. The storm had bypassed this shore; the whale skins had been abandoned to the storm's powerful tides, however. The tides had washed them inland past the high embankment and walls, ground the skins with their racks onto the greater rocks and matted, thorned vegetation beyond, dragged them back to the low-water mark and wrapped them around the remaining racks and poles.

He had seen Carnot's body, retrieved by Nogura and Tatsumi.

But for a patch of soaked and dead snug, there had been no trace of Kammer. The Ihrdizu would not come down from their shelter, nor would they let anybody in; he had tried to enter and had been repelled by fierce females at the gates, screaming and wielding flensing knives. The females had scored their long horizontal thoraxes and legs and were bleeding profusely.

This was not what he had wanted. He had seen senseless accusation in Tatsumi's eyes, and it burned; this was not what he had wanted, but it was what he had feared.

The odor rising from the demolished skins reminded him of Kammer's smell. Odor of sanctity. He sniffed and adjusted his filter to reduce the smell, but not before he saw flashes of color. Kammer stood on the beach beside him, drowned, dead-looking. Then Kammer was not there.

Philby shook his head and cursed. The carpet-whale smell was drugging him, making him see things. That had to be the explanation. He backed away, trying to keep his calm, finish his analysis.

An hour before, the silent Japanese woman had given him copies of tapes. In his own transport, he had watched and listened to the recordings made by Tatsumi's cameras. He had boosted the audio and replayed Kammer's last words. He had magnified the last few moments of Carnot's existence, and seen what he thought was Kammer—an enhanced but still-blurred image—wading into the sea beyond the Ihrdizu horde and the carpet-whale skins.

Philby shook his head, beyond sadness. He knew what would happen next. Word would spread among the Ihrdizu, from village to village. It would reach Carnot's temple sites. The story of Carnot and Kammer, who had received their martyrdom and apotheosis, would spread; how far, who could say? Ultimately, it might fade, for it was alien, and the Ihrdizu might have cultural immunity.

Kammer's last words echoed in his thoughts as Philby retreated from the ruined racks and tide-scattered shreds of himatid skins. He had called the Chujoans "Masters," but with special meaning.

Kammer had surmised something, or confirmed something, and

had made a discovery on the beach. What had he discovered or confirmed? His words were tantalizing but not at all clear. *"They're the ones. They're the ones, and you're killing them!"* Surely he didn't mean the carpet whales?

Thompson's footsteps on the shingles brought Philby out of his reverie. "The Japanese investigation team has arrived; they were caught in another arm of the storm and delayed. They're holding a conference soon, and Tatsumi wants to . . . talk with you."

Philby nodded. She would not be pleasant to face. She saw herself as caught between two stones, dead Carnot and live Philby, who in their battle had provoked the Ihrdizu in ways neither could have specifically predicted but anyone could have intuited.

One last shred of skin lay on the upper beach. Adjusting his filter to reject all Genjian atmosphere for the time being, he stooped to pick up the shred with his gloved hand. In Genji's higher gravitation, it weighed ten or twelve kilograms, water-soaked. Examining its layers, running his gloved finger along the divisions of tissue, feeling the thick vascular tubes between the layers, he shivered as if engaged in some blasphemy.

Neck hair still on end, Philby lay the shred gently, reverently, on the wet gray stones. He slowly pushed to his feet, scanned the empty sea, and followed Thompson up the beach to the Japanese transports.

Tatsumi awaited him, polite and very, very cold.

BIRTHING POOL

BY NANCY KRESS

Mommy said they had been here too long.

How long was too long? The question didn't make much sense to Rilla. She had been on Genji her whole life. Did that mean her life had been too long? She was not quite ten standard.

"Less than a year till we go home to Earth," Mommy said, dumping mush from the food processor into a bowl and reaching for her precious spice safe. She said this often, as if she didn't want Rilla to forget it.

"I *am* home," Rilla said, but Mommy's QED chimed softly and in a flash she had left the food machine and run to the console in the corner of the field dome, where new figures and pictures scrolled across the screen.

"I'm only the fourth human born on Genji," Rilla said loudly, in case Mommy could be distracted from the QED. "Rita Byrne, Seigi Minoru, Cade Anson, and me."

But all Mommy said was, "Call your father, Rilla! He's down at the village! Tell him to come see this!"

Nobody listened to a ten-year-old. Nobody.

Still, it was all right to be sent down to the village. Tmafekitch might even be there. Rilla put on her suit, checked the tanks and translator and safety devices, cycled through the air lock, and started across the plateau toward the loose collection of Ihrdizu farms and pools and greens.

She found her father taking water samples from a birthing pool with two Ihrdizu grown-ups. Even Rilla knew that her father, or any other scientist on Genji, couldn't possibly need any more water samples from any more birthing pools. For nearly thirty years teams had collected thousands of samples from pools in Nighland, Southland, even in Farland, on the other side of the world where it was always moonless and Rilla had never been. The QED had analyzed all the sample data and then analyzed it again and again, and not even Daddy could think there was anything left to learn from the algae growing in an empty birthing pool. No, Daddy just wanted a way to talk to the two Ihrdizu grown-ups, one of whom had only just arrived in the village and mated with Tshifel, an unmarried male, a little while ago. Daddy always liked to talk to females who had just finished their mating journey, especially if they had traveled a long way to find a mate.

Rilla sometimes considered that the only mate her age in the entire Murasaki System was Seigi Minoru. He was on Chujo with his parents. *That* would be a long mating journey.

"Rilla," Daddy said. "What are you doing here?"

"Mommy says to come right away. There's something interesting on the QED."

It was hard to see Daddy's expression through his helmet, but it seemed to Rilla that he didn't really want to leave. Why not? Nothing interesting could be going on *here.* But then Daddy said his good-byes—without the translator, as what he and Mommy called a gesture of courtesy, and Rilla couldn't help noticing that his accent was terrible—and reached for her hand.

"Come on, Rilla."

But Rilla caught sight of Tmafekitch, coming around the corner of the Carnot temple. "I'll stay here, Daddy. There's Tmafekitch."

"Be careful," he said automatically, and hurried toward the dome.

"Tmafekitch!" Rilla yelled. Tmafekitch saw her and ambled over. "What were you doing?"

"Listening to the talker in the Carnot temple," her friend said. She spoke a combination of English, Ihrdizu, and the private language she and Rilla had spoken to each other all Rilla's life. All Tmafekitch's, too. With Tmafekitch, Rilla hardly used her translator at all.

"There was a talker in the temple and you didn't come tell me?" Rilla said, outraged. "What story was she talking?"

"Szikwshawmi."

"That's the best one!" In Ihrdizu, this came out "the best one to eat," since stories for the Ihrdizu were listened to with devouring attention. Daddy had explained this to Rilla, and ordinarily she got the giggles every time she thought of stories coming out of Mommy's food machine. But this time she was too disappointed. The story of Szikwshawmi was *great,* with angels appearing out of the sky to strike female Ihrdizu and give them greater strength to be warriors. Rilla and Tmafekitch had acted it out lots of times, changing parts so that each got to pounce out of the sky and each got to be given great strength and fierceness. And it was even better told inside the Carnot temple, which a man named Robert Carnot had built for the Ihrdizu to be religious in a long time ago, because if the talker sat in the right place there were thrilling echoes.

"Come, do not die on the starside," Tmafekitch said, which meant that Rilla was not supposed to be so negative. "I have something to tell you."

"What?" Rilla said sulkily. "Look at that she over there—the new one—why is she watching us so hard?"

"She has never seen a human until she came here."

So that was why Daddy had been so eager to talk to the new female. She came from a village where no scientists had been. She must have had a very long mating journey. Mommy and Daddy's field camp, after all, wasn't on Farland. It was only an hour's fly from Okuma Base, where there were plenty of humans.

"I go," Tmafekitch said, and walked away, flipping her tail. Tmafekitch was angry; Rilla realized it was because she hadn't asked what the something was that Tmafekitch had offered to tell her—what Mommy would call "a serious breach of manners."

"I am low," she said hastily to Tmafekitch's retreating back. "Cut off my tail. May I never rise to Chujo."

Tmafekitch turned around and nodded, accepting the apology. She never held a grudge. Unlike me, thought Rilla, who was currently holding several grudges against several people. But not against Tmafekitch. Never against Tmafekitch.

"I have something to tell you," Tmafekitch said, just as if the little anger hadn't happened.

"Oh, what?"

"Last dark I had a heat flush. The first."

Rilla stared at the Ihrdizu. A heat flush! "But that means you won't be a little-she any more! You'll be a grown-up! And you'll go off on a mating journey!"

"Yes. So," Tmafekitch said.

"And leave me here!"

"You will soon go off on your own mating journey," Tmafekitch said, but Rilla heard in her clicks and words and grunts and pitch—the grunts that she and Tmafekitch had invented together!—that Tmafekitch was sad about the parting, too. Well, so what! Sadness didn't help! Tmafekitch would go off to find some male, and it would have to be pretty far off because look how far the new she had had to come to find anybody to mate with, and then Rilla would never see Tmafekitch again. Never. And in less than a year Mommy and Daddy would take her back to Earth that they were so Chujo about, and Rilla would have nothing left. Nothing. Nothing.

She turned and left Tmafekitch standing there without even a good-bye courtesy, running away from the village, away from the dome, her strong Genji-bred legs standing against the gravity better than her parents ever could, not even the bulky suit much slowing her flight under the thick, gray sky.

. . .

"Let me see it again," Bruce Johnson said.

His wife Jane hit Replay, and the QED in the corner of the small dome, half research station and half home, started the incredible sequence of data again.

The QED—Quantum-Effect Device—was on receiving mode, which meant that at the moment it was doing no thinking of its own but merely acting as a terminal to receive data from the main computer at Okuma Base, atop Mount Korabachi. The QED in the field dome was capable of thinking, very smart thinking, due to fuzzy programs that could make reasonable deductions from incomplete evidence. Bruce Johnson, xenobiologist, had thought often over the last ten years that this was a good thing because on Genji all you got was incomplete knowledge. This didn't bother him. A huge ex-Texan who found it hard to sit still, either physically or mentally, he was pleased rather than not that Murasaki System still held so many facts that refused to fit together. It made for interesting theories. And now, looking at the data coming in on receiver mode, here was room for one more.

The carpet whales, those huge sluggish maybe-sentient himatids that spent their unguessably long lives in the polar waters of Genji's starside, were all swimming toward moonside.

All of them.

They were doing it very, very slowly, at even less than the two knots that were characteristic of their budding journeys. Measurement of their speed and direction came from Malachiel Holden, the half-crazy hermit researcher who fanatically studied the carpet whales from a research outpost on Farland. Well, not "hermit" any more, not since he had married Rita Byrne, the Genji-born girl young enough to be his daughter. That had fascinated and appalled Jane, who had taken to giving worried glances at Rilla and then doubled her insistence that Bruce and she and Rilla secure places on the ship arriving from and returning to Earth next year. Bruce didn't much care that Rita Byrne had married Malachiel Holden. People didn't interest him as much as Ihrdizu or himatids.

Except for Jane and Rilla, of course.

"Look at that," he said to Jane. "All of those damn carpet whales. All moving toward moonside, where they never go."

"Holden has done a beautiful job of tracking their movements. He must spend every minute of every day either at sea or running QED projections."

"Not practical," Bruce said. "But he's good, all right. Cautious, though. This is all data and images—he's not even offering a tentative hypothesis."

"Just an expense request," Jane said dryly. The allocation of resources to carpet-whale study had always been a sore point among the researchers of the Ihrdizu; the Ihrdizu at least cooperated with being researched. In their own eccentric way. "He wants a station set up at the probable point of convergence of all the whales. As soon as he can figure out what it is."

"Well, of course," Bruce said. Jane glanced at her husband. Abruptly she moved into his line of sight, not directly between him and the screen but clearly in his peripheral vision.

"Bruce—we're leaving in less than a year, right? We are leaving?"

"Will you look at that," he said softly. "Just *look* at that."

At Okuma Base, Jordan Dane, First Conciliator, stared at another set of data, this set from the moon.

"Are they sure of this?" he asked his scientific liaison, Suzy Tatsumi, a middle-aged woman of soft-spoken tact and penetrating intelligence.

"Yes, First Conciliator. They are sure."

He glanced at her, half smiling. How did she get so many delicate shades of meaning into six words? Verification ("The data is reliable"), rebuke ("They would not send it if they were not sure"), loyalty ("They on Chujo are my countrymen, after all, should you be questioning them to me?"), and conciliation ("I know it is just a Western reflex, to question data integrity, to question even superior researchers"). How did Tatsumi-san do it? *She* should be First Conciliator.

Which was a damn silly title anyway. It sounded as if he were followed by a whole line of other conciliators—second, third—like a tiered judiciary system. But there was only Dane, at thirty-five standard years one of the youngest adults on Genji, chosen by the seven different human groups in the Murasaki System to coordinate forums at which their differences could be conciliated. Six of those groups maintained clusters of headquarter domes at Okuma Base, where most days you could breathe most of the air: three domes for the Japanese expedition that had seniority on Genji. Three domes for the American scientists that had arrived twenty-five years ago. Four domes for the British-led multinational expedition five years after that. And three smaller domes belonging to smaller groups.

Among the domes, power packs hummed softly. Okuma Base had also, for the last six years, been the nexus of the information-sharing network Dane had set up. The QED in the British dome acted as a clearinghouse, not because the British equipment was particularly distinguished but because the Japanese and the Southwest American teams both found it easier to deal with the British than with each other.

That was also probably the reason Jordan Dane had been elected First Conciliator. It was a vital job, he had come to see, even though it carried no actual power whatsoever and he could not order anyone to do anything. But the post was nonetheless necessary. First, because the seven groups were so diverse—three English-speaking scientific expeditions; the large group of Japanese scientists; the pathetic remnants of the proselytizing Carnot missionaries, mostly wiped out by plague; one even weirder religious group called the Mission of Fruitful Life whose stated aim was to fill the entire galaxy with humans, however long it took; and one Spacer group who denied being colonists—there weren't enough human-usable resources on Genji to self-support colonists—but didn't seem to be anything else. They were artists, they said, but they neither wrote nor painted nor performed. They described themselves as "time artists," and from what Dane could see, they sat and contemplated time at someone's incredible expense.

The second reason a First Conciliator was needed was the twenty-year-old massacre of Robert Carnot, human, and Aaron Kammer, God-knows-what, by Ihrdizu fisherfolk, who had in turn been massacring whales. The incident had left anger, confusion, and myths. The anger belonged to the Japanese, who had seen the two Anglo factions as disrupting Genji culture to gain power and glory. The confusion belonged to Edward Philby, the self-appointed first First Conciliator, who had witnessed (caused?) the massacre and who had never been the same afterward. The myths belonged to the Ihrdizu. All sorts of myths, none of them particularly influential but all of them tenacious: that the temples Robert Carnot left behind were blessed by angels from the sky. That the humans could disappear into the sea and become carpet whales. That Aaron Kammer was not really dead but had been glimpsed in Farland.

This last, oddly, was what had driven that super-rationalist Edward Philby around the bend.

The odd thing, though, was that Philby had not left Genji. Twenty years later and he was still here, sitting with the time artists, contemplating whatever it was that time artists contemplated.

Tatsumi never spoke of him. Jordan Dane never asked her why, sensing that she would not answer, that there were things moving below the surface of her mind about Philby. He could sense things like that. It was why he had lasted as First Conciliator. And Suzy Tatsumi was naturally reticent, formal. He liked that in her; it was restful. Perhaps it was also why she had lasted as liaison to diverse sets of scientists.

He said to her now, "Who is still here who remembers that first time the snug mats formed on Chujo? Who was an eyewitness to the bioloons?" He was careful not to say the "so-called bioloons," as the non-Japanese scientists did. In nearly thirty years, no one had ever seen bioloons form again.

Tatsumi said, "Most of them returned on the second Japanese ship. But there is here a woman, Miyuki Kaneko, who witnessed it all."

"Here? On Genji?"

"No. On Chujo."

Dane nodded. He stared a moment longer at the transmitter screen, which showed a valley floor on bleak Chujo writhing as if alive. Which it was, with the bioengineered microorganisms that, together, made a mysterious sort of cloth that had already done so many things on Murasaki's worlds: Cure. Transform. Kill.

"I think we should call a general forum," Dane said. "Representatives from each group, two from those with teams on both Genji and Chujo. Transmitter linkup only for those who absolutely can't spare the personnel from either the snug watch or the carpet-whale watch. Everyone else welcome, to the dome's capacity. Call it a priority-two meeting: information sharing with possible vote on significant action."

Tatsumi nodded. She didn't look surprised. "For when shall I call the meeting, First Conciliator?"

Dane stared at the snug writhing over the floor of Chujo. The screen switched to data on the nomadic Chupchups, traveling toward the spot, even as the carpet whales traveled toward . . . something or other.

"For now," he said. "Better yet, for yesterday."

Jane Johnson stood at the edge of the plateau that held the Johnson field dome and the Ihrdizu village, and bitterly watched the water below rising up the plateau wall.

Water on Genji was always doing some damn thing: rising in tides, falling in tides, whipping into vicious sea storms, stagnating in birth pools until the smell was enough to drive you crazy, even, according to the best research theory, wiping out entire ecosystems on a systematic basis, like endless punishments of an entire race for some sin no one remembered.

She had been so enthusiastic about ecosystem research during her first year on Genji. Everything had seemed so exciting, after the confinement of the ship. She was a botanist; there had been so many new plants. New people. New possibilities. Genji had struck her as ugly, but next to the rest of it, that had hardly mattered.

How did you account for a ten-year mistake?

It had started with her pregnancy, an astonishment that had resulted from a batch of defective pregnancy blockers among the supplies. Well, with that many pharmaceuticals aboard that long, there were bound to be some defects. The surprising thing had been her fight against an abortion. She had wanted the baby fiercely, unthinkingly, and eventually Bruce had given up arguing. It wasn't as if she had been the first: Rita Byrne was already fifteen years old and thriving. On Chujo, little Seigi Minoru was almost two.

She didn't know how it had been for those mothers, but for Jane, Rilla's birth had changed everything. With her baby in her arms Jane had come to look at Genji as the hell it really was. Thick, heavy planet, dragging on her body, on her legs, on her very arms as she held her baby. Thick, soupy gray air, pressing down on them wherever they went, not even safe to breathe. Ultraviolet radiation to sear an infant's unprotected skin, swooping pseudobirds strong enough in their perverse gravity to carry away an Ihrdizu child. Or a human one.

Rilla changed everything. Under the huge dome at Okuma Base while Bruce went into the field to work, or in the research camps he insisted she bring Rilla to when the little girl was older, Rilla was a constant presence in Jane's heart, pressing on her, weighing on her. Rilla deserved better. Rilla deserved a planet where she could run outside unfettered in the sunlight, dive into clear blue water, play with little girls instead of the little-she's of the friendly Ihrdizu, who no matter how friendly could never really be friends. That was the first lesson of xenobiology: The alien is not human. Not your own behaviors, not your own motivations, not your own kind.

No woman should ever have a baby off-planet.

The tide below the plateau had almost peaked. Jane looked at the swirling water beneath her. Then she closed her eyes and arched her back slightly, not easy to do in her bulky suit. But she wasn't in her suit. She stood on the edge of a red cliff at Amilcar, and below her the Mediterranean crashed, blue as the sky. Her back was arched against the wind, which blew her hair back from her face and brought to her the scent of wild jasmine. She sniffed deeply, eyes closed, only opening them because she was so hungry for the exquisite sight of the dusty leaves of olive trees lacy against the bright, clear sky.

"I'm not going!" Rilla cried, aghast. "How can you make me go?"

Her father looked at her, not especially patiently. Behind them, Mommy was doing something to the QED, and Rilla knew why, too: so that Mommy wouldn't have to look at Rilla while Daddy told her she had to go with them to the conference at Okuma Base. If Mommy had said she had to go, Rilla could always have run to Daddy; Daddy *liked* her to be such friends with Tmafekitch. But Daddy was the one telling her. There was no escape.

"I won't go! I'll . . . I'll run away with Tmafekitch on her mating journey!"

Mommy turned around sharply, her face white. But Daddy only said, in a tone he probably thought was soothing, "Now, Rilla, you know you can't do that. How could you get food, or air tanks? And besides, Tmafekitch wouldn't take you. She has an important job to do, finding a mate so she can establish a homestead and not be a little-she anymore. She can't fit you into that job."

This was true. Rilla had already asked Tmafekitch. And Tmafekitch, waving her snorkel and clicking her feet in a way that meant she was embarrassed, had said no. The flush was all over her skin, that hateful sex flush that meant soon Rilla would never see her friend again.

"But by the time we get back from Okuma Base, Tmafekitch might be already gone!"

"She might not," Daddy said. But he didn't look at her when he said it.

Rilla burst into tears, stamped both her feet, and fled behind her partition.

Jane frowned. "When did she start doing that?"

"Doing what?" Bruce said. He still squatted on the floor, bringing himself down to Rilla's height. His love for his daughter, he often thought, should not be such a painful thing.

"Stamping both her feet like that to show she's angry. In that Ihrdizu pattern."

"I don't know."

"She never smiles," Jane said.

"Smiles are rude in Ihrdizu. You know that. The tongue is a sex organ."

"She's not Ihrdizu!"

Bruce rose. "Lay off, Jane, will you?"

"She's *not Ihrdizu.*"

Within an hour the three of them were in the flyer, bound for Okuma Base.

Dane looked around the crowded room. Nobody looked back; they were all watching the monitor showing carpet whales migrating on Genji, snug mats growing on Chujo, or both.

The scientists sat in rows on inflatable benches, reasonably orderly even under stress. Hauro Maguto represented the Japanese scientists on Genji, Miyuki Kaneko those on Chujo. Miyuki had answered eager questions almost the moment her shuttle had landed, but she hadn't been able to add much. The data coming in on transmission was fresher than her last firsthand information from Chujo. She claimed, Dane remembered, to be an eyewitness to the bioloons these snug mats had supposedly become twenty-eight years ago. Her face, as she stared at the visuals from the Chujo upland valleys, showed nothing.

Six designated representatives from the three other scientific expeditions also occupied inflatable benches, talking quietly among themselves. Other people crowded in the back, among them, Dane saw, the Johnsons. He had received three requests for berth space aboard the *Light of Allah,* due to arrive and depart Genji in eight months, from Jane Johnson. None had been cotransmitted with her husband. A bad sign. The child, Rilla, was not at the meeting; Jane had probably left her to play with the only other child on Genji, six-year-old Cade Anson.

Between the inflatable benches and the standing scientists sat two members of the Quantists: two of the nineteen that existed, including Cade Anson. Dane couldn't remember their names. They were muttering something. Prayers?

Well away from the Quantists, a woman from the Mission of Fruitful Life sat on a folding stool. She was obviously pregnant. "Go forth and multiply" meant, to the Fruity Livers, just that; they were fulfilling their mission to fill the whole galaxy with humanity, starting with Genji. What was with these people, to send a pregnant woman to do anything in this gravity? But the woman herself looked calm enough, if very uncomfortable.

No one at all had come from the small weird collective of the time artists.

"I think we should get started," Dane said genially. Faces turned toward him, first reluctantly and then with determination.

"We've all looked at the data and the images," Dane said. "I'd like to organize the meeting in three parts, if that's all right with you all." He smiled. Conciliatorily. "First, I'd like a brief summary of all the questions raised by each group by the events of the last few days. Second, I'd like to ask for possible interpretations of those events or answers to those questions, by way of sharing speculation and information. Finally, we'll determine together what needs to be done. If anything."

People nodded. Before Dane could speak again, one of the Quantists spoke. "Why isn't there an Ihrdizu at this meeting?"

Dane said, "Well, I . . . it didn't seem appropriate. We're sharing human perspectives, and we have researchers with us well qualified to share Ihrdizu ideas—"

"Not the ideas of those Ihrdizu who already believe in the Ascendancy!"

"Sit down!" someone else called. "It's not your turn!"

"*You* can speak for your culture-contaminated tame Ihrdizu," someone else said, with contempt. Dane saw the nonconfrontational Japanese wince.

Dane said, "How many people vote to invite an Ihrdizu representative to this meeting?" Only the Quantists raised their hands. "All right, let's start with the questions we *don't* know answers to. Dr. Kaneko?"

Miyuki Kaneko rose heavily. Twenty years on Chujo's lighter gravity, Dane thought. He could picture her younger, more lithe, although her present appearance—small, serene, not yet old when the average life span stretched to nearly a century—pleased him as well. Nor had he overestimated her capacity for organized thought.

She said, "One: We do not know what has triggered the snug mats to start re-forming in Chujo's highland valleys, after they have not done so for twenty-eight years. Two: We do not know whether this snug-mat formation is larger than the ones twenty-five years ago, because then no measurements were made. Three: We do not know what is in the 'books' in the library cairns, since for twenty-eight years the Chupchups have not let us examine a single one. Four: We still do not know why the Chupchups abandoned their elaborate and technologically advanced cities to live as nomads, or when, or why they seem to have no interest in the cities now. Nor in the bioengineering that, to judge from what they did to Aaron Kammer, they once knew how to perform."

There was a moment of silence; to those newer to Genji or Chujo, Aaron Kammer's weird history was almost as unsubstantiated as the bioloons.

A Quantist said derisively, "You sure haven't learned much in nearly thirty years on the moon!"

Dane said swiftly, "That is not a useful comment. Please remember that this meeting is being held on *Lorentz* Expedition property and that anyone who disrupts it can be evicted."

Miyuki said, just as if the comment had been a reasoned and constructive criticism, "It is difficult to study a people who will not acknowledge your existence, yes. We have been much distressed."

Dane looked at her admiringly. She, too, might have been a First Conciliator.

"Five," Miyuki said, and now her voice did change, taking on a slight hesitation. "We still do not know if the carvings in the abandoned cities have any meaning. Or ever did have."

Dane said, "Describe one for us, just to fill in those people who have not been to Chujo." This covered much of the room.

Miyuki said, in that same hesitant voice—the carving had some personal meaning for her, Dane guessed, that she herself was having difficulty defining—"There is one of a tigerlike creature whose tail curves around and around, forming a Chupchup face, before it comes into the mouth of the tiger to be consumed. In the background are bioloons. This is how we know the bioloon phenomenon did not happen for the first time twenty-eight years ago."

Abruptly, she sat down. Dane said, "Next?"

Kara Linden stood, a brisk, no-nonsense woman who was chief of the *Lorentz* Expedition. "There are fewer things we don't know about the Ihrdizu than about the Chujoans, of course, because the Ihrdizu are so cooperative. But they are also factual, practical, and much more hard-wired to their basic biological

DUNE TIGER – ANATOMY POSTULATED FROM CARVING FOUND IN THE ABANDONED CITIES OF CHUJO. THE DUNE TIGER SUBMERGES ITS HEAD IN THE SAND TO AWAIT PREY. SENSING A CREATURE OVERHEAD, THE TIGER WILL CLAMP DOWN WITH ITS TRIGGER HORN WHILE STABBING THE PREY WITH DEADLY RETRACTABLE DAGGERS.

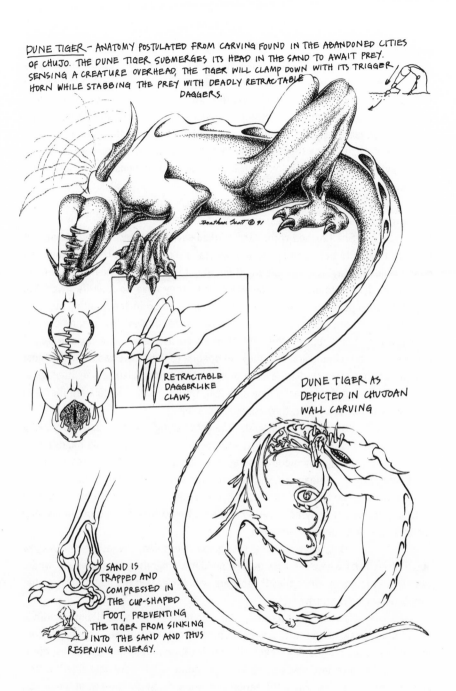

RETRACTABLE DAGGERLIKE CLAWS

DUNE TIGER AS DEPICTED IN CHUJOAN WALL CARVING

SAND IS TRAPPED AND COMPRESSED IN THE CUP-SHAPED FOOT, PREVENTING THE TIGER FROM SINKING INTO THE SAND AND THUS RESERVING ENERGY.

patterns than are humans. This means they don't question their own lives very deeply, and even their 'religions,' if I can use that word, are usually taken very casually. Religion seems to be mostly valued as a source of enjoyable stories and festivals than anything else, and even the Carnot temples"—she glanced contemptuously at the Quantists—"currently are mostly used as community recreation huts, with amiable religious frosting. Given all this, the main thing we don't know about the Ihrdizu is why they continue to regard Chujo with some reverence—as much reverence, I may add, as such a practical and no-nonsense people seem capable of."

Dane hid a grin; it was obvious Dr. Linden approved of this trait in the Ihrdizu. She might have made a good Ihrdizu herself.

She finished with, "The Ihrdizu say the Masters live on Chujo, but they are unable to define what these 'masters' are masters *of.* They say they will go to Chujo one day, but questioning them about whether this means they will go there after death produces only bewilderment. They have no afterlife myth. We have offered repeatedly to take a few of them to Chujo in the shuttle, but they always decline, with what seems a total lack of not only interest but comprehension. They are not stupid, but on the subject of Chujo they are . . . are *opaque,* and I have come to the conclusion that they are opaque to themselves as well. The most you can get out of an Ihrdizu, even a highly intelligent Ihrdizu in a technological capacity in one of the largest villages, is 'Oh, Chujo . . . The Masters are there. In time, we will go, too.' Then they change the subject."

"All right," Dane said, "the list of things we don't know is growing nicely." A few people laughed. "Who will speak to the carpet-whale migration?"

After a moment a young man stood, younger even than Dane. "I can't really say . . . I mean, Dr. Holden and his wife report to me, but not on a regular basis." The young man blushed. Dane guessed that Dr. Holden reported to this timid person only because no one else would take the job of supervising the irascible and caustic researcher.

"But, anyway," the young man ventured, "what we don't know about the carpet whales is why they're suddenly migrating to moonside, where exactly they're going, when they'll get there, what triggered the migration, or what they'll do when they arrive."

That about covered it, Dane thought. "Now, does all our ignorance constitute a crisis of any sort? Several people have talked to me"—*besieged me,* he wanted to say but didn't—"about the reallocation of research territories, given that current events have made some areas suddenly much more desirable." Everybody wanted to be near where the action was, even if nobody knew what the action meant. "Now, we had all agreed—*voluntarily*—to spread out far enough not to contaminate each others' sphere of culture." This was not strictly true; the Quantists went around contaminating everywhere they could, but nineteen people with limited resources couldn't influence very much. If the Ihrdizu had taken up Robert Carnot's Church of the Ascendancy, that might have been a different thing, but as Kara Linden pointed out, for the most part they had not.

Dane drew a deep breath: *Here goes.* "So the question before us is whether or not we want to reallocate research spheres, on what basis, and to whom, given the difference in each party's equipment and interests."

Immediately a dozen voices clamored for the floor. Several people rose to their feet, with varying degrees of clumsiness. No one could be heard. Dane simply waited; if he recognized no one, eventually they would quiet down and restore order. Unless, of course, there was a fistfight, and he didn't think the scientists would do that. The Quantists might—twenty years of frustration, starting with plague and massacre, was not exactly calming—but the scientists, eager to claim research rights, ignored the religious groups. The Fruity Livers, as usual, simply sat, multiplying.

Bruce Johnson yelled, "Ihrdizu genetic patterns..."

Somebody else called, "—informally agreed that after fifteen months..."

"—carpet whales—"

"—Chujo—"

The door at the back of the room slammed open.

Everybody turned. A woman strode in, brisk even in the heavy gravity, carrying a holocorder. Dane had never seen her before. Then, with a shock, he realized that he had: a year ago, at her wedding. Rita Byrne Holden. Her skin was burnt and mottled—the ultraviolet radiation she must be permitting herself to take in the name of open-sea research! Born on Genji, she had always had a squat, compact body heavily muscled, as human anatomy shaped itself to Genji gravitational imperatives. Now, however, her muscles in the brief indoor tunic— she and Holden must live nearly naked, when they were not in suits—bulged like a caricature of a sumo wrestler, although without the fat. She was impressive but oddly deformed. Dane would not want to have to tangle with her in a fair fight.

Jane Johnson looked at her with something very like terror.

"Listen," Rita said, without ritual pleasantries, "I've got something to show you. Holden sent me because he wanted to be sure you all saw this without any screwups or evasions."

The rabbity young man whom Holden was supposed to "report to" opened his mouth, then closed it again.

Rita plugged the holocorder into the QED, blanked the pictures on the two-dimensional screen, and turned the device on. For a moment Dane wondered how Holden, the fringe researcher, had wangled a rare and expensive holocorder, but then he forgot that, and everything else, in the three-dimensional hologram that sprang to life in the four-foot square of alloy floor in front of the QED.

Carpet whales. Twelve, sixteen, twenty of them, already arrived at the strait between Nighland and Southland, their dark hugeness reduced to absurd miniaturization by the holo. But not so miniature that he could not see that one whale had rolled over. Its ventral side, grayish white, was exposed to the sky. Above it, clearly shimmering in ribbons of red and green light, floated an enormous representation of a twisted human figure covered in snug that could only be Aaron Kammer.

Rilla looked out the window of the flyer as it skimmed over the surface of Genji toward their dome. Hurry, hurry! Oh, what if Tmafekitch had already left on her mating journey and Rilla never even got to say good-bye? Daddy had promised they would get back before Tmafekitch left, but then the stupid meeting had gone hours and hours past what it was supposed to, all because of Rita Byrne. People shouting, arguing, talking, just sitting there. A whole day, almost, and all the while Tmafekitch may be setting out to look for a stupid mate and leave Rilla behind forever.

And her parents were *still* at it, talking even while Rilla's throat hurt so much it might just break.

"Not light," Daddy said, for the hundredth time. "Exudates, gases and water, reflected and refracted through thousands of precisely placed bits of shiny minerals embedded in the flesh and acting as mirrors. All to produce a sort of holo of Aaron Kammer. Of *Aaron Kammer*! It's not possible."

"We saw it," Mommy said. She sounded scared. "It was photographable. Not a drug-induced illusion or hypnosis."

"No wonder Rita Byrne brought the pictures herself. No one would have believed her."

"A lot still didn't."

"Not even the QED could specify an exact moving arrangement of mineral embedding and exudate control to produce an illusion like that," Daddy said. "Well, all right, maybe the QED could, but . . . it's not possible. It doesn't make *sense*. How could it happen?" Unlike Mommy, Daddy didn't look scared. His eyes were bright, and his big rough hands moved restlessly over the flyer controls.

Mommy didn't answer. Rilla leaned forward, to get there sooner, or make the flyer go faster, or something. Hurry! Hurry!

"It's not possible," Daddy said.

"Will you stop saying that?" Mommy said sharply. "Obviously it is possible. The himatids did it. Genetic engineering, all that time they've been growing out there, multiplying, reaching some kind of critical mass to do whatever it is they do out there for millennia . . . it's obviously possible, because it exists!"

"Don't shout, Jane."

"I'll shout if I want to!"

Daddy said, "You used to be a researcher. Intellectual questions used to engage you."

"I *used* to be a lot of things," Mommy said, and turned her back to watch their dome approach portside.

Rilla sealed her helmet. The moment she was out of the flyer, she was running, ignoring Mommy screaming behind her. "Rilla! You didn't check your tanks or your safety devices!" Ignoring Daddy, who started to run after her, then stopped. He couldn't catch her. Not in this gravity she had been born in and he had not. *I was the fourth one born on Genji,* she chanted to herself desperately, *Rita Byrne and Seigi Minoru and Cade Anson and . . .*

The chanting didn't help. She reached the village, and there stood Tykifizz, Tmafekitch's daddy, and Rilla knew just from the expression on the small male's four-eyed, snorkeled head that Tmafekitch had already gone.

Rilla didn't even hesitate. She had filled her tanks, packed her supplies, done her safety check before they left Okuma Base, while Mommy and Daddy had been talking and talking and talking about carpet whales. What were carpet whales compared to Tmafekitch, her *friend*? Just nothing. She didn't have the translator because that might have made her parents suspicious, but probably Tmafekitch's daddy could understand her well enough without the translator. And, of course, once she found Tmafekitch, she wouldn't need any stupid old translator.

Speaking very slowly and putting in as many Ihrdizu sounds as she could—only it was hard to know which ones were really Ihrdizu and which ones were hers and Tmafekitch's!—she said to Tykifizz, "Which path did she take? Where does she search? Through whose food pond does she mate?"

She asked all the questions she could think of, keeping one eye out for Mommy or Daddy. But they didn't come. Still fighting? Or did they just think she was sulking and would be back?

She would, of course. She knew *that,* no matter how much of a baby they thought she was. She knew she couldn't really live off the Genji land, and she knew Tmafekitch couldn't really take Rilla with her. But Rilla *could* say good-bye. They weren't going to cheat her out of that.

Once she had all the information Tykifizz could give her, she started off after her friend, her lost soul mate, to say good-bye.

Jordan Dane was not a scientist. He had been chosen for First Conciliator precisely because he was not and thus was assumed not to favor any one scientific discipline over another. He had come to Murasaki System as librarian, highly trained at storing, cross-referencing, retrieving, and preserving other people's science, a QED specialist considerably less valuable at what he did than the QED itself. Looking at the screen displaying close-up transmissions of Chujoan Chupchups camped in rings around writhing vast mats of snug, Dane found himself wishing—for the first time—that he was a scientist.

Tatsumi was watching him with her quiet eyes. What she said surprised him.

"Where were you born, First Conciliator?"

"I'm a Spacer, Tatsumi-san. I thought you knew that."

She bowed slightly, apology for the inquisitiveness. "From what place?"

He smiled at her. "A habitat. It no longer exists. An accident. They were attaching antimatter thrusters to the hollowed-out asteroid, preparing to move it to a better location. The whole thing blew."

"Ah. Clayton's World."

He bowed in return, a playful mimicry. So the details had reached even Murasaki. He didn't like talking about it. But one more sentence seemed necessary: expiation. "I was away at graduate school on Earth. Harvard."

"So you are an exile," she said, so neutrally he knew he did not have to say any more. She would not probe. Together they watched the Chupchups camped around the snug vats, until Suzy Tatsumi said in her formal, pretty voice, "I think, First Conciliator, that someone should go talk to Mr. Philby."

She was shocked at how much Philby had changed.

Tatsumi looked in her mirror every morning; although the changes there were gradual, she did not delude herself that the lined face and smooth, gray-flecked hair belonged to the same young woman who had sobbed on the beach as the Ihrdizu stoned to death Robert Carnot and Aaron Kammer. She was slower, thicker, in her prime but past her bloom. Yet she was still the same person, recognizable in that mirror. Edward Philby was not recognizable. For a long, heart-stopping moment, he did not look human.

But that was illusion. Of bulk: the once sleek and well-fed body weighed no more than sixty kilos. Of hair: Philby had none left. Most of all, of skin: Philby's very brown face, neck, arms, and bare chest were covered with melanomas, as if he had sat deliberately in the ultraviolet light for a very long time. As perhaps he had. The cancers, Tatsumi could see, were killing him.

She tried to hide her shock as she approached him. He sat on a bench in front of a standard portable dome among five other domes at the time artists' "colony." He wore pants, boots, and a breathing filter. Tatsumi, who wore a full suit, thought that at this air pressure, not sea level but not mountaintop either, he must be very uncomfortable. He gave no sign of it.

"Mr. Philby," she said formally. "It is Dr. Tatsumi."

She wasn't sure what she expected. Slowly, slowly Philby rose, nodded, and led the way into the dome.

Tatsumi removed her helmet. (Was it completely safe? He looked crazed. But she stood between him and the air lock, and it was painfully obvious by how much she was the stronger.) She bowed slightly.

"I have come to see you, after all this time, to ask you once again about something. Alas, it is a painful topic: that last day on the beach, at the Ihrdizu fishing association, when Robert Carnot and Aaron Kammer died."

"In time, everything must happen," Philby said.

She nodded politely. "So say many Oriental philosophers."

"And you think I am merely echoing them. But I mean something much subtler, something derived from physics," Philby said. She remembered that he had debated philosophy for—literally—years with Robert Carnot, through ship-to-ship link. She heard, too, what she had missed in his first, five-word utterance: the cancer had invaded his throat.

"What is it that you do mean?" she said, still polite.

"For everything there is an equal and opposite reaction. That is basic physics. It is also cosmic design. For everything, if one waits and witnesses with enough patience, there is a corrective swing in events. Like a pendulum."

"Even manslaughter," Tatsumi said, using the curious Western term. She could think of no other. For what had happened on the beach, "murder" was not the right word.

A faint gleam shone in Philby's sunken eyes. "Yes. You understand."

"Not completely," Tatsumi said honestly. "You are waiting to witness events that will correct your . . . your moral guilt?"

"I bear no moral guilt," Philby said hoarsely. "I wait to see the swing of the pendulum, for aesthetic satisfaction. I am an artist."

Time artists. "But," Tatsumi could not help saying, although it was no part of what she had come to say, "an artist does not just wait. An artist participates in the process."

"We participate," Philby said. "Ask any court if the witnesses are not participants in a trial."

"But that is justice, not art."

"Ah," said Philby, "but the wisdom of our art is that we do not recognize the distinction. We know that only art creates true justice."

Tatsumi gave it up. Subtlety interested her; self-serving rationalization did not. "Mr. Philby, will you look at some pictures I have brought?"

"An artist witnesses whatever part of the design is entrusted to him."

She opened the packet she carried, hard copy from the QED.

"These are carpet whales. They are all—all, Mr. Philby—gathering at a point in the strait between Southland and Nighland. The point is as close to the sub-Chujo node as possible, the actual node being inland. This picture here shows one himatid that has rolled over to expose its ventral side. The formation in the air above is an illusion of exudates, gases and water, reflected and refracted by thousands of minute bits of shiny metal, which it must have taken the whale millennia to collect and embed at precise locations between its teeth and stomata."

Philby did not seem surprised to hear this.

"What does the illusory formation look like to you, Mr. Philby?"

He said promptly, "It's Aaron Kammer."

"Mr. Philby, you told me . . ." No. Wrong. "Mr. Philby, have you ever seen anything like this before?"

"On the beach. After he died."

"After?"

"I walked between the whale skins. What was left of the whale skins. And I saw him, just like that, red and green ribbons of light." To her shock, Tatsumi saw that there were tears in his sunken eyes. Tears of gladness. What strange ideas of absolution had been touched in his mind by all this?

She said, "Just like this you saw him. After he was dead."

"I told you so at the time, Tatsumi-san."

"Yes. You did." How cold she had been to him, how furious, how judgmental. How young. "You said something else, as well. You told me what Kammer's final words were before the . . . the massacre started."

"Yes. He said, 'They're the ones. They're the ones, and you're killing them!' "

She had remembered right. She let out her breath. "Thank you, Mr. Philby."

"Thank *you,*" he said.

"Do you need anything? Pain blockers?"

"You have brought me everything a time artist needs."

He was too sick to debate with, even if debating had been her style. Too sick, too old, too peculiarly shamed. Tatsumi had not known Westerners were capable of such deep, all-accepting shame. Certainly she had not known Philby was. She had been wrong. Or perhaps over the course of twenty years he had changed, grain by grain, like those flabby plants that petrify into unbreakable stone.

As she climbed back into her flyer, she thought of two things, turning them over and over like the smooth white stones in her grandmother's miniature sand garden in Kyoto. The first was what Aaron Kammer had said to her, Suzy Tatsumi, about the Chupchups on Chujo: *"Learned much myself on Chujo about understanding and standing between. Masters and slaves. Everybody's right, every-*

body's wrong.'' She had not known what he meant. Now, seeing Philby, who had been so wrong and had worked it around in his mind to a process of right that united justice and art—a process she had just contributed to with her prosecutorial questions—she was not so sure. Right and wrong looked more complex to her now. And mastery—of anything—seemed much dimmer.

The other thought was that it had been years since she had remembered her grandmother's sand garden in Japan, on Earth, her birth-home.

"I tell you, she's gone!" Jane Johnson screamed. "She's gone, looking for that damn iguana!"

Bruce Johnson stopped short. The Ihrdizu had never in the least reminded him of iguanas—where did Jane, even in her hysteria, get that? And it wasn't like her to be so ethnocentric, so utterly imperial about the aliens. . . . She was a scientist. Even if the science was only botany.

"Calm down," he said. "She's probably playing in the Carnot temple, or sulking somewhere. . . . She knows how much air is in her tanks and what her physical capacity is. You underestimate her, Jane. She'll be all right."

"Which only means you don't want to bother to go looking for her! Well, I'm going!" She yanked on her suit, crying.

Bruce suppressed his irritation. He didn't know what was happening to Jane. She had always been high-strung, but now . . .

"High emotion means an increased chance of accidents, Jane. Look, if you have to go out, just calm down first. Rilla's all right, she's a Genjian. . . . "

"What? What *did you say*?"

"I said, she's a Genjian."

Jane sobered immediately. Coldly, methodically, she pulled on and sealed her suit, ran through the safety checks. She did not look at him or speak to him until she actually had her hand on the air-lock recycle. Then she said, in a voice he had never heard from her before, "She's a Canadian child."

The QED chimed, not softly, which meant a transmission of crucial, although not life-threatening, importance. Bruce turned his head toward the QED. When he turned it back, Jane was gone.

Unnecessary. Rilla would be fine. She would be back in an hour. Unnecessary, and therefore wasteful.

"Transmission from Chujo," the QED said. A Japanese head appeared, someone Bruce didn't recognize. "This is Dr. Kenzo Ohkubo," the man said in English; Bruce recognized the slightly mechanical undertones of the QED translator. Dr. Ohkubo was speaking Japanese. "I am at temporary base near the sub-Genji point, twenty-five degrees twenty-eight minutes south, where the largest of the snug mats is growing. I wish to play for my esteemed colleagues on Genji, in which I include all scientists in reach of the information network, the recording of an interview I have just had with a Chujo Master."

Bruce whistled. He wasn't sure what impressed him more: that the Japanese, who tended to be formal and a little proprietary about scientific information, were sharing the interview, or that they had finally gotten one with a Chupchup at all. After twenty-eight years!

"We did not obtain this information by our efforts," Dr. Ohkubo said. "It was freely given. The Chujoan walked from his camp near the snug vats to our dome. When I advanced to greet him, he spoke as follows."

The camera angle shifted; it was not a particularly good picture. The image of the Chujoan wavered, steadied; no one at the temporary camp, hopeless of any real contact, had prepared for this abrupt appearance. Bruce stared, fascinated, at the noseless humanoid face with the huge gold-brown eyes, slitted mouth, and flaring, scalloped ears. How good would the translation be? For two and a half decades the Japanese had been dropping transmitters into Chujoan encampments and farm centers. This electronic eavesdropping had yielded only a meager vocabulary and the knowledge that Chupchups would not shine at cocktail parties. The QED translation program would not have much to go on.

But speak it did, forty-five seconds of trills, twitters, and growls. Bruce had the eerie impression that the Chujoan had slowed down its speech, making an effort to be more intelligible. When the statement was over, a callused, blue-fingernailed hand extended toward the camera, offering a smooth blue box about half a meter square. A human hand moved into camera range and grasped the box. Then the Chupchup simply turned and loped off.

Dr. Ohkubo reappeared. "We have run this speech through the best language programs we have. Many of the Chujoan words were new to the computer. This is the closest approximation we can make, going first to Japanese and then to English. Please bear in your mind that it may not be correct."

The voice of the translator began: "It *is/will be* *time/an animal hunted/a problem solved.* Snug travels to Genji. *Error/hunting-mistake-which-leaves-an-animal-unkilled* is *solved/hunted/built/completed.* Cities are empty because Chupchups not *inside/needful of/tied down for the kill* the cities. We eat the *beings* of Genji. The *beings* of Genji eat us. It *is/will be* *time/an animal hunted/a problem solved.*"

Dr. Ohkubo returned and said something brief in Japanese. Bruce, watching, wondered what he could have said for the translator to produce the idiomatic, resigned English translation: "There you have it."

Jesus Christ, Bruce thought. Jesus H. Christ.

Then he remembered that he was a scientist and should take the flyer posthaste to either Okuma Base or—better—where the carpet whales were gathering as close as possible to the sub-Chujo node.

Only then did he remember that Jane had the flyer, looking for Rilla.

"Poetry," Dane said. "It could be poetry. The last line repeating the first . . . "

"The only clear points," said Don Serranian, one of the physicists, "is that the snug is supposed to travel to Genji, and that something is supposed to be settled. But there's no way that snug could cross space!"

"Are you sure?" Miyuki Kaneko said. Her voice held an underlying tremor that made Tatsumi watch her closely. "There has been for generations now speculation about bioengineered spaceships."

Everyone spoke at once then. Dane tried to follow the arguments behind the positions taken by highly trained minds, none of whom agreed with each other.

"The same word carries connotations of 'time,' of 'an animal hunted,' and of 'a problem solved.' Is that threefold meaning a construct of our translator, or does it imply a fatalistic belief system in which time is measured by what events are resolved in a given span?"

"The Chupchups seem to be saying that they abandoned the cities by their own choice, because they no longer needed them. Not because the race had degenerated to a pre-city level. Which, I'd like to remind everyone, is what I maintained all along."

"What are the implications of 'We eat the beings of Genji'? The translation of 'eat' is firm, but the translation of 'beings' is tentative, level-three uncertainty—are they talking about the Ihrdizu? Are the Chujoans possibly cannibalistic? Or could they have been once?"

"The next sentence is 'The beings of Genji eat us.' That seems to imply a metaphorical interpretation rather than a literal one. Perhaps the entire message is metaphor!"

"If the Japanese would bring that blue 'book' to Genji where the rest of us could have a crack at it—"

"Ihrdizu folk sayings like the groveling 'May I never rise to Chujo' seem to me to imply an exalted state for Chujo. If it represents a kind of perfected being-hood, a Nirvana—"

"Ihrdizu ecological disasters—"

"—carpet whales—"

They were not getting anywhere, Dane saw. They never did get anywhere. Individual researches illuminated this small fact of the Murasaki biosphere, or that small fact, or a tentative connection between this and that. But they never got anywhere creating a coherent overall picture. Not in thirty years. Did that mean that humans couldn't grasp a big picture so alien? Or that there was no coherence to be grasped?

Dane didn't believe the latter.

Why not? Because he just didn't. The universe was not that fractured. Or human comprehension that limited.

"We do not really understand anything happening here," Tatsumi said in her pretty voice, and he looked at her, startled to hear his own thoughts articulated so clearly. Tatsumi smiled at him. No one else even heard her: they were all too loud with desperate speculation.

Why desperate? Dane wondered. But then he knew: contradictory elements in their adopted world made hash of the limited understanding they had already struggled so hard to achieve. The lack of understanding made them feel excluded. Genji and Chujo, by its sudden eruption of events so clear to their own species and so weird to the humans, were shutting the humans out. They felt exiled.

And he, Dane, did not? No. Why not?

Tatsumi said to him, in a voice barely above a whisper, "You, Jordan-san, already felt like an exile."

Rilla stopped walking to check her tanks. Not quite halfway used. She could walk a little ways yet. But not far. She would have to find Tmafekitch soon. Or—

She was farther away from the field dome than she had ever been, except in the flyer. The village was far behind. Around her were no birth pools, no Carnot temple, no food ponds. Only low yellow plants and marshy ground and low hillocks and the path, hard and firm, that generations of Ihrdizu had worn for trade. There were no people. Rilla didn't like to admit how much she wanted to see a snorkel waving above the vegetation. Anybody's snorkel, it didn't even have to be Tmafekitch's.

How could Tmafekitch leave without saying good-bye! How could she!

Rilla walked on a little farther. Above, Chujo was full face, the color of the sand that she and Tmafekitch used to build domes with. Chujo was streaked at one edge with white clouds. It was ugly. Tmafekitch wasn't there.

Her tanks suddenly chimed, very loud. They were half empty.

Rilla sat down on a rock beside the path and started to cry. She had to go back. She wasn't going to see Tmafekitch after all. She had to go back or she would die. She couldn't even, in fact, afford the time and energy to sit here and cry.

Life was awful. Nobody had ever told her life was going to be this awful.

Rilla got heavily to her feet, and Tmafekitch came trotting around a hillock.

"Tmafekitch! You're here!"

Tmafekitch stopped dead and clicked her feet in astonishment. Her snorkel waved in loops. She said to Rilla in their personal language, "Why are you here? Where do you go?"

"I came to find you! You left before I came back!"

"It was time for my mating journey," Tmafekitch said, still clicking and looping. "Are you going on a mating journey now?"

"Of course not!" Rilla said. This was not the meeting she had envisioned. A new thought occurred to her. "Tmafekitch—why are you traveling back toward your village?"

"I cannot go on my mating journey."

"*Cannot?*" Rilla said. She had never heard of such a thing. "Why not?"

"Because it is ****."

Rilla had never heard the word. Something odd in Tmafekitch's snorkel loops made her think suddenly that Tmafekitch had never said the word, either. But that didn't make any sense. Rilla wished she had the translator with her after all.

"Tmafekitch, what does that word mean? The one you just said?"

Tmafekitch came close to Rilla's rock. She sat down on her tail, then got up again, which meant she was thinking hard. Her snorkel looped wildly. A flock of silverbirds flew overhead, and only one of her upper eyes tracked it, so distracted was she. Finally she sat down again on her tail and put her face very close to Rilla's, as talkers often did when they came to the exciting parts in a story they were talking.

"It means time. And an animal killed after long hunting. And . . . a problem solved."

"What?" Rilla said. "What?"

Tmafekitch took her face away. The silverbirds suddenly started to screech, and Rilla looked up. A flyer approached. Mommy or Daddy. Or both. Probably furious.

"Oh, uneaten turds," she said. "Tmafekitch, are you really coming back to your village?"

"Yes."

"What about your mating journey?"

"I cannot go. It's ****."

There it was again. Rilla had never heard of anything interrupting a mating journey once it was started. "What about your heat flush?"

"Gone."

Rilla had never heard of that, either. "Will it come back?"

"Oh, yes."

"When?"

"After ****."

The flyer landed. Through the window Rilla could see Mommy, gesturing at her furiously. Nothing was going right. Except, of course, that Tmafekitch was coming back to the village. Even if that made no sense.

"Tmafekitch—how come you never told me this word before, if it's so important it can stop your mating journey?"

Tmafekitch seemed to think deeply. Her snorkel ceased all motion. A long moment went by, in which Mommy climbed out of the flyer and stalked toward Rilla.

"Because," Tmafekitch finally said, "it was not before in me."

"That's crazy!" Rilla burst out angrily.

"Yes," Tmafekitch agreed. "The Masters are sometimes crazy. They did not put the word in the Ihrdizu. Not before. Only now."

All over Genji, Ihrdizu on their mating journeys stopped, turned around, and walked back to their villages. Researchers raced to question them. Each little-she responded courteously.

"It is ****."

Fishing boats stopped fishing, stowed the catch they already had, and sailed back to their fishing ports. Two scientists, one Japanese and one Anglo, took flyers to two different ports, made ritual greetings, and asked why the boats had returned.

"It is ****," the Ihrdizu said.

A three-day festival in the Southland central valley, a gathering of two thousand Ihrdizu, came to a sudden halt. The festival-goers packed up their young and their provisions and started back to their own food ponds and birthing pools. The itinerant talkers who had come for the festival, who had much local fame but no food ponds or birthing pools of their own, each went with a different group of Ihrdizu. Bruce Johnson flew to Southland to question as many talkers as he could. Why did the festival stop? Why were the talkers each boarding with an Ihrdizu household instead of continuing on their accustomed circuit?

"It is ****," the talkers said.

"How the hell did a Chujoan word get into their vocabulary?" Don Serranian cried. "A word that apparently none of them knew before the same identical moment all over the fucking planet?"

Bruce Johnson said, "Hard-wired. Into the genetic structure. Had to be. All set for conscious access at some signal, some timing system." Johnson hardly slept, Dane thought. As tightly wrapped as Serranian, Johnson nonetheless was responding differently to this latest development. He was completely absorbed, forgetting even to eat, to bathe. Serranian, like many of the others, was frustrated and scared by events that made no sense. Johnson loved it.

Serranian said tightly, "What sort of signal?"

"How should I know?" Johnson said. He walked in tight circles in front of the QED. "Maybe astronomical, like the minute variations in light that trigger some bird migrations on Earth. Maybe internal. If knowledge was stored in the Ihrdizu brain, passed on generation after generation, until some chemical inhibitor was removed in the synapses... Yes! Yes!" He began punching keys furiously.

"Removed *how?*" Serranian yelled. "You can't just have spontaneous genetic combustion!"

"*We* can't," Johnson said gleefully. "Can the Ihrdizu?"

"No!"

"How the hell do you know? Could they have an outside trigger?"

"Like what?" Serranian was furious; Dane actually thought he might strike Johnson. Dane moved swiftly between them. A First Conciliator was not supposed to be a bodyguard, but to keep fanatics conciliated...

But Johnson seemed to calm down a little, even if Serranian did not. His next words were very soft, almost inaudible. His face shone. "An outside trigger. Yes. Tell me, Serranian—how do the carpet whales communicate with each other across huge expanses of ocean?"

"We don't know!"

"Carpet whales," Johnson said musingly, his face still radiant. "*Carpet whales.*" He started typing rapidly in QED mode, inputting to the fuzzy-logic program he had set up to coordinate event-data. After a while he leaned back and watched the screen.

"Will you look at that," he said softly. "Just *look at that.*"

Every mature carpet whale on Genji had arrived at the Southland-Nighland strait, south of the sub-Chujo node.

They blanketed the sea for kilometers with their sinuous black flatness billowing on the waves, their dozens and dozens of pairs of thin waving tentacles. The largest of the whales stretched a hundred meters long, twenty-five meters wide. There was not enough food in the sea for all the stomatalike mouths to graze on, so the himatids seemed to have simply stopped eating. They did not move much. However alien they were, it seemed obvious what the carpet whales were doing.

They were waiting.

All over Genji, the Ihrdizu returned to their villages, and waited.

On Chujo, the mats of snug grew and writhed, and, circled around the mats, the Chupchups waited.

The humans looked at each other. The fascinated ones, Dane thought, the ones like Bruce Johnson, ran data program after program, straining even the QED's powers. The others, the ones used to the orderly accumulation of knowledge that grew rather than decreased in logical connections, sat around tight-lipped—and cursed the waiting.

"I want her out of here!" Jane Johnson said to her husband. "I want Rilla on the orbital ship, away from all this! It's just too weird, and nobody knows what will happen!"

"I won't go!" Rilla said. "I want to stay here on Genji!"

Jordan Dane doubted that Bruce Johnson actually heard either of them.

"In my grandmother's sand garden," Suzy Tatsumi said reflectively to Dane, "were quiet empty spaces, bare sand or bare polished rock, as much a part of the design as the living bonsai."

For days there were storms. Powerful winds blew Genji's thick air masses. Rain whipped across the seas. In the low-lying villages, the waters rose dangerously above flood tide.

But then the winds blew themselves out, the clouds dissipated, and one of Genji's rare clear skies shone above noontime Southland. And the carpet whales, the massed and tightly packed carpet whales in the Nighland-Southland strait below Chujo, all rolled over to their ventral sides.

Signals began to flash into the sky.

Grains of metal from the seas, grains gathered over millennia and apparently stored in precisely measured amounts in precisely measured locations on the ventral surface, reflected the light of Murasaki. Clouds of gases released from millions of stomata refracted the light. Focused it. Sent it toward Chujo, which was not in eclipse with Genji and therefore was experiencing midnight, a moonside midnight clear and cloudless at the sub-Genji point.

"The light signals are of course very faint. Far too faint to activate any phototropisms in the snug mat," Kenzo Ohkubo transmitted from Chujo. He said it as if he did not expect this information to make the slightest bit of difference, as indeed he did not. They had all, or nearly all, given up expectations. What expectations should *E. coli* have about the next food to come down the human gullet? Ohkubo, thought Jordan Dane, sounded almost jaunty. He was not among the scared ones.

The electromagnetic signals—clearly more than just light—went on striking the great snug mat on Chujo. The mat stirred. "A hive mind, perhaps," Bruce Johnson said. "Or something."

All around the moonside of Genji, the Ihrdizu sat still, remembering things they had never before known.

Nearly every scientist flew, after wild negotiations for flyer space, to the Southland-Nighland strait, and agreed-upon research spheres be damned. Okuma Base was effectively deserted. Technicians remained, along with Jordan Dane, Suzy Tatsumi, and—to Dane's surprise—the Johnsons. At first Dane thought that Bruce Johnson was staying for Jane's sake. Later he realized that Johnson wanted to be near the QED, preferring to analyze data than to gather it.

Jane Johnson, tight-lipped, disappeared into the dorm dome, taking Rilla with her.

Bruce, Dane, and Tatsumi were gathered at the screen in the main dome when Miyuki Kaneko appeared on the all-channel transmission from Chujo. Unlike Kenzo Ohkubo, Miyuki's voice was not jaunty. It was perfectly steady, without shading but not empty, as white light is without color because it contains all colors.

Miyuki said formally, "To all human scientists: The Chujo team has succeeded in opening the Chujoan 'book' voluntarily given to us by the Chujoan spokesman. The artifact is a container of opaque and very hard glass. It has taken the team so long to open both because they did not wish to break it and because the method of closing, locking, and opening is unlike anything humans use. Dr. Ohkubo, who is at the snug-mat site, has asked me to describe to all of you exactly what we have found."

She drew a careful breath. "To call the artifact a 'book' is incorrect, although to call the cairns a 'library' is not incorrect. The glass box contained a pile of etchings on thin plates of glass. These are unmistakably numbered by dots in the left-hand corner of each: one dot for the etching on the top, two dots on the next we encountered. We will transmit the etchings now, with commentary on what we have learned thus far."

"*Listen* to her. Prerecorded, all of it. As good as already written the journal paper," Bruce Johnson said. He could not sit still. He danced in front of the screen, his eyes burning with excitement and fatigue.

Tatsumi, pouring tea for Jordan Dane, said, "Formality can be such a protection against disbelief."

The huge mat of snug, covering the entire floor of the valley, wrinkled, stretched, slid. The Chupchups scrambled across its surface, heading for a crevasse that billowed steam. Streamers of sulfurous yellow billowed across the mat. Suddenly, one edge of the mat reared, jerked, and leapt into the sky. The edge struck the far side of the crevasse, to join with a second leaping edge. The two waves stuck, clung, forming a seamless whole. The bioloon started to billow along the crevasse.

"Not again," Miyuki said, in the same formal voice in which a few hours ago she had recorded the contents of the Chujoan glass box. "They should not die again."

No one heard her. The rest of the team recorded, scanned for samples left behind, controlled the movements of the robot probe that would fly as close alongside the rising bioloons as Kenzo Ohkubo dared. They observed. They were scientists.

"The first etching," said the prerecorded Miyuki, "as you can see, shows two Chujoans standing with an Ihrdizu on what clearly seems to be the surface of Genji. Please look carefully at the Ihrdizu, who is a mature female. Around her snorkel is a . . . a 'necklace.' It is an actual necklace, in miniature, made separate from the etching and then embedded in the glass."

The picture of the etching held, then magnified the Ihrdizu's snorkel. Dane leaned as close as possible to the screen. He realized he was breathing heavily. Like Bruce Johnson, he thought ruefully, and glanced at Tatsumi. She went on drinking her tea, her dark eyes large.

The screen transmitted an image of a corroded lump of metal. Miyuki's voice said formally, "We all have known, of course, that the Ihrdizu once had metallurgy. This coin or medallion was found by the expedition's first ecospecialist, Dr. Katsuyoshi Minoru, twenty-five years ago. Core samples taken under choice Ihrdizu seaside villages have shown that, just as they have shown that the Ihrdizu culture flourished in waves, dying off and then being rebuilt at least six separate times. Each time, many other flora and fauna have died with them and never been replaced.

"A great question has always been: What caused the die-offs on

Genji? What upset the ecological balance so much that the Ihrdizu had to fight for prime space, by the sea but on very high ground, just to survive? What ecological disaster raced through Genji, changing everything eighty generations ago in a breathtakingly short space of time?"

The snug mat was lifting itself. Alive with purpose, rippling, its center axis bulged, pulling the rest of it along the ground with a hiss like a wave sliding up a beach. It shed pebbles, making itself lighter, letting go of its birthplace.

Beneath, in the vat, hydrogen by-products of the snug combined with other gases. The mat rose, shaping itself into a teardrop. A teardrop with pockets. From the other valleys of the volcanic ridge, other bioloons rose, each bearing a load of Chujoans clinging to the sides, scrambling into the pockets.

"They will all die again," Miyuki said. "All die! Like the successive generations on Genji, like the carpet whales slaughtered by the Ihrdizu . . . death. All death!"

Kenzo Ohkubo looked away from his recording instruments long enough to glance at her. He said quietly, "You forget yourself, Kaneko-san."

The rebuke, gentle as it was, sobered her. She watched the bioloons rise to the sky, paced by the robot probe.

"The second etching," said the formal Miyuki two hours earlier, "shows the same two Chujoans—computer analysis shows all four figures to have been etched from the same plate—standing still on Genji. This time the necklace-bearing Ihrdizu is dead at their feet. The plants around them are dead. The village behind them is in flames. The small birthing pool in the lower left corner is overgrown with what seems to be—this is just supposition—some sort of snug. It is not possible, given our current uncertainty about Chupchup culture, to read the identical expressions on the two Chujoan faces."

"Grief," said Jordan Dane at once. He glanced at Tatsumi. She put her teacup on the table; it rattled in her fingers.

"They *caused* it," Bruce Johnson said. "Dane—the Chujoans fucking *caused* the die-offs. Or that die-off, anyway. Look at that birthing pool. *Snug.* It was like the wineskin plague, only this version attacked Genji life-forms. The Chujoans were the bioengineers, and they fucked up, and they *caused* an ecological disaster!"

Dane said shakily, "You don't know that."

Johnson said, "I'm going to set a QED fuzzy-logic program right now to correlate the data and deduce the probabilities."

Tatsumi said, "He said—" She stopped.

Dane turned toward her. Her face, ordinarily the clear pale gold of good brandy, had gone white. He put a hand on her shoulder, gently, the first time he had ever touched her. "Who said what, Suzy?"

"Kammer. He said to me, after the Chujoans had covered him with that snug, twisted and deformed him . . . "

"What, Suzy? What did Kammer say?"

"'Learned much myself on Chujo about understanding and standing between. Masters and slaves. Everybody's right, everybody's wrong.'"

"Masters," Dane said. "Masters of bioengineering."

They watched the screen, waiting for the next etching.

The bioloons soared into the blue-black sky of Chujo. On the ground, the long lines of Chupchups who had not climbed onto the snug watched the others go.

Miyuki strained her eyes until the bioloons were small dots. Still they kept rising, high into the atmosphere. She put her hand over her mouth, realized what she was doing, and took her hand away. This time she would not be sick.

She would not.

Ohkubo's team had already erected the dome of double-thick

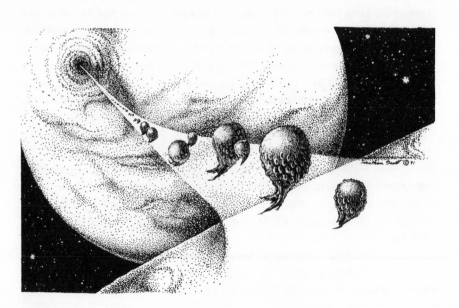

shielding material. Last time, they had had no protection. Last time, when the Chujoan bodies had started to hurl back toward the planet, still trailing streamers of snug, it had been only chance that none of the splattering corpses had struck any of the human researchers. Only the body fluids had.

She would not be sick.

Inside the dome, the researchers crowded around the screen receiving transmissions from the robot cameras pacing the bioloons. Ohkubo focused on one large bioloon, adjusted the telescopic lens, and split the screen to show transmissions both from a distance large enough to see the bioloon whole, and from a few meters away from one pocket. On the second screen, a golden-brown Chupchup face with large-pupiled green eyes stared at Miyuki. If the researchers had known enough to name Chupchup expressions, she told herself with rare sarcasm, she would have said the face was exalted.

She turned away from the screen, not wanting to see him die.

"The third etching, which you see here, is ... is ... " The prerecorded voice faltered.

"Jesus H. Christ," Bruce Johnson said, not prayerfully.

"—is perhaps stylized rather than literal. We know from the carvings in the abandoned cities of Chujo that the Chujoans are capable of stylized representation. Or perhaps the etching is literal."

A line divided the top of the drawing from the bottom. The line might have been a sea cliff, or a shoreline, or nothing at all. Above the line, the same two Chujoans—Dane did not need a computer analysis to know they were the same ones as in the first two etchings—knelt, their heads bowed, staring below the line. Below the line, a carpet whale swam, its dozens of "eyes," those sensory organs located between each pair of tentaclelike "arms," all turned toward the Chujoans. The orientation of the eyes was painstakingly drawn. The himatid regarded the penitent Chupchups, who regarded them back.

Johnson laughed, a slightly sour note. "It's a story. Just another myth, another talking."

"It's not a myth," Dane said. He wondered how he knew. "The carpet whales somehow judged the Chujoans for the mess they had made of the Genji ecology. Well, maybe not 'judged'—but got told about it anyway. Or something."

Johnson started frantically feeding data into his fuzzy-logic program.

Tatsumi said quietly, "The carpet whales made the illusions of Kammer. Of Kammer in his tatters of snug. Of Kammer dead, just as Philby saw him on the beach after the massacre."

"The himatids are very old," Dane said. "Not even Holden knows how old."

"Master and slave," Tatsumi said. "Did I ever tell you what Edward Philby said to me about time, art, and justice?"

Dane didn't answer.

"He said our great failing was that we could not recognize that they were the same things."

High in the atmosphere above Chujo, the bioloons began to change.

The robot cameras recorded it all, from several angles, at several different depths, with several different levels of magnification. There was no mistake. The Chujoans in the pockets of the bioloons, all at exactly the same moment, extended their hands straight above them, their humanoid legs straight below. They went stiff, long rigid axes of stiffness. The pockets around them grew as the snug shifted violently, then sealed itself. Each rigid human was sealed in a pocket of snug: giving warmth, conserving air. Around these rigid axes the bioloon shifted with incredible swiftness, changing shape too precisely for anyone to think it was by chance.

"What do they do?" Ohkubo cried. "They are creating an . . . an aerodynamically feasible shape—"

The gases in the bioloon's central cavity suddenly shot out a point near groundside, and the bioloon—no longer shaped like a balloon—shot forward. The electronic watchers on Chujo, all except Ohkubo, fell silent. Miyuki felt an emotion creep over her she could not name. The Chupchup emotion, her own— she could no longer name anything. She could only watch, the glass etchings dancing before her eyes.

Finally someone said, the voice hoarse, "If the bioloons manufacture more hydrogen through photosynthetic processes, maybe even other gases as well . . . "

Someone else said, "We know the snug can interact with the Chupchup body, drawing on those resources as well. . . . "

"There is a tremendous amount of energy stored in snug chemical bonds. . . . "

"At their current altitude, how much escape velocity would they need . . . "

"How much time would it take, sealed in those pockets . . . Of course, if the bioengineered process has the capacity to manufacture additional gases for breathing as well as propulsion . . . "

"How could they have calculated the right entry point, the right angle for reentry . . . No, no, it isn't possible . . . "

"How do we know what is possible? We cannot even see the inside of those . . . craft. . . . "

The bioloons continued reshaping themselves.

At the sub-Chujo point on Genji, the carpet whales writhed and twitched, changing with minute precision the electromagnetic signals beaming into the sky.

"This fourth drawing," said the formal Japanese voice, "shows a spacecraft of some sort covered with what appears to be formalized drawings of snug.

"We do not know whether snug can survive the interplanetary void, but this is partly because we do not know whether snug can take forms different from that observed on Aaron Kammer two decades ago. Bear in mind, also, that this etching, which appears to be taking the two Chupchups to Chujo away from Genji, may just be a story. A myth. Or a stylized version of some actual historical happening unrelated to the events of the other etchings but blended with them in the retelling over time. We simply do not know. The implied narrative conclusion drawn from this ordering of etchings, that the sentient humanoid race was somehow sent away from Genji and to Chujo at the behest or order of the himatids, may be completely erroneous. Silly, even. We do not know."

"Quarantine of experiment," Bruce Johnson said.

"Exile," Jordan Dane said.

Tatsumi reached out and took his hand.

The bioloons glided into the comparatively narrow strait of space between the atmospheres of Chujo and Genji.

"Shape still flattening," said Ohkubo tightly, monitoring the transmissions from the robot cameras. "I think it's gaining maximum surface area for some sort of phototropic activity, probably releasing gases. Why did we not think to send along a probe capable of spectral analysis?"

This question was a lapse of control, Miyuki thought; everyone pretended Ohkubo had not asked it. The answer was obvious, anyway. They had not sent a probe to analyze unknown phototropic reactions that might furnish propulsion capability because no one had known such an event was imminent. Or possible. Or thinkable.

How many of the Chupchups sealed in their bioloon pockets were still alive? Had their life processes been slowed by the snug to require less breathable air, less heat, less gas exchange? It seemed probable. But, then, perhaps the snug ship had speeded up the Chupchup life processes to produce *more* of these things. How would the humans ever know? Unless, of course, the ship remained in analyzable form once it reached Genji.

If it reached Genji.

"Entry into Genji upper atmosphere in . . . three minutes, forty-two seconds," someone said. "What will they do about the heat of entry?"

No one answered.

"Fifth comes an etching of a Chupchup city on Chujo. It is partially constructed. As you see, the actual hard labor appears to be mostly being performed by 'trolls'; the Chupchups are standing to the left-hand side absorbed in an undifferentiated artifact."

"'That's no artifact, that's my snug,'" Bruce Johnson said. He laughed and glanced around. Tatsumi would have said his manic gaze saw none of them. "They experimented with the damn stuff in the safety of Chujo until they got it right! I'll be damned!"

Dane Jordan said, "You are making a supposition." Tatsumi saw that he didn't believe his own words. He, too, could recognize snug when he saw an etching of it.

The Japanese scientist, Miyuki, must have been under tremendous internal pressure, to draw herself back from the recognition.

"Sixth," Miyuki said, "is this stylized picture, virtually identical to a carving, one of many, in the abandoned Chupchup city."

The animal informally named "dune tiger," now presumed extinct, glared at them from the screen. Its long, long tail stretched into a wraparound wreath that grew gnarled branches, sprouted ample flowers, twisted about itself to form a Chujoan profile, and finally curved back to be eaten by the tiger itself.

"Full circle!" Bruce Johnson yelled. "Yeeooweee! The Chupchups perfect the bioengineered solution to the ecological catastrophe *they* caused—and the cycle comes full circle. 'Masters!' Damn straight they call themselves fucking Masters!"

Dane said, "It could be just a story. . . . "

Johnson finally seemed to see him. "You don't believe that."

Dane didn't answer. Finally, he said, "No. I don't."

"What was it that Chupchup said to the Japs?" Johnson demanded. "The same multitiered concept the Ihrdizu have taken to spouting? 'It *is/will be* *time/an animal hunted/a problem solved*.' No wonder they abandoned their damn cities without any sense they'd degenerated! The lab part of the process was over! They were ready for field experiments!"

Tatsumi grasped what he was saying. For a second she went still, awed by the sheer size of it. A design for justice taking eighty generations, saving a world by exiling the perpetrators/saviors for only the most practical of motives . . . All genetically hard-wired. Justice that was genetic.

Justice? Or was it art?

Johnson said gleefully, "And we thought we on Earth understood the self-regulating nature of a biosphere! We don't know shit!"

Tatsumi could not understand why that should fill him with such pleasure.

When the bioloons hit the atmosphere, they changed again. The robot camera's telescopic lens showed a ripple over every centimeter of their surface, subtle and uniform, as if the snug were reorienting at a cellular level. The albedo increased dramatically, acting as a heat reflector and hence a heat shield. At the same time, the shape of each ship changed again. As the gravity well took hold upon the Chujoan cargo in its pockets, the ship broadened, thinned, curved in proportion to the increasing air pressure. By the time the ships were fully in the atmosphere, they were no longer ships but enormous, aerodynamically stiffened parachutes.

"Here," said the prerecorded voice of Miyuki, and even through her formal control, her listeners felt her relief, "is the last of the etchings in the Chujoan library box."

The screen showed parachutes, uneven parachutes unmistakably of snug, falling through the sky. Stylized Chujoan faces adorned each parachute. On the ground—so clearly Genji ground, the edge of the sea decorated with Genjian plants and a watching Ihrdizu—the sea surged. It was thronged with carpet whales, watching the sky. From each himatid, the artist had etched a faint line to a bioloon, a line made of flowers and plants no human had yet seen anywhere on Genji.

"Coming back," Dane Jordan said. His voice had turned husky. "Returning to Genji. Like the myth of Szikwshawmi. Angels coming from the sky to confer biological strength on female Ihrdizu." Was that what had happened once long ago?

"Guided by the carpet whales," Tatsumi said.

Johnson said nothing; he was updating his fuzzy-logic deduction program on the QED like a man possessed.

"But there's one thing I don't understand," Dane said.

Tatsumi said, with honest astonishment, "Only one?"

"If the carpet whales are to guide the Chujoans back to Genji with new bioengineered snug—if the whales are the masterminds—"

Johnson looked up, with scorn. "Masterminds! That's all wrong. They're genetically hard-wired for their role, too. None of the three races is any more in control than the others!"

"All right." Dane drew a deep breath. "But if the signal or whatever comes from the himatids . . . what happened last time? Why did the Chujoans get into their bioloons and start off into their atmosphere twenty-eight years ago, only to fall back and die? What went wrong?"

Johnson stopped typing. His forehead, sweaty with exultation, furrowed.

Dane said, "If the carpet whales maybe started to give some kind of signal, and then the whole . . . 'mission' aborted—why? Why wasn't the signal what it was supposed to be?"

"Damn," Johnson said. "I don't know. Maybe the computer can come up with something. . . . "

Tatsumi saw it. Wavy lines appeared beneath her eyelids, dizzying her, then righted. She said, "I know."

The men turned to her. Johnson said, "You know why the carpet-whale signal failed last time? Why?"

Again she saw Edward Philby, poor tormented justified Philby dying of his cancers among the time artists. He stood in the field dome and repeated the last words Aaron Kammer had said, just before Kammer died: " 'They're the ones! They're the ones, and you're killing them!' "

The ones. The carpet whales.

She said, "The Ihrdizu killed too many. There were not enough left to make the right signals."

Everybody's right. Everybody's wrong.

Cameras recorded frantically: on the south shore of Nighland, pointed at the sky; in fishing boats, as close to the himatids as the humans dared; in the sky itself, from out of flyer windows or on robot probes. No one had known what would happen, but they had known that *something* would, and the humans, Dane thought, were ready. Weren't they supposed to be? Why else had the Chujoans broken three decades of disdain to give humans the library etchings? Why else had the figure of Aaron Kammer appeared above a carpet whale in exudates and light? Why else, if not to invite the humans to watch this Murasaki System story, this wordless talking that dwarfed anything the humans themselves had offered by way of petty Carnot temples or small-scale offers to day-trip to the moon?

Dane turned to tell his thoughts to Suzy Tatsumi. But at that moment the screen in front of them, filled with sea spray from somebody's misplaced camera, switched pictures. The images flowing into Okuma Base from the sea strait had been erratic for the last hour. Everyone at the strait was too busy recording to take time to route the best images to those unfortunates left behind at the base or at field camps. They, like the scientists on Chujo or the crew in the orbiting ship, didn't count. Only the sea straits, glassy under the moon, counted. The off-site researchers took what the automatic transmitter sent, in the order the computer received it.

But now the image cleared. Johnson raced back from his QED terminal to stand with Dane and Tatsumi. None of them spoke.

The parachutes of snug hit a sudden gust in Genji's treacherous, thick atmosphere. The affected bioloons wobbled. Light, focused by millions of tiny reflectors embedded in the upturned ventral sides of carpet whales, flashed toward the parachutes. Immediately the parachutes adjusted shape, the snug expanding or contracting at the cellular level, until the chutes once more rode the wind.

The parachutes began to close at the bottom, meter by meter, until they once more became the shape of organic balloons. On each balloon, pockets bulged. Something within the pockets stirred faintly. The robot cameras, at extremely close range, showed the tops of the pockets begin to unseal.

"The gravity," Dane said aloud. "So much greater than Chujo. Bones not developed for it, muscles . . . Unless the landing of every one of those is perfect, the Chupchups won't survive. . . . "

The image changed again, this time to the southern shore of Nighland, meters from the nearest carpet whale. Ihrdizu were wading into the water from the beach, hundreds of them. They submerged themselves to the tops of their tentacles. A few actually touched the edge of a carpet whale, which could bring its huge shape so close to land only because of its weird flatness. The Ihrdizu were laughing.

Light, reflected in exudates, danced and beamed from the carpet whales. A peculiar noise filled the air, louder than the laughing Ihrdizu or the lapping waves, a high-pitched rising and falling wail that might have been sonic signals. Might have been keening. Might have been cheers.

As the bioloons came closer to land, most of them aimed at the sea, the carpet whales began to submerge. One-third, half, two-thirds of each himatid, the portions farthest from the beach, sank under the water, leaving wide stretches of open sea between the remaining visible sections of whale. The light signals from these intensified. The noise rose in pitch. The first of the bioloons splashed into the water.

And the himatids guided the rest of the Masters home.

EPILOGUE

Rilla stood near the birthing pool with Tmafekitch and her mate, a purplish male named Frikatim with a long snorkel and one extra toe. Rilla felt a little shy of Frikatim, whom, after all, she didn't know very well—how could she? She and Daddy had only been in the village a few days. Tmafekitch had had months and months to get to know Frikatim, and she must like him, or she wouldn't be having a baby with him, would she? Rilla didn't know if she liked him or not. As long as he let her have these ten days with Tmafekitch, these ten days Daddy had promised she could have, Rilla didn't really care if Frikatim was there or not. It wasn't as if she were jealous of her friend's mate. Much.

She knew why Daddy had let her have the ten days, moving his field camp clear over by Tmafekitch's adopted village (after they found it). Rilla knew why. But she didn't like to think about the reason.

Tmafekitch made a sudden noise, a high clear click that meant she was startled. She took a few steps into the birthing pool, then crowded closer to Frikatim. In the pool, the tough membrane of the egg sac began to wobble.

Rilla said, "Is the baby coming?"

Tmafekitch answered, in their own private language, "Soon!" and waved her snorkel in circles.

"I'll get the Master!" Rilla cried, glad to have something to do.

The Master was staying in a sort of dome made of woven plants and daubed mud, since this village, unlike the one Tmafekitch had been born in, had no Carnot temple. A curtain of snug hung down in front of the doorway. Rilla knocked on a li-plant stem—the Masters had seemed to understand without any trouble the human custom of knocking—and the snug pulled apart. The Master came out.

He carried a stick covered with crawling snug. Rilla looked at it furtively—would it grow a new kind of plant Tmafekitch and her baby could eat? One Master had already made a plant with bright red berries that Tmafekitch said were delicious, although of course Rilla couldn't eat them. She kept her glance at the writhing stick very fast. She was never really comfortable with the Masters. Unlike the Ihrdizu, they seemed to have no interest whatsoever in a little girl.

She said to the unsmiling face, so much farther above her than Tmafekitch's would have been, "Tmafekitch. Baby. Now." That was how the Masters liked you to talk to them: the simplest Ihrdizu words, in the smallest number that would convey the information.

The Master didn't say thank you—they never *did,* Rilla thought resentfully—and started toward the birthing pool. Rilla followed. The Master walked too fast for her to keep up, which was supposed to indicate something wonderful about their bodies. That the bones or muscles or heart or something were actually changing to adapt to the gravity. Rilla couldn't have cared less. Even a Master should say thank you.

She had to admit, though, that the Masters had been good for Genji. She didn't understand it all, but Daddy said that since the Chujoans returned, Genji was being transformed from the bottom ecological layer up, for greater stability and abundance. Well, Rilla didn't know about that, but she did know it was prettier. There were thicker plants, and brighter flowers, and more food for the Ihrdizu, and the sea had more bits of colored plankton floating in it. Rilla even liked the patches of snug that crawled freely around the tidal pools, sometimes venturing onto paths, although they gave many humans the creeps.

Like Mommy.

She had to see Mommy this afternoon, because the new ship was leaving for Earth tomorrow and Rilla would never see her again. It was only right, Daddy said, that Rilla see her one last time. She hadn't seen her much, because Mommy had never come down off the ship in orbit since the day the Masters had sailed out of the sky from Chujo. That old ship was too damaged by its trip to Genji to ever leave again, so it just stayed in orbit, and Mommy just orbited along with it. Everything Mommy knew about the Masters, she had watched on screens.

Rilla hated to admit to herself that she didn't want to see Mommy.

So instead she hurried along the path to the birthing pool, and by the time she got there the baby was tearing at the inside of the egg sac with its tiny sharp claws. Tmafekitch and Frikatim watched anxiously, their front legs in the pool up to their tentacles, not helping but making encouraging bleats and clicks. Everybody knew you mustn't help a baby out of its egg sac. If you did, it might not be strong enough to live.

But the baby *did* get out. It tore the sac and stuck its snout through, and then its front claws, and then pulled its claws back in and stuck out its little tentacles. It kept struggling until its back claws were free, and then it stood in the shallow of the birthing pool where Tmafekitch and Frikatim had fed it for so long with bits of plants and secretions and their own shit, which Daddy said was good for eggs. The Master had pissed in the pool, too, every morning. Now the Master picked up the baby and gently shoved a bit of special snug down its throat and another bit, a different color, under the flap of its tympanum. Then the Master handed the baby to Frikatim, who would care for it while Tmafekitch hunted and protected them.

Frikatim's snorkel waved proudly. He sat full up on his tail. Tmafekitch and even Rilla crowded close to stroke the back of the squealing baby. It was such a cute little-she! Rilla put a finger between the teeny flukes of its tail, and the baby flipped it in pleasure. Rilla stroked it again while the Master watched, inscrutable, and all of a sudden Rilla was crying at the little-she, at being with Tmafekitch again, at the beauty and excitement of a new life on Genji.

"Hello, Jane," Daddy said.

Rilla tightened her grasp on his hand.

Mommy looked calm, which was more than she had looked the last time Rilla had visited her. She sat in a small room on the ship, a room even smaller than Rilla's partitioned cubby in the field dome. Two walls of the room were painted to look like a place Rilla had never seen. The sky was the wrong color, a sort of garish blue, and the plants were too tall and thin, and very strange-looking. Rilla shrank closer to Daddy.

He said, "I've brought her."

Mommy didn't even look at Rilla. But Rilla knew she saw her. Mommy hurt, that was why she didn't look at Rilla, and seeing Mommy again, remembering how Mommy had combed her hair and read her stories, Rilla hurt, too. So much she thought she couldn't stand it.

But all Mommy said was, "I've been reading the original exploration teams' journals, Bruce."

"Oh? Why is that? I thought you read only things set on Earth."

Mommy didn't say why. "I read Toshio Tatsuhiko, Yukiko Arama, Emile Esperanza, Nicole Washington—even Aaron Kammer. The presnug Aaron Kammer. The human."

Daddy's mouth turned down.

"And you know what?" Mommy said. "They all reflect the same concern. They all cared so much about not causing ecological and cultural imbalance on Genji and Chujo. Were so fucking *concerned* about human contamination. And all the time we humans were completely, totally irrelevant. Don't you think that's funny?"

Daddy said, "I'm not sure it's true."

"Yes, you are. You know it. All the ecological balances, all the cultural disasters, were caused by the Murasakians themselves. Not by us. And now they're being corrected by the Murasakians themselves, and not all our science or religion or so-called 'art' or anything else has made the slightest difference to the whole weird process. Isn't that true?"

Daddy was silent.

"How does it feel to be completely irrelevant, Bruce? How do you stand it?"

Daddy glanced down at Rilla. "That's enough, Jane. Please don't start again. . . . "

"And do you know why we're irrelevant on Genji and Chujo? *Because it's not our system, Bruce.* We can't even eat the food, breathe most of the air— we don't belong here. Even our science doesn't belong here. Science observes things *in order to effect beneficial change,* Bruce. You knew that once. There is nothing we can ever change here. Nothing."

Daddy said, his voice thick, "Not again, Jane. I brought Rilla here to say good-bye. Just that."

"Just that. 'Just that.' A First Conciliator you bought and paid for decides who gets custody of my daughter and you—"

"That's not true, Jane! Not even a word of it!"

Rilla saw a place to say something. Holding on to Daddy's hand very tight, she said, "I wanted to stay on Genji, Mommy. I *wanted* to. I told Mr. Dane that."

Mommy didn't say anything. Suddenly she hugged Rilla so tight Rilla couldn't breathe. "Mommy! You're hurting me!"

Abruptly, Mommy let her go. Then she was pushing them out of the cabin, closing the door. "Go! Go! Take her!"

Daddy picked up Rilla, who was too old to be picked up, and ran down the ship corridor. He didn't stop until he got to the shuttle bay, where he set her down, knelt, and brought his face close to hers. "Rilla—are you sure? There won't be another ship from Earth for at least three years standard, you know. Are you sure?"

Rilla said, "I'm sure."

"And I . . . I know I'm not the best father for you, I get so caught up in my work . . . "

Rilla hated it when he got like this. It was so much better when he just *did* the work, letting her do what she wanted to. She was all right, she had Tmafekitch and the other Ihrdizu. . . . When Daddy got like this, she almost despised him. That feeling frightened her. So she said coldly, "Don't start again, Daddy. Please."

After that, Daddy got quiet. Rilla felt herself grow quieter, too. But it wasn't until they were in the shuttle, returning to Genji, that she spoke again.

"Daddy—I didn't tell Mommy that Mr. Dane isn't going to stay on Genji. I was going to, because I thought she might want to know who else was going to make the trip with her, but then I didn't. Was that right?"

Daddy brushed his face with his hand. "That was right, Rilla."

"Daddy—are we unimportant to Genji, like Mommy said?"

Daddy sucked in his cheeks. "Yes."

"Then . . . then why are you staying? I mean, I know why *I'm* staying, because I was born here"—*Rita Byrne and Seigi Minoru and Cade Anson and me*—"but why are you? If you're completely unimportant to Genji?"

Bruce Johnson looked out the shuttle window. The great ship was in low orbit; beneath them Genji's clouds swirled thickly, covering and uncovering an expanse of bleak sea, multicolored land.

"Because Genji is important to me."

Suzy Tatsumi laid the bunch of flowers on Edward Philby's grave, telling herself it was a ridiculous and sentimental thing to do. Certainly Philby would have thought so. The body, cremated, was not really buried under the rough stone marker, and the tide would come up in a few hours and carry away the flowers anyway. But they were "new flowers," the first the Chujoans had engineered, and Tatsumi wanted them to be there.

Jordan Dane waited in the flyer. She knew he still had much to do before both of them boarded the shuttle tomorrow for the ship, but he showed no sign of impatience. He was, she thought, always and forever, a patient man.

"All done?"

"In my grandmother's house in Kyoto," Tatsumi said as the flyer lifted, "was a painting on rice paper. It was very old, and she was very proud of it. The painting showed a mountain beside a sea. It was done in the old style: very spare, quick, light brush strokes. In the foreground were plum blossoms. I would stare at the painting for hours when I was a child. What I remember—although it is difficult to know if memory is accurate—is that the mountain and the sea and the trees filled me with peace. They seemed completely calm, caught forever in a moment of perfect balance."

"I see," Dane said.

"I think you do," Tatsumi said, in her pretty voice. "Jordan, where will you go when we reach Earth?"

"I have eleven years to think about it," he said. He did not look at her. "I have never seen Japan."

"You would very much like Kyoto. At least, the Kyoto I remember. Of course, Japan may be very different now."

"Do you expect it will be?"

"Not in its essence. That does not change. And of course there are excellent facilities for the writing of your book."

"I would very much like Japan if you were there," Dane said.

"It is very different from a habitat. Or from Genji."

"I would hope so," Jordan said.

The flyer skimmed over a cliff and then over the sea. Below them drifted a mass of the new plankton the Masters were breeding, dull red. It was fast-growing, of high nourishment to several breeds of Genji sea life, genetically malleable. Bruce Johnson had exulted in the new plankton.

Suzy said neutrally, "I am twenty years your senior, Jordan."

"I don't think I should want to come to Kyoto if you were not."

"It is not usual for a young man to value a . . . a formal balance over, let us say, sexual youth. Or riotous adventure."

Dane looked again at the drifting mass of plankton, which had not existed two months ago. At the bioloon floating in the air in the far distance above Nighland. At the manic report Bruce Johnson had turned in correlating QED fuzzy-logic deductions about the bioengineered spaceship, the Masters' cities on Chujo, the genetic alteration of plankton and land fauna, the sudden vocabulary acquisition of the Ihrdizu, and his wife's refusal to set foot on Genji. The report also covered the origin of carpet whales, which Johnson maintained had been created by the Chupchups. Three Japanese researchers had filed angry and derisive counterreports, calling Johnson's speculations "irresponsible science-mongering," a term completely opaque to Dane. Maybe it was the translator. Johnson had counterattacked. Resource allocations for Malachiel Holden's carpet-whale studies were affected by the politics of this and six other scientific feuds dumped on the First Conciliator, with Holden's resources being cut by a third. Or increased by a third—the outcome was not yet clear. Holden and Byrne were screaming anyway, just in case. Three Quantists had declared the Chujoan return to be a "Return," capital R, and had set about building more Carnot temples. Two of the time artists had moved into a Carnot temple to hold what they called a "court of time": Dane had failed to find out exactly what this involved. The ship from Earth was bringing a mixed scientific and missionary team. The ship was called the *Light of Allah,* and most of the people aboard, after eleven years together, seemed to be engaged in blood feuds with each other.

"Riotous adventure," Dane repeated, and laughed, and reached for Suzy's hand.

After a moment she laughed, too.

The new First Conciliator stood ready to greet the first team of scientists off the shuttle. It was actually the shuttle belonging to the old ship still in orbit; apparently, the shuttle on the *Light of Allah* had been damaged in some unspecified accident in transit. The First Conciliator found it hard to picture this: surely not even a space-bored crew would have reason to try to make use of a shuttle while traveling at an acceleration slightly greater than one g? What could they do with it? These questions had not thus far been answered.

The shuttle touched down on the plain not far from the sub-Genji point. The main base on Chujo had, of course, been shifted to here after the startling events of eight months ago. And now that the new First Conciliator had been chosen, Dune Tiger Station would replace Okuma Base as the center of joint decisions for the humans in the Murasaki System.

If you could call what Miyuki made "decisions."

The shuttle air lock opened, and the first ten embarkees, in full suits, stepped onto the soil of Chujo. Miyuki moved forward, greeting first Captain Salah Mahjoub, then each member of the scientific team. Before greeting the last man in line, she braced herself.

Even through his faceplate the resemblance was startling. The old pictures she had seen... just the same. The light, sandy hair, so out of place among the dark-complexioned team. The slightly crooked nose, gray eyes, too-small chin.

She said in English, "You are welcome to the Murasaki System, Mr. Kevin Kammer-Washington."

His eyes burned with his special interest in this place: the boulder-strewn valley with its deep crevasses, the self-managing fields, the ruins of the Chupchup city on the horizon.

"Thank you, First Conciliator," he said. "I am very eager to become a part of Chujo."

APPENDIX A:
DESIGN FOR TWO WORLDS

BY POUL ANDERSON

Hoping to keep the science in this book as "hard" as possible, I have picked a real star, close enough that it could be reached in human-scale time without going faster than light. I also wanted to avoid those within such a radius that everybody else has been using. Since big, bright stars are implausible (to put it mildly) as suns of habitable planets, this gets us to the red dwarfs. Some astronomers raise objections to these, too, which I will get to shortly, but to my mind this constitutes a challenge with the potential of generating some interesting worlds.

The star in question has only a catalogue number, HD36395 (or $-3°1123$), for it is of magnitude 7.9, well below naked-eye visibility, in Orion (RA 5^h26^m, dec. $-3°42'$). The parallax is $0.''163$, which translates to just about 20 light-years and gives an absolute visual magnitude of 9.03, corresponding to a luminosity of 0.0213, or about 1/47, Sol's. The spectral type is M1.

Twenty light-years is not enough of a distance to change the constellations much. Some stars in the Orion vicinity may show a little displacement. Sol is in Ophiuchus, of magnitude 4.08, visible without instruments but unimpressive. There does not seem to be any rule governing the orientation of stellar rotation axes and orbital planes, so I am arbitrarily supposing this system is so arranged—at this moment in galactic history—that north is in the general direction of Sheliak, Beta Lyrae, about 57° off our north celestial pole. Of course, each of the planets has its own north, but this sector is approximately right for all of them, unless some writer wants to give one a radically skewed revolution or rotation.

A spacecraft traveling at one Earth gravity acceleration, turn-over (commencement of equal deceleration) at midpoint, would cover 20 light-years in 21 years Earth time, but, because of relativistic effects, only 11 years plus a couple of months in ship's time. A 2-g boost would cut the latter time to 6.25 years. Perhaps people could take this much without ill effect. It would be harder on the circulatory system than on the bones and muscles; but medications to help might be developed. Bussard ramjets and/or antimatter fueling will theoretically make such spacecraft possible—though thinking about problems of engineering, what the ship *cannot* do, as well as human organization and relationships en route, yields material for many stories. If the ship was much slower, I at least would want suspended animation, unless life span had been enormously increased. I no longer believe "generation ships" are feasible.

THE SUN

The astronomical data above are not really as exact as they may look; obser-vations have their probable errors. What follows is, to be honest, even less precise. It represents what I have calculated using formulas for relationships among such quantities as luminosity, mass, color index, diameter, and temper-ature. Besides necessarily embodying the uncertainties of the primary data, these formulas omit important factors, notably age. Fortunately, red dwarfs evolve very slowly, so that this generally matters much less where they are concerned than it does for larger stars. I have carried out my results to more significant figures than is justified, but we may as well use these; they're as likely to be correct as any others in the same ballpark.

The mass comes out to be 0.333 Sol's, just one-third. The di-ameter is proportionately larger, 0.82 Sol's, because red dwarfs are less dense. Seen from the distance of the hypothetical planets to be discussed, it has an angular diameter of 1°40′12″, or 3.67 times that of Sol seen from Earth. The photosphere temperature is 3,396 K (cf. Sol's approximately 6,000 K), which makes the wavelength of maximum intensity emitted 8,500 Å, in the near in-frared (cf. Sol's 3,300 Å, in the near ultraviolet).

At this point I must emphasize that the term "red dwarf" is misleading, as are color names for most kinds of stars. We would not see a dull crimson ember. A temperature of 3,396 K is well above that of old-time carbon-filament incandescent lamps (about 2,400 K) and not far below that of a carbon arc (about 3,900 K). Our star is certainly less brilliant than Sol. You could look straight at it for a little bit longer without suffering permanent eye damage, but only a little bit, and you wouldn't want to. Its light has a yellowish tinge, and at the distance of our imaginary planets there is significantly less than Earth gets, but human vision is so adaptable that ordinarily this won't make any important difference. Think of being in a normally well-lighted twentieth-century room after dark. The paucity of ultraviolet radiation does have its very noticeable effects, which we'll get to later.

It is thought that stars like this have considerable solar winds, in volume if perhaps not so much in energy. If you blanked out the disk of ours, you'd see a larger corona than Sol's, a spectacular sight indeed. On the other hand, flares and prominences are probably smaller and fewer. There are doubtless sunspots, but it seems to be anybody's guess how big and many they are, or what kind of cycle they go through. My own guess is that this kind of activity, too, is less than on Sol, but that occasionally a large and highly energetic flare occurs.

Age and composition are equally problematic. As a general rule, which must have individual exceptions, the older a star is, the poorer it is in "metals" (elements heavier than helium). Bright ones like Sirius are so short-lived that we can set an upper limit on their ages and those of any companions, which presumably formed together with them. However, the dim ones change so slowly that we have no such clues other than their spectra, which are not always very helpful. HD36395 is in our immediate neighborhood, and its rather modest velocity with respect to us suggests that it hasn't drifted in from a remote and very different region. Subject to correction, I assume it is about as old as Sol, whose age is a bit under five billion years, and has a similar metal content—which means that its planets resemble ours to that extent.

At this point, rather than continue entirely in so abstract a vein, some ideas about nomenclature may be in order. I suppose the mythologies of Earth will long since have been used up on closer planetary systems that are also of interest (if not within the solar system itself, the way things have been going). At the same time, if people intend to pay much attention at all to a given set of worlds, they'll want names for them, and it will be helpful to have those names bestowed according to some system rather than at whim.

With Karen Anderson's help, I have christened HD36395 Murasaki, for the famous Japanese writer (*floruit* A.D. 1000), and its planets for characters in her *Genji Monogatari*. The two on which we shall concentrate are called "Genji," for the hero of the novel, and "Tō no Chujo," for his close friend; the latter can correctly be shortened to "Chujo." Doubtless there are other planets in the system, of less interest because they have no life; probably they number fewer than Sol's retinue. Giants could be named for the two emperors in the tale, Ryozen and Suzaku. Other male characters include Sochi and Yugiri; females include Asagao, Aoi, Omiya, and Jokyoden.

PLANETS

Today it does seem likely that the majority of stars, at least, are accompanied by lesser objects, and that in many cases some of these objects are large enough to be called planets. How common life may be is another matter. So far the solar system has proved disappointing, and one school of thought holds that the necessary conditions are so strict that Earth may be unique, or close to unique, in the universe. I doubt this very much, but for present purposes will assume that life involves proteins in water solution. Conceivably something radically different exists, but the former is the conservative, "hard" assumption.

By far the largest number of stars are red dwarfs, so if biopoesis cannot occur around any of these, the incidence of it is enormously reduced. The most telling objections, and possible counterarguments to them, are as follows.

1. Their radiation is too poor in ultraviolet to energize the chemistry that leads to life and later makes complex, high-energy organisms possible. *Answer:* Organic molecules of significant complexity have been identified in interstellar space. Without much UV to break them down, they can accumulate on planets, and there react with each other. Moreover, the planets themselves offer such energy sources as cosmic radiation, radioactivity, heat, and lightning, so they might generate their own prebiological molecules. We do not today know how fast chemical and biological evolution could proceed on that basis, but the fact seems to be that the formation of an ozone layer on Earth, vastly reducing the UV at the surface, did not slow it down much if at all. Besides, presumably life could employ more labile molecules than ours, with the visible wavelengths supplying sufficient energy. I shall make that assumption here.

2. The planet must be at such a temperature, for extremely long periods of time, that water exists in liquid form on its surface, neither all frozen nor all vaporized. The region around a red dwarf in which it receives just the right amount of energy for this is so narrow that surely very few orbits throughout the universe happen to occupy any. *Answer:* It ought to occur occasionally. More importantly, greenhouse effect, about which more later, broadens the zone considerably. Indeed, Earth would be frozen solid were it not for this. Hence the situation isn't really implausible.

3. If the planet is close enough in, the tidal drag of the sun, which follows an inverse cube law, will produce a locked rotation, whether 1:1 as Earth has done to its moon or 2:3 as Sol has done to Mercury. The dark side will get so cold, in its permanent or very long night, that atmosphere, or at least all water, will soon freeze out, and not much will melt or sublime by day. At best, the whole world will be as arid as our Antarctica. Life couldn't develop or survive

with so little moisture. *Answer:* Atmospherics is not an exact science yet, but full of surprises. Global circulation might actually keep the dark side warm enough. But a more picturesque possibility is that of a double planet, two worlds swinging around a common center of mass that orbits the sun, thus enjoying a sufficiently rapid alternation of night and day. I grant you that this is doubtless rare, but it is the situation I propose to develop, with Genji and Chujo being the companion globes.

What kind of orbit around Murasaki do they share? We don't today know what determines such quantities. I could put them at a mean distance of 0.1459 a.u. (astronomical unit, where Earth's from Sol = 1.0 a.u.) so that they get as much irradiation from their sun as we do from ours, albeit with a different spectral distribution. However, that seemed awfully close in—and not really playing the game! I finally settled on 0.2233 a.u. This is still a smaller orbit than Mercury's (0.387), but the gravitational field has the same strength, so it seems reasonable that planets could condense there. Genji-Chujo is, I suppose, the innermost of any noteworthiness; outer worlds are distributed according to some kind of Bode-Titius rule, and the scale of the system in general is smaller than Sol's.

At this distance, our associated planets receive 0.4272 the irradiation Earth gets, comparable to Mars'. As mentioned earlier, the sun appears three and two-thirds times as wide as Sol seen from Earth. The tidal force of Murasaki is about 1.72 that of Sol on Mercury. Whether this would produce a 1:1 rotation, I'm not sure; it's quite a bit less than the drag of Earth on Luna. Doubtless it would at least have slowed the rotation down greatly, were it not for the double-planet situation.

The sidereal year of the companions is 0.1829 Earth's, or 66 days, 19½ hours in Terrestrial terms.

Now the question arises how planets receiving no more energy than this can support life. As observed earlier, we must invoke greenhouse effect, which implies a substantial atmosphere. How much is it reasonable to give a world whose size is the same order of magnitude as Earth's? All or nearly all primordial gas must have been lost early on, and a secondary atmosphere outgassed. If the amount of this was proportional to mass, we get the interesting result that air pressure down at the surface was then proportional to the square of g, the gravitational acceleration at that surface. (A recent and rather heterodox idea is that we got much of our water from small comets. The latest evidence seems to have discredited this, but even if it is true, a planet should attract comets proportionally to its mass.) This argument is, though, pretty academic. Atmospheres evolve, and the cases of Earth, Venus, and Mars show how radically different they can become.

Since Genji and Chujo are of approximately Earth mass, I assume they both have plate tectonics and that this, along with other factors, has caused most of the original carbon dioxide to be fixed in the rocks. Life has also been at work; both atmospheres now contain oxygen, nitrogen, and argon in approximately Terrestrial proportions, with carbon dioxide, water vapor, and methane the most significant trace compounds.

Let us start by considering mean planetary temperatures. Earth's is about 288 K (15°C)—which, when one looks at the range of temperatures found in reality, shows how artificial that "mean" is. Yet we need some such figure as the basis for further thinking. The absolute temperature, T, should be a roughly linear function of albedo, A, or rather of the quantity 1 − A; of greenhouse effect; and of the fourth root of irradiation. I have found the thoughts of Frank Chadwick and his associates very helpful in this connection.

Albedo is an overall figure, depending on how much of what kinds of surface the planet has. Water reflects more light than rock but less than ice, etc. If cloudiness varies, so will A. Given their characteristics, to be detailed later, I estimated the mean A for Genji as 0.35, a little more than Earth's, and for Chujo as 0.15, about like Mars'.

Greenhouse effect is still more a matter of guesswork and arbitrariness. It should be crudely proportional to the amount of atmosphere per unit area, but we are discovering here on Earth—we are likely to find out the precise details the hard way—what a difference very slight-looking variations in such quantities as CO_2 content can make. The present case is further complicated by the fact that the greenhouse gases will keep much of Murasaki's radiation out! Nevertheless, the wavelengths that get through will result in heat being trapped, especially if our planets have a little more carbon dioxide in their airs than Earth does.

Once again weighing the various factors as best I could, I derived a mean temperature of 293K (20°C) for Genji, 278 K (5°C) for Chujo. Rough though these results are, they indicate that it is reasonable to suppose the two planets support life.

At this point I should admit that none of their characteristics came to me through divine inspiration. It was all very much a business of cut-and-try, converging by successive approximations on the desired result—and more often than not, this or that assumption, while promoting the possibility of a habitable world, had other consequences that surprised me. This is one of the things that makes planet-building fun.

The Genji-Chujo pair has a center of mass that orbits Murasaki at the given mean distance of 0.2233 a.u. The eccentricity is about 0.02, slightly more than for Earth but its effects small compared to those of other factors. Precession and nutation of the combined orbits and the planetary rotation axes must be considerable and have important effects, such as changes of regional climates, over geologically short periods of time. Being larger, Genji is proportionately closer to the center of mass and swings through a smaller course.

The mutual orbit of the planets is not in the same plane as that of the center, but is in the present epoch inclined 4°29' to it. The planets are separated by an average distance of 156,262 kilometers, about 40 percent of the Earth-Luna figure. The eccentricity of this orbit is 0.06, which means that, although they are in locked rotation facing each other, they librate somewhat. This has effects on their atmospheres, hydrospheres, and lithospheres. The period is 3.78 Earth days, or 90 hours, 43 minutes, 12 seconds. Thus the year = 17.6 planetary days.

Their tidal forces on each other are huge. The locked rotation minimizes the effects, but they are there, both because of libration and because of their action on air, water, and rock. The tidal force of Murasaki on either amounts to 13.6 times that of Luna on Earth, and this is of course fully manifested in the course of a rotation period.

Hence Genji and Chujo cannot always have been in locked rotation and will not always continue so. Genji especially is being slowed down by frictional losses in its seas, driving the two globes farther apart. However, precisely because the forces are so large, straits where the losses are especially great are geologically short-lived. On a human time-scale, Genji and Chujo have been as they are with respect to each other for a long time and will stay that way for another long time.

I will now discuss the general physical characteristics of the two planets separately. Some of the quantities already mentioned, such as the shared rotation period, derive from them.

GENJI

This is the larger partner. Letting "E" stand for "times that of Earth," it has a mass of 2.77 E and a mean density of 1.1 E, which means its mean diameter is 1.36 E, or 17,349 km. Like Chujo, it is little flattened by its rather slow rotation, but has been measurably (though not perceptibly by the unaided eye) deformed by the gravitation of the other world, so that it is slightly egg-shaped with the point toward the latter. Escape velocity is 15.98 km per sec; cf. Earth's 11.2. Standing on a level plain, a person of average height would see the horizon about 5.6 km off, compared to 4.8 on Earth. The surface gravity is 1.50 E. Humans in good condition can tolerate this, though they have to be wary of falls—indeed, acquire a whole new art of walking, running, and throwing—and cannot carry loads as large as they could at home.

The inclination of the axis to the shared orbital plane is 3°17′. Even taking into account the inclination of this orbit, it does not lead to much in the way of seasons anywhere. At sea level, climates range from hotter than Earth's tropics to coolish-temperate in the polar regions; there are no ice caps. Given the lesser irradiation, slower rotation, and denser atmosphere compared to Earth, winds are generally light, though they have more force for a given speed. Spectacular lightning storms are quite common. Other things being equal, waves on deep water travel some 20 percent faster than on Earth, which joins with the powerful, complexly shifting tidal forces to make for violent, treacherous seas.

The distribution of water and land surface is similar to Earth's, 0.8 to 0.2. There is more cloudiness and precipitation. Given the greater density gradient of the atmosphere, clouds do not generally form very high up. What uplands exist are therefore usually clear-skied, and overlook extensive lowland cloud decks—which, however, are not permanent like Venus', but change and often break up for a while.

Highlands are comparatively few, though, and no mountains are as tall as Earth's best. Plate tectonics and other diastrophic processes operate more strongly, because of the greater planetary mass, generating many earthquakes and pushing strata up; but they have a stronger gravitational field to work against, and erosion by the heavier atmosphere helps bring down their creations faster. Most coastlands are regularly inundated by the enormous tides, which often produce savage, dangerous bores.

The sea-level atmospheric pressure is 3.1 bars. Given its Earth-like composition, this is too much for humans, unless they have devices to reduce it before they breathe. The lowest endurable altitude, and it not really safe, is about 2,100 meters, where pressure has fallen to 2 bars, and you don't get a comfortable 1 bar till you're at about 5,800 meters, an altitude seldom found and a cold, arid, sparsely begrown environment. Because Murasaki light contains much less blue than Sol's, the sky looks darker than Earth's, dusky grayish. From sea level, on a clear night, you see far fewer stars even on "starside," the outer hemisphere, while on "moonside" the brightness of Chujo washes nearly all out of vision.

The tidal drag of Chujo = 917.3 times that of Luna on Earth. Though the locked rotation minimizes the consequences of this, you do get tremendous slosh effects in some seas as Genji librates, and of course big tides follow Murasaki around the world. Because of gravitational deformation, most of the highest country on Genji is on moonside, concentrating around the area below Chujo.

Seen from Genji, Chujo has an angular diameter of 4°24″, which is 8.5 times that of Luna or Sol seen from Earth. When it is full, it gives 66 times the light of full Luna, or about 0.0001 that of Sol on Earth. It does not eclipse Murasaki every noon, and some eclipses are partial or cover the sun only briefly. Maximum eclipse durations occur twice a year, 1 hour 6 minutes during which the sun is entirely hidden. (The time from first to last contact adds about 20 minutes.) At such times the darkened planetary disk is surrounded by a red ring of refracted light.

CHUJO

I will run through the features in pretty much the same order. Both its mass and its density are appreciably less, especially the former. (As for the latter, I was guessing again, but guessing on the basis of what we observe in the solar system.) The mass is 0.758 E, the density 0.9 E, leading to a mean diameter of 0.94 E, or 11,922 km. Escape velocity is 10.05 km per sec. Flat horizon distance is 4.7 km, substantially the same as on Earth. Surface gravity is 0.85 E, which poses no physiological problems for humans.

The inclination of the axis to the shared orbital plane is 25°28'. Taken together with the inclination of the orbit itself, theoretically this increases summer temperature by some 34°C and reduces winter temperature by some 19°C. These figures must not be taken literally; the calculation is exceedingly crude, and among other things, the shortness of the year will prevent such extremes. However, it does join with the generally dry surface and thin air to indicate violent swings of weather. Windstorms are frequent and strong, though lightning, rain, and snow are scarce.

Land and water distributions are almost the reverse of Genji's: 0.72 to 0.22, with polar caps and other ice fields covering the rest of the surface. Clouds are slight and the ice is generally dusty; together with the desertlike ecology of most regions, this accounts for the low albedo. Skies are usually clear, except when dust storms arise. Sometimes the dust is glittery powdered ice, at least in part. What clouds occur are oftenest cirrus, high and thin in a dark purplish sky. Starside nights are wonderfully starry.

In general, Chujo is a world ranging from chilly to intensely cold, though temperatures about like a warm summer day in Earth's temperate zones can be briefly experienced in the lower latitudes. Most of the water is locked in permafrost and buried glaciers. Topographical and geological evidence indicates that this was not always the case and will not always be so. Much less well buffered than Genji or even Earth, this planet is subject to effects of orbital and rotational shifts, which, astronomically speaking, go on rather rapidly. It has had its warm, wet cycles in the past and will again in the future.

With almost as much tectonic activity as Earth and with less gravity and erosion, Chujo has many elevated tablelands and great mountain ranges, some of which exceed anything Terrestrial. In the present epoch there are no proper oceans; seas are small and mostly wide-scattered. A number of them are intensely briny, as are many marshes. Dried riverbeds and sea bottoms are common. Although Genji's tidal force on Chujo is about 1,210 times that of Luna on Earth, its effects are mainly apparent in the mountainous character of moonside and in the frequency of volcanoes, a "ring of fire," girdling the planet on the border between moonside and starside.

The sea-level atmospheric pressure is 0.71 bar. This is equivalent to 3,660 meters on Earth. Not all humans can acclimate to it, and everybody finds its dryness uncomfortable. Nobody can go much higher without artificial help. At an altitude of some 6,000 meters pressure has dropped to one-half, quite insufficient for us.

Genji has an angular diameter in the sky of 6°20′24″, about 12.27 times that of Luna seen from Earth, and when full gives 321.6 times the light, about 0.0006 that of Sol on Earth, ample to read by and even see colors. It eclipses Murasaki oftener than Chujo does, the maximum duration of totality being 1 hour, 35 min, 12 sec. The red ring then seen is somewhat thinner and fainter than it is around the eclipsed Chujo.

LIFE

Although organisms and, indeed, ecologies are quite different on Genji and Chujo, it is astounding how similar the biochemistries are, beginning with the genetic codes. The variations are not much more than would be expected on a single planet such as Earth. It is thought that this is due to primitive spores having been carried between the planets, from high in the atmosphere, by light pressure, the Arrhenius process. Murasaki light and wind would be less disruptive than Sol's. Which world life started on is debatable, considering how Chujo, especially, has changed with time. Perhaps it began independently on both and swapped around; there are some anomalous life-forms, especially on the microscopic level.

Fundamentally this biology involves proteins in water solution, as on Earth, but for the most part they are not the same proteins or even all the same amino acids, while such classes of compounds as lipids, sugars, etc., that life also uses are still more different from ours. In a general sense, the key molecules are more labile than on Earth, as they must be to use the lower-energy quanta that this sun mainly offers. Ultraviolet is as deadly to Murasakian life as hard X rays are to Terrestrial. Since the planets have no ozone layers to speak of, the—fortunately infrequent—large flares on the sun can bring disaster to exposed regions.

Fire might be thought to be still more of a hazard on oxygen-rich Genji, but most plants there have evolved to be not readily combustible. Some are, their reproductive cycles depending on it. On the whole, animals are apt to be worse injured by a burn than we are.

Obviously, humans and other Terrestrial creatures can get no nourishment from this life, and most tastes terrible while some is outright poisonous. The converse holds, of course. Thus people need fear no native microbes, and any damage suffered from large animals will be essentially accidental.

On both planets we get vegetable and animal kingdoms as on Earth, with corresponding ambiguities. (In their book *Five Kingdoms*, Margulis and Schwartz recognize that many on our planet.) Most vegetation photosynthesizes, thereby supplying the atmospheres with their free oxygen. For this it does not employ chlorophyll, but a molecule activated by red and orange light. Consequently most leaves, stalks, etc. are yellow. Humans have dubbed the compound "xanthophyll." Strictly speaking, there are two distinct forms, one found on Genji and one on Chujo, which gives a clue to early evolution on those worlds; but the variation between the molecules is not great. The shades and tones of yellow are as many as are the greens on Earth, and, just as with some Terrestrial plants that are not green because of pigmentation, some here are other colors, especially blue.

Presumably due to the shortness of the year, no deciduous plants have developed on either world. The botany of both is as complicated and fascinating as ever Earth's was. Some Terrestrial adaptations are lacking, and some here have no Terrestrial counterparts.

However, I will concentrate on the animal life of Genji. It is every bit as various, intricate, and alien as the vegetation. As was to be expected, nothing has evolved that can properly be called a fish, reptile, bird, etc. Still, form follows function, and many structures are analogous to those on Earth.

This includes the basic design of many multicellular creatures. Like ours, they are essentially cylinders, taking in nourishment at one end, where the major sense organs are, and excreting wastes at the other end, with appendages in between that are more or less cylindrical, too. (I am reminded of the childish riddle, "What is the difference between a stovepipe and a crazy Dutchman?" Answer: "One is a hollow cylinder, and the other is a silly Hollander.") Such organs as male and female gonads, eyes, ears, lungs, etc., together with such structures as exo- and endoskeletons, scales, teeth, wings, horns, etc., have evolved. The endoskeletal animals all have just four true limbs, the same as on Earth. Yet differences of detail are countless, especially when one studies what is below the surface, and often these differences are quite radical—as they can be on Earth.

Two things immediately strike the human observer newly arrived on Genji. One is the vast proliferation of winged creatures, of every size from nearly microscopic insectoids to hoverers larger than our ancient Quetzalcoatlus. Although the planet's gravity is higher than Earth's, the great air pressure more than compensates, making conditions very favorable for flyers. All classes have representatives, even the ichthyoids, some of which have developed oxygen storage enabling them to leap from the water and flap for a while.

The other feature is the absence of anything at all analogous to our mammalia. Live birth and a primitive sort of homeothermy do occur in some beasts, and one order combines them, though it is no more conspicuous than mammals were in our Mesozoic; but placentas, lactation, and hair are quite unknown. There has been no "reason" for them. Despite regional climatic changes through geological time, Genji seems never to have had any glacial era; probably the dense atmosphere and huge hydrosphere are too good a buffer. Also, given the small axial tilt and the dearth of any real highlands, there is much less zonal variation than on Earth.

(Where mountains do exist, conditions change far more rapidly with altitude, because air pressure drops faster. Thus uplands become populated by specialized plants and animals, often in successively higher ecological belts that have relatively little interaction with each other. Mountains being short-lived, these organisms have not had the chance to evolve much beyond their special adaptations; they are mostly small and rather primitive.)

Nonetheless, animals have developed numerous remarkable features—in two species, actual intelligence. I will discuss these species at some length. Not only are they of particular interest to us, but each typefies its general kind in the same way that we typefy the less specialized mammals.

THE LAND GENJIANS

Also known as Ihrdizu, and sometimes by other names, all names being in some degree inaccurate, these are the more numerous race, probably the more advanced, and certainly the easier for humans to make contact with. Temporarily, therefore, I shall just call them the Genjians, as if they were the only sapients on the planet.

The ancestral form originated in a coastal area. It has been pointed out that the gigantic tides inundate most littorals. The water is turbulent and tricky, but by bringing up minerals from below—as well as by receiving material brought from inland by erosion—it supports a rich variety of life. The proto-Genjian lived an amphibious existence, going ashore at low tide or swimming up to the marshes; it nested and hunted in the great mats of "floating forest"; it dived below in search of prey, but also climbed rocks and cliffs when these reared above high water. This life put a premium on agility, the capability of grasping and holding, sharp senses, and quick wits.

The modern sapient is a quadruped, with five clawed, prehensile digits on the hind feet. The four on each forepaw have smaller claws, almost like nails. The blue-gray, smooth-skinned body is somewhat torpedo-shaped. At the rear is a strong tail with two muscular horizontal flukes. It does the propulsion when the Genjian swims, whether on the water surface or below; the limbs then act as rudders. Ashore, the being uses the tail as a support when it sits upright, or as a formidable weapon in case of need. The head is continuous with the body; there is no neck. The lipless mouth has front teeth meant for snapping and slashing, back teeth meant for grinding; this is an omnivore. An adult female is about two meters long from snout to tail end, and masses some 100 kilos. The adult male is seldom more than a meter and a half long and is rather slenderer.

The beings are not amphibians like frogs or toads, but perhaps they are more analogous to these than to anything else Terrestrial. Ordinarily they are poikilothermic, seeking either sunlight or water to regulate body temperature; but they can "turn up" their metabolism to a high rate and commonly do, being on the whole as active as humans, though better at sitting still when that is called for. Activity helps keep them warm. At need they can "burn" fat directly for heat energy or to support a burst of furious motion, when their speed can be cheetahlike. Lacking sweat glands, they could not survive long in a hot desert, but there are hardly any such on the planet. Nearly all lowland environments offer water, shade, or mud for wallowing.

The head also bears the signs of the breed's aquatic origin. On top is the "snorkel," a small trunk that can be lifted for breathing while the being is submerged; valves can close the passages. It is not the olfactory organ, but it does have a certain thermal sensitivity, helping to track down prey or find one's way in a dense fog. A tympanum on either side responds to sound waves; leathery flaps can be drawn across for protection. This is not as efficient at hearing as the human ear—for one thing, it has poor directionality—but the thick atmosphere, conducting sound fast and well, compensates to a sufficient degree. Four eyes are spaced around the head behind the mouth, thus giving full vision even though the head cannot turn. They are round, have a variety of colors in beautiful agatelike patterns, and possess remarkable dark adaptation. (Many nights are cloudy, Chujo shines on only one hemisphere, and to this day Genjians are often well underwater for many minutes on end.) The eyes are set in telescoping sockets and can be extended several centimeters, enabling the owner to see both above and below water at once or to see past his/her own bulky body when sitting on shore. After being brought down flush with the skin, they can be covered first by a tough, semitransparent protective membrane, then by opaque lids. Often, wishing to concentrate on something, a Genjian has only one or two eyes open.

Two slender tentacles, each terminating in three digits, grow from below the tympani. These were originally sensory palps somewhat like the whiskers of catfish, for use deep in the water; they developed into food collectors and so eventually into boneless but fairly strong "arms" with "fingers." Neither these tentacles nor the forepaws are by themselves as good as human hands, but when a Genjian sits upright the combination is at least as dextrous, and when he/she is being four-footed the tentacles serve perfectly well for such jobs as carrying things or, for that matter, throwing a missile or wielding a simple tool.

The tongue is a larger and more complex organ than ours, with a variety of functions. Its rough upper surface cleans up meat like a cat's; its sides are covered with ciliary chemosensors, so that it both tastes and smells; and it is the male organ of copulation, by which he passes his gametes into the female reproductive tract. At such times its secretions pleasure him as the friction and subtler chemical cues do her. Before you think this is disgusting, consider that *our* male organ doubles as a sewer pipe.

The female lays an "egg," a soft though tough bag about the size of a man's fist, at fairly regular intervals. Despite this equivalent of menstruation, Genjians do not seem to be permanently in low-grade rut like humans; xenologists have seen nothing to suggest purely recreational sex. Desire seems to originate in the female, who courts the male in ways that vary from society to society. After the first adolescent experiments have led to an infant, this arousal apparently is triggered by the stage of development of the youngest offspring; its death leads to the quick production of a new one, whereas if it is in good health there will be a few Terrestrial years between reproductions. This spacing is, however, quite variable, and dependent on a number of factors understood little or not at all. Genjians enjoy sex when it happens, though, inevitably, they surround it with still more mystique than humans have done. They are about as monogamous by nature as we are, whatever that means. Care of the young clearly has more to do with pair bonding than sex does.

A fertilized egg-sac contains the zygote afloat in fluid and the rudiments of certain simple chemical-processing organs. It has been dubbed an "external uterus." The female places it in some kind of small, quiet, watery environment such as a pool or a hole scraped in marshy soil. Both parents then "feed" it, putting organic matter in the water. This includes food scraps, rotted vegetation, etc., but much of it is their own excrement, which during this stage contains nutritious matter. (Rabbits on Earth have a similar ability to vary the quality of their droppings.) The female exudes a fluid from her genital tract containing enzymes that help break it down, and symbiotic microbes are also involved. Otherwise, the male is mainly in charge. As an intelligent being, he gets the satisfaction of doing his duty, but his ancient ancestors must have been responding to stimuli that still have their subliminal effects on him; perhaps odoriferous compounds act as pheromones. Thus both parents are, so to speak, directly involved in gestation, and this undoubtedly has profound psychological consequences.

Blotting up the nutrients from the degraded organic matter, the egg grows and develops together with the zygote. How long until "hatching" depends on conditions. Ideally, it is just a matter of a Genjian year or two; but nourishment may be scarce or it may be necessary to carry the egg away from danger. In such cases, development can be suspended for a considerable time without harm. The male normally does the guarding and tending, and, in primitive milieus, the fleeing or hiding. This may be one reason why he is smaller and more agile than his mate, who in most cultures has been the one to go out and hunt or work the farm. When the young finally claws the sac open and emerges, it cannot quite be called either altricial or precocial. It can eat solid food and move around freely from the start, but is small, ignorant, and dependent on its elders for a long period of care.

In their wet Urheimat, the proto-Genjians never mastered fire and made rather little use of stone. Shells became the principal material for tools and weapons. Some were of animals, some were of plants, especially a genus of large nuts that spread themselves by floating freely about within flinty casings. Instead of fire, perhaps the key invention was footgear. Evolved for swimming and climbing, the creatures were now enabled to walk far inland, encounter new challenges, and spread across the globe. Eventually they did start to use stone and fire, and some got to metallurgy.

For communication, the Genjians make considerable use of body language, notably the flexible tentacles. Since the dense, humid, usually warm air carries odors well, body exudations and even fragrances artificially produced have a certain importance, too, particularly for conveying emotional subtleties. Mainly, though, like us, they talk. We hear the speech as a set of grunts, barks, coughs, belches, rumbles, and quavers; the Genjian voice lacks the range and precision of ours. Nonetheless it can evidently say anything for which a concept exists.

One can no more generalize about Genjians and make sense than one can about humans, but xenologists have gotten some preliminary impressions, subject to correction as more is learned. They have many cultures around the planet, technologically ranging from "paleolithic" upward. Most are based on agriculture and—more importantly—aquaculture, raising both domestic plants and animals in lakes, marshes, estuaries, and bays. In some areas they have draft animals, but none for riding, which is to be expected; some of the draft animals are swimmers pulling boats or small ships, though sails are also known. Considering their anatomy, they have not been very successful with oars. For details about those of them that have reached an industrial stage, see Frederik Pohl's contribution.

Nowhere is there a city. In the more populous regions, single homesteads and thorps that seem to house extended families are spread through an area. Its inhabitants frequently get together at a "fair," which can roughly correspond to the old Icelandic Thing as well as being a mart and social meeting ground.

Individual Genjians, especially females, can quarrel; the quarrels can become deadly; in a number of cultures, apparently this can lead to clan feuds, and homesteads bristle with defenses. Yet war as we have known it seems unheard of. Therefore, so is the nation-state; after all, preparing for wars and waging them is its *raison d'être*. Genjians of the more sophisticated societies do have loyalties beyond immediate kin, but these seem to be relatively abstract: religious ties, trade links, and relationships less comprehensible by us. Public works such as roads, dikes, and harbors are carried out and maintained in these societies, but not at the behest of kings or bureaucrats. Instead, such activities appear to be, by some kind of traditional consent, the duty and prerogative of certain organizations whose membership is hereditary, though adoption into them is a solemnity often performed; they are supported by "user fees" in kind or, in a few regions, coin.

This does not mean that Genjians are natural-born libertarians. If anything, they are more obedient to a set of rules and rituals than most humans, and transgressors are subject to sanctions ranging from payments to an aggrieved party to outlawry and death. Social relationships are intricate. Perhaps the fact that they never live together in crowds helps preserve the prescriptions for interaction when they do meet.

Their religions are, so far, still less understandable by us. Advanced cultures studied to date seem to have had their philosophers but never any prophets, and nowhere are there indications of god-persons; yet a sense of pervasive spirit appears to be universal. It has been ascertained that in societies that live near mountains, these are always regarded with awe and veneration, and many aged individuals ascend them to die.

MORE ABOUT GENJI

Geography

Most of the land surface is on "moonside," the Chujo-facing hemisphere. The huge continent that English-speaking humans call Nighland does extend an arm into northern "starside," the opposite hemisphere. South of it are the somewhat smaller continent Southland and the considerable land mass Great Island. These have their plains, mountain ranges, rivers, lakes, etc., as on Earth. No mountains match the highest of Earth's, though some are tall enough to have snow and glaciers. Because of the rapid decline of air pressure with altitude, such ranges often form sharp ecological borders, with plants and animals quite different on the two sides, as well as climates—weather barriers, too, being more marked than on Earth. Occasional deep valleys have been thus isolated for long times and curious developments have occurred in the life-forms there. However, except for certain desert regions near the middle of Nighland, most lower-lying country is rather uniformly cloudy and rainy. Along the coasts there is much fog, and frequently wind and the great waves of the tides will act to fill the air with drops of brine.

Starside is largely oceanic, like our Pacific basin on a bigger scale. It, too, is surrounded by a "ring of fire," many volcanoes and islands of volcanic origin along the boundary between the hemispheres. This is the result of Chujo's pull, varied by libration, on plate tectonics. (The same effect occurs on Chujo, but much more marked.) Near the middle of Genji starside is the continent called Farland, a little larger than Australia. Archipelagoes and isolated islands are found in both hemispheres.

Ocean currents, westerly winds, and cyclonic winds are less plentiful and strong than on Earth; a real cyclonic storm is a very rare event. Global air circulation is dominated by the tendency to form Hadley cells versus the tendency for air to move from the night to the day side. The slow rotation does provide some westerly component. (By convention, humans define "north" and "south" in a given planetary system so that all, or most, bodies rotate from west to east.)

Life

The vegetable kingdom has developed analogues of gymnosperms and angiosperms, trees, shrubs, vines, flowers, etc. Trees are generally short and stout, to resist the slow but heavy winds and the pull of gravity. There is no worldwide equivalent of the grasses. In some regions, stalky plants with certain similarities of appearance, except for the color, occur; but the most widespread and diverse family is that of the yeisenae (named for Mamoru Yeisen, the botanist who first described them). Low-growing, with small leaves, these commonly cover the ground with a tough mat, through which only certain other kinds of plants are able to pass seeds—usually by way of some animal that grazes or burrows—and thrust up shoots.

Some plant names, bestowed by humans or translated from a native language, which suggest appearances and functions: redlance, clinger, nightwort, groundvine, shadowfruit, cat-o'-nine-tails, bluecap.

Actually, the traditional Terrestrial system of kingdoms, phyla, classes, orders, genera, and species does not work very well on Genji. Perhaps because its thick atmosphere and vast seas buffer it efficiently, the planet does not seem to have suffered much if anything in the way of mass extinctions like Earth, and evolution has radiated from a wild diversity of primordial types. Herewith brief mention of two conspicuous "superphyla," with a third to be discussed later in more detail.

The moonside sapients already described belong to the *tetroptes* (singular *tetrops*), characterized by the basic cylindrical, four-limbed, four-eyed body. One phylum within this possesses a true neck and thus a distinct, movable head. This phylum contains most of the tetroptic bipeds and flyers.

The *astromorphs* have a basic shape suggestive of a starfish, though one "arm" is actually the head and there is an internal skeleton. They include both quadrupeds and bipeds, aquatic and land species—all, however, air-breathing and two-sexed. (I almost wrote "bisexual," but that's another word whose proper meaning these days is slipping from our grasp!) To them belong the largest flyers on the planet, the dinopteryxes. The truly huge ones, outdoing our own old Quetzalcoatlus, are essentially hoverers like our condor, but some raptors are not much smaller and correspondingly formidable. Certain arboreal forms are comparable to our simians, perhaps even in intelligence. The astromorphs occupy parts of Nighland and Southland, and all of Great Island except for what the sapients introduced when they arrived there. In general, the tetroptes are more successful and have displaced most of the astromorphs except for those that took to the air or the trees.

Some animal names (including entomoids, ichthyoids, etc.): silverbuck, slithe, buzzbuzz, mountain dragon, spitcat, skyranger, nightghost, fenris, joker.

The moonside sapients

Already described, these tetroptes are commonly known to humans as land Genjians and Nighlanders—both misnomers, since they are not exclusively dwellers on land, they are not confined to Nighland, and they are not the only intelligent Genjians. In one of their major dialects, the word for "person" is, roughly rendered into our alphabet, "ihrdizu," which is used by many humans, generally capitalized. Plurals are formed according to complex rules; that corresponding to "people" is, approximately, "io-ihrdizu," but most humans simply make the singular double as the plural, analogously to English "deer."

Although technologies and ways of life differ widely across the planet, there is only one language, admittedly with a range of dialects. Fred Pohl discusses this and other details at length. Otherwise, remarkably from our viewpoint, little cultural leveling has occurred. The species just doesn't seem to breed missionaries or conquerors. Of course, societies do borrow from each other whatever they find attractive, especially in arts and philosophies.

This degree of mutual tolerance probably does not spring from natural-born saintliness, but from instincts formed in the course of evolution. Perhaps ancestral animals operated more in family groups like lions than in gangs or packs like Terrestrial simians. The Ihrdizu do all seem to be less aggressive when acting collectively than humans generally are; the demands of the collectivity on the individual usually appear to be less, though individuals are amply aggressive and self-aggrandizing. Yet they can't really be called a race of individualists either. In many ways they cooperate more readily than we do.

The Ihrdizu reached starside in prehistoric times by migrating to the far end of Nighland, but not until well into their Iron Age did they begin navigating the world-ocean there. When they hunted the carpet whales or killed off himatid calves and tads (q.v. *infra*) wholesale in the course of planting colonies on Farland, it was largely because they did not recognize these as intelligent beings. The realization came very gradually. It was accompanied by neither racist rationalization nor liberal guilt. Few if any Ihrdizu felt the slightest inclination to make recompense, let alone restore any territory. However, most found the himatids interesting, which alone gave reason for preserving them, and as time went on, some Ihrdizu established mutually profitable partnerships with groups of calves for the exploitation of littoral resources.

Efforts to communicate with the carpet whales have not yet gotten far, perhaps because most of their thinking involves concepts for which no Ihrdizuan language has any words—or perhaps because the carpet whales aren't interested, or perhaps because as they grow old they actually do sink into intellectual sluggishness.

The starside sapients

As said, the starside of Genji is essentially oceanic. There are many islands besides the small continent Farland, but they are proportionately fewer than in our Pacific basin, because tides flood the lower ones and wear them down to reefs—geologically speaking, about as fast as tectonics can push new ones up. Thus isolated, whole kingdoms and superphyla have been free to develop without being overrun by others perhaps more efficient. The most interesting animals among them are the himatids.

The basic form is neither the cylinder nor the starfish but the ribbon or plate, an organism just a few cells thick, taking in nourishment and oxygen on the lower (ventral) side and excreting on the upper (dorsal) side. Most such creatures live in the water, which supports their weight, but forms somewhat analogous to slugs exist on land, and there are many kinds of airborne "flying wings." (The most beautifully colored of these are apt to be extremely venomous.)

The largest are the "carpet whales," which grow to enormous sizes, grazing on the equivalent of plankton and krill. They concentrate toward polar waters, where currents bring up the most minerals, but certain kinds migrate and thus may be seen throughout the hemisphere. Several distinct orders of these exist, the result of convergent evolution. The following is the sapient.

Like others, it has a rudimentary homeothermic capacity, burning food energy fast at need to keep warm, but usually it gets along well enough; the upper layers of sea on Genji never do grow as cold as on Earth. The sketch shows the basic shape, a smooth, glistening black ribbon, bluntly pointed at the ends, with fifteen "arms" on either side, each slightly more than half as long as the body is wide. The fore and aft pairs are specialized for communication. Between each set of two arms is a simple "pinhole-camera" eye. (It is lidless and subject to damage or loss but, being simple, can readily be regenerated. Though a single eye gives a poor image, the ensemble supplies plenty of information for the neurons to process.) Wastes come out of exudant cells on the back or top side, in the form of gases and liquids that air and waves bear away; the manner of this provides important sensory input. The belly is covered with "mouths," which are actually more like the stomata of Terrestrial plants, each supplied with a "tooth." More on this later. Here it is worth observing that, in a way, the himatid perceives the world through its entire body to a degree and in a fashion not really imaginable by humans.

One could call the creature hermaphroditic, since there is only one sex, but it takes two to reproduce, by a process somewhat analogous to bacterial conjugation. Both partners then bud off their young. Mating takes place in arctic waters (for the sapient species), after which a herd migrates south and buds near the shores of Farland and neighboring islands. (Farland has evidently sat on its plate for an enormous time, with shield volcanoes replacing what erosion washes away.) A reproductive cycle takes several Murasakian years, the actual length depending on how favorable conditions are; a carpet whale mates and buds when it has accumulated enough reserve tissue.

The young come off a parent by the scores, tiny wrigglers that swim ashore by the same undulations as their elders but then crawl up on land and adopt a sluglike existence, feeding on vegetable matter, small entomoids, carrion, and whatever else they can get. They hook themselves along by the "scales" at their "mouths," which will grow much less in proportion and eventually function entirely as teeth. A himatid can wrap its ventral side around, or against, anything—a small patch of itself for a small object, a larger patch or the entire body for a larger object. Tubules among the dorsal cells then grow rigid by turgor, which change in osmotic pressure controls, to give a strong grip. The sapient kind and its near relatives can also clutch with "hands," to be described later. The teeth tear as the belly ripples, and the mouths exude acid and enzymes to dissolve food, which is then blotted up. Also, "arms" and "hands" can press food against "mouths."

English speakers refer to this stage of the organism as the "tad." Naturally, it is a prey for other animals, and the great majority perishes. Meanwhile, though, the survivors are growing, and as they do, they develop better organs and a whole new layer of cells in the middle of their leaf-thin bodies, which will eventually combine the functions of our brain, spinal cord, and higher nervous system. The toughest, most alert, and luckiest live until they have grown too big to get around readily on land. They then make their way to the tidewater regions. There chemical cues, comparable to those that call a salmon back to its spawning grounds, bring them to the older juveniles already living in the water. English speakers call these the "calves."

They are of every size, depending on age, from the newly arrived recent tads—perhaps 40 cm long and 10 cm wide—to the preadults, 4 or 5 meters in length and correspondingly wide. At first the new tads grow fast, acquiring full intelligence, then the rate of growth slows down, and it takes some thirty *Earth* years to reach the next stage. The calf can move through the water remarkably fast when it wants to. It can dive and it can climb onto rocks, clinging by some of the arms, lifting the upper part of the body into the air. It can clamber around in the "floating forests," which are also found on this side of the planet. It can go briefly ashore, and can function out of the water indefinitely if at least half the body remains submerged.

Except for the two pairs fore and aft, each flexible arm ends in a circular "palm" surrounded by eight boneless "fingers" with "pads" on the ends. A palm is covered with hairlike processes making a surface akin to fuzzy Velcro, while a pad is covered with others that can be stiffened by turgor to make a surface like hook Velcro. Thus the himatid can grasp fingers-to-fingers or, more strongly, fingers-to-palm, in a variety of combinations. The clasp is harder to break than one might expect—weaker, of course, than that of a human hand or an Ihrdizuan tentacle, but then as many as twenty-eight can be brought to bear. It should also be remembered that, on the whole, himatids have evolved in competition only with other himatids. The prehensile body, with its rasps and solvents, is a formidable supplement.

The two front and two rear arms have basically similar "hands" that can be used to grasp at need, but less effectively, because they have specialized to produce sounds. The calf snaps fingers, scratches them together, rubs them across palms or across arms, etc., hardening or softening the ciliate hooks as desired. The resulting language(s) is (are) in principle not altogether unlike the "talking drums" of old Africa. Water carries the sounds well, and the himatid hears, in effect, with its whole body. It can also hear, less well, through the dense air.

In general, besides the eyes, sensory information comes in through the entire "skin," tactilely and chemically. There is no brain as such, but the neural cell layer, and more rudimentary cells elsewhere, do the job of one, as well as handling other nervous functions. The himatid probably thinks more slowly than a human, but perhaps more profoundly, with more nuances.

The tidewater regions are a changeable, often violent, always challenging environment. In the present case, natural selection has led to actual intelligence—by way of "manual" dexterity, the coordination and the wits to make good use of it, linguistic ability to warn others of danger and cooperate with them. The sapients obviously have neither fire nor metal, but they make use of animal tissue, wood, stone fragments, shell, etc.

Obviously, too, the "selfish gene" doesn't work here. No concept of kinship exists. Tads arrive anonymously and are received by the calves, who raise them in a sort of extended family. Small and agile, the young can go where older, larger individuals cannot, to flush out small game, harvest sea plants, and so on. In return, the older calves protect them from perils and educate them. The more a young calf has learned, the better it can in its turn help provide and protect. Predation is a constant menace, not only by locally evolved beasts like the "carpet shark" but also by tetroptic and astromorphic swimmers whose ancestors came from moonside.

Calves habitually live in bands, each occupying its own territory, such as a given fjord or the waters around a given island. In many cases, a band has pretty well succeeded in clearing its territory of dangerous animals, though of course from time to time new ones swim in from outside. They have developed arts and ceremonies, about which humans so far know virtually nothing. Likewise mysterious are laws, customs, religions, etc. Trading goes on between communities; there is probably no single organization trading far, but sometimes goods pass "hand to hand" from end to end of Farland or throughout an archipelago.

Growing all its life, eventually a himatid gets too big for the rough, reef-choked tidal waters. It moves out to sea and becomes a carpet whale, growing larger yet, apparently indefinitely. When it has reached sexual maturity, the life cycle begins anew.

As huge as they are, and traveling in herds, the carpet whales have essentially no natural enemies other than parasites and disease. They no longer hunt but graze, and have no further use for tools or weapons. It is not known to humans or Ihrdizu just how they do spend most of their time. They do not seem to interact with the calves in any way. Yet probably they don't drift off into animal otium, unless perhaps at great ages. After all, it is they that do the reproducing, and sexual selection has probably been a strong factor making for intelligence, as well as the survival pressures on tads and calves. Could the carpet whales be a species of philosopher?

When the Ihrdizu arrived from moonside, it was a catastrophe for the himatids. They were killed wholesale, driven from their home grounds, sometimes enslaved if they were sapients. Eventually there began to be some concern for them, practical rather than sentimental—as discussed earlier. Technological civilization is utterly alien to them, and aside from the occasional working partnerships they have assimilated no important part of it, just such tools and gadgets as they can use in otherwise unchanged lives. This leads many Ihrdizu to maintain that the himatids are, after all, merely clever animals. Other Ihrdizu, though, believe the carpet whales possess mystical insights.

CHUJO

Life

Although in general there is much less life on Chujo than there was in the warm, moist part of its cycle, it is, after all, an entire world, with enormous variations between regions. Moreover, here on Earth life is actually more abundant in some areas than it appears to the superficial observer—for example, in the Arctic or in the deserts of the southwestern United States. Chujoan ecologies have undergone a terrible winnowing, with many forms becoming extinct; but others have survived, and some are actually doing better now than before—those suited to cold, aridity, briny water, etc. The transition was apparently quite rapid and happened not so long ago, perhaps ten thousand Earth years, so evolution has not had time to make radical adaptive changes. However, a number of distinct new species have already developed out of older ones as modifications of size, color, diet in the case of animals, and so on.

Macroscopic animal life does not have the diversity of basic types found on Genji, and indeed exhibits the same fundamental structure as that on Earth: cylindroidal, with a head containing a brain, two eyes, two ears, a mouth;

the limbs are four and the sexes two; tails are usual though not universal. The most striking difference is in the air intake. Rather than possessing a nose, the ordinary animal has two slits on either side of the neck. Protected by flaps of muscle like opercula, they somewhat resemble gills, but except on the aquatic types they are not. Among land animals, usually the tongue, partly covered with ciliate chemosensors, detects odors as well as tastes.

At present the herpetoids and other poikilothermic sorts are not doing so well, their survivors being found mostly in the tropics, but many theroids are widespread. These are not actually mammals, the differences in anatomy and chemistry being manifold, but are in effect rather similar. Homeothermic, they give live birth and the female lactates. Hair has not evolved, and quite a few species have scales, which in some cases are so delicate and intricately barbed as to suggest feathers. Temperature regulation is assisted by a vascular network just below the skin analogous to the rete mirabile in the feet of our birds; and a furry covering is not needed against the feeble ultraviolet of Murasaki.

Like mammals on Earth, the theroids have proliferated into a variety of herbivores and carnivores of all sizes, shapes, and functions; they include the flyers. A human gets an overall impression of a tendency toward gracile build, emphasis on speed and agility, but this is only a tendency and graviportals do occur, some larger than on Earth (as the lower gravity allows).

Some animal names: highjumper, hellbat, tricorn, dune tiger, gigantothere, ripper, snakehound, burrowbunny, kobold, peri.

Only one society of the sapient Chujoans appears to remain, numbering perhaps a million individuals though it is impossible for humans to conduct a census. Thus we have just a single race of them to describe.

At first glance the being looks humanoid. It (he or she) when adult stands quite tall, averaging two meters or a little more, though much of this is in the long, thin-shanked but strong-calved legs. The chest is broad and deep, padded out by adipose tissue in both sexes; at the center is a single nipple, nonfunctional in the male but of similar appearance. The soles of the feet have thickened and the three remaining toes grown short and stubby so that the foot, almost always kept bare, somewhat resembles a hoof. The hands each have four digits; controlled by a muscular pad in the palm, either of the two outer ones can serve as a thumb; the blue "nails" are actually the last of the ancestral scales. Otherwise the skin is smooth, of a dark golden-brown hue that varies with blood flow just underneath. All excretion is through the same tube. The male genitals are retracted when not in use. Above the neck and its air slits, the head is ovoidal, with two large, scalloped, movable ears, two large eyes that seem to be all iris (of assorted colors) and have a nictitating third membrane, a mouth with lips, and with teeth mainly designed for meat although the being is an omnivore (cf. our bears).

Obviously, the voice sounds nothing like ours. We humans hear the language—seemingly the only remaining language—as a set of trills, twitters, and occasional growls; but it is quite as complex as any of ours, phonetically and perhaps also semantically. Almost as striking to the human is the relative lack of sexual dimorphism. Male and female look almost identical except during mating. Yet no signs of homosexual behavior have been noticed. It appears that the Chujoan is not permanently rutty like a human, but desire in the male is aroused by certain odors given off by the female—who also does most of the courting, which involves singing and dancing suggestive of Terrestrial birds. What arouses the female is uncertain; it seems to happen fairly often, more than reproduction requires. Probably she has some kind of internal cycle, which may be regulated by nutrition, state of health, etc., and probably, as among us, sex is as important for its pair-bonding effects as for producing offspring. Chujoans seem to mate for life and stay pretty monogamous. The sexes seem to be equal socially, with perhaps a slight female dominance; however, they do have various rites (and celebrations?) that they carry out separately.

The species was once found all over the planet, like mankind on Earth, and has left countless relics, small and large. Shortly before the global climate began to change, the most advanced societies had reached a technological state more or less equivalent to our Hellenistic era and/or its Chinese contemporary. There was one very important difference. The society that dominated northern starside had developed clear glass, which led to optical instruments, and, probably aided by this, a remarkable practical knowledge of genetics, which it put to intensive use.

Its abandoned cities still stand, some of them in recognizable condition. Not much metal was used in construction, given the low gravity, so the successor society has not plundered them for this, nor has it any need to quarry the stone. Wind, frost, drifting sand, invading desert brush and animals have not yet leveled all these wonderful buildings. They include low, colonnaded structures with high-pitched roofs and soaring towers, in a style suggesting some blend of our classical, Oriental, and Gothic motifs. (Not grotesque, however it may sound. In the Oakland hills is a Greek Orthodox church whose architecture is equally eclectic—one of the most beautiful buildings I have ever seen anywhere.)

Agriculture had replaced much industry. Plants were bred to produce great varieties of food, plus fibers either strong or elastic, ready-made textiles and writing materials, pharmaceuticals—almost anything; some actually extracted metals from lodes of ore or natural aqueous solutions. Correspondingly specialized animals existed. Then there were the plants, animals, and microbes to meet various needs of these, maintaining an ecological balance. (For example, ground cover kept out weeds, fungoids made otherwise defenseless leaves distasteful or poisonous to browsers, small burrowers loosened the soil for roots . . . and, of course, all these required their own nourishment.) The most spectacular "caretakers" were the "trolls," as humans have called them. These were bred from the Chujoan equivalent of great apes. They occupied territories in the vast agroforests, living in bands like chimpanzees, eating fruits and leaves and small creatures; but plants valued by the Chujoans were not to their liking, and disease was set to break out whenever their numbers grew too great. Their function was to attack and drive off any large animals that appeared before much damage could be done; they were more xenophobic than pit bulls, and a lot smarter.

Some remain. A troll resembles a Chujoan in the way that a chimp or orang resembles a human—not so tall but much wider and thicker, with long arms, comparatively small head, and huge jaws. It is not arboreal, though it can climb when it wants to; its legs are shorter than a Chujoan's, but aided by its arms, it can get across the ground almighty fast. Anything sizable other than a Chujoan, it attacks, in bands. It is cunning; even the gigantothere turns aside from its flung stones. Chujoans are careful to smear themselves with a certain odorous extract before approaching troll country; it reinforces their natural smell and prevents misunderstandings.

Remains of irrigation and other large public works show how this civilization tried to keep going as conditions worsened. Insofar as analogies may be drawn to human history, it probably turned itself into something like the labor-intensive despotisms of our early Near East, Far East, and South America. The effort failed, and indeed everywhere else on Chujo the sapients apparently died out. (Perhaps survivors migrated to these parts.) Probably the rulers foresaw that failure was inevitable, and set themselves to working out a new way of life.

Dying back, the self-managing fields and forests could no longer support city populations. However, fragments of them endured, especially in the tropics and near the seas—which are found mostly on starside. Also, life suited to cold and aridity was moving south from the arctic. A much-reduced sapient population could take up a pastoral, nomadic existence.

Thus it may appear that a great civilization has died and its descendants have reverted to primitivism, like descendants of the Mayas in the jungles of Yucatán. But that does not seem to be the case here. After all, these are not humans and this is not Earth. The changeover was carefully planned and executed. Insofar as human explorers have been able to communicate with Chujoans, they have found no sense of downfall. The ancestors are admired, but in somewhat the same spirit as we admire classical Greece; we have gone on to something quite different, which we feel is in most respects better, though the Greeks might not agree if they knew.

The Chujoans live in "tribes," each with its own territory, most migrating according to seasons. As short as the seasons are, these are not simple north-south movements, but follow a complex pattern in which subunits move about so as to optimize use of the territory. For example, a tricorn herd in the lower tropics keeps moving simply so as not to overgraze any pasture, while a herd of peri follows the quickly moving spring and summer of the northern temperate zone north for leafage, then moves south eating the fruits of fall and the roots and bulbs of winter. A subtribe may pause in its cycle to seine a lake for ichthyoids and then move on. (The shores of the shrunken seas, with their powerful tides and intensely salty marshes, would not support "fisher" communities.) While a group moves, hunters range around to collect supplemental wild game.

The herds are kept chiefly for meat, though some use is made of bone, skin, etc. The herders go afoot, aided by their snakehounds, though they do have baggage animals and, where terrain permits, draft animals pulling light wagons. The Chujoans erect tents when they camp. If they do not eat food raw, they usually grill, bake, or stew it (see the Miscellaneous Notes). Most tools and weapons are of stone, wood, and other natural materials, but metal implements, carefully maintained, are still in use where they serve best.

Subgroups meet periodically in their travels, and whole tribes get together every few Murasakian years for negotiations. They seem quite cooperative; a tribe that has suffered misfortune, such as a murrain in its livestock, receives help from others more fortunate, and humans have found no evidence of any that ever attempted conquest of its neighbors. The arrowfowl, more flexibly trainable than the passenger pigeon, provides quick communication over large distances. It is not clear whether anything corresponding to a central authority exists.

Although austere, this way of life is not impoverished. From the remaining ecoplantations, tribes carefully harvest most of what they want. Only metal is really scarce, and not much is needed. Literacy seems to be universal. A caravan has space for some books, materials for writing and picturing, etc. Throughout its territories are cairnlike repositories, inviolable, attended to at every visit. These are libraries, as well as storehouses of specialized tools and materials; a little more on this is in the Miscellaneous Notes. Obviously architecture, engineering, and suchlike activities are no more, but besides literature and graphic art, there is a wealth of music, dance, handicrafts such as embroidery, and things more esoteric to us. The Chujoans have retained knowledge of past history and scientific discoveries. They continue to make updating observations in astronomy and other fields. Thus they know that their world goes around one sun, accompanied by another that they never see. There are hints that Genji is central to their religion, assuming they have what we could call a religion.

In short, human nomads have always been fringe people of civilization, depending on sedentary industries for many of their needs. This is not the case on Chujo. The nomads *are* the civilization.

To humans it is a very strange one in many other respects as well. Fred Pohl has some ideas about this.

MISCELLANEOUS NOTES

At noon on Chujo's moonside, Genji should be dark, but in fact glows faintly in the daylit sky because of Chujo-light on its clouds and seas. The dark parts of the disk are thus discernible beside the sunlit parts until midnight, when Genji is full; they range from dull blue-gray at the edge toward the bright white-and-blue of the sunlit side, and the boundary of the crescent is blurred. When Genji eclipses the sun, its disk does not go totally black, again because of reflections (high albedos), but does become quite dark, surrounded by a red ring of sunlight refracted through atmosphere. When Chujo passes between the sun and Genji, bluish-gray darkness creeps across the disk of the latter, which at totality glows with a dull coppery hue.

The same phases occur for Chujo as seen from Genji, although Chujo is generally less bright, a buff color on which a couple of seas glint and occasional clouds make white streaks. At solar eclipse the red ring is thinner and at planetary eclipse the coppery shade is somewhat brighter—since, although Genji's disk is larger, its more extensive atmosphere refracts sunlight better.

The Chujoan nomads do have some ceramic vessels, prepared, like their metal implements, during stopovers at certain sites. These sites normally include a library—repository of books, etc., carefully sealed against pests when not in use—and assorted workshop facilities. They can quite safely be left alone, theft and vandalism being essentially unheard of.

Like our American Indians and others, Chujoans can also cook with water in the equivalents of bark pots and leather bags, using heated stones. "Stew with dumplings!" proposes Karen; from the ancient plantations they can still harvest starchy foods that need little or no preparation (such as threshing or milling) prior to cooking.

Appendix B:
MURASAKI'S WORLDS

by Frederik Pohl

In constructing stories for Murasaki's worlds, we have a total of four intelligent races to consider: the Ihrdizu and the himatids of Genji; the Chujoans; and the humans.

Since presumably most of you will be writing from the viewpoint of a human character, let's take up the humans first.

All of this takes place in some future time, far enough in the future that interstellar space travel is possible, though very far from cheap or easy; near enough so that the human characters are not very different from ourselves.

Probably most of us don't need to specify dates, but for the sake of consistency for those who do, here are some:

A.D. 2219 Robot probe (sent by Japanese) first arrives in the Murasaki System, begins sending data back to Earth.

A.D. 2239 Messages (sent by ordinary radio, at light speed) from robot probe received in Earth system. Japanese decide to send a manned ship there.

A.D. 2242 Japanese begin to construct ship in Low Earth Orbit. Will take three years to complete and fit. However, at the same time—

A.D. 2242 The Spacers (see below) have listened in on the probe reports and they, too, have decided to explore the system. The Spacers convert a hull intended for transport within the solar system to interstellar use. This pisses the Japanese off, but there's nothing they can do about it.

A.D. 2244 Spacer ship starts out to Murasaki.

A.D. 2245 Japanese ship starts out to Murasaki. The travel time for each is about 21 Earth years. (Subjectively 11 years for the ship crews, because of time dilation at relativistic speeds; see Poul.)

A.D. 2265 Spacer ship arrives in Murasaki System and begins exploration.

A.D. 2266 Japanese ship arrives.

A.D. 2286 Earliest date when radioed reports from Spacer ship can be received in Earth system.

Ad lib: Other expeditions launched from space or Earth, arriving whenever you like *after* A.D. 2266.

No doubt Murasaki's is not the only stellar system investigated by robot probes, but as of the date of first launch above (at least) all the others have come up empty as far as habitable planets are concerned.

LIFE ON EARTH

At this point in the future there are nearly 20 billion human beings alive. Nineteen billion of them live on Earth itself. Some 20 million people live in sealed-in lunar and Martian colonies; all the rest, nearly a billion in all, live in O'Neill-type orbiting habitats. Each habitat has an average population of 100,000, and there are nearly 10,000 habitats somewhere in solar space. (Once the first few were built, it was relatively cheap and easy to make more, using off-Earth resources.)

The habitats are widely scattered. A few hundred of them are in Earth or lunar orbit; the bulk are in solar orbits. About 6,000 are between the orbits of Earth and Venus, at convenient distances for maximizing solar power without being too close to the sun for comfort. (The primary industry of these is tapping solar power to make, for example, antimatter.) Most of the others are out near the asteroid belt, for access to minerals, with scatterings orbiting Mars, Venus, and (small ones, specially built) Jupiter and Saturn. There is a thriving commerce among the space habitats, with fusion- or antimatter-powered spacecraft. These spacecraft never land on a planet, of course; cargoes for Earth (including people) are frequently dropped like an Apollo capsule; cargoes, and people, going from Earth to space are launched in any of a number of ways (see below), including shuttlelike ferries.

The principal primary energy source is solar power, and there is a lot of it. All the space habitats have deployed arrays of mirrors and thermoelectric (or other) generators to supply themselves with electrical power for heavy-industry smelting and manufacturing (with raw materials from, for example, the asteroids and minor satellites for minerals, and from comet nuclei for elemental hydrogen, oxygen, carbon, nitrogen and their compounds), and for their own domestic use.

The habitats also export energy. As above, many habitats in solar orbit use the power to manufacture antimatter, which is then used for (among other things) spacecraft propulsion. Those in near-Earth orbits sell electricity to Earth by microwaving it to rectennae on the Earth's surface. (These power satellites are visible from Earth's surface. In fact, they are the principal objects visible in Earth's nighttime sky; they have probably made optical and radio astronomy from Earth's surface extinct disciplines.)

Earth is heavily dependent on this import of energy from space, which is a source of strain in Earth-space relations.

Although even at this time only a tiny fraction of the sun's radiation is captured and used for human purposes, the proportion is increasing all the time. Our sun is on its way to becoming a kind of Dyson sphere.

As there is a lot of power, there is necessarily considerable wealth. The wealth is not equally distributed among all classes of people, though. There are rich and poor everywhere. The 19 billion people on Earth have an average living standard about equal to a late-twentieth-century American's, with a great many much wealthier individuals (as well as many very poor ones). The economic situation of the people in space is more like a late-twentieth-century Kuwaiti's, for the same reasons. Nobody is desperately poor, and the rich are incredibly rich: space is where the resources are.

A natural question arises: If space is such a neat place, why doesn't everybody go there? There are two reasons: 1) it's not easy to get off Earth (see below); 2) living in space is *dangerous;* it is not the environment humans evolved to live in, and small accidents can be lethal.

There is no "world government." There are half a dozen superpowers on Earth, as well as a great many smaller "countries," most of which are client states to one or another of the superpowers. The space population is administratively fractionated (every habitat is a law unto itself), but the various habitats and colonies tend to unite together to present a common front in their dealings with Earth for economic reasons, like the oil sheikhs of OPEC days.

As to the nature of national governments on Earth, etc., there is very likely a great spread, as at present. Some are libertarian, some police states, some parliamentary democracies punctuated by revolutions—what you will. The only one I wish to establish as dogma is Japan (because Japanese discovered the system). Japan is a parliamentary monarchy, like England; the royal family goes around visiting hospitals and judging cake contests. It is no larger geographically than it is now; the Japanese do not admit aliens to citizenship. But many of the Earth-orbit habitats are all-Japanese and are considered prefectures of the nation, like Okinawa. Adjacent Asian states (China,

Korea, etc.) are Japanese clients—political independence but economic thralldom, like a Canadian's view of the United States.

The ecology of Earth is much poorer than in our time. There have been damages from various causes. There may have been a few nuclear wars a couple of centuries ago, and there certainly was a lot of tsurris with ozone depletion, CO_2 warming, acid rain, soil loss, toxic-chemical and radionuclide pollution, etc. But the human race has gotten used to it, and most of the scars are now pretty well healed. Most rich mines are pretty well depleted by now. Necessary raw materials are either grown (textiles, pharmaceuticals, as well as food), extracted from the sea (by specially bred plants concentrating whatever they want), or imported from space. Recycling of basic metals is universal and important.

International relations are not notably more friendly than they are now, but there are no major wars. This is because of MAD: everyone is vulnerable to mutually assured destruction with everyone else. All of the space colonies are fragile, and everything on Earth is open to attack from space (possibly by shooting an asteroid at it). There are lots of tensions and disagreements, and occasional minor wars—perhaps about at the scale of the Falklands War; perhaps there is also a continuing element of terrorism. However, people on Earth travel fairly freely around its surface, and people in space do so easily from any habitat to any other.

Traveling from planet surface to orbit, though, is another matter. On Earth some nations may have skyhooks (but only if they have possessions quite near the Equator). Other Earth nations may have Lufstrom loops, but probably of limited capacity. On the moon (possibly also on Mars, using the slope of Olympus Mons for a track) electric rail guns can launch a ship to orbit (though landing one is harder). For all other planetside launches the only way to attain escape velocity is to sit on top of a big firecracker of some kind, and that is intrinsically expensive. So, except for a very fortunate very few, Earth's 19 billion will stay on Earth till they die.

Even allowing for all the wealth and technology, to send out an interstellar expedition to Murasaki is, as Poul points out, a big-ticket venture, with a near-zero prospect of any economic return.

This means that we need to explain why our human travelers are going to Murasaki's worlds in the first place. There are two parts to this question: Why does anyone pay to build these very expensive ships? And, why does anyone volunteer to man them?

The only *rational* reason I can see for spending the resources necessary would be pure scientific inquiry. Nonrational reasons might include national prestige, or missionary fervor. Possibly Islam or the Catholic Church could get up the money to send a missionary expedition out, and under certain circumstances might want to do so, assuming they supposed the Genjians and Chujoans had souls to save. (Individual contributors are, of course, free to discover other reasons.)

As to the volunteers themselves, their motivations might be much the same—plus the possibility of personal profit for a few of the earliest, at least. The explorers returning on the first actual ship to get back to the Earth system will surely be rewarded with wealth, fame, groupies, college lecture dates, and all the other hoopla that was given to, say, Charles Lindbergh or the Mercury astronauts.

The Murasaki System was first described by the Japanese by means of a relatively cheap robot probe; that's why the planets and satellites were named after characters from *The Tale of Genji*. For that reason, the Japanese might take a special interest in sending actual human explorers there: that would be an example of a possible nationalistic reason for an exploration mission.

Terrestrial nations in general are more likely than Spacers to look covetously at interestellar space; the Terries are resentful of the fact that the Spacers have taken over most of the available real estate in the solar system, and so, somewhat like Germany just before World War I, are likely to wish for colonies of their own. (Even though they are told colonies won't be any kind of money-spinners on Genji or Chujo.) They know the economics are prohibitive, but they *want*. Spacers, on the other hand, have less of that kind of motivation, but interstellar travel is easier for them (though still certainly not *very* easy).

Any other rational or nonrational reasons for such a venture that might occur to any of you are, of course, your own to play with. It is very unlikely, however, that anyone could hope to make money out of such an expedition, in view of the terribly high cost and long travel times. No one is likely to find spices, pharmaceuticals, or rare gems worth the cost of shipping them back to the Sol system; though, of course, some people might hope to.

Outposts (as on Antarctica) are likely on both Genji and Chujo, for long-term research; self-supporting *colonies* are not. On these planets, the colonization imperatives that drove Europeans to Asia, Africa, and the Americas don't apply: because of transportation time and costs, there is no hope of finding markets for Earth products or cheap plantation labor to produce raw materials to ship back. Nor is there a "frontier" to attract pioneers. The environment of neither Genji nor Chujo is benign enough to support homesteading. (Though, here again, some people, driven to escape from some form of political, religious, or other persecution, might *try*.)

Human beings visiting Genji or Chujo arrive there after a very long trip in crowded quarters, and few of them will ever return to Earth. Their contact with family and friends left behind is either tenuous or nonexistent.

These facts will have psychological effects on your characters, no doubt exacerbating interpersonal relationships. A certain amount of personal screwiness seems probable. And all of this is of course made worse by the environmental adversities they experience after landing on Genji or Chujo.

HUMAN TECHNOLOGY

Generally speaking, human beings are still human beings, not physically much different from ourselves. There have been very great advances, of course, in such things as molecular biology. Most diseases have been prevented or cured. Healthy life spans go up to nearly a hundred years.

However, humans do not change their gender at will or grow extra limbs, etc. They look much like us—rather, they look pretty much like our movie stars. They select for benign genes in their offspring, of course, but have not bred a race of supergeniuses or physical freaks.

That's for Earthlings. It is a little different for Spacers. In space, people may be richer, but Earth people live longer; they're not exposed to the risk of lethal solar radiation from flares, or to all the other probable stresses: dietary, circulatory, bone-mass loss. And, as mentioned above, although space people don't necessarily have more accidents than Earth people, the ones they do have tend to be more probably fatal.

Computers are far advanced. "Fuzzy" programs make reasonable deductions from incomplete evidence. Smart machines, which rely on quantum-effect devices, or QEDs, are *damn* smart. (The QEDs are about 1/100 the size of current chip technology and roughly 10,000 times faster and more powerful.) This has made possible very small, and therefore relatively cheap, interstellar probes. They have a pretty good idea of what the Murasaki System is like before any human being actually gets there.

However, the people are not cyberpunks. There is no direct human-to-machine linkage, and they do not wear computer implants in their brains. (Perhaps there was a fad for that sort of thing a century or two earlier, but the people using such devices went psychotic. Or at least sociopathic—or both, like the characters in cyberpunk novels.)

THE INTERSTELLAR SHIPS

As Poul has informed us, these are propelled by antimatter drives, perhaps very sophisticated versions of the Augenstein (porous tungsten blocks through which liquid hydrogen is diffused, reacting with streams of antiprotons) or

Morgan (pion-exhaust) drives. If the Augenstein, or any other drive in which the matter-antimatter reaction is used primarily to heat a working fluid to exhaust, then a working fluid is needed; probably this will be hydrogen, and unless the ship is to store great quantities of it, the ship will need something like a Bussard scoop to collect interstellar gas along the way.

This makes several design problems. One is that the same thrust engine is used for both acceleration and deceleration—meaning, no doubt, that at the halfway point the ship has to be turned around, proceeding stern first toward Murasaki from then on. But the scoop must always face forward; so at the turnover point it must be rerigged from bow to stern—not necessarily easy to do.

Another is communication with Earth. The ship's communication antennae have to point toward Earth, and during the acceleration phase are trying to get a signal through a cloud of very hot plasma from the drive's exhaust. I doubt this is going to be easy, and it may not be possible; so the ship may be out of touch with Earth for some years.

That's not the only communication problem, however.

During the flight, communications will be hampered also by Doppler frequency shifts (not a big problem, just requiring careful tuning), but far more seriously by time dilation. Messages *from* Earth come in at half the speed of messages *to* Earth, if they are possible at all.

Power is also a problem. At interstellar distances any signal is going to be seriously attenuated, and the ship (and even the "colonies" at destination) will have limited, though considerable, resources. Probably at the Sol end of the line a large orbiting dish, roughly Arecibo-sized, will have to both receive and transmit; either it will have to be a dedicated antenna, or transmission and reception time schedules will have to be worked out in advance.

Voice communication will be digitalized and sent slowly (probably even redundantly), to be reconstituted at destination. Pictures will be even slower. Receiving them will be not unlike watching the probe pictures come in at JPL, as they build up line by line. "Motion pictures" can be sent in either direction, but they will take forever to transmit. Arbitrarily let us assume that one hour's transmission back to Earth can yield a) maybe twenty minutes of voice transmission, b) a few hundred still photographs, or c) about thirty seconds of videotape.

If explorers on Genji or Chujo wish to send a one-hour *National Geographic*-type film back to Earth they can certainly do so, but it will take five days of continuous transmission time. And it will take twenty-one years to get there.

There will certainly be no face-to-face conversations by means of interstellar videophone. Apart from the problems of slow transmission, anything anyone says on Earth takes twenty-one years to get to Murasaki and just as long for an answer to get back.

Presumably the first few ships, at least, to carry people to Murasaki will be as small as possible, for economic reasons.

That is not, however, really very small. Assume a capacity of maybe twenty-five crew. (It would not help much to make the capacity smaller, because of all the things they have to carry with them.)

The ship then needs to carry everything these people will need for an essentially indefinite period: food, air, and water (no doubt recycled, perhaps even with food synthesizers—but the food has to be synthesized out of *something*); clothes; books; tapes; pharmaceuticals, surgical stuff and other medical needs; cosmetics; games; etc.

It also needs everything they will need during exploration. Small items they will generally carry with them, like scientific instruments, probably weapons (for use against predators, if for nothing more sinister), "trade goods"— things like pocket calculators, maybe solar-powered (but maybe they don't work well in Murasaki's light), toys, flashlights (but their yellow-green light hurts the natives' eyes?), beads, etc., wristwatch radios, etc. Larger things for exploration: probably a couple of light planes for surface exploration, and no doubt a few moon-buggy things for the same reason; a food synthesizer (or a lot of food); a power plant to drive all their equipment; pressure-reducing suits and helmets for exploration of Genji, and air masks for exploring Chujo. They will also need at least one lander shuttle.

And the ship itself will need everything to make it run, plus spare parts for repairs and tools to make the repair with. This is a job for considerable mass. No small interstellar ships need apply.

(Later on, of course, ships might be really *big*. Probably some group of spacers may well decide to hook antimatter drives onto a self-sufficient 100,000-person habitat and launch it toward Murasaki. No doubt this would be much slower than a purpose-built ship, but it would sure carry a lot of people. That might be the actual ultimate "colonization" of the Murasaki System.)

A PUZZLE FOR PLANETOGRAPHERS

Although probes and space telescopes have identified other planets in the galaxy, Genji and Chujo are the only ones that seem to have life of any kind.

Is this because Genji and Chujo are co-orbiting twins, as the Earth with its moon? Is it necessary for a planet to co-orbit with another body of similar mass, with its consequent great tidal forces, in order for life to develop on it?

Some astronomers have speculated that this is true. (In fact, they have done so even in our own twentieth century.) They suggest that life cannot evolve on any planet that lacks the equivalent of a Van Allen Belt, because ionizing radiation would destroy it; that the Van Allen Belts can't develop without a strong magnetic field; that there cannot be a strong magnetic field without a molten core; that only a nearby co-orbiting large mass, constantly churning up the interior of a planet, can keep a large core molten after the surface of a planet has cooled long enough for liquid water to be stable for geologically long times.

Genji and Chujo *almost* support that theory. Genji and Chujo are the only known planets, other than Earth/moon, with co-orbiters; they are also the only known planets, other than Earth, that support life. That is too much of a coincidence to be purely coincidental.

But neither Genji nor Chujo has a strong Van Allen Belt. It is only one detail, but that's enough to wreck the whole chain of deduction.

So human planetographers are puzzled. Perhaps this is one reason why some people are anxious to study the Murasaki System at close range.

A far stronger reason is that Genji/Chujo are the only other planets anywhere in the universe so far known to harbor life. If humanity is to meet any intelligent aliens anywhere, the Murasaki System is the only place to go.

HOW HUMANS LIVE ON GENJI/CHUJO

As Poul has explained, human beings cannot get around on either planet in shorts and solar topis. On Genji, they establish "settlements" on the high plateaus. Even those are not comfortable: they're cold, dark, and bleak, but at least there they can breathe the air.

To explore the sea-level surface of Genji the humans need something like rigid diving suits. The partial pressure of oxygen at 2,000 millibars will do irreversible damage to airways and lungs if endured too long.

They may, however, expose themselves to the sea-level air for brief periods, though they risk nitrogen narcosis. It is possible that some bored humans use sea-level Genjian air as a recreational drug, enjoying the "raptures" as a kind of high. ("Low"?)

Human Life on Genji

Genji is no more than marginally habitable for human beings. Their most difficult problem is food: they can't eat Genjian organisms, and they can't easily establish farms to grow their own food. The high altiplanos where they live lack the rain and warmth necessary for farming. Conceivably they could bribe natives into farming for them at lower levels, where crops might grow, but there isn't enough blue-green light for Earthly chlorophyll to work well; artificial lighting would probably be necessary (and expensive), and minor variations in the soil chemistry would probably cause crop failures anyway—at least until some high-powered agronomists worked out ways of dealing with them.

The same food sources the people had on their eleven-year (subjective) flight from Earth would have to feed them once they land: I presume some sort of closed-cycle system using their bodily wastes to nourish plants. Such recycling systems can be quite efficient (this is far enough in the future to allow for considerable improvement in using designer genes for food plants and animals), but they would probably need constant attention; if the system fails, the people starve. (No doubt there will be redundant systems, so the people might not starve but would have to eat unsatisfactory diets.)

At 1,000-millibar elevations, the Genjian biota (as Poul points out), is sparse, tough, and small. Stunted plants, things like mosses; possibly when (very infrequently) it rains there is an explosion of "flowering" plants, as in Earthly deserts.

Getting to Genji

The interstellar ship itself does not land on a planet but orbits somewhere—around Chujo? around Genji? around both of them? The landing crews come down in smaller craft, perhaps like shuttles or the Spaceplane.

Most travelers probably leave Earth when they are twenty-five or thirty. When they reach Genji they are pushing forty (though their twins back on Earth, if they have any, are nearly fifty).

According to Poul's stats the interstellar ships travel at a uniform 1-g acceleration. Actually, I think they tend to increase the acceleration slowly. Spacers would probably want to start out at lesser thrusts; both Earthies and Spacers would likely want to build up to 1.5 g in the final deceleration period, so that by the time the adventurers reach Genji they have become more or less accustomed to its 1.5-g conditions. This need not shorten the total travel time very much, and perhaps not all ships will do it—those heading for Chujo have no need to.

The condition of the explorers when they arrive on Genji depends on how successfully they have managed the stresses of the long trip: living in each others' pockets for a decade is likely to bring out any latent psychoses. Some ships will do better than others, but the worst of them may have had mini civil wars, murders, vendettas, etc., which may carry over.

No doubt by this time in the future there will be pharmaceutical (or other) treatments for most forms of loopiness, but it is fair to assume that the treatments carry side effects (lethargy, confusion, depression—take your pick). So the voyagers do not step off onto the soil of Genji as hale and well balanced as when they took off from Earth.

Physically, both Spacers and Earthies will probably take some latter-day analogues of steroids and calcium-binders, to help stand the 1.5 g.

All Genjinauts are aware that their voyage will be long and most likely one-way. (All right, fellows, why do they let themselves in for this? Do some of them want to convert the heathen to God? Are some social misfits, even criminals? Are people drafted for this? Are they paid so handsomely that they can get their families out of poverty into affluence forever?— their families rather than themselves, because whatever the voyagers themselves are paid, they can't spend it. Is this part of the story material you will invent?) Still, *some* of them can return. It is probable that at least one or two ships will return to Earth at some time, perhaps five years after landing: they will probably want to bring specimens of some kind back for study. This means that a lucky few can go home. When they get there, those who started out at twenty-five will now be fifty or more. (Their cohort-mates left on Earth may well be pushing eighty; so no one comes back to the girl he left behind him.)

How do they decide who goes back? I think it depends on each separate shipload; perhaps there are stories there. Maybe the decision will be made by a lottery. Maybe by political decisions and various forms of skulduggery. Maybe by force majeure; or maybe whoever survives gets to return.

I assume that almost everyone would volunteer to return to Earth, since certainly those few who get back, especially the *first* few who get back, can look forward to fame and fortune—may even be elected to whatever the Senate is like at that time. Those who stay on Genji may get rivers and mountains named after them so their names will live forever, but the ones who get back to Earth will get all the chicks. (Or cocks, as the case may be.)

Of course, a lot of humans who get to Genji will die there before their normal time, by accident, exposure, violence, or simply exhaustion.

I'm not sure how much attention people on Earth pay to what's going on on Genji. After all, by the time the first ship reaches there, and the first messages come back to Earth at light speed, more than forty years have passed: half the human race will not have been born when the ship departed. And by then humanity may have other things on its mind. . . .

THE IHRDIZU

Before I get very explicit about the manners and customs of the Ihrdizu, let me go over and perhaps expand on some of the points Poul has already made about Genji.

"Sea level" on Genji is a fairly ambiguous concept, because of the vast tides; nevertheless, most Genjians live somewhere near it (partly because of their amphibious origins). Humans, on the other hand, are comfortable only at great elevations. Ships from Earth will ordinarily land on high plateaus and will establish bases where they land; so Earthmen can be on Genji for some time without the Genjians' being aware of their presence.

Humans can go to sea level if they wish, but not easily or comfortably. The easiest way would be to travel in sealed aircraft, which they would never leave, doing their exploring (and communicating with the Genjians) through robot proxies or just looking out of the windows. They could leave the aircraft for at least brief periods, but they would run the risk of nitrogen narcosis, or "rapture of the deeps," if they stayed unprotected at sea level for any length of time; they would risk bends; and probably if the exposure were of long duration or frequent there would be damage to their lungs. (Their situation at sea level is analogous to a Terrestrial skin diver working at a depth of about thirty meters.)

If they wish to walk around the surface of Genji at sea level they need to wear a sort of diving helmet, at least, with an air pump to reduce the pressure inside.

Alternatively, a human could wear an all-metal diving suit. (It could not be flexible, as were the rubberized suits with metal helmets human divers used to wear, because those suits were pressurized from within.) Both the helmet and the full suit would be cumbersome (especially in Genji's higher surface gravity), uncomfortable, and generally unpleasant, though in somewhat different ways. Some humans would prefer to go out unprotected and pay the penalty of short excursions and slow decompression, or to take their chances.

It is even worse for Genjians who might wish to visit the Earth landing ship at its altitude of 5,800 meters or so. Not only do they need something like space suits, to let them breathe, but the suits must be heated, since the Genjians are not normally homeothermic. (As specified by Poul, they do have internal temperature sources, but it is a stress on the organism to try to maintain a proper body temperature for very long.) Without artificial heat supplies, if Genjians were to remain for any length of time at such altitudes they would slow down, their ability to think would be impaired, and before long they would die.

(In fact, climbing a mountain is a recognized method of suicide. As Poul points out, sometimes aging Genjians climb mountains to die: they climb, using up their stores of fat and energy, until breathing becomes too difficult. Then they settle down, ultimately relapse into coma, and pass away peacefully.)

Genjian villages

The largest communities of Genjians amount to fewer than two hundred individuals. It is basic to the Genjian nature to be essentially self-sufficient, especially in growing their own food; a large Genjian "village" would comprise a dozen clusters of six or eight homesteads each, surrounded by their equivalent of farms, fish ponds, breeding ponds, and so on.

Their most densely populated areas (not very densely—five or six Genjians per square kilometer taken over a whole region, no more than ten times that even in a "village") are near the seashores. They can only be on fairly high hills or mountainsides, since the great tides inundate everything within some tens of meters of sea level regularly, and at peak tides can go considerably higher.

Genjian homes anywhere near sea level are unheated, at least by day. There are no winters, and the principal function of a house is to keep the rain and wind out. (Remember the vast storms that are common.) Perhaps in many of the less-developed societies the Genjians live in tents, and perhaps use that advantage to migrate when they feel like it. (More-civilized Genjians stay put, because their farms and ponds can't be moved.)

The more technologically advanced Genjian societies have much larger and more solid structures, though not necessarily to live in: factories, particularly metalworking forges and foundries, may be built with solid walls. (Or may not?)

I think in the case of the *most* advanced Genjians, they are building rather sophisticated structures. For example, they probably build tidal electricity generators, with dams and barrages.

This probably produces strains on their social patterns. Not cities, because Poul says not, but at least large-scale industrial areas, to which Genjians perhaps commute.

Genjian prehistory

The history of technology among the Ihrdizu is a little more complicated than that of humans. It goes like this:

Shell Age. Earliest settlements; tools and weapons made of shells; invention of agriculture.

Stone Age. Brief transition period, reconstructing shell tools in more refractory (but better) stone. Invention of fire.

Bronze/Glass Age. Beginnings of industry; invention of writing; more sophisticated social organizations. This is a long, long period of Ihrdizu history.

Iron Age. Brief transition period, marked with beginnings of use of electricity and magnetism—but the more primitive Ihrdizu are still in it.

Aluminum Age. The Ihrdizu go rather quickly from iron to aluminum; with abundant tidal power and wind power, they can generate electricity on a fairly large scale without burning large quantities of fossil fuel. This is the stage of the most advanced Ihrdizu at present.

These may also use electrolytically derived hydrogen for fuel.

Ihrdizu social institutions

Poul says they are not organized as nations, but through interest linkages.

Perhaps all left-handed Genjians have something in common.

Perhaps the males and the females, though mated, have different loyalties.

Perhaps there are "fan groups"—as tightly bound as, say, s-f fandom, but organized around different common interests. Sports fans? Shell collectors?

Whatever the interests are, they are as important to the Genjians as, say, religion is to us; which means that although a community of fifty or so Genjians may get along well enough most of the time, they will from time to time have pogroms or IRA-style action groups.

Gender differences

The females are larger and stronger than the males; perhaps they are the "heads" of the families.

Courtship is at the instigation of the female. When she reaches sexual maturity she leaves her home to visit other communities on her trek to find a mate. The unattached males in the community look her over, but wait for her to make the first move.

A mate-questing female first and foremost wants a mate; but she wants a *particular* male, one she can get along with, and one who is by Ihrdizu standards good-looking if possible. She also wants a congenial community—where the living is easy, and where conditions are interesting to her. Another important factor is whether there is room in the community for a new household, since Ihrdizu don't like to be crowded. This is a judgment call. The female may think there's room, but others in the community may disagree.

When a questing female shows up in a community, she is taken in by households that have unattached males.

Assuming a 1:1 sex ratio at birth, there will generally be more mature males than females, because males mature earlier; and therefore the female is in a better position to pick and choose among possible mates than the male. For the same reason, in most couples the female is older than the male. Assuming the male and female average life spans are about the same, that means there will often be a number of widowed males looking for new mates. Perhaps in some households a father and son compete for the same female.

However, at some point in their adult lives females lose the capacity to reproduce. At this point they may be "divorced" by their mates— or the mates may choose to continue with them for the sake of the bonding that has developed over the years. This is a fairly new problem for the Ihrdizu society; until fairly recently mothers didn't usually live long enough to reach "menopause."

Males are probably more prized than females as children, as on Earth, though not for the same reasons: On Genji, immature females are only temporary members of the community and spend a lot of time and energy thinking about where they will go on their mate quest. "A daughter's a daughter till she becomes a wife, but a son is a son for all of your life."

The questing female probably stays at each household in the new community for a few days, getting to know the males; this is the Ihrdizu form of dating. When she is about to enter her first real sexual phase (as distinguished from the "false heat" described elsewhere) she makes her choice of males, and they set up housekeeping—either starting a new household, or perhaps taking over an abandoned one. If the male's family is small, they may live with the in-laws for a while.

This is the basic rationalized mating procedure. However, Genjians are not all that much more rational than humans, and sometimes they fall in love, passionately and romantically and without much thought for what is socially acceptable. A female may fall in love with a male in her own community, but it is a star-crossed love. If they mate, then either they do not migrate (in which case the community thinks of the female as the Genjian equivalent of a scarlet woman and the male as the victim of an immoral female), or both she and the male leave, perhaps to try to set up a new household in an uncultivated area.

Although it is usually the female in a couple who dies first, sometimes it is the male; then the widowed female has a hard choice. She can either remain in the community, living celibate, or she can migrate like a newly mature girl. Neither course is attractive.

The attitude of a village toward a new questing female depends partly on the female, who may have special virtues (wealth? skills? personality?), and even more on whether the community considers there is room for a new household. Households with unattached males will always take her in for a visit, however.

Diurnal variations

Genji has no real seasons, but it does have day and night; the daytime temperature averages some ten degrees Centigrade warmer than night, as on Earth.

Genjians who wish to be active at night heat their homes. They don't need a *lot* of heat—only enough to raise the temperature ten degrees or so, rather than the much larger spread between inside and outside that humans need to make the inside of a house comfortable in winter. They may use fire, in which case they perhaps have floor-heating devices like the Roman hypocaust, but that is a fairly recent development and is considered effete, as central heating was in England until quite recently. More likely they employ special kinds of vegetation, which rot and give out a little heat, like a compost heap.

However, night is still a time of reduced efficiency for the Genjians; since they are pretty poikilothermic they have had millions of years to set their body clocks to operate better by day than by night. Even the most advanced Genjians are not at their best at night.

(Where predation is still a problem for Genjians, as in the case of the "savage" tribes on starside, the predators are homeothermic carnivores that do their hunting at night. This is discussed in more detail below.)

Manners and customs of the Ihrdizu

The land Genjians, known as the Ihrdizu, are a single species. They can certainly interbreed and do so on occasion, but they are not a single community. They do not divide themselves into "nations," nor do they have more than one real language. Nevertheless, there are differences in customs and lifestyles among them. These are not marked by national borders but change gradually with distance. So do local dialects of the one common language, so that a land Genjian whose home is on the shore of an inland lake would have some trouble communicating with one living in an elevated valley or on the tidal shores of the ocean. (He would also find some of the customs surprising.) Some "tribes" are quite advanced in machine-using and metallurgy, others relatively primitive.

(Poul comments that a planetwide language requires special explanation—why didn't it diverge into mutually incomprehensible tongues, as on Earth? The principal reason is that the Ihrdizu females in particular do a good deal of migrating, sometimes over long distances, and that works against the differentiation of language.)

The first land Genjians humans encounter call themselves the Ihrdizu. Human explorers use that name for all members of that species. This is an error, actually, since different varieties of land Genjians call themselves by different names; but humans stick with that name for all of them. (Just as Europeans called all Native Americans "Indians," regardless of whether they were Algonkians or Navajo.)

Poul's description of Ihrdizu ways is gospel. However, what he describes is not necessarily universal; it is the norm, and there may well be individual variations—"perversions," perhaps. For example, some male Ihrdizu will want sex even when it's out of season.

Ihrdizu, like humans, use a variety of recreational drugs. Some, like caffeine, perk them up. Some are intoxicating; some are hallucinogens.

In some Ihrdizu societies there are modesty tabus. Because the tongue is a sex organ, it is concealed. These Ihrdizu don't smile; they are shocked when humans do. Possibly the more prudish Ihrdizu do not eat in public.

The farther apart the tribes are, the more their norms of behavior may vary. The starside Ihrdizu and the moonside Ihrdizu may be quite different in many ways. The differences among them are as marked as the differences among, say, a shopkeeper on Rodeo Drive, an Inuit, a Harlem street-gang kid, and a Tibetan.

However, Ihrdizu aren't xenophobes. Au contraire. They are attracted to, rather than repelled by, "foreignness." This is probably the result of the nature of their mating customs, as will be explained below.

The following material applies particularly to the moonside Ihrdizu, and among them to their most advanced communities.

Ihrdizu names

I agree that Earthmen will name features for themselves once they get there, but I think on occasion they will use Ihrdizu names, too.

Some Ihrdizu names, I think, will be common words (after the Earthly example of "Painted Desert," "Death Valley," "High Tor," etc.), and Earthmen will simply translate the names into English. Other Ihrdizu names they will attempt to reproduce phonetically. (No doubt with only partial success. I am reminded of the story of how the state I live in got its name. Some French travelers asked the natives what they called this place, and the Indians obligingly told them: "Ee-en-wah." So the travelers, being what they were, wrote it down phonetically as "Illinois.")

As to what names the Earthmen will invent for themselves, I think that depends on what sort of society they come from. If from religious communities, perhaps saints' names; perhaps names of their own home localities ("New South Tokyo," etc.); perhaps after historical figures. At least in the early stages, probably each expedition will have some features of its own to name.

The Ihrdizu family

Since the Ihrdizu young need parenting, but not suckling, they can be taken care of by either parent or, indeed, by Ihrdizu other than their biological parents. This frees parents to do other things: they use baby-sitters. They take turns with each other's children: the hippie communes of the sixties would be at home here.

When Ihrdizu grow up they either take over the duties of their parents (if they are male), or leave for another community (if they are female). Ihrdizu females are in heat only at certain times; when a young Ihrdizu female is almost adult she experiences a "false heat." This is the signal for her to leave and seek a mate. It becomes a ceremonial occasion, as her family and friends bid her good-bye: something between a bar mitzvah and a bridal shower.

She then wanders until she reaches a place where she knows no one; then she looks for a mate. She may have to travel a hundred kilometers or more.

Ihrdizu political institutions

Ihrdizu grow up without the model of the nuclear family, and especially without the image of a particular adult as lawgiver and family head. As adults, they do not look to a chief or head of state for authority. If you can say "Take me to your leader" to an Ihrdizu he will, perhaps, take you to the person who beats time for a local orchestra.

Ihrdizu do have elections or town meetings to decide on public matters, but they don't vote for individuals. They vote on issues, and voting "yes" implies a commitment to the action decided on. For example, they may vote to dam a river, and then those who voted in favor must help.

The results of a vote are binding on all Ihrdizu affected, but in different ways. Those who have voted against the dam are required only to refrain from interfering in its construction. Those who have voted for it are obligated to contribute to it, either by labor or by money. (This is their only form of taxation.)

The "elections" may affect everyone in a particular area, in which case all Ihrdizu except immature females vote. (Even the youngest males can vote as soon as they are old enough to get about on their own; but the immature females are going to leave the area as soon as they are sexually mature and are not permanent members of the body politic.) Some elections are on specific issues that affect only people who work at a certain trade, or have certain special interests in common, and then they are the only ones who vote.

Rarely, an issue may arise that affects all Ihrdizu everywhere—the first contacts with Earth people may create such issues.

Voting is done by individuals—when possible in the same place at the same time; if that is not possible, by radio, so that everyone votes at once, perhaps all over the planet, regardless of local time.

Ihrdizu laws

There are two basic civil laws:

1. "Pay Back."

2. "Don't Interfere."

Both mean just about what they say. An Ihrdizu who borrows something, or asks a favor, must repay it; it is a terrible offense to fail in that, and an Ihrdizu's word is his bond. That's "Pay Back," and it also applies to injuries.

Noninterference means toleration of almost any kind of behavior—except where it interferes with one's own life. (For example, an Ihrdizu who chose to take drugs could do so freely; but if his behavior bothers someone else the other person can require him to stop or go elsewhere.)

There are also "religious" observances and trade customs that have the force of law, but only for those who subscribe to them.

Crime and punishment

A few Ihrdizu are sociopaths; they break the laws and try to get away with it.

These are caught and punished. Capture is done by groups of neighbors, as a kind of posse (but limited in its powers by the basic "Don't Interfere" injunction). Punishment is neither imprisonment nor a fine. For comparatively minor offenses it can be a beating. For the worst crimes (for example, a long record of lawless behavior), the offender's snorkel is chewed off by one of the persons he has harmed.

Since the snorkel is important to an Ihrdizu's well-being, he is then left seriously impaired. Among other things, it is the snorkel that does the scent-marking (see below).

There are no Ihrdizu police. If someone commits a criminal act any other Ihrdizu can apprehend him, and call on all other Ihrdizu to help if necessary and to decide on punishment if that is indicated.

However, there is a class of Ihrdizu who function as circuit judges—or, better, as rabbis. They travel around, interpreting and expounding the law. They are the guests of any Ihrdizu they choose to stay with, for as long as they wish to stay.

Queerly, they are almost always former criminals. They are also widows or widowers with only grown children: they have no family.

They have no authority to make any decisions, but only to clarify the interpretation of the laws. They do not touch on matters of "religion."

Property

Ihrdizu mark their property by scent-marking its perimeters. They also scent-mark their possessions. They can leave, for example, a valuable tool out in the open for long periods of time and no one will touch it, as long as they visit it to refresh the scent marking as needed.

Entertainment

Ihrdizu get together for dances; and to sing in eisteddfods; and to witness (and act in) sort of Greek plays. Each play is based on a historical incident, and the audience always knows the lines as well as the actors: they function as a chorus, and sometimes like the audience at a midnight showing of *The Rocky Horror Picture Show*.

Their dances are very athletic, within the bounds of their physiques, and they involve a certain amount of pouncing from concealment.

Their singing is quite horrible to Earthly ears. So is their music, which is largely percussive. But the sound of the words in their songs is quite beautiful: much use is made of onomatopoeia, rhyme, and alliteration.

Ihrdizu games and recreations

Many Ihrdizu enjoy hunting, even when they don't need to do it for sustenance—like humans. They hunt (as their primitive forebears did) by lurking in the shallows near the edge of a body of water, with only the snorkel exposed, waiting for some unwary prey to come by. (The Earthly analogy is to an alligator, waiting mostly submerged, with only the nostrils and eyes above water as it hunts.) When prey does appear they burst out of the water in a flurry of spray and foam and grab it, again like an alligator.

Young Ihrdizu do this as play, sometimes in their domestic food ponds—perhaps upsetting their parents.

Adult Ihrdizu recreations are related to this wait-and-pounce strategy. Their games, which are not card or board, are something like a sophisticated form of hide-and-seek. The principal one, which is like bridge or chess in the Western world of Earth, involves each player taking a small object (they are special game pieces, like carved chessmen) and hiding it in a game area. It is usually played by two to five Ihrdizu. The players are allowed to move their pieces about, and as soon as one player has located all of his opponents' pieces he pounces and grabs them.

The name of the game is "Find." Some Ihrdizu play it a lot, obsessively, like chess nuts. Depending on the number of players it is called "A Find of Two," "A Find of Five," etc.

When a lot of Genjians get together, at perhaps their equivalent of a fair, some of them will play a Find of Twelve or more. This game will go on for a long time, and spectators watch avidly as the players move about, trying to deceive each other with bluffing moves and conversation.

Ihrdizu fashions

Ihrdizu do not generally wear much in the way of clothing, except to protect themselves against inclement weather (heavy rain or strong winds). They do ornament their bodies in the way Moroccan women use henna, drawing complicated designs over all exposed flesh.

When they are heavily ornamented they are more likely to cover themselves with some sort of garment out of doors—to protect the ornamentation, as some humans wear hats to protect their hairdos.

Sexual characteristics of the Ihrdizu

In addition to the traits already described by Poul, there are a couple of others that need to be mentioned.

When male Ihrdizu reach puberty their tongues swell, making their speech thick and harsh until they get used to it. (Like an adolescent boy's change of voice.) This is embarrassing to them, and they try not to talk much in this period.

Female Ihrdizu have a "sexual skin," like the flushing posteriors of some Earthly primates: it changes color when they are about to come into heat.

Lower orders

Poul has given us a number of other Genjian organisms, to which I wish only to add a few notes. One of the prey animals is a sort of large-jointed beetle, ten centimeters long; it has flexible joints between the sections of its carapace that it can inflate. It swallows air when threatened, and does so occasionally for the sake of spreading to new territories: when inflated it is blown about by the strong winds.

A big herbivore has what appear to be feathers for skin covering. It does not fly; the feathers are its armor against predation. (Feather armor was used by the warriors of the Shoguns; closely layered feathers absorb a lot of kinetic energy.)

Major predators are homeothermic carnivores. They do their hunting at night, when the poikilotherms are relatively immobile.

There are whole species of special *starside* predators that operate in total darkness (rare on moonside Genji). These have evolved echolocation to help catch their prey. (This is a pretty probable evolutionary development, since on Earth both the suborders of the bats, micro- and megachiroptera, have this trait, although they appear to have evolved independently of each other, as do such more distantly related animals as some birds, shrews, toothed whales— and blind human beings.)

Extrapolating a bat's echolocating capacity to an Ihrdizu-sized animal, the predator would be able to detect an object a meter in diameter at two hundred meters distance in total darkness.

A few predators may also have heat-sensing organs, like some Earthly snakes, but they would not be very useful in locating poikilothermic prey. Perhaps more likely, some prey animals may have them as a defense mechanism, to warn of the approach of homeothermic enemies.

There are some Genjian animals as similar to Ihrdizu as apes are to us. The Ihrdizu call them "not-men" in their language. They, too, have the sexual tongues. As these organs are very strong and agile, they use them for feeding.

Certain "plants" have co-evolved with the Ihrdizu, and these plants have come to rely on the Ihrdizu, the "not-men," and similar organisms to fertilize them (as insects fertilize Earthly plants). The basic process of fertilization is pretty much the same as on Earth; the male and female gametes unite to produce the zygote. They secrete a kind of tasty mush deep inside their fleshy "petals"; it is rich in proteins and vitamins (or their Genjian equivalents), and very important in the diet of the animals.

The civilized Ihrdizu also cultivate these plants. They can be prepared in many ways in their cuisine, but they are most relished when eaten raw and indeed still on the vine.

These plants come in two main varieties. One is called "malefood" and can be eaten on the vine only by male Ihrdizu. Another, with its "nectar" less deeply concealed, is called "motherfood." (The tongues of female Ihrdizu are smaller and less muscular than those of the males.)

When a male Ihrdizu eats malefood, some male gametes (like pollen) stick to his tongue as it rubs against the equivalent of the "anther." When he eats another, the "pollen" is carried to the "pistil" of the other plant, where some of the male gametes unite with the female gametes of the second plant to produce cross-fertilization. (Of course, these structures are not the same as in Earthly plants, but they fulfill similar functions.)

The "flower" of malefood resembles the sexual parts of a female Ihrdizu. The taste is like the taste of the female in heat—think of it as resembling both caviar and champagne. Eating malefood is both a kind of masturbation and a limited aphrodisiac; it is what keeps the male Ihrdizu going when his female is not interested, or when he has not yet obtained a mate.

Of course, a female Ihrdizu could cut a plant open and eat any part of it she wishes, but the flavor is not as attractive to her as to the male.

Motherfood is also a plant, fertilized in the same way, eaten indiscriminately by both sexes; but it is particularly important for females since it contains nutrients necessary to the production of progeny.

A proper Ihrdizu household has malefood and motherfood plants growing all around it. Because of the lack of seasons there are always a few ripe fruits, and these are delicacies, served to honored guests.

The Ihrdizu diet

In addition to malefood and motherfood, they eat a great deal of a kind of primitive plant that resembles terrestrial algae. (Of course, it isn't algae; but it has a number of characteristics in common. It doesn't store energy in specialized structures like seeds, fruit, or tubers, so the whole thing is eaten. It is slimy to the touch, quite featureless, and grows on stagnant water rich in nutrients; so human beings will call it Genji-algae, or just algae.) Genji-algae is normally eaten raw and fresh, but can be dried and preserved as a kind of biscuit.

An algae pond, too, is found in every proper Ihrdizu household. It is generally fertilized by the Ihrdizu's own excrement and general household wastes. (The birthing pond described by Poul is a smaller and more carefully tended version of the same.)

Ihrdizu eat other plants, and fruits and nuts, and meat. They eat almost any kind of meat. They may even eat each other; there are no cannibalism tabus. When an Ihrdizu dies, the funeral ceremonies are related to the possibility of eating him. First he is ceremonially bled and gutted. The blood, along with his intestines and digestive tract, is cooked into a sort of paste that is then deposited in the family's algae pond. The rest of his body is cere-monially smoke-baked: placed in a sort of smoker oven and left there overnight. (By that time most organisms, including disease germs, have been killed.) If the Ihrdizu was in reasonably good shape, his flesh is then removed from the bones. The meat may be eaten (then or later—the smoking preserves it fairly well), and the skeleton ceremonially sunk in the nearest good-sized body of water.

Dead relatives are eaten as a kind of ritual meal—at the funeral, or on special occasions: the eating of the dead is to the Ihrdizu something between the eating of the Host at Communion and the Thanksgiving turkey. There is one other important ritual meal. As Poul has described, the Ihrdizu can alter the composition of their excrement to nourish their offspring. They do something of the same sort at their mating ceremonies: the male and the female each produce an edible turd and exchange them.

These customs do vary somewhat from group to group. The exchanging of turds is pretty universal. Funeral ceremonies are more flexible. More primitive Ihrdizu, particularly starside Ihrdizu who generally live near the shores of oceans or large tidal lakes, may simply tie the body of the deceased to heavy stones and sink it in shallow water, where the crablike "crustaceans" will eat it (after which they eat the crustaceans).

Ihrdizu gender

The Ihrdizu recognize three sexes: male, immature female, and mature female. Immature females are called "girls," mature ones "mothers." This is reflected in their language, which has four genders in pronouns: it, its; he, him, his; she, her, hers; and a set that does not translate well into English but is taken to be little-she, little-her, and little-hers.

A female Ihrdizu who has passed the time of fertility can be referred to as either "she" or "little-she." The former is honorary, the second pejorative.

Male Ihrdizu are sexually mature almost at birth. By the time they can walk, talk, and feed themselves they can impregnate a female—though they can't ordinarily find a mate until they are several years old.

Genjian diseases

Genjians, including the Ihrdizu, are subject to the same range of disease organisms as humans, and are infected in much the same way. A common disease like a cold affects the snorkel, making it tender and inflamed as a human nose. This is particularly unpleasant for the Ihrdizu, who depend on the snorkel for many things. (An Ihrdizu with an inflamed snorkel can't scent-mark his possessions properly.)

Ihrdizu are prone to bone and joint diseases—arthritis and osteoporosis in particular, which are especially handicapping in their higher surface gravity. Old Ihrdizu have to be very careful of falling, and their joints hurt. Their joint diseases are aggravated by certain diets; malefood is particularly bad. (Like Earthly gout, this never kills but only causes pain and limits mobility. An Ihrdizu with arthritis may be a subject of ridicule.)

Genjians, including Ihrdizu, frequently suffer from internal wormlike parasites. The only way to get rid of them is to starve them. The Ihrdizu restricts his diet until he is rather anemic and the parasites die—but he almost does, too.

No Genjian disease is normally communicable to humans, but one might imagine a mutant virus if necessary.

Poul did not go into Genjian cytology, so he did not mention that Genjian organisms often have multiple nuclei, like human osteoclasts. This leads to a Genjian disease unknown on Earth. In the Genjian equivalent of mitosis, or cell division, each of the nuclei separates as fine threads and migrates. Sometimes not all the nuclei are included in a cell division, with unpleasant consequences: this is their equivalent of cancer.

Ihrdizu views of Chujo

Ihrdizu will be fascinated by Chujo, since it is about all they can see in their skies other than Murasaki itself. (There are not many stars even on their starside, because of the dense and cloudy atmosphere, and essentially none at all visible from their moonside.) They will recognize it as "another Earth." They will be very curious about its starside, and there will be a lot of mythology/religion about it. (Primitive Ihrdizu may think it is where they go when they die. The more sophisticated ones probably have telescopes—though not very good ones, and seldom with good seeing. Still, with them they have possibly detected at least some very large artifacts on the surface of Chujo (ruins of cities?) and may think that the surviving Chujoans still live on the starside.)

Since no Ihrdizu have achieved spaceflight, this pent-up curiosity makes them very interested in their human visitors from space. Probably they think at first that the human beings come from Chujo's starside; then, when they understand that the humans come from a quite different part of the universe, the Ihrdizu beg to be told about (or even taken to) Chujo.

The Ihrdizu have long-established names for the visible features on Chujo. Many of these names will be because of fancied resemblances to something familiar in Ihrdizu life. (Perhaps "The Egg Pond," a craterlike feature, "The Horny Tongue," a mountain range, etc.)

Which leads to—

Telling time on Genji

Moonside Ihrdizu don't usually carry watches. They don't need them; they've got Chujo and Murasaki. From Murasaki-rise to Murasaki-set they tell time by Murasaki's elevation in the sky; it is easy to estimate how far it has risen because Chujo is hanging there to measure it against. If they want more precision, they could create their own "clock" anywhere. Since the axis of rotation of the two-planet system has little inclination relative to the pole of the ecliptic of their joint orbit around Murasaki, all days are pretty much the same length, so a stick thrust vertically into the ground would be a pretty accurate sundial.

However, they don't really need even a sundial. They have one up in the sky. The Ihrdizu can trace the passage of time by the progress of the sunlight terminator across the face of Chujo, all through the night and indeed through most of the day. Each "hour" has a name, depending on which prominent feature of Chujo the terminator has just reached; the hour is named after the object.

(All of this is limited by their heavy cloud cover, but still, even a glimpse of the sky will tell them what they want to know.)

The starside Ihrdizu, who are perhaps more primitive, don't carry watches either. By day they mark the passage of time by the elevation of Murasaki in the sky, and they sleep at night.

The deep sea

Ihrdizu, like humans, cannot dive too deeply in the sea, even with their equivalent of scuba gear: they, too, suffer from nitrogen narcosis. They get delusional.

This leads them to superstitious beliefs about the depths of the sea. As with the surface of Chujo, the deeps have mystical meanings for them.

The biomes of Genji

Poul has already described most of this, so I will just add a few additional remarks.

One can distinguish twelve main biomes on Genji: upland, lowland, tidal, and deep-water, each differing with climate (tropical, temperate, cool), though the temperature differences are not nearly as marked as on Earth.

On Earth, the separation of continents has meant a good deal of local diversification. On Genji, this is less marked. Because so many species are at least partly aquatic, and because there are stronger winds and so many flying animals to carry seeds, spores, etc., around, there is much more transport of new species from one part of the planet to another. So a biome on the starside of Genji has organisms very like those on the moonside.

Adaptations of Genjian plants

As on Earth, some plants have evolved defenses against being eaten by animals: stinging cells (which may or may not be effective against human beings), foul (to a Genjian) odors—humans may be crazy about them; thorns; sticky secretions, etc.

Adaptations of Genjian animals

Defenses against predation include mimicry, hard shells, electric shock, poison glands, etc.

THE HIMATIDS OF GENJI

As Poul points out, the himatids are poorly understood by either the Ihrdizu or humans. It's not at all easy for humans to study them anyway. Since they by definition live at sea level (or below), humans can visit the habitats of the himatids only by teleprobes or in considerable risk and discomfort.

The other way to look at it, though, is that it isn't much harder for humans to study himatids than to study Ihrdizu; very possibly before long the humans will know more about some aspects of himatid life than the Ihrdizu do.

Ihrdizu and himatids

As we know from Poul's writings, the Ihrdizu enslaved himatid juveniles when they first encountered them. Enslavement was not easy. The Ihrdizu could not really chain the himatids, nor could they hold their families hostage for good behavior, since the himatids have no conception of kinship. The Ihrdizu had to work harder for their slaves. They controlled many shorelines. They captured tads as they came ashore and began training them, by punishment and favor, as dogs are taught tricks. Many tads could not or would not learn, and those the Ihrdizu killed. The others did simple work for the Ihrdizu, helping to tend the algae plants, driving prey to Ihrdizu hunters, and so on; by the time they were juveniles, these trained tads knew no way to live except to serve the Ihrdizu.

When the enslaved tads went out to sea there was friction between them and the free juveniles, who had lived out their tad lives on small islands and shores not inhabited by Ihrdizu. The free juveniles tried to persuade them to give up the Ihrdizu, and many did; but enough remained true to their training to continue to serve the Ihrdizu.

The more civilized Ihrdizu do not enslave himatids anymore, but a few more-primitive groups continue the practice. These groups also have a taste for himatid flesh. In particular, when an elder himatid, in the carpet-whale phase of existence, comes near one of their shores they set out in fleets of boats to drive and tow it toward land. If they are successful and it is beached, or caught in a narrow bay, they eat it—often enough while it is still alive.

It is known that the adult, carpet-whale himatids communicate with each other over great distances in the sea, but what they say to each other no one knows. Not even the juvenile himatids. The himatids grow more intelligent as they grow older, by simple multiplication of nervous tissue; the adult language is too subtle and complex for calves to comprehend.

Humans (and some Ihrdizu) have various theories about the huge adult himatids. Some think they may be philosophizing. Others that they are artists, and their main purpose in life is to sing and speak gracefully and poetically to each other. Still others believe that with advancing age they go mad, or suffer the himatid equivalent of Alzheimer's; but most students agree that no one really knows.

The himatids have one physiological trait Poul did not discuss. As they metabolize, their waste products give off certain molecules that human beings find pleasurable—even addicting; they are like psychedelic drugs. (It has no such effect on Genjian organisms.)

It is possible that some humans enter into raptures under the influence of himatid exudations and feel that they are en rapport with the himatids.

THE CHUJOANS

As Poul has told us, the proper name of the second planet is Tō no Chujo, but as my WordStar program makes a hash of putting macrons in the proper place, I'll just call it Chujo.

For the purpose of the overall story line, we assume that humans will first visit Genji (since it is apparently the more hospitable planet).

Chujo is thus relatively unknown at the point in time from which our stories take off; it seems to me that stories involving Chujo will be basically stories of exploration, and that it is up to the individual writer to decide what his explorers discover. So I will add only a few "first impressions" to what Poul has already provided.

The Chujoans have had to adapt to the much more hostile present environment.

They wear heavy clothing. Their favorite garment is a kind of living skin, perhaps vaguely like the himatid's, that generates a little warmth.

Their name for themselves is a sort of trill, best rendered by human beings as a whistle through the teeth that sounds something like *fweess-chupchup;* the first syllable is prolonged on a high note, the second and third run together lower in pitch. Humans sometimes refer to them as "Chupchups," or Chujoans, or simply "the apes."

Although their environment is harsh, their lives are not unduly arduous; the remains of the self-sustaining farms and their herds give them plenty of food. It seems to human explorers that, with a little more exertion, Chujo could easily support a much larger population of the Chupchups, as it clearly did before the climatic change. But the Chupchups don't seem to want to increase and multiply.

Communication between humans and Chupchups is very poor. The few humans who visit Chujo have barely scratched the surface of the Chupchup language, and have only the cloudiest notion of what Chupchups think, or want, or do with their lives. The best theory is that the Chupchups are a race of *philosophes* whose primary interest is to think about the *meaning* of things. They seem to have long ago understood the fundamental principles of cosmology, evolution, entropy, and so on, and now devote their minds to creating a grand, unifying Theory of Everything. They are intrigued by human machines but have no interest in learning to use them, or in adapting them for their own lives.

As Poul has told us, there are about 1 million Chujoans. One human investigator thinks that is not an approximate number. He believes that there are *exactly* 1,048,576 Chupchups at all times, divided into 1,024 tribes of 1,024 individuals each. (And subdivided within the tribes to 32 families of 32 members each.) It appears that these numbers are immutable. It is not clear how the numbers are maintained: either new children are conceived when there is a death in the tribe, or when a new baby is born another member of the tribe dies, by suicide or ritual murder.

The Chupchup society is a confusing mixture of authoritarian centralism and individualism: the main purpose of any Chujoan's life seems to be for him to perfect his own understanding of himself, his world, and the universe.

As far as anyone has yet been able to determine, Chupchups do not seem to have a religion in any Earthly sense. They do not appear to believe in a God or a hereafter. Best guess: What they believe in is rightness. It seems that the most important question for any Chupchup to decide is when it is right for him to die.

Why Chujo is so mysterious

Living Chujoans are not immediately detected, either by the Ihrdizu or by humans from space. Since the interstellar ship undoubtedly has surveillance equipment at least as good as twentieth-century spy satellites, and since Chujo's atmosphere is rarely clouded enough to hide anything, why aren't the Chujoan communities, baggage trains, and so on seen immediately?

There are two answers to this. One is simply time. Chujo is, after all, a whole planet—it has more land area than Earth—and the more resolution in a camera, the smaller its field of view.

The other answer is that the Chujoans prefer to live in the woods. The reasons for this are three. First, the "trees" protect them to some extent from dust storms. Second, the "trees" are a source of food—the equivalent of nuts and fruits, and probably things like truffles, fungi growing among the roots. Third, the worst predators don't come into the forests.

A fourth reason might be simply that they like it that way, because they are Chujoans.

The ruined cities, on the other hand, are certainly large enough to be quite easily visible. They have in fact been observed, even by the Ihrdizu—sort of. Some are completely buried and can only be detected by observing vegetation growth patterns in the soil above them (as buried archaeological sites can sometimes be located by aerial reconnaissance on Earth). Others are partly buried, and the parts above ground have sometimes been worn away by time and dust storms. Nevertheless, a few ruined "cities" have actually been seen and charted.

What is not seen ever is their inhabitants.

There aren't any actual city-dwellers any more. The surviving Chupchups don't live in the cities that have been discovered, since the change in climate has put those cities in harsh environments, and the survivors have long since migrated to more benign ones. (Still, there may be a few old cities surviving from the Golden Age of Chujo where some tribes still live. Perhaps they are on starside. If the first interstellar ships take station in Low Genji Orbit, Genji being the more interesting-looking planet, Chujo's starside won't be easily observable by them—and not by the Ihrdizu ever.)

Individual Chupchups have in fact been seen by the mapping scans from the interstellar ships—as have most Chujoan animals much larger than a cat—but they have not been identified as intelligent, or related to the city builders. Such sightings are very rare. With only about a million Chujoan sentients on the whole planet (and most of them generally hidden in the forests), only a few thousand could be visible at any given time. Think of maybe a dozen human beings in the state of Kansas: how many would you see from orbit?

So what is known about Chujo and its people is far less than what remains to be discovered—presumably by you.

ABOUT THE AUTHORS

FREDERIK POHL, after a career spanning more than fifty years that is unmatched in the history of science fiction for its many-sided nature, remains a vital creative force in the field today, maintaining a vast popularity among science-fiction readers and the admiration of his fellow professionals. Pohl has been a magazine editor, a book editor, a literary agent, a futurologist known as a keen student of scientific and sociocultural trends, and a novelist famed for his multivolume "Heechee" saga and for his satirical book *The Space Merchants* (written in collaboration with the late C. M. Kornbluth), among much else. He won the Nebula Award in consecutive years for his novels *Man Plus* and *Gateway* and is a six-time Hugo winner, winning three awards as an editor and three more for his own fiction.

DAVID BRIN leaped into prominence with his second novel, *Startide Rising,* which was published in 1983 and won both the Hugo and Nebula awards. Since then, with such books as *The Postman, The Uplift War* (a Hugo winner in 1988), and the recent long novel *Earth,* he has consolidated his position as one of the most successful of the newer science-fiction authors. His work is marked by vigorous and vivid writing, deep insight into the speculative side of scientific thought, and a pervasively optimistic view of the future. His short story "The Crystal Spheres" brought him an additional Hugo trophy in 1985.

POUL ANDERSON made an immediate mark in science fiction with his first published story, "Tomorrow's Children" in 1947 (written in collaboration with F. N. Waldrop), and has been a conspicuous and widely published figure in the field ever since. His best-known novels include *The High Crusade, Three Hearts and Three Lions, Tau Zero,* and the recent awards nominee, *The Boat of a Million Years.* Among his profusion of shorter works are the classic novellas "Call Me Joe," "Goat Song," and "The Queen of Air and Darkness." He is a three-time winner of the Nebula Award, for the last two stories and "The Saturn Game," and he has won seven Hugos for his fiction, a total that no other writer has surpassed.

GREGORY BENFORD, a professor of physics at the University of California, Irvine, has since the early 1970s maintained a highly successful career in science fiction, producing works of great originality and power. Among his many books are the memorable novel *Timescape* and such highly regarded works as *Great Sky River, Tides of Light,* and *In the Ocean of Night.* In collaboration with David Brin he published the well-liked novel *Heart of the Comet* in 1986. He is a two-time Nebula winner: for *Timescape* in 1980 and for the novelette "If the Stars Are Gods" (with Gordon Eklund) in 1974.

GREG BEAR's first science-fiction stories were published in the late 1960s, when he was still a teenager. From that precocious beginning he has gone on to a significant career as one of science fiction's most original thinkers, with an enthusiastic readership making his books best-sellers in many countries. Among his works are the novels *Eon, Eternity, The Forge of God,* and the recent *Queen of Angels,* as well as dozens of novellas and shorter stories. He is a three-time winner of the Nebula Award (for the novella "Hardfought" and the novella "Blood Music," both in 1983, and the short story "Tangents" in 1986.) "Blood Music" and "Tangents" brought him Hugo Awards as well.

NANCY KRESS began her writing career in the 1970s with three fantasy novels—*The White Pipes, The Golden Grove,* and *The Prince of Morning Bells,* but it is as a science-fiction writer that she has primarily been known—particularly for the powerful novella "Trinity," a Nebula finalist in 1985. She won the Nebula Award in 1986 for her short story "Out of All Them Bright Stars." Her most recent novel is *An Alien Light.*